shayla black

"Scorching, wrenching, suspenseful."

—Lora Leigh, #1 *New York Times* bestselling author

"Thoroughly gripping and . . . so blisteringly sexy."

—*Fallen Angel Reviews*

"Searingly sexy stories that always leave me wanting more."

—Maya Banks, *New York Times* bestselling author

sylvia day

"Boldly passionate, scorchingly sexy." —*Booklist*

"Intense . . . graphic love scenes." —*Publishers Weekly*

"Emotionally charged, unbelievably sexy."

—*Romance Reader at Heart*

shiloh walker

"Wickedly sexy and wildly imaginative!"

—Larissa Ione, *New York Times* bestselling author

"Mind-blowing . . . Scorching hot." —*Romance Junkies*

"Some of the best erotic romantic fantasies on the market."

—*The Best Reviews*

Hot in Handcuffs

shayla black

sylvia day

shiloh walker

BERKLEY SENSATION, NEW YORK

THE BERKLEY PUBLISHING GROUP
Published by the Penguin Group
Penguin Group (USA) Inc.
375 Hudson Street, New York, New York 10014, USA
Penguin Group (Canada), 90 Eglinton Avenue East, Suite 700, Toronto, Ontario M4P 2Y3, Canada (a division of Pearson Penguin Canada Inc.) • Penguin Books Ltd., 80 Strand, London WC2R 0RL, England • Penguin Group Ireland, 25 St. Stephen's Green, Dublin 2, Ireland (a division of Penguin Books Ltd.) • Penguin Group (Australia), 250 Camberwell Road, Camberwell, Victoria 3124, Australia (a division of Pearson Australia Group Pty. Ltd.) • Penguin Books India Pvt. Ltd., 11 Community Centre, Panchsheel Park, New Delhi—110 017, India • Penguin Group (NZ), 67 Apollo Drive, Rosedale, Auckland 0632, New Zealand (a division of Pearson New Zealand Ltd.) • Penguin Books (South Africa) (Pty.) Ltd., 24 Sturdee Avenue, Rosebank, Johannesburg 2196, South Africa

Penguin Books Ltd., Registered Offices: 80 Strand, London WC2R 0RL, England

This book is an original publication of The Berkley Publishing Group.

Cover photo by Claudio Marinesco.
Cover design by Rita Frangie.
Interior text design by Kristin del Rosario.

PUBLISHING HISTORY
Berkley Sensation trade paperback edition / July 2012

Library of Congress Cataloging-in-Publication Data

Black, Shayla.
Hot in handcuffs / Shayla Black, Sylvia Day, Shiloh Walker.—Berkley Sensation trade paperback ed.
p. cm.
ISBN 978-0-425-24769-3
I. Day, Sylvia. II. Walker, Shiloh. III. Title.
PS3602.L325245H68 2012
813'.6—dc23
2012012365

PRINTED IN THE UNITED STATES OF AMERICA

10 9 8 7 6 5 4 3 2

CONTENTS

Arresting Desire

shayla black

For my parents. You're not big readers, and you're very practical, so the creative process is a bit of a head-scratcher for you. Thank you for not freaking out when I left my safe, comfortable day job and for realizing this "whole book writing thing" really makes me happy. While I don't use my very expensive education in the way you anticipated, I know it's contributed to my success and my life. Your love and support mean a lot.

chapter one

He stood at the back of the smoky club and watched with a grimace as four mostly naked men danced around the sitting redhead he hadn't quite forgotten in the last two years. A bawdy song about loosening up some girl's buttons throbbed over the speakers in the background.

"Well, well, well. If it isn't Blade Bocelli," a familiar voice drawled.

He turned to find Nicki Sullivan wearing a red lacy corset, a tight leather skirt, and five-inch fuck-me pumps—along with a huge, glittering wedding ring. She leaned against the club's back wall, giving him a teasing smile.

"You know my name is Jon." He grimaced. "Drop the cheesy Blade, huh? My days undercover with the Mafia, posing as your Uncle Pietro's right-hand bitch, are done."

"You clean up nice in Armani. Guess the FBI prefers its agents in suits." Nicki looked up and down with a grin. "But you looked good in leather."

Jon didn't give a shit what she thought. "You share that view with your husband?"

"I said you looked good. I didn't say I wanted to fuck you. Mark is the only one, and he knows it." She crossed her arms over her chest. "You're a long way from Jersey. What brings you back to Vegas?"

"I need to talk to you, and like I said over the phone, I didn't want any potential for being overheard." He glanced at the stage again, holding in a curse when one of the male dancers gyrated his junk in the pretty redhead's face. When she giggled, Jon clenched a fist.

"Something wrong?" Nicki asked, all innocence.

"You didn't tell me your sister would be here."

She shrugged. "You didn't ask."

No, but he'd wanted to. Lucia DiStefano was everything he had no business wanting and embodied nearly every fantasy he'd ever had. She wasn't tall or stick-thin. She wasn't a man-eater who knew twenty ways to get off in three minutes. She was highly intelligent, more *National Geographic* than *Vogue*. Jon had itched to awaken the sensual woman under Lucia's polished surface the second he'd laid eyes on her while working undercover here two years ago.

"Her comings and goings are none of my business," he said finally.

"But you want them to be," the sultry brunette returned. "Especially the coming."

Absolutely. Fuck, was he that transparent? "I need to ask you about something your father may have left you in his will."

"What are you looking for?"

Wasn't that the million-dollar question? Or in this case, a lifetime sentence. If he didn't get it answered fast, his brother might die in a maximum-security prison for the murder of a federal judge he hadn't committed.

"I'm not exactly sure. I suspect I'm looking for some form of media he used to store security footage. A DVD, a flash drive, an SD card . . ."

Nicki snorted. "The feds had his office bugged for years. You're one of them. Can't you just prowl through your own files?"

Great thought, but . . . "I looked through their evidence. I found nothing. Literally. Whatever we once collected is gone. Shortly after

I looked, my boss told me not to sniff around for anything related to Judge Casale's murder."

"They know your brother was convicted of that."

"Stefan didn't do it."

"Because he's such a choir boy?" She raised a dark brow.

"I'm under no illusions. My brother was once your father's favorite assassin, and no one in the Mafia is a choir boy. But Stefan didn't kill that judge."

"He tell you that?"

"My brother hasn't said a damn word."

But Jon knew Stefan well. If he had pulled the trigger and planted two bullets in the judge's head, Stefan would be agitated and itching to get back to his "family." The fact that he seemed content to rot in the pen told Jon that his brother was lying low for some reason. But there was no chance that Jon was going to let Stef piss his life away. If Lucia's father, Nicholas DiStefano, had ordered someone else to knock off Judge Casale, he might have kept a record, some evidence—something that could exonerate Stef. Since, by all accounts, Nicholas and his wife had been estranged for a while, who else but his daughters would the man have entrusted with his worldly goods after his murder?

"Well, my father has been gone a few years now. Lucia and I have been through his things. I didn't find any recording devices or security footage that I can recall."

"All of his possessions are accounted for?"

Nicki sighed. Clearly, she didn't like these questions. "I have no way of knowing. I loved my father, but he wasn't the sort of man who let anyone get terribly close."

True enough.

"We never found our grandmother's jewelry, which upsets my sister most. Since Lucia was a little girl, Mama Antonella had promised my sister her engagement ring and her mother's locket. They weren't among my father's belongings, though. None of it is hugely valuable. It's just sentimental."

Nicholas DiStefano hadn't been dumb. He'd known that someone in the Gamalini crime family, most likely his own brother, had wanted to take him down and become boss. Maybe he'd stashed the jewelry and his security recordings together? Jon looked down to the stage, where one G-string-clad dancer hovered over Lucia and kissed her cheek. Jon had the immediate urge to give the douche bag a slow, painful beating.

"Any theories on what might have happened to the jewelry?" he asked Nicki, forcing himself back on task.

"It's not like my father needed the money, so he wouldn't have pawned or sold it. At this point, I wonder if my Uncle Pietro grabbed it for his stupid cow of a daughter. But I don't know."

One thing Jon did know for sure? Pietro DiStefano was looking hot and hard for something that had belonged to his deceased older brother. Maybe money. Or one of the man's many accommodating mistresses. But it could also be something more incriminating. Either way, Jon had a week's vacation to save his brother from a life—and probable death—behind bars.

"Look . . ." Nicki glanced at the stage, then raised a brow as one of the male dancers kissed Lucia's neck.

Jon ripped his gaze away from the scene. "What?"

"If you came all the way to Vegas just for some hidden media storage stuff, you're wasting your time. If you came about my sister . . ." She crossed slender arms over her chest and grinned. "Then your timing is perfect."

"She looks occupied to me." Crap, he hadn't meant to sound jealous.

"Not yet. You know she's turning twenty-five tomorrow?"

Jon swallowed. No, he hadn't known, but it reinforced the reasons he'd left her untouched two years ago. Though he was barely ten years Lucia's senior, twenty-five sounded damn young to him. Given their differences in life experience, that ten years might as well be a hundred.

"So your dancing goons down there are a birthday present?" He nodded to the stage.

"Nah. My employees just like her."

"Well, then she won't be spending her birthday alone." And wasn't that a bitch?

"Maybe not. But she likes you more." Nicki's direct stare challenged him.

Jon knew that. God, didn't Nicki realize that he'd had to force himself to leave Lucia once before? Twenty-three had been too young for what he'd wanted to do to her. He'd taken one look at her then and known that she was a virgin. Glancing at her giggling embarrassment around the male strippers currently thrusting their dicks in her direction, Jon wondered if anything had changed.

"Your sister is beautiful and kind. She deserves someone great who will come home to her every night, kiss the kids, and snuggle up with her on the couch. That's not me."

"I didn't ask you to marry her and knock her up. I only meant that maybe you'd take her out for a drink or something and talk."

"Where do you think that talking would lead, Nicki?"

She shrugged. "Maybe to just a nice evening. Maybe to bed."

He shot her a skeptical glance. "You're encouraging me to sleep with your younger sister?"

Shifting her weight from one platform to the other, Nicki sighed. "She's still a full-fledged V-card member, but probably not for long. I'm . . . worried about her."

Jon was far more worried about what would happen if he spent any time alone at all with Lucia DiStefano. She made him hungry. And after too many tense, sex-related cases, his strings were pulled damn tight. Knowing that she was still a virgin . . . Well, everything about her was so sweet and pure. And couldn't he use some of that in his life?

Great, except he'd sully her all up. He couldn't bear to be the one to disillusion a girl as tender as Lucia.

"Want to know what I did on my last case?" Jon asked Nicki. He was sure that she didn't, but he was going to tell her anyway. "I ensured that one of my analysts trained properly to pose undercover as a submissive at a BDSM resort. I watched her get naked. I watched her get spanked by one man . . . and get off at the hands of another—at the same time. I saw her publicly flogged and fondled, then I had to send her to a place where orgies and whippings are common. Your sister's idea of racy is probably reading *Lady Chatterley's Lover* aloud at a book discussion group of her fellow academians. Don't get me wrong; I'd be a lying motherfucker if I said I didn't want to be the man to take Lucia's virginity, but she deserves someone who hasn't lived too long on the edge. Trust me, I'm doing her a favor."

"Oh, get over yourself." Nicki rolled her eyes. "So she's been sheltered. That makes her corruptible, not breakable. I'm only telling you this because I know you have some feelings for her, and I think you'd make her first time better than any drunk slob she's going to meet at that stupid singles' resort she's jetting off to for a week. But you know what? If you're determined to be all self-sacrificing and white knightish, then let her go to the Bahamas and get her brains fucked out by a stranger. I'll slip a box of condoms into her suitcase and tell her to have a good time." Nicki shoved away from the wall. "You're welcome to stay for cake. If not, you know where to find the door."

"SO, DR. DISTEFANO," Ashley whispered in Lucia's ear, "are you going to make a meal out of him or just ogle him like a decadent but off-limits dessert?"

Sipping her daiquiri, Lucia tore her gaze away from the hunk embroiled in conversation with her sister and tossed a glare over her shoulder at Ashley. "I'm just trying to figure out what he's doing here. I haven't seen Jon Bocelli in two years."

Ashley's blue eyes widened. "*That's* the guy you've been crushing on? Oh, I can totally see why you've been hung up all this time. He's *hawt*! It doesn't matter why he's here. Go for it! You're twenty-five and never been—"

"I don't need a reminder that my hymen is probably growing cobwebs," she whispered furiously.

She stared at Jon, still unable to believe he'd come here. He'd likely flown out to Vegas for something related to a case, since he'd talked to Nicki first. Certainly, he hadn't come for her. She'd made no impact on him two years ago. Most likely, she made even less of one now.

Lucia needed to get over him and move on with her life. Despite their frequent arguments during the summer they'd spent here, only Jon—with his hard body wrapped in sleek Italian style, black leather, and commanding vibe—had aroused her. In the past, he'd swaggered his way around Nicki's club, Girls' Night Out, looking hotter than any oiled-down pretty boy on stage. He reminded her of the Doms she read about in the erotic romances she devoured one after the other. Nothing had changed in the last two years, except his attire. His presence still filled a room and made her shiver. But he'd left his undercover assignment—and her—and walked away without a word. Why was he here now?

"Jon Bocelli is *so* out of my league. Heck, he's out of my universe." He could—and probably had—hooked up with any number of sexy, confident, experienced women. "Wanting him is a bad habit I should quit. I just need the right twelve-step program."

"Maybe not . . ." Ashley whispered. "Every time you're not looking at him, his eyes are all over you. Those glances of his could singe the chrome off a fender."

"You've had too much to drink. If he's looking, he's probably wondering how Nicki could possibly share genes with such a frumpy sister."

Ashley smacked her arm. "You are *not* frumpy. If he thought you were, he wouldn't stare like he's dying to eat you up." She anchored a hand on her hip and sent her a sour glare. "You do this, you know?"

"Do what?" Lucia scowled into her daiquiri glass before finishing the last sip.

"Undermine yourself. I've seen it a hundred times with you. You talk, you laugh, you sparkle with a guy. The minute he acts interested, you clam up, shut down, and your personality leaves town. Why is that?"

Lucia rolled her eyes. Why did Ashley have to drudge this crap up tonight? "I know when men are being polite. They aren't interested in me sexually. They like to talk to me. I'm a good listener. I laugh at their jokes. But they always ask out someone thin and cute who doesn't have an IQ that puts her in the 'freak' category. Trust me, the one-two punch of being thirty pounds overweight and enjoying a healthy debate about whether Alexander the Great or Napoleon was the more brilliant military strategist scares them off. If, by some miracle, they're still interested despite the thunder thighs or the fact I earned a PhD at twenty-one . . . well, the family name drives off the rest."

Pursing her glossy red lips together, Ashley sighed. "You're the one who puts a stop to anything beyond friendship. That one"—she nodded at Jon—"isn't thinking anything about your thighs except how much he'd like to be between them. I guarantee it."

"He's probably looking at you," Lucia said. And that would be normal. Ashley stood tall and slender, with long, blond hair tumbling down her back in tousled waves. She was every man's walking wet dream.

"Nope. Bocelli likes curves, especially breasts, which you've got plenty of, lucky thing."

"You've never met the guy. How would you know?"

"Because every time you turn in his direction, he looks at yours." Before she could object, Ashley cut her off. "How about a friendly bet?"

"Okay." Lucia turned her back to Jon and frowned suspiciously. "What?"

"When he talks to you, engage him in conversation, flirt, give him the green-light vibe. If he backs away after that, I promise to proofread your latest research article. Deal?"

Tempting offer. Ashley was a killer with copyediting marks and a red pen. And this last article she'd finished was so, so important to her professionally.

"All right. But I'm telling you, he's only staring because he's wondering why I squeezed an ass so big into a black dress so tiny. Last time I listen to you for fashion advice, by the way."

Ashley grinned. "Honey, please consider the possibility that he genuinely likes you, that you make him hard as hell, and that he's trying to figure out how to get your panties off."

"Sure." Lucia rolled her eyes. "Every scrumptious bad boy in Vegas is trying to figure out how to get me into bed."

"That wouldn't surprise me in the least, Doc," murmured an all-too-familiar gravelly, Jersey-accented voice that went straight to her belly and bloomed into a wild, sensual ache.

Jon Bocelli.

Oh my God! She gasped. He'd heard her?

Lucia could feel him now, hot at her back, mere inches away. The musky spice unique to him alone wrapped around her, intensifying the ache in her gut into something with claws that had dug in deep long ago and refused to let go.

She turned, hoping somehow that her senses had deceived her.

But no. There he stood, all six-plus feet of him, clad in a midnight blue shirt, black slacks, and matching suit coat.

The slam of her heartbeat kicking into overdrive thumped like a sledgehammer against her chest. Lucia swallowed, fighting the ache low in her belly, spreading between her legs. Helplessly, her gaze climbed up his sculpted torso, past the golden sinew of his throat visible through his open-collared shirt, gliding over the five o'clock shadow that spelled danger, lingering on his full mouth, which would have looked just as at home on a sultan, a gigolo, or the cover of a magazine. Finally, she made her way to his dark eyes. His stare, relentless, self-possessed, hungry, and not remotely teasing, made her suck in a breath. The sense of leashed control he gave off absolutely melted her.

"Talk to him," Ashley mumbled in her ear.

Talk? Lucia could barely find the presence of mind to shut her gaping mouth, let alone think of a witty rejoinder.

"All right, everyone!" Nicki spoke into a small microphone, breaking the tense moment. "Time for the birthday girl to open gifts."

Jon flicked his gaze to her sister for a moment, breaking the spell. Lucia released the breath she'd been holding.

"Guess I . . . should go," Lucia murmured. "It was good seeing you."

His gaze drilled into her, hot, intense. "I'm not leaving yet. I need to talk to you."

About what? "Sure."

"Lucia!" Nicki prompted into the microphone at center stage. Her mountain of a husband, Mark, stood behind her, hand resting protectively around her waist. "Get up here, birthday girl!"

Doing her best to balance on four-inch heels, Lucia made her way to Nicki's side, mindful of her little black dress—which was just barely shy of indecent—and sat in the waiting chair in the center. Nicki thrust a fresh daiquiri in her hand. Lucia promptly consumed half of it, nervous when she noticed Jon's gaze lingering on her.

"Start unwrapping!" Nicki demanded, pulling Lucia out of her thoughts.

Setting aside the other half of her daiquiri, Lucia stared at the smattering of brightly wrapped boxes, some little, some big, all around her. She dove in.

From a group of the dancers who worked at the club, a gift certificate for a day of pampering at an upscale spa nearby. From Nicki and Mark, a gorgeous pair of pearl earrings and a matching pendant. Amid the scattering of boxes, one that had no wrapping paper and no card snagged her attention.

Her father, God rest him, had never wrapped any of her gifts or given the folks at Hallmark a dime.

Lucia frowned as she picked up the rectangular box.

Definitely odd. It barely fit on her lap. The cardboard of the box was a bit dulled, as if it was old. The edges were even frayed.

Lucia frowned. "Who is this from, do you know?"

"Oh, sorry," Nicki piped up. "That arrived this morning from Dalton Cahill."

"Dad's estate attorney?"

Nicki nodded with a shrug thrown in. "I thought that was weird, too. But I signed for it."

They only heard from Dalton Cahill whenever business pertaining to the assets her father had left behind arose. But he'd never contacted them in a personal way. Certainly, he'd never observed their birthdays. Cahill had all the warmth of a used car salesman crossed with a cobra.

Frowning, Lucia pulled away the heavy strapping tape around the faded box and lifted the lid. She peeled back the tissue paper, feeling the outline of something hard and square with rounded edges. She dug deeper inside and wrapped her fingers around the metallic outline. Lifting it free, she found a photo in a sleek silver frame. The image was raised in the center, and the sides of the frame slanted down, giving the photo a three-dimensional effect.

The picture itself was of her father, looking as he had shortly before his murder, standing next to his brother, her Uncle Pietro, arms around one another, both smiling as they stood outside an Italian restaurant called Celeste's. She'd never heard of the place. But seeing her father looking so vital, standing beside the man she was certain had orchestrated her father's death, torqued something in her stomach. The hot sting of tears stabbed at the back of her eyes.

Nicki wandered closer, leaned in, then hugged her. "Oh my God . . ."

The moment her sister's arms came around her, Lucia lost it, and tears fell. With one hand, she clutched the picture to her chest. With the other, she covered her mouth. But even that didn't keep the sobs in.

"Why would Cahill have sent this to you?" Nicki frowned. "And why a picture of him with Pietro?"

"Are you okay?" Mark moved in behind her, his brows lowered in concern, eyes gentle.

Lucia wiped at her tears. "Fine. I'll be fine. I just . . . I didn't get anything in the way of personal mementos when my father passed away. So this is a shock."

"And really unusual," Nicki murmured.

Exactly. Why had her father's attorney sent her such a thing, especially after all this time?

"Have you spoken to Dalton Cahill lately?" Nicki asked, practically reading Lucia's mind.

She shook her head. "He just left me a message a few weeks ago and asked if I'd be coming to Atlantic City anytime this summer.

He wanted to have lunch. I left him a voice mail telling him that I was coming here."

Snagged by the weight of a hot stare across the room, Lucia looked up. Jon stood there, over six feet of testosterone. He drilled her with a questioning gaze, part concern, part crowbar. He had questions about something and intended to get answers.

Nearly lost in the wad of tissue paper on the floor of the stage, she glimpsed a piece of paper she'd missed before, taped to the bottom of the box. Grabbing the little scrap, she ripped it off and opened the handwritten note from Dalton Cahill.

"What does it say?" Nicki prompted impatiently, leaning over her shoulder.

Miss DiStefano,

Shortly before his death, your father asked me to pass this box and its contents to you on the occasion of your twenty-fifth birthday. Therefore, I am forwarding this box to you at his behest.

Best,
D. Cahill

Her father had asked his attorney to do this *before* his murder? And years after his passing? Cold shock cascaded through her. It made no sense . . . Then again, many of her father's actions hadn't. Always cloaked in secrecy, in kind evasions. She knew he'd been trying to protect her from his big, bad world. She missed him in death, even if she hadn't understood him in life. They'd shared a familial bond. She'd loved him. And in his macho Italian way, he'd loved her, too.

Fresh tears filled her eyes, and Lucia swiped at them. This was a birthday party, a celebration of life. Ashley hadn't flown all the way to Vegas to be sad. Tomorrow, they were going to the tropics to get their tan on and find hot guys at Erotics Anonymous. Now wasn't the time to weep. She'd been through the grief process, and had learned to deal with life minus her dad. But every once in a while, a new pang would assert itself, and she'd feel the sadness weigh her down.

Maybe she was looking at his gift all wrong. Her father had given her a memento so she could remember and celebrate, not so she could mourn.

Yes, but . . . why *this* photo? Why now? One thing she and her father had in common was the love of a good puzzle. Maybe she was supposed to figure out why Dad had sent this to her. Was it a message from beyond the grave?

chapter two

"That's a really special gift, Lucia," Nicki said with a too-bright smile, clearly trying to lighten the mood. "I know you'll treasure it. But there's more fun to be had tonight. It's a celebration. Let's dance!"

The deejay started playing a bubble-gum pop song by Katy Perry about Friday night. Jon blocked it out and watched as Lucia hugged the framed picture to her chest and fought more tears. Nicholas DiStefano may have been a Mafia dirtbag and Stefan's boss for years, but he'd been this sweet woman's father. Her confusion and pain were visible. Jon's chest buckled at the sight.

Until five minutes ago, he'd been just about ready to write this trip to Vegas off as a wild-goose chase. Walking away from Lucia again was going to be a blow. Though seeing her again thwacked him like a two-by-four in the chest, he'd been prepared to leave her once more.

Now . . . his every instinct was on high alert. He couldn't ignore a dead man arranging a birthday gift for his daughter posthumously without investigating. It didn't add up. Why not leave this gift to her in his will? Or with his personal effects? Certainly, the girls would have found it after he'd gone. Instead, almost as if he'd known his murder was imminent, Nicholas DiStefano had arranged with his solicitor to leave this picture to Lucia years later.

From everything Stefan had said about his boss, DiStefano had been smart and calculating. It stood to reason that the man had left this gift for a specific cause. But what? He scowled. And why leave it to his younger daughter? Jon had no evidence to suggest that Lucia had been closer to her father than Nicki. They were very different women, but they were both caring and warm. If Nicholas had loved the girls equally, why leave a memento to Lucia and not Nicki? Why bypass the party girl and leave something to . . .

That was it. He'd chosen Lucia because she was a genius. Jon's heart rate picked up. That present must have some deeper meaning. He felt it in his gut. Granted, it was a long shot that anything this picture revealed could help Stef, but it was better than no shot. Right now, this was his only lead.

No way was he leaving Vegas now. Or Lucia. Maybe that was the best part of all . . .

When another tear rolled down her cheek, Jon jumped onto the stage and knelt in front of her. "Lucia?"

Standing this close, her confusion and grief were tangible. When she blinked up at him, his chest tightened again. He wiped the tear from her cheek, then tucked a strand of her hair behind her ear. Her thick lashes lowered, brushed her rosy cheek, then lifted again, revealing a golden gaze that jolted him and raced through his system like a drug.

Jon gritted his teeth against a sudden surge of desire—to both touch and protect her. He had to focus on her unexpected gift. Every minute his brother sat in prison was dangerous. Pietro DiStefano must know that Stef had all kinds of dirty details on him and would talk for the right deal. Jon doubted that Pietro would leave him alive. Stef had survived by his wits—so far—but he couldn't count on that lasting forever.

"I'm fine." Lucia swallowed and sent him a brave—but totally false—smile.

"You sure?" he chided gently. She wasn't his to punish for fibbing, and she probably needed his comfort now more than anything.

She nodded and set the photo in her lap. "I don't mean to be weepy. This is one of the few pictures I have of my father. Getting it was really . . . unexpected. It just hit me."

Jon resisted the urge to wrap his arms around her and draw her close. Instead, he stared down at the image. "I understand. Have you been to the restaurant where the picture was taken?"

Lucia shook her head. "I don't even know where it is."

"Newark." With every moment that passed, Jon became more certain that this gift shouldn't be taken at face value. "Good food."

"I—I had no idea. I never knew that he even traveled to that part of New Jersey." She frowned.

About now, Lucia had to be asking herself why her father had sent her a picture of himself in front of a restaurant she knew nothing about, standing next to the very man who had likely killed him. Jon couldn't agree more.

"I think there was a lot about your father that you didn't know."

"That's an understatement." She stared at the picture again. "Growing up, I was told that he owned a string of dry cleaners and nightclubs in Manhattan. During brief breaks from boarding school, I'd hear kids whispering that my dad was a Mafia boss. I always laughed—until you investigated my family."

"I didn't do it to hurt you."

But it had, and the pain on her face said so. He wished he had the right to pull her into his lap and console her, but he was here for his brother, not himself.

Lucia sighed. "You were doing your job. I just wish you'd been able to prove who killed my father."

"About that . . . Is there someplace quiet we can talk?" He held out his hand. She hesitated, then took it. He tried not to notice just how damn soft her hands were and how fucking good she smelled. He had to get his dick out of the equation and focus.

But Lucia's soft little mouth was so close. He could almost taste the fruity drink she'd been imbibing earlier. Her breath hitched. The idea of being alone with him made her slightly nervous. Jon's blood pumped at the thought.

Their gazes locked, unblinking. The long, silent moment drew on. The background music and people faded away, and he itched to crush her mouth under his and touch her all over. Damn it, he was trying to keep his head, but her awareness of the attraction raging between them made his skin flare with heat, his desire rise dangerously. Lucia's eyes widened, as if she knew every nasty, sweaty, lusty thing he wanted to do to her . . .

He didn't have the luxury of closing his eyes and refocusing, not when he had to convince her to let him examine that picture. But he wasn't thinking about investigating as he rubbed the back of her hand with his thumb or glanced at the gorgeous swells of her cleavage pushing up from the deep *V* of her sexy black dress. Below that, the lush curves of her hips and sleek thighs had him clenching a fist. He felt his mental restraints snapping loose. She had maybe five seconds to break this spell before he lost control and kissed her.

"The bar is in the back," she managed to choke out.

The music throbbed back there, powered by a whole system of speakers meant to project throughout the club.

He shook his head. "Someplace quieter."

His demand took her aback, and Jon intentionally gentled his face. She might be a woman, but in her experience with men, she was a girl, and he had to be mindful not to scare the hell out of her.

"M-My sister's office—"

"Is right above the deejay booth. You know it's pounding in there."

And it was also visible to everyone in the club. Jon didn't want all those prying eyes as he examined the photo. Having worked undercover here, he knew the building housed some normally vacant apartments upstairs.

She nodded, and Jon stood, tugging her with him. "Come with me. I know just the place."

He was asking her for her trust. She nodded and rose to her feet, giving it.

That fact wasn't lost on him. On some level, she not only felt safe with him, but had unconscious submissive tendencies. Fuck, with the right amount of time and the right situation, what he wouldn't like to do with that . . .

But there was nothing right about now.

Gritting his teeth, he jumped off the stage to avoid all the dancing couples blocking the stairs at the far end, then turned to Lucia, arms raised expectantly, ready to catch her.

She bit her lip uncertainly. "I'm too heavy."

He set his face into unyielding lines. "Bullshit. Jump."

"I'm not sure I can in these heels."

"I'll catch you," he promised. "Trust me. Hand me the picture and jump to me now."

Lucia paused for a single moment, then did as he instructed. She landed against him, her breasts smashed against his chest. Automatically, his arm wrapped around her waist, his fingers hovering over the curve of her gorgeous ass.

Shit, he'd never been this close to her, and it was overloading his system. Two years ago, Lucia had skewed his self-control. Now she crushed it. Against his will, he tightened his grip on her and he buried his face in her hair. *Fucking strawberries.* That's what she smelled like. And some sort of purely female musk that made him ache to shove her against the nearest wall and have his way with her . . .

He sniffed again, and that musk was stronger, more pungent.

Then he realized what that meant. Lucia was aroused.

Every instinct he had as a man shouted to get her naked and slide between her legs.

Let her go to the Bahamas and get her brains fucked out by a stranger. I'll slip a box of condoms into her suitcase . . . Nicki's rant rang in his head. His gut tightened. Lucia probably should find a guy closer to her own age and explore her sexuality. But the thought of anyone else touching her, helping her out of her clothes and taking her virginity, made him downright murderous.

Shit, he really was strung too tight. He had to let go.

Jon stepped away from Lucia stiffly and gestured toward the back of the club with what he hoped was an encouraging smile. She hesitated for a second, then started walking. Swaying would have been a better description. In that tight dress, her hips shifted and rolled with every step. The tight material hugged her ass, and he couldn't look away. He barely managed to stop himself from shoving her inside the stairwell, pushing her against the wall, and kissing her senseless. Instead, he nudged her through the stairway behind the bar, letting the door close behind them, and flipped on the lights so they wouldn't trip.

But watching her every step up was torture. After three flights, his dick throbbed behind his zipper. Lust, aggression, need—they all seared through his veins. He did his best to swallow them down and prowled around the top floor until he found a familiar door and the sparsely furnished apartment he'd lived in two summers ago.

Ignoring the perfectly useful bed in the next room, Jon turned on the lights and led Lucia to the sofa. He sat her at one end and resisted the urge to plant himself right beside her. Instead, he settled on the other end. With the picture in his lap, he glanced into her uncertain face.

"It's been a long time, Doc."

Jon frowned. That wasn't what he'd meant to say. He'd stood

down some of the most soulless killers and sex offenders and never groped for words. This woman tied his tongue in knots.

"It has. How have you been?" Her face said that she genuinely wanted to know.

"Busy. A lot of ugly cases." He nodded, searching for some way to reduce the tension, get back on task. Make her smile. Yeah, he'd like that. But he came up blank, so he gripped the frame and asked, "No idea why your father would have left this for you?"

"None. I also can't fathom why he would have asked his attorney to give it to me now, like this."

Jon hesitated. The fact that she had a vacation planned tomorrow—where she intended to let complete strangers buy her drinks and seduce her out of her innocence—didn't bode well for persuading her to pursue this cold case with him. But he had to try since it could help his brother. He was pretty damn sure it would ultimately help her, too.

"Consider the reasons he would send this to you, Lucia, and not your sister."

"It's already occurred to me that it's some riddle I'm meant to solve. My father wasn't a warm man, but when I was little, I'd crawl into his lap, and we'd work puzzles together. All kinds of puzzles—crosswords, anagrams, word searches, jigsaws, three-D models. As I got older, he'd challenge me with riddles and different codes to break." She smiled. "He was really proud of the fact that, if I'd worked as a code breaker in World War Two, I would have been able to break the Japanese and German codes." Then her smile died. "I didn't see as much of him when I went off to boarding school."

"When was that?"

"I was nine." A faint smile flitted across her lips. "Before then, I didn't realize that *War and Peace* wasn't what the average middle schooler chose for a book report."

"Isn't nine young for middle school?"

"I started skipping grades early. But even then, the teachers didn't know what to do with me. If they challenged me enough, all my classmates made fun of me. Heck, they did anyway."

"So your parents sent you off to Westover?"

Lucia cocked her head, sending him a sharp glance. "How did you know that?"

Jon looked down. Was that a flush he actually felt crawling up his face? Wincing, he rubbed the back of his neck. "I . . . um, did research on your whole family. For my undercover work a few years back."

That skeptical rise of her brow damn near made him squirm, but Lucia didn't challenge him outright. "Dad and I had summers and holidays together, and we'd always do puzzles. Then I started my doctoral program, and my schedule got crazy. He grew more distant. But I still have the last code he gave me to break. When I solved it, the result said, 'I love you, little girl.' He was gone a month later."

Lucia closed her eyes to rein back her pain, and Jon couldn't be immune. He'd lost his own father damn young, as well as countless friends and coworkers. He understood grief.

Scooting closer, he grabbed her hand and rubbed her shoulder. "I know it's hard to dredge all this stuff up. I'm sorry to do it so close to your birthday."

She forced a smile. "It's sad, Jon, but I'm not going to break. I'm really not fragile."

Exactly what Nicki had said earlier. Good. If the purpose of her father's gift was what he suspected, she was going to need a whole lot of fortitude and backbone. It could be both emotionally trying and dangerous.

"The problem is, if your father was trying to say something, we don't know what. Would you mind if I examined this picture a bit more closely?"

"I meant to do that after the party."

Jon heard her subtext: She wanted to do it alone. Freeing his brother was important to him, but he didn't want to trample all over Lucia's grief.

He handed the framed picture back to her. "I can step out and give you a few minutes—"

"That's okay." She bit the inside of her cheek, then nudged the picture back into his hands. "You go ahead."

She trusted him, and he shoved aside the implications of her sharing this moment with him—or he'd have her naked in nothing flat.

Instead, he turned the frame over and quickly saw that it had been waxed shut. *Unusual.* But no mistaking the thin veneer of clear wax melted all around the seal. Had Nicholas DiStefano done that in an attempt to make sure his attorney didn't tamper with it? Perhaps. He'd been abundantly cautious, which made sense in his line of work.

Withdrawing a pocketknife from his jeans, Jon flicked open a blade, then carefully broke the seal. The solid backing, wrapped tightly in blue velvet, came loose. He pulled it off without issue and inspected the back of the picture. The older generation sometimes wrote names, dates—anything important—there. But the back of this photo was a pristine white, as if it had been printed from someone's computer and deposited directly into this frame.

At the bottom of the frame, however, sat two objects that made certainty hum through his veins. He was on the right track.

Lifting the first, a small piece of paper with a series of random numbers written in pencil, he handed it to Lucia. "This mean anything to you?"

She took the item, wonder sprawling across her face. "It's a cipher. He wants me to solve for a message. This will tell us exactly how to decode the cryptovariable once we determine it."

"Cryptovariable? A document he based the cipher on?"

"Exactly. Once we determine the cryptovariable, we bump it against the cipher, figure out the pattern, and solve. But I have no idea what document he might have used. He chose different ones every time." She smiled wistfully. "He liked to keep me on my toes."

Next, Jon dug into the picture frame and found a little silver key. He held it up. "This looks like it belongs to a padlock."

Lucia peered, too. "You're right. I have no idea where that lock might be, though. He never mentioned one that I recall."

As grief moved across her face again, Jon took her hand and squeezed. "My guess is that we'll find answers, and maybe even the lock, somewhere near Celeste's."

"Yes." She stared at the picture. "That would be like him."

"This could be dangerous." It was only fair to warn her.

She scowled. "I'm naïve, but not an idiot."

"Do you know what role Pietro played in your father's death?"

Lucia speared him with a sharp gaze, a bitter determination crossing her face. "I suspect he's responsible. I can't prove it now. Someday I will. Did he ever tell you that he had something to do with my father's death when you worked undercover in his organization?"

"No. He was all innuendos. An elbow and a chuckle, but nothing firm. He definitely didn't grieve when Nicholas died. That's suspicious, but wouldn't hold up in court." Jon hesitated, searching for the right words, but not finding them. "Look, I'm sure you've figured out that your father may have sent this picture to you as part of a puzzle to help solve his murder."

"Of course. He wasn't sentimental, and if he'd wanted to give me a gift, he'd have given me some shiny bauble." She laughed softly. "I don't think he ever really understood women. He presumed all of us thought that diamonds are a girl's best friend."

Jon had already figured out that Lucia didn't fall into that category of female. “So you have a whole bunch of jewelry you never wear?”

Her thick, dark lashes swept across her cheeks again as she grinned. “It’s pretty, but . . .”

“Nicki appreciates that sort of thing far more than you.”

She nodded. “My mom always sent me books. I was way happier to receive her packages. But I hear what you’re trying to tell me. Pietro being in this picture—he and my dad weren’t really close—is odd all by itself. The fact that my father gave this picture to *me* in this way, with a cipher and the key to a padlock . . . I’d already figured he was trying to tell me something important.”

“Your father believed that Pietro would off him, at least according to my brother. To protect his interests and keep you from learning the truth, he may be willing to kill you, too. My question is, are you willing to follow this clue and investigate? I’ll help you.”

“As soon as I get back from”—she bit her lip—“vacation. I’ll, um . . . call you, and we can hook up. I mean, get together and—”

“That’s not going to work, Lucia. It’s been almost four years. Do you really want to wait longer to solve this? We have no way of knowing if your father arranged to have this clue sent now because it’s time-sensitive. I can’t help you after this week. I’ve only got now.”

She frowned. “The Bureau put you on this case with a time frame?”

Lucia might not appreciate his honesty, but he was going to give it to her. “I’m on leave. This is personal.”

“Your brother?”

He nodded. “Stefan isn’t safe in prison. He might deserve to do hard time for all the lousy things he’s done, but he doesn’t deserve to die by some thug skewering him with a rusty, makeshift blade in the prison yard. He’s all the family I’ve got left.”

Regret crossed her pretty face. “I can’t bail on Ashley at the last minute. She's taken time off, spent a lot of money . . ." She sent him a grimace that pleaded his understanding. "If you want to get started while I'm gone, I'll pick up where you left off when I return. I'm good with research, and—"

"No." In some ways, that would work better, Jon conceded. He liked to work alone, and Lucia had no experience with dangerous situations. But chances were, he was going to need her help with that cipher. Nicholas hadn't sent these clues to the police or the FBI. He'd sent them to his daughter. Something in her memory or her skill set would likely be the key to understanding what the man had left behind. And she wouldn't be safe working these clues without a protector. She was going to need him, too.

"You have to come with me now."

"Jon, I just explained . . . It's not possible. As soon as I get back, great. In fact, I'll have the rest of the summer to devote to this."

"I don't. Neither does my brother. And frankly, I don't think your father would have wanted you to put off solving his murder so that you could run off to some hedonistic resort and let a sloppy drunk you barely know tear off your clothes and take your virginity." It was dirty pool, and Jon knew it. But he couldn't manage polite now.

No, that wasn't the only reason. He also refused to sit by idly while she let someone else fuck her. There, he'd admitted it. Jon had left her once. In the back of his mind, he'd always hoped that their paths would cross again, and she'd be older, more prepared . . . Faced with the possibility of letting her slip through his fingers a second time, he was unwilling to let her go. She might not completely grasp everything he wanted, but she was a grown-up girl. And he wasn't backing down again.

Lucia gasped. "That's low."

"That's the unvarnished truth. Or are you going to try to tell me differently?"

She gritted her teeth. "My sister told you where I was going and what I planned to do. Damn it! It's none of your business. You had your chance. Two years ago, I all but threw myself at you, and it was so goddamn embarrassing that you didn't even once notice—"

Jon was all over her in an instant, slanting his mouth over hers, silencing her with a searing kiss. He didn't test the waters or gauge his welcome; he just forced Lucia's lips to part under his, prowled inside, and made her take all the hunger he could shove into that kiss.

Under him, she gasped, then clutched the lapels of his suit coat, pulling him closer. God, she tasted like rum and tropical fruit and pure lust. A hot surge of desire pumped through him, and he didn't think twice before he covered her body with his. He wrapped his arm around her and planted his hand on her voluptuous ass, bringing her body directly against him, notching his cock against her.

She moaned as he took even deeper possession of her mouth. There wasn't a hint of resistance or rejection, and Jon felt like he would crawl out of his damn skin if he didn't touch her soon. Her every curve pressed against his body, and he felt her breasts tighten until her nipples stabbed his chest. Her tongue curled around his, seeking and soft. He demanded more of her, taking her lips in another scorching kiss that had her arching and wrapping her arms around his neck.

His cock, already hard, turned to stone—unyielding and heavy. The teeth of the zipper all but branded a painful pattern into his dick. Fire charred his veins, and he had no idea where he'd find the restraint to back down.

Shit, this was getting out of hand. He wanted her, but not on a sofa after sneaking away from a party like guilty teenagers. Not by pushing their clothes aside and fucking her with all haste and zero finesse. No, he wanted her on a bed, naked, mentally ready for the fact that he would take her tenderly and make her first experience sweet—before he started tying her to his bedposts and pushing her boundaries, one after the other.

Jon tore his mouth from hers, panting. "Believe me, Doc, I noticed."

Lucia blinked up at him, speechless for a long moment, her breathing slightly heavy. "You never gave me any indication—"

"I was undercover, and your uncle sent me to be Nicki's watchdog. The minute you hit Vegas, that order included you. He'd have killed me and ruined the investigation if I'd so much as looked at you too long. Trust me when I say I noticed you. And I wanted you."

A becoming little flush crawled up her cheeks. A moment later, he saw the wheels in her head start to turn. Then her eyes narrowed, and she glared at him. "You're just saying that to gain my cooperation. It's convenient to want me when you need my help for your brother's case." She grabbed the picture frame and its contents, shoved it all back together with shaking hands, then sprang to her feet. "God, for a smart girl, I can be so stupid."

As she darted for the door, Jon started after her in shock. "What the hell are you talking about? My desire for you has nothing to do with this case."

"Right." The sarcasm in her tone matched the way she yanked the door open. "You know what? I have a roomful of people who genuinely care for me and want me to be happy, and I've taken time from them to let you dupe me. I'm done. You know the way out."

She thought he'd manufactured passion to gain her cooperation? As soon as he could, he'd show her just how wrong she was. "Stop."

Lucia froze for a long moment, the door open in front of her as she glanced over her shoulder at him. Her delicate face was taut with anger, mouth pursed. But she'd heeded his command. Damn, that went straight to his cock.

"I need your help. That has nothing to do with how much I want you."

"You gave up two years of your life for a mission. After that, pretending to want me to further your cause must be a piece of cake. I'm not opening myself up so that you can just leave again. Goodbye, Jon." She marched into the hall and slammed the door behind her.

Anger and determination fired through Jon's veins as he chased her into the hall, running around her to block her path to the stairs. "I *will* do anything to get my brother free. But I'm also going to prove that I truly want you. We're going to follow these clues your father has left us—this week. You're not going to run off to the Bahamas and let some total stranger take what I want." He grabbed her arms. "What you want to give me."

If anything, she got angrier. "Get out of my way."

"No. Come with me."

"Go to hell."

"You're leaving me no choice, Lucia . . ." Before she could question that statement, he bent and shoved his shoulder into her soft belly, then hoisted her up on his shoulder.

"What are you doing?" she shrieked.

"Exactly what I promised." He braced himself with one hand on the handrail. With the other, he palmed her upper thigh to balance her.

God, he couldn't wait to get her naked and supine. He might not be the best man in the world for her virginal sensibilities, but he'd treat her damn better than any random asshole she'd pick up at a singles' resort for a one-night stand. Together, they would follow whatever clues Nicholas had left. Jon hoped and prayed that the Mafia boss's clues also proved that Stefan hadn't killed that judge. Even if they didn't, she would solve the riddle her father had left her, and he couldn't let her walk into potential danger alone.

Lucia was screaming when he hit the bottom of the stairs on the first floor and emerged into the club. Suddenly, the music stopped, and he could feel every eye in the place on him.

"Jon?" Nicki approached, raising her brow at him.

"I'm taking your sister with me for a while. We have unfinished business."

"Nicki, you cannot let him do this. It's ridiculous! This is against my will. I'm going on vacation tomorrow with Ashley. We've paid for Erotics Anonymous, and—"

He'd heard enough of this speech. Jon ended her tirade with a slap to the ass.

"Damn you!" she snarled.

Her sister just smiled. "Check in when you two come up for air. Have fun!"

"You did *not* just condone this, Nicki!" Lucia shouted. "It's kidnapping!"

"I think she did, Doc." He grinned. He might get to help his brother *and* have the woman he'd wanted for too damn long.

"Ashley!" Lucia called out.

Her friend bopped over and bent, revealing a huge grin spread across her face. "Go have fun."

"You're okay with this, too?" Lucia sounded incredulous.

"Sure. I don't need you to hold my hand at Erotics Anonymous. I know exactly what to do." She wiggled her brows. "We'll catch up after I get back."

Jon searched the room, looking for anyone who might object. Nicki's husband, Mark, was the only person he spied. "Got anything to say?"

"Be good to her. She deserves it."

Jon nodded. "Absolutely."

Lucia squirmed on his shoulder, kicking and grumbling as she tried to get away. He swatted her ass again and headed out of the club, into the hot Vegas night, and right for his rental car.

"You cannot just carry me out of this club and—just how do

you intend to get me to New Jersey? The minute we hit the airport, I'll scream to every security officer within a hundred-foot radius."

"Thanks for the heads-up, Doc. I've got a great plan B. In the meantime, you can spend some time discerning how to find the cryptovariable your dad left for you . . . and thinking about all the ways I'm going to touch you as soon as we find a bed."

chapter three

Lucia crossed her arms over her chest and released a shuddering breath as she watched Jon flip a bunch of knobs and buttons in the little cockpit, powering the little passenger plane down. Icy terror slowly slid out of her bloodstream.

"You can remove your death grip on the armrests. It's over."

She looked down at her hands and realized they were white with tension and half numb. Letting go, she shook them out. "That scared the hell out of me."

"I'm an experienced pilot, Lucia. I got you here in one piece."

"I don't like flying much, and I like little planes even less."

"I didn't intend to scare you. I'm never going to hurt you. You know that, right?" Jon lifted a brow at her, his dark eyes glittering. "I think you're mostly pissed that I picked you up and carted you away from your birthday party."

"I didn't exactly consent."

She'd figured that Jon had balls. A guy would have to in order to work undercover for the FBI in a Mafia sting for over two years. But to pick up a woman in front of her family and friends and all but announce that he intended to take her virginity? He had to be crazy.

"Sorry. I'm used to fighting criminals, who are rarely polite. My social skills must be rusty."

She crossed her arms over her chest. "I want to go back to Vegas. My plane to the Bahamas leaves in the morning."

"You're staying with me, we're going to solve this riddle, and I'm going to make sure you don't once regret that or anything else we do this week. Are you hungry?"

"No." She winced. God, she sounded petulant. Damn it, she didn't like how much being near the man and hearing his authoritative voice heated her up, made everything between her thighs throb. She should be furious with his high-handed tactics. And despite what he claimed, she feared that his "desire" was nothing more than a calculated gesture to gain her cooperation for his investigation. She needed to keep that in mind the next time he touched her.

"Yes, you are." He turned to her in his pilot's seat, jaw clenched. "Look, we have serious work to do, but I'm also going to make time for you. I want to make your first time tender and sweet—"

"You're assuming I'm saying yes."

He shrugged those massive shoulders. "Fair enough. When I have you under me and I'm kissing every inch of your body . . . well, if you're not interested, feel free to just say 'no.' But if you keep lying to me, I'm going to paddle your ass until you learn to be honest."

"You roll *that* way?" Her heart stuttered at the thought that he might be exactly the sort of man who could fulfill all the kinky fantasies she'd never told anyone.

Jon raised a brow. "If you're asking whether I'm dominant, the answer is yes. Not every minute. Not every time I have sex. But generally, yes. Furthermore, I think you're submissive, and we're going to get on really well together."

Submissive? Yes. She'd figured that out long ago. While she enjoyed all kinds of literature, Lucia had read more than her fair share of erotic romances in the last five years, most BDSM-themed. She already knew that she responded to the idea of a dominant man. But being spanked? She shivered. Yes, his purred threat aroused her. Would the reality excite her as much? Maybe. Either way, she felt compelled to push back. She might be submissive, but she wasn't a doormat.

"Go to hell," she said through clenched teeth. She'd try submitting someday, preferably to a man who wasn't simply using her and her desires to further his own ends.

Jon laughed. "Now you're just being bratty and asking to be punished. And I'm kind of looking forward to it. After years of considering you off-limits, I'm really happy to know that, soon, I'm going to introduce you to every pleasure my filthy mind can think of."

The engine of the plane finally ramped down, and Lucia tugged off her seat belt, then darted out of the cockpit until she reached the cabin of the small passenger plane. She stood near the door. "Let me out. I'm taking a taxi to Newark and catching the next flight to the Bahamas."

"Don't you know every time you say that, it's like waving a red cape in front of an angry bull's face?" He followed her to the door and opened it, then pressed the lever for the hydraulic stairs to descend. "We've had this discussion. You know the answer. And regardless of what you told me, I know your stomach is rumbling. It's nearly midnight here, so Celeste's will be closed. We'll be there when they open the doors for lunch, but until then I'll find something to sate that hunger before I spend a few hours fulfilling the other."

Hours? He assumed they were going to have sex tonight? She wanted to. Her pussy burned and pulsed at the thought of Jon being the first man inside her and giving her pleasure. She'd always wanted him. But if he was really just sleeping with her to help his brother, how pathetic would she be if she let him?

She whirled on him. "Just drop the pretense. You don't have to butter me up. If it's that damn important to you, then I'll stay and see if anything my father left behind will help your brother. But don't bother lying about—"

"Stop." Jon grabbed her wrist and jerked her closer, then pressed her palm directly on his erection.

Thick. Long. Hard. Heat shimmered through her, almost flattened her. Lucia struggled to breathe. Her jaw dropped.

"That feel like I don't want you, Doc?"

Oh my God . . . Finally finding the gumption, she jerked her hand away. Her palm burned. "Can't guys breathe and get erect? I'm not flattered."

Jon laughed, the deep, rich rumble of his voice pinging through her body. She was horrified to realize that her nipples had peaked at the sound. "Basic respiration doesn't excite me, Doc. Sexy little professors with attitude do. Who sold you a bad bill of goods?"

"No one." She marched down the steps, shaking all over and clutching the picture from her father. "I'm aware of my faults. You don't need to pretend that they don't exist."

Jon didn't say anything for a long minute. Beside her, he looked as if he was mulling her words over—and like they left a bitter taste in his mouth. "I'm not pretending. There's not a damn thing wrong with you. Don't think for a second that men don't see or want you. Maybe you've been dealing with chicken shits who are threatened by your IQ. I don't know. But I think you're sexy, and I don't want to hear you tear yourself down again. Are we clear?"

She blinked up at him, not even bothering to ask if he was serious. Clearly he was. He thought she was sexy? Really?

With a decisive nod, as if that settled the issue, he pulled out his phone and spoke low. She could barely hear him over the wind, but what little she did hear sounded like some code or spyspeak.

They walked through a deserted terminal, and Lucia was surprised to find herself at a small airport, clearly used only for private planes. Jon took her hand and dragged her through the little building. She begged a moment in the restroom and tried to calm her racing thoughts. As soon as she emerged, he dragged her to the front of the terminal. Magically, a sleek black Lincoln awaited them.

"That was fast."

He shrugged. "It pays to have friends."

Without another word, Jon opened her door, and she scooted into the plush interior. He climbed in behind her, planting himself right beside her, his hand on her thigh.

"Bocelli," the driver greeted, his blue eyes shining in the rearview mirror.

"Wade." Jon nodded. "Good place to stay in town? We'll be here for a few days, I think."

"I got just the thing. Sit back, I'll have you there in twenty." He drove into the dark night, making his way out of the little airport and onto a relatively deserted street.

"With room service?" Jon asked. "She hasn't eaten yet."

"Yeah. Kitchen might be closed, but I'll hook you up."

Jon leaned forward and slapped Wade's shoulder. "You're all right, man."

"I'll remember you said that."

Laughing, Jon sat back and slung his arm around Lucia, angling her back against his wide chest and between his legs—and brushing his fingers over the swells of her cleavage. "Isn't she pretty?"

She held her breath, wishing to hell her skin wasn't tingling where he touched her. She tried to squirm away from his grazing fingertips, but he clamped his free hand around her thigh and tightened his arm around her shoulders, keeping her in place with a silent command. His fingers caressed her flesh, easing down to the edge of her bra and just beneath the lace. Her breath caught, and wide-eyed, she glanced at Wade, who watched in the rearview mirror. She was frozen except for her suddenly heavy breathing. What the hell was Jon doing?

"Gorgeous." Wade's voice sounded like black silk, low and smooth. "Natural breasts that large are a total turn-on, and her hips . . ." He hissed. "They were made for gripping during a long, hard fuck."

Jon's hand on her thigh began creeping up, shoving the hem of her dress up as he went. Her mouth fell open, and his fingertips brushing up her thigh left a trail of fire. What was he doing to her?

"Exactly. Anything about her unattractive?"

She tried to elbow Jon, but he sat too close to get in a hard blow.

"Not a damn thing. If you didn't have your hands all over her and weren't obviously staking some claim, I'd be asking the pretty thing to spend a little time with me."

"Fuck off," Jon volleyed back with a smile.

"Message received." Wade laughed.

"Could you two not talk about me as if I'm not here?" Lucia asked them.

But deep down, she was pleased. This was his way of both telling and showing her that she was desirable. The knowledge made her glow.

"We know you're here, Doc." With his grip, Jon nudged her thighs apart. His fingers crept up higher, so close she could feel the heat of his skin on the other side of her rapidly dampening panties. "I like you here."

Wildly, Lucia wondered how much Wade could see in the rearview mirror. And why his eyes on the two of them turned her on. She swallowed hard.

Jon breathed along the side of her neck, sending a shiver down her spine and a starburst of tingles along her skin. Heat flared through her flesh. Her will began to crumble. Unconsciously, she let her head fall to the side, giving him more access to her throat.

"That's it, Doc," he whispered. "God, you smell good. I can't wait to get you alone. I'm going to spend half the night figuring out every way to make you come with my mouth. The other half I'm going to spend inside you."

She whimpered at his words. Her sex clenched, wept, ached. Everything he said dug inside her and tore down more of her defenses. His hand crept higher still on her thigh, almost . . . there. Would he go even higher, actually touch her? Would he feel how wet she was? She held her breath.

"Lucia, look at me," he demanded in a whisper, leaning around her side to make that possible.

With heavy lids, she opened her eyes and turned slowly, looking at the fierce passion stamped across his face. Her body flushed hot, bloomed open for him.

He was right when he said she wanted to give herself to him. Until she'd looked at him, she'd never known the ache to have a man. Jon had left her—but the need never had. Having him back here only ramped up the desire again.

She couldn't wait to feel him, to have his hands on her. Lucia arched, purposely pressing the secret, untouched part of her against his fingers and crying out at the electric touch that revved up her body.

Jon cupped her mound possessively, pressing his fingers in slow circles over her. "You're wet, Doc."

God, he could feel her through her panties. Lucia closed her eyes. "Yes."

"And so hot. Is this pussy mine?"

She gasped, trembling, trying to find the words to answer. She had no experience with desire, with anything this overwhelming. Sensation drowned her mind, and for the first time in her life, Lucia felt only her body, her pleasure, and it was a revelation. Unlike the rest of her life, she didn't analyze it, she just let events unfold. There was no doubt in her mind that Jon Bocelli was going to be her first lover—and that no other man would ever measure up.

"Lucia? Look at me." As her eyes fluttered open again, she realized that she didn't remember shutting them. Now she sensed Wade's gaze on them through the mirror, but it was Jon's dark, commanding stare that captured her. With a glance, he caressed her mouth, then settled on her eyes. "You look beautiful. C'mon, Doc. Give me what I want. Tell me, is this pussy mine?"

"Yes," she breathed.

"Good girl. I'm going to need more of it. More of you," he whispered against her neck, making her shiver once more. "Lift your back away from me."

Lucia didn't stop to think, she just complied. It was as if all her inhibitions and worries went out the window. Jon had told her how he felt, had even shown her she was desirable. He still wanted her, even when she offered to help him with his brother. He told her what he wanted; she didn't have to wonder if she was doing anything wrong or displeasing him. With him, pleasure was as simple as breathing. It was also deep as an ocean, and its currents just kept pulling her under and under to the dark place where her body throbbed and waited and ached only for him.

When she eased away from him, he removed his hand from her mound, and she mewled a protest.

"Shh. Patience, Doc." He smiled softly as he unzipped her little black dress down the back, all the way to her hips. The black fabric slithered apart. Jon pushed it off her shoulders, revealing her black lacy bra. Cold air hit her overheated skin and was almost welcome. It made her nipples even harder.

"Fuck, that's pretty, Doc. Know how many fantasies I've had about you?" he growled in her ear.

Stunned, she shook her head. He'd thought of her?

"I'll bet even you can't count that high." He smiled. "Want my hand back on your pussy?"

"Yes," she panted.

"I do, too. Take your bra off for me, and I'll touch you again."

Would he touch her breasts? Lick them? Suck her nipples? Or just stare with that inscrutable, intense stare? She wanted any of those, all of those, but . . .

Lucia flicked her gaze to the rearview mirror and whispered, "What about him?"

"You want him to watch?"

At first she'd found it arousing. Now . . . Lucia bit her lip. "No. I want to be with just you."

"Good answer." Jon flicked a button, and up went a privacy partition of darkly tinted glass.

Lucia caught one last regretful blue-eyed stare in that glass before the partition closed completely, leaving her alone with Jon. She trembled. Now she was completely at Jon's mercy, totally under his spell—and she didn't want to be anywhere else.

Slowly, she angled toward him, then reached behind her and unclasped her bra. As she pulled it away from her body, her heavy breasts spilled out, nipples dark and taut. As Jon shoved it in his coat pocket with a grin, his rapt gaze immediately fell there, and he caressed the side of her breast, his thumb swiping across her nipple.

Lucia froze as pleasure rushed her. She gasped, arched—a silent plea for more.

"Sensitive nipples. Hmm . . ." He thumbed the little bud again, a slow, calculated swipe back and forth.

"Yes." She could hear her own voice trembling, her desire dripping in her breathy tone.

"You're not getting that bra back until I say so." He kissed her shoulder, nipped at her earlobe. "I've got all night with you, and I think it's a safe bet that you won't see it again until tomorrow, Doc."

He intended to keep her naked all night? She swallowed. The idea should alarm her. With big breasts, she rarely went without a bra. She usually slept with one, in fact, for the support. But the idea of being bare and available for Jon turned her on even more. She nodded.

"Good. Now give me your panties. You don't need them, either."

Reach up under her dress and remove the only barrier between him and her wet sex? Give him total access . . . Lucia stopped thinking after that realization. She wriggled her hips and lifted her skirt, catching the bottom of her little black panties and pulling them down.

The second the fabric cleared the hem of her dress, Jon took over, yanking the panties down her thighs, over her knees, until he tugged them off her completely. He gripped them in his fist with a triumphant smile. "These are soaking, Doc. You're wet for me."

How could she deny it? "Yes."

"I'm going to take advantage of that." He pressed a long, lingering kiss to her lips, dipping inside for a languorous tasting that melted her all over again.

"Please," she whimpered. She might be appalled later. Her pride and backbone would eventually balk at how she'd allowed herself to be reduced to monosyllables, but right now she was too lost in the moment—in him—to care.

"You just wait, Doc." That didn't sound like a threat, but a promise, and Lucia couldn't wait.

He tucked the damp panties into his coat pocket, too, and patted just outside. "These are mine, just like you're going to be soon. All of you."

He hovered, his stare raked her up and down. Lucia couldn't ignore that her lips felt swollen, her breasts tight and needy for his touch. Her dress had fallen to her waist, its hem just barely covering her sex. The leather under her butt would probably bear a puddle when she got up, she was so wet. If she could see herself, she'd probably be shocked, but she wasn't about to object.

Suddenly, the car stopped. Wade rapped on the other part of the partition. She looked out and saw a quaint little hotel with Old World charm to her left.

Jon cursed. "Put your dress back on."

Numbly, she thrust her hands into the sleeves, wondering how much longer it would be before he took it off again. He zipped it back up for her, then rapped on the partition. It buzzed down slowly, and Wade's blue eyes met hers in the mirror once more.

"I called ahead," he said from the front seat. "All you have to do is walk in, flash some ID, grab a key, and . . . whatever you're going to do then. Have fun."

"Thanks, man. I owe you."

"I'll remember that, too."

Jon laughed. "I know you will."

He climbed out of the vehicle, onto the dark sidewalk, then turned and held out his hand.

This was it, for real. If Lucia went with him, he would remove her dress completely, lay her down, and explore every inch of her body. He'd make her take him deep, probably more than once.

Sex, when she'd thought of it with a nice stranger she could direct and control, hadn't made her heart race. Sex with Jon wouldn't be like that. He'd dominate. He'd demand. He'd tell her how it was going to be. He'd make her wet and panting and needy—and there wouldn't be a damn thing she could do about it. That both excited and scared her.

It was probably good for her to be so far removed from her tightly controlled life.

She slid her hand into his, blinking up at him, asking him for . . . she wasn't sure. Not mercy, exactly. Not love. She knew better.

Whatever she asked for, though, he understood. "I've got you, Doc."

Lucia believed him. He was strong, capable, smart, brave, determined . . . perfect. This wasn't forever, but she couldn't have wished for any other man to be her first. She smiled as she exited the car and stood beside him.

Gripping her hand, he used his other to shut the car door, then thumped the roof twice with his palm. Wade honked once and drove off.

The night closed in on them, and Jon turned watchful, scanning his surroundings alertly in a slow slide up and down the street. Then he tugged on her hand. "Let's go."

She couldn't see the exterior of the inn well in the dark, but the inside enveloped her in warmth and cheer right away. Tuscan themed and decorated in rich woods and earth tones, the place felt welcoming.

But as she walked toward the check-in desk, Lucia became acutely aware of her bare nipples brushing the slightly rough fabric of her dress, making them even harder. With each step, she got even wetter. Jon turned to her, wearing a wicked little smile, as if he knew exactly how being naked under her dress made her feel. As he arranged for room service in one hour and grabbed the key, Lucia felt her moisture slide down to the insides of her thighs. As they headed to the elevator, that moisture spread, lubricating her skin where her thighs rubbed together. God, she'd be a mess by the time they got to the room.

As the elevator doors slid shut behind them, enveloping them in privacy, Jon pulled her against him, her back to his front. His thick erection prodded her lower back as he pressed her into him with a groan. She wriggled back on him, and his grip on her tightened.

"Doc . . . you don't want me out of control."

But she did. He'd melted her into a puddle of need. While he was still capable of signing the registrar's book and ordering food, she was damn near blind with lust. She wriggled again.

"Last warning . . ." he growled in her ear.

The sound shivered down her spine, and she shook her head, refusing to heed it. Instead, she plastered her back to him, throwing her head on his shoulder, and gyrated on his erection again. "Jon, please."

He hissed and dropped his hand to her thigh. Quickly, it climbed up, up to her hip. Lucia held her breath as his fingers dipped under the hem of her dress and right between her soaking folds. Unerringly, his fingertips found her clit and grazed her sensitive nub. Sensation swelled. She leaned into him with a moan. Jon nipped at her neck, teeth scraping, lips and tongue soothing. With his other hand, he cupped her breast through her dress, rolling her nipple between his thumb and index finger. All the feelings joined up right between her legs and sparked. Blood rushed through her body. From occasional masturbation, Lucia knew she was close.

The ding of the elevator interrupted, and she could have cried. As the doors parted, Jon dropped his hands and eased away. His cool control frustrated Lucia—until she realized an elderly couple stood on the other side of the door with a polite smile.

"Excuse us." Jon grabbed her hand and led her down the hall, dimly lit with faux sconces. When he reached the end of the hall and shoved the door open, he pulled her inside and shut the door behind him. "Wait here."

Then he drew a pistol from the small of his back.

chapter four

Lucia's eyes widened. All this time, he'd been armed? As he disappeared into the bathroom, checking the tub and behind the door, she frowned at herself. Of course. He was an FBI agent. The organization's culture was high on guns and danger. He probably expected trouble as they unraveled her father's clues, which made sense. If Pietro was guilty, he wouldn't want this secret uncovered. If he'd killed his brother to elevate his own mob status, he'd think nothing of killing his niece to protect it.

A moment later, Jon returned, flipped on the light in the narrow hall, then secured each of the three locks on the door. He came at her with burning eyes, slowly prowling forward. That fiery, commanding gaze insisted that she heed him, and as he advanced, she retreated until her back hit the door. He braced his hands on either side of her head and leaned in, putting his face mere inches from hers.

"Want out?"

He was giving her every opportunity to bail if she wasn't ready to give up her virginity. He'd already spelled out what would happen if she stayed, but he wasn't going to press her if she didn't want to have sex.

"No."

Dark triumph crossed his face as he backed up a step. "Turn around, Doc."

No reason. No explanation . . . just a command. Lucia could have studied it to death, but that didn't suit her purposes. She didn't have to know anything except that she could trust Jon and he'd do everything he could to make her first experience as good as possible.

She nodded, then turned her back to him. Jon moaned and placed his big, hot hands on her shoulders, planting a row of burning kisses along the back of her neck that made her want to rub against him and beg.

Instead, his hands slid down to her hips. "Behave, and I'll reward you."

And she'd bet his idea of reward would be beyond pleasurable. "Yes, Sir."

He hesitated. "Sir? You've done some reading?"

"I have."

"Excellent. I'll be putting your knowledge to good use soon." He didn't say another word, just lowered her zipper. The quiet hiss filled the room, along with her heavy breathing. The cold air hit her skin, but he covered her with those warm palms, slowly sliding the dress off her shoulders, down her arms, over her hips . . . then into a pile at her feet.

Lucia was acutely aware that she was naked, that Jon Bocelli could see her back, her wide ass, her thick thighs. She closed her eyes, her heart thundering in her chest.

"Disappointed?" She had to ask the question.

He gripped her hips again and pulled her body against his. "If this wasn't your first time and I weren't trying to be tender with you, I'd spank your ass for that question." His hand skated down her backside, gently groping and feeling. The lights shined down on her, and there was nowhere to hide. Jon seemed to like what he saw, groaning and kneeling to place a kiss on each of her round cheeks. "No more self-doubt. I know exactly what I'm getting, and there's no woman I want more, Lucia."

When he stood and turned her to face him, and she saw the sincerity in his eyes, she shoved her fears to the back of her mind. Not all men wanted a twig. Not all men found her intelligence intimidating. Not all men thought her lack of experience was strange. Nicki had been telling her these things for years, and she hadn't really listened. But now she understood that it only mattered what Jon thought. And he seemed to like her just the way she was.

Everything hit her at once: the gravity of the pending moment, his weighty stare telling her that this night was important to him, too, and the unbending certainty that she'd fallen totally in love with Jon Bocelli. He'd probably walk away again; they lived in two different worlds. But tonight was theirs, and she'd cherish her memories even when she had to move on without him.

"I want you, too." She stared up into his dark eyes, feeling caressed, enveloped by him.

He took her hand and led her deeper into the room, past a plush terra cotta sofa and a pair of leather club chairs, then to the giant canopied four-poster bed. The bulky, imposing mahogany was almost at odds with the soft gold and cream comforter and lacy pillows.

Jon flipped on the lights and turned down the bed. Automatically, Lucia walked toward him, nervous and eager to be his, at least for the night. But as she walked past him, she frowned. "You're . . . overdressed."

Raising a brow, he sent her a hot stare rife with challenge. "You feel like doing something about it?"

Absolutely. Lucia smiled.

Pausing in front of him, she lifted her hands and pushed the suit coat off his shoulders. With a grin tugging one corner of his mouth, he helped her by shrugging out of the jacket. He caught it with one hand and folded it over the back of a nearby chair. Then Lucia set to work on his pristine dress shirt, one button at a time, revealing a wide swath of muscles, dusted with dark, coarse hair across his chest, narrowing into a narrow path down his ridged abdomen. He was so male everywhere, so . . . everything that made her breath catch.

Tugging the shirt from the waistband of his pants, she watched as he eased out of the garment and draped it across the back of the chair, over his coat. He toed out of his shoes and doffed his socks, setting them aside.

"Don't stop, Lucia." The words were soft, but the command was unmistakable.

"Yes, Sir," she whispered, perfectly at peace.

This was the right move, with the right man, in the right way.

She set to work on his button and zipper, easing his pants down his narrow hips and muscular thighs, also dusted with dark hair. He was big and imposing, a total testosterone bomb. But she knew he would never hurt her.

He stepped out of his pants, and from the pocket, he extracted a little packet, and set it on the nearby nightstand. A condom. God, why hadn't she thought of that? Even in her most naïve moments, Jon was taking care of her.

"Thank you. I—I'm not on birth control."

He nodded at her. "I'll do everything possible to keep you safe in every way."

Lucia closed her eyes as a fresh wave of need crashed over her. Jon would make some lucky woman a great husband someday. She yearned to be that woman, but knew better. He'd always been career focused, and now he had his brother to worry about. She had critical papers due. "Publish or perish" was the motto of all true academics. With fresh tenure, she had to try to keep up with her more seasoned peers.

"Do you need me to take over, Doc?"

No. She wanted to do this. He'd removed every stitch she wore, bared her for his gaze. She wanted to do the same to him.

Even through his dark cotton boxer briefs, she could see the outline of his thick erection. She'd never seen a live penis, but that didn't matter. He wasn't expecting a sexpert, just someone willing to let him touch her and learn.

Gathering her nerves, she curled her fingers around his waistband and eased the underwear down his hips, pausing to draw the elastic away from his hard . . . The word "erection" didn't seem imposing enough for the long, hard column of flesh with the flushed, swollen head.

"You're staring at my cock."

"Everything is so new. I didn't . . ." She shook her head. *His cock*. Okay, that was what she'd call it. "I want to touch you."

"I'd be disappointed if you didn't."

Jon was every kind of perfect, and she was so glad now that she'd waited and never had the kind of fumbling-in-the-back-of-the-car experience her sister and her friends had talked about. This would be sublime.

Her hand trembled as she lifted it to him, but she wasn't nervous. A pinging excitement had overtaken her and given her a delicious case of the shivers. When her fingers curled around him, she gasped. She'd expected hard flesh, but not the softness of his skin, not the sheer heat he put off in such measure that she could imagine, with Jon by her side, in her bed, she'd never be cold again.

He jerked and groaned as she wrapped her hand around him and squeezed gently. She gave him an exploratory stroke, up to brush her thumb across the impatient purple head flaring above her grip, then with a drag of her palm back down his shaft to the heavy male testicles below. He closed his eyes, his entire body tensing, fists clenching. Lucia smiled. He was nearly a foot taller than her and outweighed her by at least seventy-five pounds. He was bigger, stronger, and could drop her to her back and mount her quicker than the blink of an eye if he chose. But he stood here and let her have complete power over him, allowing her whatever time she needed to grow used to him, feel comfortable. And she adored him for it.

Again, she stroked him. Unbelievably, he swelled in her hand. Grew even harder, visibly longer and thicker. Soon, this would be inside her, a part of her. She shivered again as that ping of excitement became more like a seismic tremor.

"Lucia . . ." he groaned. "Fuck, Doc, you have no idea how many times I've thought of this."

"I have, too."

His eyes flashed open. He looked surprised—in a good way. "Yeah? What else?"

Did she dare? Tonight might be all they had. No way was she going to let him go with regrets. She'd better go for broke and fulfill all her fantasies.

Slowly, she sank to her knees. Jon's eyes flared with heat as he slid his fingers possessively through her hair and fisted the thick auburn strands, holding her just shy of his waiting cock. "Are you sure you want this?"

"Please." It was almost a whimper.

Using his hold on her hair with one hand, he wrapped the other around his shaft and guided her mouth to him. "Open up. Use your tongue and suck—Oh, yeah . . . Just like that. Fuck, Doc. That's perfect. Holy shit."

Lucia smiled to herself and redoubled her efforts. From studying anatomy—she'd loved the sciences—she knew where he'd be most sensitive, so she focused on swiping the nerve-laden head with her tongue on every upstroke, then taking as much of him in her mouth as she could. When the head hit her throat, she swallowed on him, both for his pleasure and to push back her gag reflex. Then she hollowed out her cheeks and sucked as strongly as she could manage, running the tip of her tongue along the underside, nudging that spot just under his crown. And because she'd listened to her girlfriends talk about giving head, she knew that Jon would like her hand on the heavy fall of his testicles.

His grip in her hair tightened, pulling just slightly. The sting was anything but unpleasant. Funny, she'd always been a cerebral creature, but for the first time in her life, she experienced herself through the physical, as if she could finally comprehend the outside world by using the inherent gifts of her arms, legs, and skin—and her glorious sense of taste. On her tongue, he registered as salty and masculine. And perfect. Though she knelt to him and laved him, his pure pleasure in her act made her feel so feminine, almost powerful. How much satisfaction would it give them both if she stayed here and made him climax in this way? The act was so intimate, and she couldn't help thinking that she'd feel so close to him afterward.

But that wasn't on his agenda.

When he pulled away and lifted her to her feet, she moaned. "Jon . . ."

"Stop, Doc. You're damn good at that," he panted.

Lucia grinned shyly. "Beginner's luck?"

"We've established that you read."

"And pay attention to what my friends have said about their boyfriends . . ."

Jon growled. "Don't want you hearing about other guys' sex lives."

The possessive statement jolted her with pleasure. "Trust me, I'm only thinking about you right now."

"Good girl." He caressed her cheek, then looked past her to the bed. "Get on. Flat on your back. Spread your legs for me."

The dark command in his voice both aroused and scared her. He wasn't the lover who'd been putty in her hands a few minutes ago. He was now completely in charge, his nearly black gaze like a drill penetrating all her bravado to see to the soft woman underneath who not just wanted his passion, but needed his tenderness.

He caressed her hip. "I'm riding a thin edge, Doc. But you can trust me. I'll never hurt you. I'll work like hell to make it good for you."

With a nod, she eased onto the bed, conscious of the generous flare of her hips, the less than flat curve of her belly. Jon liked her as she was, though. He'd be disappointed if she couldn't get past herself to follow a simple command. Lucia forced herself to spread her legs.

She could work up her courage, but there was one issue she couldn't discount.

"It's going to hurt." She bit her lip.

He sat on the edge of the bed and took her hand. "For a second. That's unavoidable."

"You speaking from experience?" In an odd way, she hoped that he was.

"Sorry, Doc. I grew up in a rough neighborhood. My dad was gone. Mama worked two jobs to feed Stef and me. I started taking odd jobs when I was ten, and by the time I got enough spare time in my day to think about sex, most of the girls I knew had been around the block a few times." He shrugged. "I didn't think at my age that I'd be having this first with anyone."

"At your age?" She swatted his arm. "You're hardly ready for assisted living."

His gaze grew serious. "I'm thirty-five, chronologically. In experience, I'm fucking Methuselah. I don't deserve to touch you."

She sat up, shoving aside the fact that her boobs probably sagged and her stomach likely pooched. Instead, she just put her arms around him and brushed a kiss over his mouth.

"I come from a family you have every right to hate. I have an IQ that put me in the freak category when I was very young, so my social skills ensured I said the wrong thing at least once a conversation. Sometimes, I still do. Boys saw me as a pudgy nuisance. When all my classmates were sixteen . . . I was eleven. When we graduated from high school, three of the girls were visibly pregnant. That was the week I got my first period. Don't start me on college. Even when I finally got a figure, all the guys called me 'jail bait.'" She shrugged. "Chronologically, I'm twenty-five today. But I guess in a lot of ways, I'm still a baby to you. If you'd rather not do this—"

Jon covered her mouth with his and shoved her back to the bed, mounting her in a second. His tongue delved deep, taking total possession of her. Lucia opened to him, clung, wrapped her arms around him. He wedged his hips between her thighs, and she felt every inch of his steely cock pressing against her slick folds, probing, sliding, prodding her clit until she gasped and arched up to him.

"You're definitely not a baby, Doc. I can't look at you like anything less than a sexy woman I can't do without touching for another second."

Every word wiped away her insecurity and sadness. He managed to open up everything inside her, and she mentally threw the doors open to her body—and her heart. "Then don't."

He lifted himself onto his arms and glanced down her body, his gaze turning hotter with every sweep. "Not rushing this."

Jon lowered himself to her, this time a bit farther down her body—right to her breasts. "These are a wet dream." He plumped one with one hand and kissed the side of her breast, his exhalations hovering over her nipple. She shivered and felt every sensation acutely. It was as if her body was completely attuned to him, suddenly swelling, rising, blooming just for him.

"That's it, Doc," he whispered just before he sucked her nipple into his mouth.

Instantly, she moaned and thrust her hands into his inky hair. Thick, glossy, perfect to hold on to as he took her apart one lick, suck, and nip at a time. Blood rushed to her nipples, and it only made him devour her more. She'd never been more aware of any part of herself, but no escaping how the sensitive little pebbles cried out for more. And every pull of his lips on her made a trail of fire flame right toward her sex. It clenched, ached with emptiness.

"Jon." She sounded desperate because she was. If he stopped now, if he didn't give her what her body craved . . . God, she was about to crawl out of her skin. Everything underneath felt hot and foreign and on the verge of an orgasm unlike anything she'd ever been able to give herself, batteries or not.

"We're going to get there, Doc," he murmured as he pressed his lips to the heavy underside of her breast, then laved his way up to her nipple, covering it and taking it in the hot depths of his mouth as he stared. Just stared. His dark gaze fused to hers, so connected she knew the rhythm of his breathing, of his heartbeat, of the blood racing through his body with the force of his desire.

Then he started kissing his way down her body, prying her thighs wider. His gaze never left hers. Pressing hot kisses over her belly, he gripped her hip with one hand—and lifted one of her legs over his shoulder, his dark eyes promising bed-scratching, back-arching, scream-worthy pleasure. Lucia's heart stuttered, skipped a few beats. She knew exactly where he was headed, and the thought sent a jolt of desire sizzling through her body. Her sex wept. She could feel it. No way he wouldn't see it as soon as he looked—

"You're so wet," he groaned as he stared at her slick folds. His thumb grazed the top of her mound, just above her clit, and she arched up, trying to put that touch just where she wanted it.

"Not yet." He held her in place and leaned in, breathing hard.

Lucia writhed against his tight hold. She loved his possession, his control of her, but her body hungered for more. She couldn't stop writhing and moaning when his hot breath caressed the most intimate and untouched part of her body. After twenty-five years of waiting, of being such a good girl, she wanted to be so, so bad.

"Jon!" She tugged at his hair, pleading. "I need you. Touch me. Something."

He palmed her ass and lifted her off the mattress a fraction, settling himself deeper between the *V* of her thighs. She looked down her body to him, and he wore a devilish smile.

"The anticipation can be half the pleasure."

"I've been anticipating for my whole life. I feel like I'm about to burst. My sanity is unraveling as quickly as my patience. Please . . ."

He brushed his thumb across her wet flesh, pausing to rub a little circle over her clit. "I'm going to take really good care of you, Doc. On my timetable. Now close your eyes."

No way she couldn't obey the deep command in his murmur. He didn't have to speak loudly to get her attention.

And then she felt the wet warmth of his tongue sliding into her folds, drinking of her juices, weaving a clever path up to her clit, where he laved and flicked, swirled, nudged, teased—then sucked.

The blood rushed through her body, roared into her head. Her heartbeat felt like an anvil against a steely breast, hard, loud, reverberating. And the pleasure buried her like an avalanche. Lucia had lived her entire life by complicated associations, metaphors, unraveling history's most important moments, looking for every nuance of meaning and finding a soft satisfaction when she found personal understanding in the moments that had shaped mankind. In this moment, she couldn't string two words together that didn't end with "please" and desperate pleading to Jon to let her fall deep into the looming pleasure.

And she couldn't find the voice to beg. The ache between her legs coiled and clawed higher. She whimpered, gripping him. Jon was in perfect control of her body, ruthlessly pushing her up the pinnacle to a place she'd never been before, pausing or slowing his ministrations until she went wild, bucking and thrashing under him. Only then did he give her more, taking her again right to the very edge of pleasure, then backing away, soothing, shushing her demands with a soft touch. Once he'd dragged her back from the precipice and breathing became part of her ritual again, he'd dive in once more, hungry, unapologetic, determined.

Lucia had never known anything like this—suspended from reality, so trapped inside her body while achingly aware of his every move and breath. The waiting . . . God, he held her in the palm of his hand, and his sure hands and little smile told her that he was terribly comfortable with that fact.

"Jon, please. *Please!*" she panted, every muscle in her legs tingling, trembling. A pleasure unlike anything she'd ever known was *right there*.

"I know, Doc. I want at least this to be really good for you. I don't know how much you'll be able to enjoy penetration the first time." He grazed her clit rhythmically with his thumb, let off, then fingered each side of the little nub, awakening yet a whole new set of nerves. Back and forth, back and forth. Lucia bypassed begging and pleading, heading straight for tears at the merciless way he took her apart. Then he sucked her in his mouth one last time. "Come now, pet."

As if his soft demand unlocked all the barriers to her body, every door and window inside her burst wide open. She let out a high, keening cry as the pleasure crested, wracking her as she shuddered, whirling and dizzy. Black spots danced in her vision. Her hearing stopped working entirely for a long moment, as if her body needed all its resources to process a climax this monumental.

And Jon stayed with her, using his fingers and mouth, until she rode the orgasm to its rough, shuddering crash at the end. She landed back in her body with a tumble, aware of her chest sucking in gulps of air, her heart rattling against her breastbone like a native drum . . . and languid satisfaction curling through every one of her limbs. Her brain? Not interested in coming back online.

"Oh. My. God." She sagged against the bed, wiping at her damp brow.

Jon stood and palmed the condom. "Last chance. I'll leave you here, if you want."

Her gaze snapped up to him. Was he insane? Come this far and not feel him deep inside her, not fulfill one of her darkest wishes? No way would she not have every chance to give him back even a tenth of the pleasure he'd given her.

"There's only one thing I want." She spread her legs in invitation. "One person I want. Now, Jon."

He didn't hesitate again, just stood, donned the condom over that sizeable cock, and slipped between her legs. "Keep with me. Tell me how you're feeling. Fuck, I don't want to hurt you."

"It'll just be a moment, right?" She opened her arms, curling them around his neck.

"I swear, I'll make the pain worth the pleasure."

"I know."

Jon stared, those dark eyes delving into her as he took her hips in his hands. She curled her legs around him as he probed against her slick opening. Unbelievably, just being near him started the rising tide of desire again. That little ache clawed its way behind her clit once more. Her heart picked up the pace again, as if the last marathon of pleasure had only been a warm-up.

Then he sank into her slowly, inching through tissues that had never known intrusion. The barrier of her virginity stopped him, and he sighed.

"Look at me. Nowhere else." He took one of her hands in his, lacing their fingers together.

At Lucia's nod, Jon eased back, holding her hip in a hard grip. That and his shuddering breath were her only warnings before he thrust hard, ripping through the barrier and shoving deep inside her. A tearing pain assailed her. She cried out, body tensing. The echoes of that pain arrowed down her limbs and tore through her body. And still he kept shoving in until he was fully immersed inside her. Then Jon sat perfectly still, focusing completely on her with his watchful gaze.

He did nothing. A second passed, another, one more . . . With each moment, the pain diminished, replaced by an achy tenderness between her legs. She'd be sore later, but now that he was inside her, the wonder of it overtook her. She could feel his heartbeat both against her chest and deep inside her sex. He brushed her hair off her forehead, caressing her reverently. The last of the pain-induced tension drained away.

"You okay?" His voice sounded as if he'd dragged it through gravel behind a speeding car. The effort to hold back was clearly costing him. That he'd take such effort for her was so damn endearing. As if she needed more reasons to be in love with him.

"Great. Really." Except an ache moved in between her legs and settled in. And it wasn't pain, but need. She frowned, wriggled, arched up to him.

Jon hissed in a breath, eyes squeezing shut. "I'm trying to stay still for you, Doc. Let your body get used to me. Just a bit longer."

A bit longer, and she'd go insane. "Now, Jon!" She planted her feet on the bed and lifted herself up to him. "I've waited twenty-five years for this. I've told you I'm not breakable. You've been so patient. Don't you want more? Take it."

He smiled and brushed a soft kiss across her mouth. "Yes, ma'am. You're awfully bossy, and I'm letting you be right now. Don't get used to it."

Did that mean he expected to take her to bed again? Lucia was giddy with the thought. This might not be forever, but he wasn't in a hurry to leave her yet. And she'd take that—at least for now. If she had her way, however, he'd make love to her, realize that he truly cared about her, and never want to let her go.

Fat chance, but it was a lovely fantasy, and she was going to milk it for all it was worth.

JON HOOVERED IN a deep breath and tried to clear his head. It was either that or turn into a raving wild man above the soft curves of Lucia's lush body and plow into her tight pussy over and over. He couldn't do that. She deserved tenderness her first time. God knew he wasn't usually the gentlest of lovers, but he was determined to make this everything she'd waited for.

Maybe then she wouldn't run off when this was over. Maybe they'd have time to explore what might be between them.

Grasping her thighs, he lifted them to his waist, and she curled her legs around him. Experimentally, he withdrew. Her body tugged at him, clung, gripping so tight. Fuck, his eyes were rolling into the back of his head. And when he eased back in, she welcomed him deep, slick flesh easing the way, then clenched him even harder. Shit, he wasn't sure how long he could last through this unrelenting sensual torture. But he was determined to give it his all to make her come at least once.

He rolled over, still deep inside her, until she sat astride, thighs hugging his hips. Oh, hell. Wasn't that a gorgeous view? Lucia was all woman, with her soft, flushed face, her heavy breasts with their tight rosy-brown nipples, the small waist, a little curve to her belly, and those hips that fascinated him so much. Her instinct kicked in, and she rooted around on his cock, raising and lowering herself, hands braced on his chest, giving him one hell of a cleavage show. But he was transfixed by her face, those flushed cheeks, the gasping wonder of her wide eyes. She showed every expression—even the occasional twinge of pain—as he planted himself even deeper inside her pussy, but discomfort quickly changed to overwhelming pleasure as she rose up and eased down again.

Beneath her, he tensed and widened his stance—then fucked her slowly from beneath, the aim and cadence of his stroke designed to hit that sensitive spot inside her over and over. Jon established a slow, deep stroke, a steady cadence deep inside her. Within seconds, she dug her nails into his shoulders and moved with him, helping him undo the last of her composure.

"You look so sexy, Doc. Being inside you is better than any fantasy I could imagine. That's it . . . Move with me." He grabbed her hips and picked up the pace. "Fuck. I feel you tightening, pet."

"Jon!"

"I'm here. Take it. Feel it. Let it go."

"I don't—" She looked at him with wide-eyed amazement. "This is different. Oh God . . . Oh!" She panted, then closed her eyes.

Her obvious arousal climbing was one hell of a turn-on for him, and he kept giving her one deep plunge of his cock after another. Her pussy fluttered, then clamped down.

"Come for me, Lucia!"

She screamed, and he increased his pace from beneath her, pounding relentlessly against her most sensitive spot. Fuck, he could feel her swelling, her nails in his skin. But it was the desperate pleasure in her helpless stare that really turned him inside out. God, she was everything he'd imagined and more. Innocent, but not totally shy. Educated, but untried. And uninhibited.

Fuck, he had to get deeper.

Rolling Lucia to her back, he planted his knees on the mattress and gripped the insides of her thighs, pulling them even wider apart. Rising up over her, he tilted her hips up and prodded that one spot inside her unmercifully. It would still be sensitive from her last orgasm. But Jon wasn't taking any chances. He covered her abdomen with one hand and prodded her clit with his thumb, fucking into her in short, deep strokes.

She gasped and shook her head back and forth, bucking wildly underneath him. "Yes! Oh my God, yes. Don't stop. Please," she begged. "I'm going to . . ."

Yeah, she was. She did—with a long growl of a moan, scratching at the sheets, and throwing her hips up at him. Around his cock, he felt a warm gush of fluid coat him, easing his way even deeper in her pussy.

Watching Lucia thrash underneath him and then cry out his name was the most erotic experience of his life. No spanking benches or blindfolds necessary, just a beautiful woman who had a foothold on his heart opening herself up to him with utter trust and passion.

Just like that, the last bit of his heart he'd kept unencumbered suddenly belonged to her. He was one hundred percent in love with Lucia DiStefano, and having her under him, coming for him . . . it was too much.

The pleasure rushed through his bloodstream, pumping into his system, as he shoved his cock into her again and again—then exploded, disintegrating, fucking melting at the pleasure bending his body and his brain, remaking him altogether as he emptied inside her with a shout and a shudder.

Though he'd used her hard, Lucia took everything he gave. Even more, she wrapped her arms around him as he collapsed against her, welcoming him as he breathed hard against her fragrant skin. She spread little kisses across his neck and shoulders.

"Thank you," she whispered. "That was perfect."

"No, you are."

Her sleepy smile went straight to his heart. Then she closed her eyes, cuddled up against him, and drifted off. Jon held her closer. Yeah, he was a goner. No way could he let this woman get away again. Once they solved this mystery of her father's, he was going to lay his cards on the table and pray that she felt the same.

chapter five

Lucia stepped out of the hotel lobby late the next morning, again in her little black dress. Jon hovered beside her, the cipher and key her father had left her in his pocket, watchful and ready for anything. He was nothing like the tender lover he'd been last night. And a few hours later. And again this morning as she'd crawled from the shower. Every step she took reminded her of how sore she was and how demanding he'd been. But she wouldn't trade a moment of their time together for the world.

As they walked down the street toward Celeste's just before eleven, the happy cocoon she'd been in dissolved. Nerves dive-bombed her stomach and gnawed at her composure. Her father had been trying to tell her something from beyond the grave, and she didn't want to fail him. Jon had also made it very clear this could quickly turn dangerous. He'd made her promise to follow his instructions explicitly and immediately if it did.

As they reached the old brick building with the little white sign that proclaimed, CELESTE'S: A FAMILY-OWNED BUSINESS SINCE 1967, a woman with salt-and-pepper hair, dancing dark eyes, and a pleasantly round face opened the door and let them in.

Her gaze lit on Jon with a smile. "I remember you. You no come to see me for a long while, eh? So handsome." She patted his face.

Lucia swore she could see Jon blush. "Thank you, Celeste."

"My daughter, she is still single . . ." The woman flashed another grin, then her eyes lit on Lucia. "Ah, but I see I am too late. Lucky girl. And *che bella donna*!" She winked.

How sweet of Celeste to call her beautiful. With a conspiratorial glance at Jon, Lucia held her hand out to the woman. "I'm Lucia DiStefano. I think you knew my father?"

"Ah. Of course." Celeste embraced her in a tight hug as if welcoming long-lost family, then stepped back, misty-eyed, and crossed herself. "God rest your father. Always he was kind to me and my family. He spoke of you with such pride."

That warmed Lucia. Nicholas DiStefano hadn't been a demonstrative man. He'd never really told her that he was proud. But she had no doubt that Celeste had spoken the truth, and it comforted Lucia to know that her father had noticed her accomplishments.

"Thank you. I miss him." She swallowed down lingering grief. Jon grabbed her hand, thumb caressing the back for reinforcement. She worked up the courage to ask Celeste, "Did he leave anything here for me, perhaps? A piece of paper of any kind?"

Celeste reared back, then hit her forehead with her open palm. "Mamma Mia! But of course. Follow me . . ."

Excitement chugging, Lucia followed Celeste as she led them through the modest dining room with its checkered tablecloths and pristine white napkins, into the kitchen. The smell of roasting garlic, basil, and oregano simmering with rich, ripe tomatoes blended with the heavenly yeasty scent of freshly baked bread. Her stomach rumbled, and Lucia thought wryly of the room service food that had gotten cold while Jon had pinned her to the bed and taught her a host of new ways that he could make her whole body glow.

As Celeste led them into a little office in the back, she sat behind a battered desk and riffled through a filing drawer. "God bless your father. He eat here nearly every week for thirty years. He was like family."

Lucia frowned. Yet he'd never brought her here. She'd never even heard of Celeste's. Though her father's nature had been secretive, she had to believe that hadn't meant that he'd loved her any less.

Celeste continued to search her drawer. "Always he brings his associates. They drink and laugh. And tip well." She laughed, and then her smile fell. "Your father, he help my son scare away the street thugs who try to make us to give money for protection. He thank me for a good meal every time. And he come to my husband's funeral five years ago. Afterward, he hug me so tight and tell me, 'If you or your children need anything, call me.' "

Really? Her father had always been an enigma, kept a distance she really hadn't comprehended between her and himself. As an adult, she guessed it was because he wanted as much room between her and his mob associates—his way of protecting her. On the one hand, she was envious that this woman and her family had known him well enough to call him a friend. On the other hand, envy aside, it warmed her heart to know he truly had the kind heart she'd always suspected. No, she knew he hadn't been an angel, but he'd been her father. She'd loved him, as Celeste clearly had.

"Ah, I find it for you. Here." The older woman held the envelope out to her.

Lucia took it slowly, fingers wrapping around the slightly yellowed edges with a pounding heart. "Thank you. Do you remember when my father gave this to you?"

"Not long before his death. I hear him tell another that he does not trust everyone around him . . ."

That instinct had been right. Lucia wished that he could have prevented his murder. Damn it, she wished he'd told her of his suspicions, though she knew logically that she could have done nothing to save him.

"I appreciate you keeping this for him and giving it to me."

Celeste nodded and ambled to the door of her office. "I leave you here to read your letter, eh? I stir my sauce and serve you a plate. You look hungry."

Jon nodded, looking grateful. "I always love your lasagna."

"I make it for you." Celeste smiled. "Lucia?"

She was hungry . . . and yet now that she held words that her father had written just for her shortly before his death, she wasn't sure she could eat a bite. But she didn't want to offend her father's friend. "Lasagna is great. Thank you."

The moment Celeste closed the door behind them, Jon fused his gaze to hers. "Talk to me. Your voice is shaking. Afraid? Nervous?"

God, the man was so attuned to her moods. "Nervous. This moment has gravity. It's like I'm going to read what he says, then I'll have to say good-bye all over again."

With seemingly little effort, Jon grabbed her around the waist and lifted her into his lap as he sat in Celeste's office chair. It creaked under their joint weight, but held as he brought her close to his chest.

"I know, Doc. This is hard, and none of it is fair. But he wanted you to do this for a reason."

Lucia nodded. "And I need to honor his wish, even if I don't understand it."

With trembling fingers, she opened the envelope and withdrew a piece of heavy stationary in a crisp white. She recognized the slanted handwriting inked in black as her father's immediately. A wave of longing rushed up to her. She wished she'd understood him better, that they'd been closer. She'd always imagined they'd have more time together.

But she didn't, and now she had to choke back her regret and move forward—for him.

My dearest Lucia,

A thousand words cannot express my regret for leaving you so soon. I leave you this task, my clever little bambina, because you alone will understand my message and do right with it. Think of all I taught you. I am counting on you and am so proud.

Love,
Papa

Tears filled her eyes. Lucia blinked to clear her vision, but they kept coming back. Jon was with her instantly, drying them away.

"Don't cry, Doc. He loved you."

"I miss him."

"Of course you do. You always will. He helped give you life and represented security for you. He protected you and loved you in his way."

She released a shuddering breath. Jon was right. "This is one hell of a cryptovariable for this cipher. But I need to do this last thing for him."

Jon hesitated, then nodded. "I'll be with you, watching out for you."

Protecting her in case danger reared its head. She knew that was what he meant. Still, she couldn't help loving him for it.

"How does it work?" he asked. "What was his system?"

"He kept this one simple." Lucia clutched the note and pointed to the first few items on the cipher. "See these three numbers grouped together?"

"Twenty-four, one hundred twenty-one, seventy-two." He frowned. "Those aren't numbers that correspond to letters of the alphabet."

"No." She laid the two papers out side by side and started counting. Within a few moments, she knew for certain that she understood. "It isn't twenty-four exactly. He's really saying second word, fourth letter. He never counted salutations or closings, just the body of the letter. So the second word, fourth letter is—"

"U," Jon said, grabbing a piece of paper and a pen off Celeste's desk. "What's next?"

"One hundred twenty-one is a bit trickier. But since the first word doesn't have twenty-one letters, we're safe to assume he meant twelfth word, first letter."

"S."

"Exactly. Next is seventy-two."

"E." Jon frowned. "Use? He wants you to use something?"

"That's the end of the word. See how he ended the line and continued his cipher directly below? That's his indication of another word."

"Let's keep moving."

A half hour and two plates of piping hot lasagna later, they sat back, staring at Jon's scribbles on the pad, and he read them again to make certain he hadn't misunderstood. "Use key to open space twenty-eight at Newark Storage Solutions. Give to FBI."

Jon pulled the key from his pocket. "This must open the lock at the storage facility."

Lucia nodded. "Agreed. But who else knows about this storage facility and has simply been waiting for the person with the key to open it?"

Good question. "Likely the person with the most to lose. The person who killed your father—Pietro. We can't prove that . . ."

"Yet. Hopefully with this"—she palmed the key—"we will. I just wonder what we'll find."

Jon wiped a bit of sauce off the corner of her mouth, then kissed her. "Let's find out."

* * *

THE TRIP TO Newark Storage Solutions took barely three minutes by taxi, long enough for Jon to text an FYI to his boss and a fellow agent in the area, so they would stand by for backup—just in case. The sun shone down brightly in the cloudless sky. It was a perfect day . . . and yet as the driver dropped them off, Jon didn't like it. The hair on the back of his neck stood up. He was watching carefully and hadn't spotted anyone following them. That didn't mean someone wasn't lying in wait.

"Please let me put you back in the taxi, Doc. I'll handle it from here."

Resolutely, she shook her head. "My father wanted me to find this. There might be another puzzle to solve. That would be his style."

Swallowing a curse, Jon relented. He couldn't refute her. Yeah, he could get the Bureau involved, but there would be delays and red tape, and he didn't have time for that.

With a wave, he sent the cab driver off.

The moment Lucia spoke with the facility owner, who opened the gate to admit them, Jon wrapped a protective arm around her waist and walked with her down the narrow paths past one corrugated orange door after another, peering at the black numbers above. For her sake, he hoped this was the end of the trail and that this gave her the peace she sought. If it at all helped with Stef's case, it would be a huge bonus. Time was running out for his brother, and if this lead proved fruitless, he was going to have to start from scratch. But he wasn't giving up.

Nor was he ready to let Lucia go. He had no notion whether this had been just a pleasant interlude for her, a way to fulfill a fantasy. Did she intend to simply go back to her fancy private school in the fall and resume her life without him? They'd both carefully avoided discussing the future, focusing instead on solving the riddle her father had left behind. But now that the end was seemingly in sight, Jon couldn't stop thinking about tomorrow. The picture without Lucia in it wasn't one he wanted to contemplate. Could she live with his job, the danger, the separation, the adrenaline?

"Here it is." Her voice shook, and she drew in a huge breath.

"I'll unlock it for you."

"No. He wanted me to do this, and I won't let him down."

Jon knew exactly why Nicholas DiStefano had been proud of his daughter. Smart, yes. That was a given. But her backbone impressed him. She could have hidden her head in the sand and decided that whatever her father wanted uncovered would be safer buried forever. But no. And she insisted on being the one to do it. No crying, no hand-wringing. Not that she wasn't afraid, but she faced it head-on. He had to admire the hell out of that.

Slowly, Lucia released a shuddering breath and tried to steady her hands as she fit the key into the padlock on door number twenty-eight. It popped open, and she pulled it free of the mooring. Jon bent to throw the door up. Sunlight shafted under the metal door as he revealed the insides one inch at a time.

Concrete. Emptiness. Just an echo as they stepped in the ten-by-ten space that contained nothing except one little box in the corner.

Lucia stared at it like a snake, transfixed but terrified. Jon understood. This meant potential danger. Whatever was in that box had been a secret her father had probably died for. But it also meant she had to face his death again and say another good-bye.

She didn't hesitate, just walked over to the metal box and bent. "There's a combination."

And they were out of clues. Damn it. "Any ideas? Your birthday, maybe?"

Immediately Lucia shook her head. "He didn't like being obvious. He wouldn't pick birthdays or addresses . . ."

"May I?" He held out his hands for the box.

Without a word, she handed it over. He inspected the top, blowing off the thick layer of dust, glancing at the sides. When he rubbed his fingertips along the bottom, the disturbance of the smooth surface made him frown. He lifted up the box and peered at the bottom, hearing something metallic rattle around inside. The investigator in him knew they could call in a team and just pry the son of a bitch open. But he was technically off the clock, and this was Lucia's gig until he knew he had something worthy of calling in his boss and a whole team. For all they knew, this box contained nothing more than family mementoes or had already been raided. It didn't look like it . . . but until he knew it hadn't been disturbed, he had to play along.

The appearance of three letters carved into the gray metal surface along the bottom of the box made him frown. "LRD."

"My initials. Oh, he used to do this when I was little. It's a Caesar Cipher. It's also called a Caesar Shift Decoder. It lets you decode text by shifting each letter a certain number of 'steps' along the alphabet. Since he didn't specify, I'll assume he used one. So that would mean that A becomes B, B becomes C, etc."

Jon had heard of this cipher. "So L becomes M, R becomes S, and D becomes E. This is a numeric padlock, though."

"The letters probably represent the number of that symbol in the alphabet. M is the thirteenth letter."

"So the combination is thirteen, nineteen, five?"

She didn't look convinced. "That's my best guess. Just knowing what I knew of my father."

He handed the box back to her. "Want to do the honors?"

Lucia's face turned pensive and reluctant, but she nodded and she reached for the metal square. "Yes."

Moments later, she had the lock in hand and had dialed out the combination they'd puzzled their way into. To his shock, it popped open on the first try.

"Oh my God," she breathed. "It worked."

Jon brought her against his chest. "You knew your father better than you thought. He'd be really proud of you today."

She smiled up at him, and wasn't that the prettiest sight he'd ever seen, her chocolate eyes swimming with proud, poignant tears, her mouth still swollen from his kisses.

"Open it," he urged. "You've earned it."

Prying off the little lock and handing it to him, she lifted the lid—and gasped. Jon peered inside. There sat a platinum filigree engagement ring that looked very old, the ornate detail ringing a carat and a half of lovely round diamond. Beside it rested a locket in a warm yellow gold with two emeralds encrusted on the front, topped with a little diamond and a few etchings to mimic the shape of a flower. It was suspended on a short chain decorated with shimmering crystals and onyx beads.

"I've been searching for my grandmother's engagement ring and my great-grandmother's locket since Papa's death." But it was the iPod beside those two items that she reached for first.

Scooping it up, she pressed the button to turn it on. Nothing. Not that Jon had expected anything. He went digging in his pockets. "It's been sitting dormant for a few years, Doc. The battery's dead."

"Yeah." She nodded, clearly nervous. "I should have realized that. I'm just—"

"There's a lot going on. Here." He handed her the little portable charging device he carried around for his iPhone.

Her eyes lit on it, and relief crossed her face as she clipped the little charger onto the device. He was glad to make her smile, but . . .

"We shouldn't investigate the iPod here. Let's take it back to our room." In fact, Jon was certain that his boss would be very interested in this development. But he wanted to be in a safe place to look at the contents first.

"I've waited years already. I've solved the riddles he left for *me*. I have to hear what he wanted me to know."

Jon hesitated. Her plea was passionate and emotional. But that impending sense of danger rolled over him again. Whatever was on that iPod may have gotten Nicholas killed. He'd hidden it this thoroughly for a reason. He'd told her to give it to the FBI. Besides, standing out here in the open, they were awfully vulnerable. Other than a single security gate, intended to keep cars more than people out, the area was totally accessible to anyone.

"Lucia, we're not safe here. Let's get secure—"

"Two minutes. Please. If we haven't seen anything interesting yet, I'll shut it off. We'll be fine. If Pietro had any idea where my father had hidden this, he would have already come and taken it. And I don't think we were followed."

"We don't know that for sure, Lucia."

"You're being paranoid."

He raised a brow at her. "Better paranoid than dead."

She stood, watching him, measuring his words. That look on her face told him that she was going to argue.

Jon had had enough. He'd stepped back and let her solve the riddle her way. Now they were entering his territory. As much as he'd like to grant her wish, he couldn't afford to be soft with her when it came to safety. "Whatever is running through that pretty head of yours, Doc, don't say it. I picked you up and carried you out of a situation once. You can be damn sure that I don't have a problem doing it again."

LUCIA CLUTCHED THE iPod in her hand. She didn't doubt Jon meant that. Nor did she discount the fact there could be danger. But there was danger in waiting, too. Every moment they didn't know what her father wanted to say was another moment the truth remained in the dark.

"Two minutes," she insisted, then pressed a few buttons.

Jon opened his mouth to argue—but closed it when he saw her father's face come into view on the little screen.

Lucia clapped her hand to her mouth to hold in a cry. It was footage from a security camera in his office in the back of one of his dry-cleaning facilities, date stamped about a month before his death. She held her breath, even as grief pressed down on her while she watched images of her father shuffle a few papers.

Then Pietro walked into the scene and shut the door behind him. "We need to talk about Casale."

Her father didn't lift his head, didn't reply.

"You listening to me?" Pietro demanded.

"I heard you."

"Fucking do something!" Her uncle pounded his fist on the table. "The asshole is getting out of hand, making more demands. He's not denying the warrants and wiretaps like we're paying him for."

"He can't look too obvious. He's done his best to minimize the shit. We've had this conversation. It's over."

"The hell it is! You're getting soft. This whole fucking organization is going to come down around our heads, and you're still going to be telling me to stay patient."

Her father finally lifted his head and speared his younger brother with a glare that promised the fires of hell. "It's not going to fall down around us. I know exactly what I'm doing. You remove Casale, and we've got no advocate behind a federal bench. All those dirty damn cops you've got stashed all over Jersey will only get you so far. Leave it alone." He got to his feet. "I've got a meeting, so get the hell out of here."

"Yeah? With who?"

"None of your business." Her father streaked a hand through his dark hair, sprinkled now with gray. "Lock up on your way out."

He exited the scene, the door slamming behind him. Pietro cursed, then began pacing. Up one side of the office, then back down the other. Finally, he yanked his phone out of his pocket and dialed a number. "Yeah, it's me. We gotta act. Casale's got to go." Pause. "No. I've got a plan. On the first of every month, Stefan Bocelli visits the good judge's house to pay him off. Next time he does, be waiting. As soon as Bocelli is gone, finish the judge. We'll plant the gun on Nicholas's lapdog later. Double-tap him to the head, just like Bocelli would. His prints are likely all over the house. You phone in an anonymous tip, say you're a passing neighbor." Pietro laughed. "Bingo. No one will be sorry to see Stefan go down the river."

Lucia reared back and looked at Jon's face. She'd read the accounts of Judge Casale's murder, enough to know that it had been an open-and-shut case against his brother, based purely on circumstantial evidence. "That might be enough to free your brother."

He blinked once, twice, gripping the iPod so tightly, his knuckles turned white. "Maybe. I hope so."

"What?" Pietro barked into the phone on the video. "Yeah. It's time to get big brother out of the way, and I know exactly how. This organization needs to run right for a fucking change. I'll take care of it. Keep your fucking mouth shut. Later."

Pietro flipped the phone shut, and the iPod's screen went momentarily dark before flashing to the menu.

Lucia tried to suck in all the information, and it rolled around in her brain over and over in the heavy silence. "I knew he had something to do with my father's murder. The police never tried very hard to solve it. They saw my father as nothing more than a career criminal not worth their effort."

Jon wrapped an arm around her and brought her against the

vital warmth of his hard chest. "This isn't conclusive, but it might be enough to reopen his case and my brother's." He lifted his head and looked around. "We'll make some phone calls as soon as we get back to our hotel room. Let's go."

Quickly, Jon sent a short text before he took the iPod and shoved it into his pocket. He was right—they should contact people who could help his brother and put Pietro away.

"Are you sending for backup or something?" she asked.

"Yes. I'd put them on alert when we arrived. Now I'm asking them to move in."

She looked at the jewelry her father had left for her in the metal box wistfully. "And these?"

He lifted the familiar pieces and put them in her hand. "It goes against procedure, but they have no bearing on the case. Take them. It's our secret."

Even after finding such a huge bombshell, Jon found a way to make her smile. After donning the jewelry, she lifted the metal box. "Should I leave this here?"

A long moment later, he nodded. "We need to stay light, be ready to run."

In truth, she didn't see how danger could find them now, but she supposed anything was possible. She put the box down. "You didn't exactly abduct me in the right shoes for that."

He peered down at her platforms and grinned. "But they're sexy as hell."

"Thank you." She didn't mean that only for the compliment, but for all his tenderness, his help, his general goodness.

"No words necessary," he murmured, then planted a quick, soft kiss on her lips.

It was over too soon, and as they left the storage facility, Lucia wondered, after all this was over, what came next for her and Jon? She loved him, but he couldn't possibly be ready to hear that. After all, he'd walked away from her once before. So where did that leave them?

They exited the unit. Jon tugged the metal door down, and Lucia locked it behind them.

Side by side, they walked to the main gate of the storage facility in silence, Lucia waving at the owner through the office as he let them out with the press of a button. As soon as they cleared the front to wait for their taxi to return, a rustling behind them caught her attention.

She whirled but Pietro grabbed her arm and dragged her back against the front of his body, planting a gun to her temple. She gasped and looked at Jon with big eyes, her heart pounding madly. He'd drawn his gun and pointed it at Pietro, but her uncle wasn't tall, and there was almost no way Jon was going to get a shot off without hitting her. They all knew it.

"You thought I didn't know, little girl?" Pietro laughed low in her ear. "You're a smart girl about books, not men."

"You mean criminals," she growled back at him.

"Lucia . . ." Jon warned her, his tone telling her not to provoke him.

"No!" She wasn't being too brave, just furious. Of course she knew there was every chance Pietro would kill her. But there was no way she was going down without a fight, and if she could distract him so that she could get free, even better.

"I know you killed my father." She was so angry, her voice trembled.

"You found the tape Nick captured. If I'd known he was keeping videos of everything in that office . . ." Pietro growled. "But since I offed him, the organization has thrived. The Gamalini family needed a new face. Nick had gone soft, and everyone from the associates to the underboss"—he pointed to himself—"knew it."

"And you also framed my brother for Judge Casale's murder," Jon said.

Pietro lifted a shoulder in a halfhearted shrug. "Oh, there's the traitor. You fucking Fed. Yeah, I had to get Stefan out of the way first. If I didn't, he would have killed me. Everyone knew he was loyal to Nick, through and through. He'd have done anything to protect my brother. It was easy enough. Now . . ." he said to Jon. "No more flapping your jaws. Put your gun down." He jammed the gun into Lucia's temple. "Put it down now!"

Heart racing, blood pumping icy cold with fear, she pleaded with Jon not to listen. The second he complied, Pietro would kill them both. But Jon couldn't do it alone; she was going to have to help. Thank God Mark was such a big believer in self-defense. He'd taught Nicki and her how to keep themselves from being overpowered. And he'd made her brush up when she announced her intent to vacation at Erotics Anonymous.

Holding the key to the storage unit tight in her palm, she shifted it until it rested between her fingers. She took a deep breath, knowing she'd run out of time. This might be her death, but she wasn't going to go down without a fight.

As Jon scanned Pietro for an opening, Lucia used her free arm to elbow her uncle in the gut hard, putting every ounce of her strength behind the blow. With a grunt and a whoosh of air, he gripped his belly, the gun in his hand momentarily faltering. She used the opportunity to ram her fist—and the key—into his thigh.

"Ouch! You bitch!" Pietro snarled, gripping his thigh with one hand—and grabbing her wrist with the other before she could run away.

With his grip loosened, she whirled around and kicked at the hand holding the gun. She heard the crunch of bone. The gun fell to the ground, and he grabbed his hand with a scream.

"You broke my fucking finger!" Still, he dove for the gun.

But she was faster and snatched it up in her grip. After a quick glance, she verified that the safety was off and aimed the gun at Pietro.

Jon walked up beside her, weapon pointed right at her uncle. She glanced his way, and he nodded, giving her a raised brow and a smile. "Impressive."

"Thank you," she said stiffly. She didn't dare take her eyes off her uncle. Instead, she crept closer and snarled at him, "You didn't think I had any fight in me, did you? You thought I was a bookworm with no common sense, and that you could get the better of me easily and make Jon comply, too, with the promise that you wouldn't hurt me. Sucker!"

"Your father would be rolling in his grave if he could see you now. It's manly, your behavior. You know how much he liked women to be feminine and sweet."

"Are you really going to try that tactic? You killed him. I'd say he has a hell of a lot more reasons to be rolling over in his grave for that than anything I've done."

Pietro growled, revealing a row of uneven white teeth in his dark face. "I did it myself, pulled the trigger. Nothing was better than offing the older brother who'd always cast a shadow over me, always thinking he was better. I enjoyed it. I stood at his funeral with my arms around you girls and I laughed at every one of your tears."

"I hate you." She clenched her free fist. Jon gripped her elbow, holding her back. "Hate you in a way that I didn't think I was capable of feeling, but you aren't going to goad me into losing my temper so that you can get the gun back. But I'm going to give you a little payback." Gritting her teeth, she kicked at Pietro, landing a blow right in the balls. Her uncle dropped to his knees, cupping his genitals. "That's for my father. And this"—she slapped him across the face—"is for me."

Jon pulled her back. "He's down. He's not going anywhere. And lots of FBI agents in suits are on their way to collect your uncle."

"You can't prove anything. It's all circumstantial, and my word against yours. Everyone will know that you've been trying to frame me to free your brother for years."

With a smile, Jon leaned into Pietro's face. "The difference now?" He pulled his phone free from his suit pocket, all lit up and showing that it was recording. "While your niece was beating your ass, I managed to get your confession on tape."

AFTER AN EXHAUSTING afternoon and early evening spent answering the FBI's questions, recounting every detail of the day she and Jon had spent figuring out and following her father's clues, a very nice female agent had brought her back to her hotel. Jon had been separated from her hours ago, and she didn't know if or when he'd return.

After letting herself into the room, Lucia flopped onto the bed, hungry and exhausted. But she'd gladly skip both food and sleep if she could be with Jon. He'd taken her virginity on this bed and cemented her love for him. Now that he'd saved his brother, what happened next? Two years ago, he'd left her without a word. Maybe . . . now that he'd achieved his goal, he had no further use for her. Lucia hated to think of their time together as the means to an end for him. Nor did she like to demean herself. But she had to be honest. For all the sizzle between her and Jon, expecting more than he'd given her was probably foolish.

Still, she wasn't going to give up.

Best to figure out how to get back to Vegas, so she could get some sage advice from her sister, then head out to give Jon Bocelli a piece of her mind. She'd gotten closure with her father, as well as gathered evidence to put Pietro away finally. That counted for a whole hell of a lot.

But Jon had made her want so much more.

Shaking her head, Lucia made a few phone calls, including one to the airline, then another to her sister. Lucia was almost relieved when she got Nicki's voice mail. She'd rather tell her sister what was going on in person, so she could be both scolded and hugged when necessary. Now she could just spend a little time figuring out her plan.

After setting the phone down, she took a scalding shower that soothed some of her thoughts. Wearing a towel and scented lotion, Lucia opened the bathroom door in a puff of steam.

And ran straight into Jon's wide chest.

He'd ditched his suit coat along the way, slung his tie around his neck, and clearly raked his fingers through his inky hair more than a few times. He looked tired, but was still the most gorgeous man to her. Her belly tumbled over. No matter where their lives took them from here, she'd never forget everything he'd done with and for her.

Lucia swallowed down a lump. "Hi. So . . . it's over, huh? We did it. You saved your brother. I avenged my father." She held out her hand for him to shake it. "Thank you for everything, Jon."

He cocked his head, then pinned her with a dark stare of displeasure before glaring at her outstretched hand. Lucia dropped it to her side, having the sudden feeling that she'd poked a dangerous male animal.

Jon grabbed the knob to the bathroom door behind her and shut it, then stepped forward, pinning her between it and his formidable body. "Think you're going somewhere, Doc?"

"I'm catching a flight back to Vegas in the morning."

His expression turned thunderous. "Were you going to talk to me before you left?"

"I didn't know if you were still in town. And I wasn't aware that you gave a damn. Two years ago, you skipped out without saying 'gotta go,' 'good-bye,' or 'kiss my ass.' I figured this was same song, different verse."

"You figured, huh? Without consulting me?" Jon drew in a deep breath and stared at the ceiling, jaw clenched. "We're not communicating here, Doc. I admit that I left you once before. I didn't think you could handle what I wanted from you. Hell, even two days ago I had my doubts."

Oh, now that just pissed her off.

"I was a virgin, not an idiot. Save me your big, bad Dom speech." She rolled her eyes and tried to push past him. "I'm a grown woman who can make my own decisions. I can certainly handle whatever you dish out."

He squarely blocked her path. "Oh, we'll see about that, pet—as soon as you let me finish what I was saying."

Lucia stared, measuring, a little ribbon of worry curling through her. She'd provoked him. But hadn't some part of her wanted to? "I'm listening."

"Since I picked you up and removed you from Girls' Night Out," he began, "you've proven to me that your inexperience was only an issue in my head. You're brave and dedicated, and you adapt well. I held back today when Pietro confronted us to let you work out your demons with him. If he had so much as harmed a hair on your head, I'd have blown his head off. I was prepared to. My trigger finger was itching. But you handled him all by yourself."

He sidled closer, nudging his thigh between hers. She couldn't be immune to him. She gasped, trembling. "You handled me last night."

The deep rumble of his voice alone made her wet, not to mention the memories of their time together in this room.

"Two years ago, I'd convinced myself that you were a naïve girl who couldn't cope with my life or wants. You've proven to me that you're a hell of a woman, Lucia. I'm proud of you. There's no way I'm letting you get away this time. I love you. You'll only get rid of me if you tell me that you can never love me in return."

Lucia gasped, blinked. *Really? Seriously?* She probably looked foolish, standing there with her mouth agape, but Jon had just said . . . "You love me?"

He cocked his head, and a smile played at the corners of his mouth. "You're a smart girl. Put together the clues. What do you think?"

Her mind raced. "You don't live far from here, do you?"

His smile told her that she was catching on. "Not far at all."

"You could have just gone home, instead of coming here to see me."

He planted his palms on either side of her head against the door and leaned in. He eyed her towel like it was the most offensive piece of fabric he'd ever seen. "Exactly."

"If your cohorts let you go at the same time they released me . . . you've had time to think about this."

"Absolutely. And plan a speech . . . with a few other surprises."

A speech that started with dropping the "L bomb." He'd done some thinking about this. What other surprises could he have in store? "I'm guessing that you don't make a habit of telling women you love them."

Jon raised a brow at her. "Try never."

"Ever?"

He shook his head. "Not once. Doc, you make me remember not to look at the world through such jaded eyes. With you around, I see everything differently, and it's a wonderful place again. For the first time in years, I've got something to look forward to. I've got hope. For that alone I could love you, but you're also an amazing woman . . ." He stared at her. "So are you going to break my heart and send me packing?"

God, he couldn't tell how she felt? Maybe he needed reassuring, just as she did. The thought was a little endearing. "I'm not going to send you packing. I love you, Jon. And I've never said those words, either."

He smiled with his whole face—his whole heart—and even in the shadowy hall, she could see love warming his dark eyes. He cupped her cheek, then lowered his mouth to hers for a sweet, lingering kiss. Joy suffused her, spreading through her like sunlit heat after a long winter. That was probably cheesy and too poetic, but for her, so true. She rubbed her cheek against his and wound her arms around his neck, drawing in that masculine scent of him that was both a comfort and a turn-on.

He kissed her jaw, her nose, her lips one last time. "That makes me really happy, pet. I can't wait to get deep inside you again and show you how much . . . just as soon as we address your assumptions and your smart mouth. Drop the towel."

Lucia felt her eyes flare wide and her breath catch. "If I do, I'll be . . . Oh, you want me naked."

He raised a dark, expectant brow at her.

"Sir," she added, unwrapping the towel and letting it drop to the floor.

With a dangerous grin, Jon picked it up and tossed it behind him, onto a nearby chair. She stood completely bare under his relentless gaze, a cool, air-conditioned breeze drifting over her skin, making her nipples harden. Just his rapt gaze traveling all over her made her wet. Without a word, the silent seconds ticked by until she felt achy, aroused, and ready. She shifted from one foot to the other, then back again, trying to ease the need.

"Hold still," he demanded.

"I've got this ache . . ." She grimaced, trying not to move.

"That I just want to make bigger until you get incredibly wet, beg me to fuck you, then scream my name and claw my back as I satisfy you."

The ache behind Lucia's clit swelled and throbbed at his words. She sucked in a breath. *Pretty please* . . . she wanted to whimper. Instead, she stayed still and ate him up with a hungry stare.

He dragged a thumb across her mouth. "I can't wait to feel whatever promise is lurking in your eyes. But first, I've got three questions for you, Doc."

She couldn't help it; she licked at his thumb. "Yes, Sir."

He gripped her chin and sent her a solemn stare. "Are you willing to remove your great-grandmother's locket, if I give you something equally meaningful and stunning?"

Her heart stuttered, then chugged in a crazy rhythm. If he meant to give her a symbol of their bond, she was sure her long-dead ancestor would approve. With shaking hands, she reached up and removed the vintage locket. Jon held out his hand, and she set it in the middle of his palm. Carefully, he put it in his trouser pocket, then withdrew a little blue box with the words TIFFANY & CO. on the front and gripped it.

"We don't have witnesses, but this isn't any less binding, Doc." He cupped her cheek and looked into her eyes. "Lucia Rose, will you wear this for me always as a symbol of your promise to honor and obey me, as I care for and cherish you through all our days?"

It took her a moment to process his request. "You're . . . asking me to wear your collar?"

"Yes. I'm asking you to be exclusively mine. This is sacred in the BDSM community."

Even if she hadn't read about it, she could hear the gravity in his voice. "I know."

"I've never done this. I've never wanted to. But you changed everything for me. Will you wear this?"

Lucia bit her lip. Everything she knew about the lifestyle was from fiction. This man had been gentle with her so far, but he had depths he hadn't shown her yet. A darker side. She felt it, but he'd kept a tight leash on it last night. If she agreed, someday he would spank and flog her, cuff her to his bed and use her in whatever way he wished. He might do any one of a million things that played into her fantasies. And she couldn't lie; it scared her a little. But deep in her soul, she craved the sort of Master who would care for her. And Jon was offering her everything she could have ever hoped for. Even at his delicious, commanding best, he would see to her safety and pleasure. He would make everything good for her.

Besides, she wasn't ready to let him go. If this was the way he wanted to continue their relationship, she wouldn't turn him down.

With her heart racing and joy bursting, she nodded. "I'd love to."

"Kneel, pet."

Slowly, there in the narrow hall with Jon's voice and scent surrounding her, Lucia got to her knees, naked before him. She bowed her head.

He stroked her hair softly, filtering her curls through his fingers just before he fastened something cool and heavy around her neck. "Perfect. I look forward to keeping, protecting, and loving you." Then he guided her to her feet, opened the bathroom door, and flipped the light on so that she could see the platinum chain with the dangling, diamond-encrusted heart nestled in the hollow of her throat, with a little lock right in the middle.

A smile curled up her lips into something happy. "It's beautiful."

"That's a twenty-four/seven mark of my possession, pet. Don't take it off without permission."

She wouldn't want it any other way. "Yes, Sir. I mean, Master."

Groaning, he gripped the vanity and pressed his erection into the small of her back. "Hearing that word roll off your sweet tongue is going to get you fucked, pet."

Lucia giggled. "Promise?"

Pressing kisses along her neck and shoulder, he whispered in her ear, "Absolutely."

Then his hands roamed up her hips, over her stomach, to cup

her breasts and tweak her nipples. The locket rested above them, his glistening stamp of ownership shimmering under the stark lights. She melted against him, feeling sublimely happy.

With a soft curse, he forced himself to step back and reach into his pocket again. He withdrew a little black velvet box, and when he opened it to reveal a beautiful engagement solitaire, she gasped. "Y-You're asking me to . . ."

"Marry me, yes. It's the same question as before, Lucia. The collaring was for us, something private. This is for the rest of the world. But I want you in every way I can get you. Will you make me a very happy man and become my wife?"

"You're sure you're ready for this?"

He turned her to face him and cupped her nape with his warm, encompassing palm. "I never forgot you, Lucia. But I told myself I was doing what was best for you. In the last two days, you've made me see what I was giving up. If you had gotten away from me again, it would have been like a never-healing wound. I would have come after you again and again until you said yes. Is it too soon for you to make this sort of public statement about us to your family and friends?"

"No. When I met you two years ago, I knew what I wanted. I just wasn't courageous enough to go after you. This time . . ." She paused, then sent him a coy smile. "You know I was going back to Vegas just long enough to talk to Nicki, gather my things, and figure out how to hunt you down. I wasn't letting you get away twice, Jon Bocelli. I was willing to take off all my clothes and beg you."

"You know just what to say to get my attention, pet." He groaned, nuzzled her neck, and pressed his cock against her. "So . . . will you marry me?"

"Of course. I'd be honored."

He slipped the gorgeous solitaire on her left finger, pressing his forehead to hers briefly. Then he guided her over to the bed, sat down, and held her hands as she stood, watching him.

Lucia frowned. "What's your third question?"

"Would you rather have your spanking with a bare hand or a paddle? I'll give you a choice—this time. Don't get used to it."

A little thrill raced through Lucia. "Spanking? What for?"

"Planning to leave without talking to me. But if you really just meant to regroup and come back for me, I might be willing to withdraw your punishment. For now."

She shivered as heat curled through her. A spanking from Jon Bocelli sounded divine. "You don't have to do that. Maybe we could try both and see which one I like better?"

With a laugh, he winked at her, then patted his lap. "I like the way you think, pet. Lie here and we'll try both. If you're good, there will be an extra reward for you."

She cupped his face in her hands and brushed a kiss across his mouth. "I've already gotten everything I've ever wanted. I love you, Jon."

"I love you, too, Doc. I couldn't be a happier man now that you're finally, truly mine."

On Fire

sylvia day

This one is for my dear friends,
Shayla Black and Shiloh Walker.

Here's to many more years of
friendship, laughter, and commiseration.

ACKNOWLEDGMENTS

To all the readers who've enjoyed the Shadow Stalkers mini-series so far, I hope you love this new installment! Thank you for buying my books, sending me your notes and e-mails, and otherwise being totally awesome. I appreciate you.

chapter one

Darcy Michaels adjusted her gloved grip on her toolbox and picked her way carefully over the charred remains of her favorite candy store. Around her, firefighters moved through the smoldering ruins, checking every crevice and corner to be certain the fire was completely extinguished. Water dripped from the blackened walls and ceiling to puddle on the floor below, and the smell of smoke and burned sugar clung to her nostrils and skin, sinking into the very fiber of her uniform.

"Third one in as many weeks," James Ralston muttered behind her. "I'm sorry, Darcy. I know you loved this place."

She stopped and faced her mentor, her chest gripped in a vise of pain. Like the two previous fires, this blaze had destroyed a location that was dear to her and had held precious memories. She'd celebrated her twelfth birthday at the Sweet Spot candy shop, and she stopped by every Friday to stock up on the sour lemonade straws her sister had turned her on to.

Focus on the details, Darcy. Don't lose it now.

"Whoever the arsonist is," she said, "he's not going to quit. He's been doing this too long. It's in his blood."

The frequency of the acts and the terrible brilliance of the timed-delay incendiary devices being used spoke of someone who'd had time to perfect his madness.

She couldn't help feeling violated, despite knowing how irrational that response was. As much as she'd wanted to leave Lion's Bay as a kid, she couldn't even contemplate abandoning the sleepy seaside town now. The same memories that had driven her parents to move away kept her bound to the area.

"I don't know what to make of it." Jim's forest green eyes were warm with compassion and intent on her face. "We don't have any new residents and it's the off-season. Tourism is down. Anyone not from around here sticks out like a sore thumb."

She turned in a slow circle, her trained gaze following the burn patterns he'd taught her to read.

"This guy didn't just crawl out of the w-woodwork," she said, startled to hear her voice cracking. She cleared her dry throat. "I think we need to bring the big guns in on this."

"Miller's doing a good job. He's meticulous and thorough." He touched her elbow lightly. "You don't want to be the one who steps on his toes."

Darcy nodded, acknowledging the sensitive nature of her relationship with the town's sheriff. "I know, but I think he needs more resources, and I think he's too stubborn to ask for help."

The last time the Feds had come in, they'd run roughshod over Chris Miller and his deputies, cutting him out of the loop while draining his limited resources. She remembered that tense time all too well, because the murder they'd been investigating had been the tragedy that brought her home. "And frankly, Chris's ego is the least of our problems."

"Let's gather the evidence, then we'll discuss the next best steps." Setting his hand on her shoulder, Jim gave her a reassuring squeeze. "Maybe you should stay with someone tonight?"

Reaching up, she set her hand over his. He knew her so well.

She wanted a particular kind of support, the kind where someone was nearby if she needed them but out of her way if she wanted time to just retreat with her thoughts.

Her gaze met Jim's and he read her mind. "My couch is always open to you, Darcy. You know that."

She nodded. "Thank you."

"Anytime."

Turning away, Darcy looked for a place to set down her kit and begin.

ROLLING OVER WITH a sigh, Darcy looked at the clock over Jim's fireplace mantel and noted the time: quarter after five. It was still dark outside and she'd been tossing and turning all night, too wired by her restless thoughts to catch the sleep she desperately needed. There was something about the fires that was niggling at her, but she just couldn't place it. Turning it over and over in her mind wasn't bringing the answer she was looking for to mind.

Sitting up, she rolled her shoulders back, knowing what had to be done. She wanted her treasured equanimity back, and the only way to make that happen was to find the psycho who was stealing it from her and see him in a cage. The sooner, the better. A possible pissing match between authorities wasn't going to be enough to hold her back. So far no one had been hurt, but their torch was barely catching his breath between fires. If he kept to his established pattern, they had only days before he struck again.

A warm exhale over her toes brought her attention to the handsome German shepherd sprawled on the floor at the foot of the couch. When her brief relationship with Jim had fizzled out, she'd felt the loss of his dog keenly.

"Thanks for watching out for me, Columbo." Reaching down, she scratched behind his ears.

The residents of Lion's Bay were paying her to provide the same service to the town—to watch out for them and keep them safe.

She wasn't going to let them down.

chapter two

Deputy U.S. Marshal Jared Cameron waited until the Lion's Bay sheriff sucked in a deep breath mid-rant, then he glanced at his partner.

"This winner is all yours," he drawled, turning on his heel and leaving Deputy Trish Morales to it. She'd been assigned to him for just that reason: she had the patience of a saint and he had no patience at all. Especially not for defensive, posturing small-town authorities who whipped their dicks out and started marking their territories the moment he rolled into town.

"I'm not done. Where the fuck is he going?" Sheriff Miller snapped, followed by a far more modulated reply from Trish.

Idiot. Nothing trumped the U.S. Marshals Service's silver star.

Jared closed the sheriff's glass inset door behind him just to shut out the man's voice. Pushing the irritation from his thoughts, he started through the bull pen toward the exit when an unexpected and unwanted complication walked into the station. He took scant note of her initially, but something drew his attention back.

Grudgingly he slowed, then came to a stop. Whoever she was, she was a bombshell. Not in the physical sense. In that regard, she was of average height, slim, and moderately proportioned. Her face was free of cosmetics and her brown hair was pulled back in a casual ponytail. If he'd been looking at a photo of her, he wouldn't have looked twice. But in the flesh, watching her move, was what snared him.

She was hot monkey sex in a brown paper wrapper.

The secret of her was revealed in the sensual fluidity of her body and her heavy-lidded, bottle green eyes. The primitive male in him recognized the attraction instantly, completely disregarding his brain, which didn't have time for this sort of distraction. Unfortunately for him, the blue uniform slacks and embroidered white button-up shirt she wore told Jared he had no chance of avoiding her unless he wanted to switch with Trish and take point with Miller instead. He was stuck with deciding which part of his anatomy was going to be the least controllable: his fists or his dick.

Maybe he'd be lucky and she would be happily married with kids, therefore not the least bit interested in getting sweaty and dirty with him.

She was lost in conversation with the female deputy manning the front desk when he approached. The glance she shot him was cursory, just as his had first been with her. Then it snagged. Her focus zeroed in, sliding over his body from the top of his head down to his scuffed work boots and back up again. When her gaze collided with his, she sucked in a breath and licked her lower lip.

Fuck. He was screwed. His brain was screaming at him to turn his ass around and take his chances with the sheriff instead. Assaulting the local authorities for getting on his last nerve would garner him less trouble than playing with the sizzling awareness arcing between him and the sexpot fire inspector.

"Here he is," the deputy said unnecessarily, pointing at him.

Jared thrust out his hand and introduced himself. The moment his palm touched the bombshell's, his blood rushed south and gave him a semi. He looked at her left hand almost desperately, cursing the lack of a wedding ring. A simple gold band would've killed his interest right then and there.

"Darcy Michaels," she replied, in a voice pitched high enough to be *this close* to girlish. "I'm a fire inspector with the Lion's Bay Fire Department."

The pretty blond deputy at the front desk smiled at him with the same invitation she'd given him when he first walked in. "Darcy's the one who asked me to put out the information about the arsonist."

The blonde was the type of woman he preferred to fuck—attractive enough to stir the most superficial interest and easy enough to want nothing more than a good time. Darcy Michaels was rousing something far deeper, igniting a hunger that was full-bodied and complex. The kind that overrode a man's better sense.

Giving himself a mental kick in the ass, Jared caught the inspector's elbow and steered her toward the exit. "Let's go."

They'd barely stepped outside when she said, "You got here quick, Deputy."

He considered her voice. It was a cross between Marilyn Monroe and Jennifer Tilly. If anyone had asked him that morning what he thought of girly voiced women, he'd have said they annoyed the shit out of him. It was just his damn luck that Darcy Michaels was the exception. Every time she opened her mouth, his mind went straight into the gutter.

Harder, Jared. Deeper . . .

Christ. His teeth grit.

"We have to move quickly," he bit out, trying to regain his focus. "If he keeps to his pattern, he'll burn something else before the week is out. What have you got so far?"

She gestured down the street to a brick-faced fire station. "My office is over there. Do you have a suspect in mind? You came because you recognized the MO, right?"

"It's similar to a known arsonist, yes."

"We're three weeks in with him. Where was he four weeks ago?"

"No clue."

Frowning, she persisted, "So there are intervals between bursts? How long?"

"Twenty years. Give or take."

She stumbled to a halt. "Are you kidding?"

He scowled for a variety of reasons, one of which was that her arm had slipped free of his grasp when she'd stopped abruptly. "Why would I?"

"Is he a recent parolee?"

"Escapee," he corrected. "Seventeen years ago. He torched a bathroom in the courthouse during an appellate hearing and escaped in the ensuing clusterfuck. Haven't seen hide nor hair of him since. But the supervisory deputy marshal in the Seattle office helped to apprehend Merkerson the first time, and she recognized the pattern."

Darcy's frown cleared. "Merkerson. That's it! I've been trying to place the MO. He was way before my time, but we studied him briefly in school. What the hell has he been up to all these years? How has he stayed under the radar?"

"He might have been incarcerated under a false name or out of the country. Or he might have trained a junior asshat to follow in his nutjob footsteps. It doesn't matter. We're going to nail the bastard." Grabbing her elbow again, Jared urged her toward the fire station.

"The hell it doesn't matter. In just three weeks, he's torn this town apart."

He heard the fury underlying her words and made note of it. Personal involvement clouded judgment. One of the many reasons why spending time with her was a really bad idea. He was already feeling the effects. While his brain was working the case, his body was straining toward hers, wired and revved and hot to screw her raw.

They were about to cross the street to the fire station when he urged her into a corner diner instead.

"I missed lunch," he explained, hoping low blood sugar, not his hormones, was responsible for handicapping his common sense. He could fix the former.

"I just ate. But I'll grab a shake."

Another mark in her favor, he thought. A woman who might not be counting every damn calorie she put in her mouth.

He nearly groaned as visions of other things she could do with her mouth swept through his testosterone-muddled mind. If he'd needed any proof that he was working too hard and not playing enough, he had it now. He should take the blond deputy up on her offer and ease himself down a notch.

Reaching the counter, Jared grabbed a menu from beside the register and ran a quick glance over the limited offerings. It was a burger-and-fries joint, with a couple salads thrown in for the calorie-conscious.

A waitress in a '50s uniform with "Ginny" embroidered over her heart approached with her notepad and a smile. "Hey, Darcy. You brought the Fed with you. Bet Miller's in a snit. I know how he gets when outsiders come in."

"How do you know everything?" Darcy looked genuinely impressed. "I just found out that the Marshals Service was here not more than five minutes ago."

Ginny shrugged. "Prime location for news. Welcome to Lion's Bay, Marshal."

"Deputy," he corrected, his attention returning to the menu. "Thanks."

"How are you doing?" Darcy asked Ginny with the easy familiarity of old friends.

"Better. Just had a new security system installed this morning. It's supposed to sense heat and alert the alarm company. And I had our existing fire alarms rechecked a couple days ago to make sure everything is working properly." Ginny jerked a thumb over her shoulder at the bulky-looking chef visible through the kitchen pass-through. "Tim joked about retiring on the insurance if the place burned. He slept on the couch last night for that one."

"Oh, hell. Ginny, I'm sorry. I—"

Jared stepped into the conversation before she could say anything further. "Proactive, thoughtful steps, Ginny. Good job. If your burgers are half as good as your planning, I'll order a double."

Ginny grinned at the praise. "Big strapping man like you, absolutely."

"Suggestions?"

"Depends. Hot or sweet?"

"Both. I'm starved."

"One chipotle bacon BBQ double-cheeseburger and fries coming up. Everything on it?"

"Yeah. And two of whatever kind of shake Inspector Michaels wants. All to go."

Jared paid the bill, waving off the five-spot Darcy pulled out of her pocket.

Closing the register, Ginny stepped away to make the shakes, leaving Darcy standing there with a grim expression. He gestured her over to a red vinyl booth by the window.

"So," he began when she sat. "How often has Lion's Bay had cause for the Feds to come in?"

One of her brows arched and she sized him up. The caveman in him beat his chest at the challenge. Damn it, he hadn't been this interested in a woman in a long, long time.

It was a good thing she had some fire to her. When he got her beneath him, he wasn't going to be gentle . . .

Fuck that. What the hell was he thinking? He was *not* going there.

"Just once," she answered.

"When?"

"Three years ago."

"Why?"

She hesitated just a second, but he caught it. "A local woman was murdered."

"What made that interesting?"

Her lips pursed and her eyes took on a hardness that startled him.

"Don't glare at me, Darcy. It's a valid question. The Feds have bigger fish to fry than a small-town murder. What caught their interest about this one?"

She exhaled in a rush. "The MO was a match to a serial killer they were looking for."

From the moment Darcy had spotted Jared Cameron in the police station, she'd known he was going to tear through her orderly life like a whirlwind.

His looks had knocked her back first. It had taken everything she had to keep her mouth from falling open when he'd walked up to her epitomizing the description of tall, dark, and dangerous. Then, he'd swept her right out the door, his touch sending tingles racing up her arm and through her body. Now she was sitting across from him, faced head-on with how seriously freakin' delicious he was. Her mother would call him a "cool drink of water," but Darcy wouldn't. Every time their eyes met, her mouth went dry. Despite his purely professional discourse, the way he looked at her with those electric blue eyes was with raw animal hunger.

And damned if she didn't want him right back. It was a primal response she couldn't suppress. Socially, he was gruff and abrupt, so she was inclined to imagine him screwing her senseless without talking. Sweaty, grasping, grinding fucking. That's what he radiated with his agitated energy and fierce gaze, and she was sold. It had taken his force-of-nature energy to make her realize she'd been dead for a while. A no-holds-barred one-night stand was just what she needed to knock the dust off.

"Which serial killer?" he asked in that clipped rough voice that brought to mind golden whisky in a crystal tumbler. He brushed back a lock of inky black hair with a careless hand, and she couldn't help but notice the veins coursing along his powerful forearms and biceps. He was perfectly built to her tastes—lean, ripped, and not the slightest bit bulky.

"Some guy from the Midwest who carved Mayan symbols in his victims' torsos."

"The Prophet." Jared leaned back in the booth, the casual pose doing little to soften him. "Counting down to doomsday. Sick fuck."

Her brows rose. "Is that your professional opinion?"

"In my professional opinion, he was a whack job. And so is this guy torching your town."

She almost smiled. Jared Cameron was a blunt object, no doubt about it, but it made her feel better knowing he was here. She couldn't fathom anyone getting anything over on him.

"Listen." His fingertips drummed on the table. "You can't carry around guilt and blame for these fires."

"I'm not."

"Bullshit. The waitress tells you she's taking steps to protect her property and you start apologizing like it's your fault."

Darcy's hackles rose. "This is a small town, Deputy. People around here aren't exactly rolling in the dough. She spent—"

"The name's Jared. Use it."

"You're just full of charm, aren't you?"

"You don't want charm, and we're talking shop."

"How the hell would you know what I want?"

"Because I want the same thing." He leaned forward and lowered his voice, his blue eyes burning like flame. "I want it so badly my dick's been half hard since the moment I saw you."

Arousal swept through her like a sudden fever, flushing her skin. No man had ever talked to her so crudely, so there'd never been a chance for her to learn it turned her on. Now she knew, and she couldn't help but wonder if he'd be vocal in bed. Just thinking about him growling raunchy and obscene statements while screwing her made her ache with desire. She struggled not to squirm, but she couldn't resist goading him for more. "And what is it we both want, Deputy?"

He didn't move a muscle for a moment. Then his lips curled on one side in a wickedly carnal smile. His eyes glittered with fierce, hard lust. "You want a sheet-clawing, back-arching, mind-blowing fuck, and I want to pound my cock into you until I've come my last drop."

Darcy sagged into the seat back, her hand lifting to her throat. "Whew."

Her pussy throbbed greedily, the tender folds slickening with her growing hunger. She'd known the man less than twenty minutes, but she was suddenly quite committed to knowing him even better. Well, his body, at least . . . "You're on. My workday ends at six."

The deputy's nostrils flared. Anticipation sharpened the blades of his cheekbones and made the precisely drawn lines of his beautiful mouth harsh. She could say, in all honesty, that he was the most gorgeous man she'd ever seen.

"I'm gonna regret this," he muttered, scowling at her.

Oddly, his reluctance about wanting her only spurred her desire to have him. It betrayed how intense his attraction to her was, so much so that he couldn't fight it even though he wanted to. And she responded as any red-blooded woman would to the ferocious sexual need of a deliciously handsome, potently masculine creature: she provoked him.

Leaning forward, she whispered, "No, you won't. You'll be seeing stars when I'm done with you."

"Christ." Grimacing with discomfort, he arched his hips up from the seat and adjusted the fit of his jeans.

"Back to the shoptalk," she said, inwardly smiling with female triumph and heated expectation. "Ginny spent money she likely doesn't have on safety precautions that won't do her a damn bit of good. You know how Merkerson works. If he goes after this diner, he'll do it in the bright light of day right under her nose."

And later, after the diner closed and the streets were quiet, the devious little time bomb would explode and engulf the structure in flames within moments.

"You heard what she said," Jared argued, rallying. "She feels better. And whether or not the modifications she made were necessary in this particular instance, they were still smart."

"It's my job to help make her feel safe, and clearly she wasn't feeling that way."

"Right." His gaze bore into her. "And people should sleep with their doors open because we have law enforcement."

"Not quite the same thing." The residents had been horrified at the first fire but trusted her and Jim to deal with it. The second fire had made things a little shakier, but they'd still been sure an arrest was imminent. By the third fire, people stopped thinking the authorities were just a step away from catching the arsonist and they started thinking about fending for themselves.

"Get over yourself, Darcy. Unless you totally fucked up the evidence collection and analysis, you've done your job and you're continuing to do your job by sending for help when you need it. Pat yourself on the back and give props to the people who are thinking forward instead of backward."

"I'm not sure if I like you or not."

"Don't like me. Let's keep this simple."

She nodded without hesitation. After all, she was willing to indulge herself with him precisely because he was just passing through. Anything more than sex was beyond her at this point in her life. "Works for me."

He was on his feet before Ginny reached their table with a take-out bag of food and a cardboard drink carrier. "Let's go, Inspector. We have a lot of work to get through between now and six o'clock."

JARED SET THE take-out bag down on the desk in Darcy's office and swept the narrow room with an examining glance. As he dug out his foam box, he considered the logistics of nailing her on the six-foot-long folding table set beneath the window that looked into the firehouse's heavy apparatus bay. Unfortunately, its flimsiness wouldn't hold up to the abuse, and it certainly wouldn't be professional, although a quickie would do a lot to restore his concentration. He didn't trust her desk, either, with its ultramodern glass top artfully balanced on a network of thin chrome bars.

"Miller's bark is worse than his bite, by the way." She reached around him for her shake, and he breathed her in, smelling warm clean woman.

The sheriff was in his mid-thirties and an obvious devotee to free weights, but he was no threat. Jared had spent six years with Delta Force before he'd joined the U.S. Marshals Service's elite Special Operations Group. There wasn't a human alive he couldn't severely maim or kill.

"My partner will deal with Miller. Even if she feels like killing him, she'll restrain herself." He took a bite out of his burger before occupying one of the two chairs in front of her desk. Pausing mid-chew, he mumbled an awed, "Holy shit."

Her lips curved around her straw. "Damn good burger, isn't it?"

He swallowed. "Insanely."

It was nearly as good as she looked when she smiled. *You'll be seeing stars when I'm done with you.* Fuck of it was, he was inclined to believe her. She was doing a number on him already without even trying. What would she do to him if she put some effort into it . . . ?

She rounded the desk and pulled open the top drawer of the filing cabinet. His gaze moved from her to the wall of cantilevered glass and chrome bookshelves behind her. Either the city invested a lot in the comfort of their civil servants or she'd spent her own dime dressing the space up. He was inclined to think that the utilitarian gray metal folding table and chairs were provided courtesy of the city. The run-of-the-mill filing cabinet, too. But the bookshelf unit and matching desk were all her—strong, eye-catching, and sexy. And the indulgence suggested that she spent a lot of time working . . . or felt the most at home in her office.

His gaze caught on a silver-framed picture on a shelf behind her. It was a snapshot of her when she was younger, wearing a cheerleader uniform and standing with her arm thrown across the shoulders of a mirror image of herself dressed in a band costume.

"You're a twin."

She pushed the drawer shut and returned to the desk, setting three manila folders on the glass. "Yes."

He wondered if her sister was anything like her. Maybe Darcy was the naughty twin. The thought made his overeager dick harden all over again. The word "naughty" thought of in conjunction with "Darcy" seemed to have that now-predictable effect on him.

"Shall we start with the first fire?" she asked, moving right along.

He resumed eating and nodded, but found himself slightly irritated by her lack of elaboration, which was a stupid response. Keeping things simple meant keeping them impersonal. He should be glad she was on the same page.

Pulling the bottom file free, Darcy opened it and began to carefully spread out photographs on her desk. Aside from a quirky blown-glass pen holder and red metal toolbox, there was nothing cluttering the pristine surface.

Jared chewed on a perfectly crispy French fry and studied the crime scene photos. She began to explain what he was looking at.

"The fire began at approximately ten o'clock in the evening. The owner locked up at eight. It started here," she pointed to the third picture, "in the hallway outside the restrooms."

"It was a brick-faced building?" he queried, noting the rubble.

"Yes. Florinda's Dance Studio took over the old firehouse after the town moved all the civil services into this one area and called it a town square." Darcy pulled another photo out of the file, this one a close-up framed with an L-square ruler, and set it in front of him. "See these curled aluminum shavings? They tested positive for traces of white phosphorous. It's likely that the incendiary device was hidden in a soda can dropped into a waste bin."

"Interesting."

"You know what I think is interesting?" Setting her palms on the desktop, she leaned forward. "An arsonist who picks a brick building. There are buildings in Lion's Bay that have been around for over a century. Good, old-fashioned wood-sided and shingled structures that would light up like a match, in areas where other buildings nearby would light up just as quickly."

He'd been thinking along those same lines. "Any possibility this is insurance fraud?"

"With the extra fires being a deflection? The incendiary device is too sophisticated for a dabbler. Our subject is a pro."

"Right. Go on."

"Structure number two was an old animal shelter, built mostly from cement block." Darcy slid the photos from the first fire into a neat pile and put them away before grabbing the second folder. She set the new photos out with care. "This location is very out of the way, but there's a lot of vegetation. It might've gotten ugly if we hadn't just had days of rain that saturated the area."

Jared dragged one of the photos closer. "You received the anonymous tip about this fire, correct?"

"Yes."

After he examined the images, she put them away and showed him the most recent property casualty.

"What was this place?" He eyed the unidentifiable twisted shapes that lined the floor along the walls.

"A candy shop. Those weird-looking things used to be the plastic bins the candy was kept in. The store shares a wall with a costume jewelry shop. The sophisticated fire alarm system ensured we responded quickly. The jewelry store sustained only minor damage."

Shutting the lid of his empty food container, Jared stood and moved to the map pinned to the wall. Three red arrow stickers marked spots. "Are these where the fires took place?"

"Yes."

He heard her put the files away while he studied the seemingly random locations. Different parts of town, different types of businesses. He sucked down the rest of the best shake he'd ever had, and said, "Let's head to the dance studio."

"It's been three weeks. There's nothing left to find."

"It's not evidence we're looking for." He met her gaze as she straightened. "The subject saw something in these targets that we're not. If we're going to get inside his head and anticipate his next moves, we need to figure out what's catching his attention."

"I've pored over everything until my eyes bled. I can't see anything but random chaos."

"A fresh perspective never hurts." *She's reluctant to go back,* he realized, wondering why and hoping that seeing her at the location would give him a clue.

"Hey."

Jared turned toward the open doorway and the man who leaned casually into the frame there. His uniform of short-sleeve white dress shirt and navy slacks was the same as Darcy's, except for a few extra patches on the sleeves and some gold braiding.

"Hey, Jim." Darcy quickly introduced them.

Chief Fire Inspector James Ralston straightened and shook Jared's hand, taking his measure with a sweeping glance. "I just heard that Darcy called in the cavalry. Hope you can help us nail this bastard."

"Working on it."

"Do you want to take over?" Darcy asked. "Deputy Cameron wants to check out the studio. You'll be more help to him than I'll be."

"You'll be fine." Ralston's eyes softened when he looked at Darcy. "And I can't go anyway. The mayor has me reinspecting all the public buildings as part of a planned overhaul of the alarm systems."

"Panic's spreading," she muttered, pulling a set of keys out of her pocket. "Don't let them keep you out all night."

"I won't, but I may be late. Let yourself in if I'm not there."

She shook her head. "Thank you. I'm fine."

Frowning, Ralston asked, "You sure?"

"Don't worry about me. I'm good."

"Okay, then. See you tomorrow."

The man left, but Jared's jaw didn't relax even then. "He's a little old for you, isn't he?"

Darcy paused in the act of rounding her desk. "Excuse me?"

"He's what? Forty? Forty-five?"

"We're not talking about this." She walked right past him.

Damn it, when she got stern in that voice of hers, it made him hot. He'd just reached the point of being too occupied by his work to pay attention to her sex appeal, then Jim Ralston had fucked it all to hell by showing up and starting a territory war.

Jared followed. "How long has it been over between you two?"

"Long enough."

"For you, maybe. Not for him."

"You're way off base." She strode right out of the open bay door and into the parking lot, making a beeline for a city-owned pickup truck with emblems on the door and a light bar on the roof. "He was there for me during a rough time in my life. It was never serious and it's been over for nearly two years—not that it's any of your damn business."

"The hell it isn't," he shot back, rounding the front end and yanking open the passenger door. "If he's going to be a problem, I have a right to know."

"He's not a problem. Drop it."

"That bit about you letting yourself into his place was like a dog lifting his leg."

She met his gaze through the window. "You don't have any right to my personal history. You don't have any rights at all where I'm concerned. You're a possible good time and that's it. And even that's debatable at the moment."

"Is it, now?" He glanced at his watch, then slid into the truck and slammed the door shut. It was four thirty. "Let's go."

chapter three

Darcy got behind the wheel and slid the key in the ignition, her thoughts roiling. Backing down from Jared Cameron wasn't an option. At the tiniest show of weakness, he would steamroll right over her. And the alternative—keeping him at a distance—wasn't an option she considered for more than a second. She wanted him. Badly. Almost desperately, if she was being honest. So, as overbearing and aggravating as he was, she was inclined to put up with his social Asperger's if that's what it took to have him in her bed.

They drove to what was left of Florinda's Dance Studio in silence. Jared's gaze slid back and forth over the city, taking everything in. There was a story behind his precise focus, something that explained the edge to him that set him apart from other law enforcement officers she'd met. He was hyperaware and highly perceptive. He moved like a predator, with an economy of movement and lightness of stride. And he never let his guard down.

A man hunter. That's what he was. Someone had spent a lot of money training him to be dangerous. The military, she guessed.

She parked on the street in front of the studio and got out. There were already bulldozers on the lot and giant Dumpsters to collect the rubble. Her stomach clenched tight with grief and sadness so thick it was hard for her to swallow past it.

Sucking in a deep breath, she joined Jared at the curb. He turned slowly, examining the surrounding neighborhood.

Darcy steeled her resolve and moved forward into the roofless ruins, trying to picture the place as it had once been. She was sorry it had been so long since she'd last visited. Her memories were cobwebbed from childhood. There were only faint echoes of bygone times when she and Danielle had playfully competed against one another and shared ballerina dreams.

"Adults or children?" Jared asked, breaking into her reverie.

"Excuse me?" She looked at him.

His gaze narrowed. "Are you okay? You don't look so good."

"Gee, thanks."

"Cut it out. You look"—he frowned—"sad."

"Both adults and children," she answered, skipping over the too-close-to-home comment. She was recovering her composure by the moment. Thanks to him, and the aura of strength and security that surrounded him. "And all styles, from ballet to hip-hop to ballroom."

"You were a student." It wasn't a question.

She took a deep breath, knowing it would be useless to deflect him. Nothing slipped by him. "A long time ago."

He nodded. His hands went to his hips as he looked over what was left. "Considering the size of the town, how large were the classes?"

"Five to fifteen students. The owners used to be professional dancers. People came from all over the country to study with them." She pointed at the quaint motel across the street. "They had arrangements for out-of-towners with the Daniels family."

"We'll have to dig into those former students."

"Sheriff Miller has been working on that."

Jared nodded. "Morales is on it, then."

At her questioning glance, he filled in, "My partner."

She watched him walk the perimeter of the crumbling brick walls, his cool cop's eyes taking in everything. Her chest tightened as her past combined with her present, but she put it aside and answered his questions.

Nearly an hour later, he glanced at his watch and pointed out, "It's quarter to six."

There was a wealth of promise in those words and the heat in his eyes.

Darcy nodded. He would dull the pain, at least for a little while. "Let's go."

THEY MADE A quick stop at Darcy's office, where she grabbed the files Jared had perused earlier and swapped out her work truck for a convertible BMW that was incongruous in a town filled with pick-ups and modest compacts.

She glanced at him, showing no doubts or trepidation. "Your place or mine?"

"Dinner first?" he asked, because he wasn't a completely one-track-minded Neanderthal. Okay . . . he was. But he didn't want this go-round with her to be his last. If he was going to ignore his better sense, he might as well do it all the way.

"Dinner later."

Fuck yeah. "Your place, then. Mine is a motel with paper-thin walls."

"Right." She backed up with speedy precision, and the sleek sports car purred out of the parking lot.

"Drugstore." He met her gaze when she glanced at him. "I didn't come prepared for this."

She got to the store quick but declined to go in with him. "It'll be all over town in a half hour anyway, but I'd rather not encourage the spread if I can help it."

Once he got inside the store, he realized quickly that she hadn't been kidding. The woman at the register eyed his purchases with an avid gaze and smiled at him with a delight that rankled. If he'd been any less impatient, he would have had Darcy drive him to the next town to buy condoms. As it was, he made it in and out of the store in less than ten minutes, dropping the bag on the floorboard between his feet when he slid back into the passenger seat. Darcy was turning back onto the street before he got his seat belt on.

Jared leaned his head back against the headrest and closed his eyes, relishing the slow simmer in his blood. He hadn't been this eager to get into a woman's pants in a very, very long time. He was also inordinately curious about Darcy's home and what it would reveal about her. "How long have you lived in Lion's Bay?"

"My whole life, except for a brief stint around college."

There was something in her voice that made him open his eyes and look at her. She'd released her ponytail from the elastic band, freeing the chocolate strands to whip around in the evening air. Her head was tilted in a way that could be described only as deeply sensual. She *sought* the feel of the wind rushing over her skin and through her hair as she would a lover's caresses.

He took a deep, slow breath. Darcy was clearly a tactile woman who wanted to be touched. And he was going to touch every inch of her, inside and out.

They pulled up to a small, dated, one-story ranch-style home. It was so diametrically opposed to what he would have pictured her gravitating to that he thought they'd made another pit stop at first. Then she pulled into the carport on the side of the house.

He frowned. She was modern, sexy, and fierce. He'd gotten that impression from the way she decorated her office and from the car she drove. But the house she lived in was retro and uninspired. There was a story there. He'd dig it out.

He followed her to the back door with a deliberately moderated stride, stretching out the last moments of delicious anticipation. There was nothing in the world like the buildup to a mind-blowing orgasm, and there was no doubt that he was minutes away from having the first of many tonight.

Darcy preceded him up the utilitarian cement walkway to a matching set of three steps and a small porch. She was through the door before he reached the tiny staircase. He climbed slowly, his cock getting harder with every step he took.

When he reached the threshold of the open door, he paused. Took another deep breath. Let it out. He absorbed the fact that somewhere over the course of a few short hours, fucking the sexy fire inspector had become damn near necessary to his sanity.

On an intellectual level, he understood the pull between them. He'd spent most of his life studying human behavior and pinpointing how best to hunt and kill men. He was well aware that they were all animals at their core, creatures of instinct and hormonal impetuses. He and Darcy had an explosive attraction at that base level, and neither of them was inclined to fight it. But that didn't mean he was taking it gracefully. He needed control and unadulterated reason, and Darcy was fucking with both of those. He was hanging on by a thread, and knowing that it was going to snap at any second had him edgy and frustrated.

She stepped into view, unabashedly undressing in the living room. Only the kitchen stood between him and her, the pathway delineated by the preparation/cooking area to his left and an older, sturdily built wood table to his right.

Her shirt was already off and her arms were reaching behind her, unclasping a sensible bra that was notable only for its color—black—and the saucy red bow that nestled between her small breasts. "Are you going to stand out there all night, Deputy?"

She was running in overdrive. Christ. Not that he minded, but . . .

Actually, he did mind. He was too wound up to just fuck her into a good time and get shown the door. He wanted his fill, needed it, so he could get his damn brain out of his pants and back in the game.

His T-shirt was already clearing his head when he crossed into the house and kicked the back door closed. He threw the dead bolt and turned back to her, tossing the condoms on the dining table before dealing with his holster, badge, and belt.

Darcy continued to strip while he did, her movements rushed and without artifice yet still sexy as hell. Those heavy-lidded eyes . . . the flushed cheeks . . . the glistening parted lips . . .

Everything about her screamed "sex" to him. He almost tripped in the process of toeing out of his boots, and forced himself to stand still while he tore open the button fly of his jeans. The freeing of his engorged cock was such a relief he groaned, a sound he repeated with more vehemence when she kicked off her panties and set her hands on her hips. Waiting. Naked. Ready.

He grabbed one of the two boxes of condoms and ripped it open, snagging a string of foil-wrapped packages in grasping fingers. Prowling forward, Jared separated one square and caught the rest between his teeth, deftly suiting up as he closed the distance between them.

Wide-eyed, she backed away. Her chest heaved with panting breaths; her tongue darted out to wet dry lips. He pursued her to the couch, watching as the backs of her legs hit the edge of the cushions and she sprawled into them.

He shoved the coffee table aside with a push of his foot, his focus solely on her and the feminine hunger that poured off her in waves of near-tangible heat. She stared at his dick with an avarice that made his balls tighten. His jaw unclenched on a deep inhale, releasing the condoms to fall to the floor.

Crowding her into the corner, Jared caught the back of the sofa with his left hand and cupped her pussy with his right, looming over her.

"Oh!" she gasped in that little girl voice that drove him crazy.

"Good," he growled, his fingertips gliding through silky moisture. "You're wet and hot. Primed for fucking."

Her neck arched back as he parted the lips of her cunt and massaged her clit. "Yes. Do it."

Bending his head, he caught her upraised lips before he thought about it. Kissing wasn't an act he much cared for himself. Or so he'd thought. But then his mind had shut off at some point between the unhooking of her bra and the removal of her panties. He was eating at her mouth as if he could sate his hunger that way, devouring her, delving into the silken recesses with a greed he couldn't control.

Her low moan only goaded his ferocious need. He sucked on her tongue as she licked into his mouth, sliding the circle of his lips up and down the slender protrusion, relishing the way she shivered and slickened the hand massaging her pussy.

With eyes half lidded with desire, Jared lifted his head and watched her as he pushed two fingers into her, watched the way her swollen lips parted on a gasp. He penetrated her slowly, deliberately, holding her gaze with his so that he owned her pleasure. He took her to the knuckles, then withdrew, biting his lower lip at how tight and plush she felt. How slick and hot.

"Umm," he purred, his dick aching with the need to be where his fingers were. "Open your legs wide, Darcy. Let me get to you."

Her lithe thighs spread gracefully, her heels lifting to the couch and her knees falling open. Presented with a beautifully pink and depilated pussy, Jared felt his tenuous control slipping by the moment. He pumped his fingers deep and fast, over and over, fucking her pretty juicy cunt until she was grinding her hips into his hand and making sexy little noises. She cupped her tits in a kneading grip, her fingers tugging at the hard little nipples, her breath escaping her arched throat in mewling pants.

All the while he hovered over her mouth, teasing her with tantalizing flicks of his tongue, staying just far enough out of reach that she couldn't have the deep French kiss they both craved. It would be too much, he'd lose his mind and his restraint, and he needed her to come first. Needed to ease the desperate tightness of her pussy. Because once he got into her, all bets were off.

"Yes." She gasped, her slim torso glistening with perspiration. "Yes, I'm going to come . . . *Oh, God . . .*"

Darcy fell into climax with a violent full-body shudder, her cunt clutching at his working fingers with a strength that nearly set him off. He dropped to his knees, his mouth replacing his hand, his tongue spearing through her tender convulsing tissues. He consumed her like a man possessed, burying his face in her silky wet core, tonguing her cunt until she came again. And again. Her short nails clawing at the sofa as she cried out words he couldn't hear over the rushing of blood in his ears. He couldn't get enough. Needed more of her taste, her pleasure, her surrender.

Her damp palm pressed to his sweat-slick forehead, pushing him away. "Jared . . . Jesus . . . I'm going to pass out before you get inside me."

Fuck that. He'd eat more of her pussy later, when she was too wiped out to argue and his dick wasn't throbbing like a son of a bitch. Damned if she'd check out before he got his cock in her.

Wiping his mouth on her inner thigh, Jared rose and caught the back of her leg over his arm. He pulled it high and wide, opening her completely.

She grasped him in both hands, making him wince as the pleasure of her touch threatened to send him over the edge. Her gaze stayed with his as she positioned him at her opening, sliding the crown around in her wetness before notching him into her tiny slit.

"God, Darcy. This is gonna be so fucking good."

The weight of his body was the force behind his entry. As his cock sank into her cushioning pussy, his breath hissed out in agonized pleasure. He'd never been so hard or his body so tense.

Whimpering, she writhed beneath him. "Jared."

The way she said his name, in that breathless girly voice, did him in. He dug his feet into the floor and he drove deep, spearing into her with a mindless thrust. Her back bowed, crushing her small breasts into his chest. The feel of her pressed against him was like a punch to the gut. His abdomen clenched, his blood raged, and his adrenaline spiked. Her cunt quivered around him, massaging his tormented dick, stealing any possibility that he might've reined himself in.

He groaned, his hips churning against hers. "You feel amazing . . . so damn tight and plush . . ."

Darcy's teeth sank into his shoulder, her hands clutching at his waist. The bite of pain was perfect, enough to jolt him out of the haze of near-painful pleasure and goad him into moving.

Shoving his arms beneath her, Jared caught her to him, crushing her against him from shoulder to hip. With her pelvis tilted up to cradle him and her body completely restrained by the bands of his arms, he possessed her completely. He gave a tentative thrust, withdrawing partway, then shoving back inside her.

She released his shoulder, her head falling back to once again arch over the armrest. She moaned. "Do that again."

"All night," he promised darkly, taking her with another fierce stroke, watching the need flare higher in the depths of her jade green eyes. "You won't remember what it felt like to go without my cock inside you."

Darcy's cunt clenched around him and he broke. Rearing back, he lunged hard and deep. His tempo increased, faster and faster, until he was riding her relentlessly. Pounding into her. Nailing her to the couch with powerful drives of his hips.

In a distant part of his mind, he knew he was taking her too roughly, working her snug pussy too hard, but she was taking everything he had to give her and demanding more.

"Harder," she gasped, throwing her hips at him. "Deeper. Ah . . . you're so big. It's so good . . ."

It was beyond good. She was killing him with her enthusiasm—the raking of her nails across his back, her heels in the backs of his thighs spurring him on, her silky tissues rippling up and down his aching cock. And her voice, which rivaled the rhythmic slap of his heavy balls against her damp flesh as the most erotic thing he'd ever heard.

"You're driving me crazy," he growled, unable to stop fucking her, needing to get deeper inside her. He was bottoming out with every plunge, filling every inch of her, his eyes rolling back because she was deliciously tight and scorching hot. The softly feminine smell of her skin was going to his head, intoxicating him, making him dizzy. Just when he thought he might blow it and go off without her, she began to tense.

"Oooh." She shivered violently. "I'm going to come again."

"Do it." Jared bit down on her shoulder, relishing the way she jerked and tightened around him in response. He grunted as she pulsed in tiny spasms. "Just like that . . . Milk my cock. Ah, hell . . ."

She climaxed with a cry, the delicate tissues that hugged him tightening into a velvet fist before convulsing in the milking grip he'd demanded of her. Pinning her shoulders, he held her immobile and jackhammered through her orgasm, his own spiraling like molten metal down his spine and pooling in his balls.

His head fell back on a serrated groan, his body bowing as her pleasure fueled his, enflaming him. Cum spurted from the tip of his cock with a ferocity that rocked him, stinging his eyes and tightening his throat. His straining muscles burned and quaked, his entire body rigid as he emptied himself into the condom.

He might have lost his sanity in that mind-blowing moment if not for Darcy. She was right there with him, meeting him stroke for stroke.

chapter four

Despite the sweat that ran in rivulets down her overheated body, Darcy missed Jared's weight and the feeling of him inside her the moment he rolled away.

He collapsed on the seat beside her, his chest heaving with deep, gulping breaths. His eyes were closed, his head pressed into the sofa.

"Holy shit," he said finally. "I can't feel my legs."

She closed her eyes, telling herself that rapid separation and focus on pleasure was the way to go. Keep it simple. They were just screwing. And since it was phenomenal, she couldn't complain.

His lips brushed over her shoulder. "I was rough and you allowed it. Thank you."

Soothed by the gesture and sentiment, she kept her eyes closed and smiled.

He shifted. His mouth sealed over hers without warning, stealing her breath. Frozen for a moment, it took a few soft licks of his tongue to kick-start her brain. When she opened to him, he kissed her with a gentleness very much at odds with the impatience with which he'd taken her body. His hand cupped the back of her neck, his fingers pushing into the sweat-dampened roots and holding her just where he wanted her.

The stroke of his tongue along hers was soft and slow, the press of his lips firm but not hard. It was a lush, hot, wet melding that curled her toes.

When they parted, they were both breathing hard. Their gazes met. A long, somewhat awkward moment passed.

She cleared her throat. "I need to take a shower."

"I bought a bag of Epsom salts, in case you'd like to soak." Jared pushed to his feet. "Bathroom?"

Startled by his thoughtfulness, she managed to point down the hall. "Left side."

He set off, presenting her with a view of a really gorgeous ass. Her gaze was riveted to its rhythmic clenching as he walked away, her heartbeat elevated by the realization that she'd pushed such a gloriously masculine creature to his limits.

Taking a moment to collect herself, Darcy stood and moved into the kitchen, realizing as she went that Jared had known the state of her body before she did—she *was* slightly sore. Breaking a year-long abstinence with a hard, pounding fuck with a well-hung man would do that to a woman, she supposed.

She was just digging through the shopping bag for the salts when she heard the rush of bathtub water surging through the house's old pipes. He had purchased men's combo hair/body wash and razors, too, which gave her an odd flutter of delight—he'd planned on staying from the get-go. She wasn't going to read anything into it, but it was nice to know he hadn't planned on yanking his pants back up as quickly as he'd dropped them.

When she joined him, Darcy found the bathroom door open and her new lover leaning over the triangular-shaped tub, testing the temperature of the water. He glanced at her as she filled the doorway.

"Now, this room," he said, "fits you."

"I had the bathroom redesigned after my parents moved out."

She'd hired a contractor to gut the closet in the adjacent den to expand the home's one bathroom into something she could live with. The room was still small, but it now accommodated a separate bath and shower, instead of the combo tub with showerhead that had been there before. The café au lait walls and tile, paired with accents of eggplant, gave the room a warm modern elegance she found soothing.

Jared held his hand out for the Epsom salts.

An odd tenseness spread through her tummy. "You came prepared. I take it riding a woman hard is par for the course with you?"

He stilled, his extended fingers curling into a fist. "Not really, no."

She stepped closer and handed him the bag. She hoped his answer meant she got to him in a unique way, especially considering how he so easily devastated her.

Looking almost . . . chagrined, Jared dumped a heaping handful of salt under the running water. "I have a sister with no concept of TMI," he said gruffly. "You might know what that's like."

She nodded.

"She said salt baths worked wonders after overenthusiastic nights. It seemed like a good idea to grab some, considering where things were heading." He gestured her over. "Is this too hot?"

It wasn't. With a grateful, slightly bemused smile, Darcy stepped into the small corner tub and sighed her delight. "Thank you."

Turning off the water, he stood. He grabbed his toiletries and moved over to the floating glass shower stall. She relaxed into the neck pillow she kept on the ledge and watched as he stepped beneath the oversized showerhead. He was tall, but the flexible arm adjusted for that, and soon enough he was putting on a show she would have paid top-dollar for.

Completely oblivious to her avid perusal, he soaped his hair and chest, his hands roaming over his gorgeously ripped body with brisk efficiency. The scent of his soap filled the air and she swallowed hard, her mouth watering. A flush swept over her skin that had more to do with her new lover than it did with the heat of the bathwater.

Jared Cameron was her darkest sexual fantasies in the flesh, his thick biceps flexing as he moved, his abdomen and pectorals clenching as his arms lifted to scrub at his hair. Soapy water sluiced down his tanned skin, making her pussy clench in renewed hunger.

When he turned his attention to washing his genitals, stroking his long thick penis in one hand and rolling his scrotum with the other, Darcy couldn't ignore the pulsing between her legs any longer.

Laying one leg on the lip of the tub, she cupped her slick pussy and massaged the tender knot of her clitoris. The fingers of her other hand caught a nipple in their grip, rolling and tugging the aching point, sending shards of delight straight to her womb. She made a soft noise of need and his head lifted abruptly, catching her in the act of pleasuring herself.

She bit her lower lip in a deliberately provocative come-on, feeling sexy and naughty as his desire rose in response to hers. His cock thickened in his hand and she arched her back, remembering how the hard length felt moving inside her.

His resultant scowl wasn't what she'd expected. Neither was the haste with which he finished rinsing off and vacated the shower. As he strode out of the bathroom with her towel wrapped around his lean hips, she wondered if she'd crossed a line.

Deflated and embarrassed, her hands fell away from her body. She sank her head beneath the water, submerging herself as long as her lungs would allow.

When she came up for air, Jared was there. Standing by the tub with his arms crossed and a new condom rolled over his raging erection. She quickly swiped the water off her face with her hands, blinking up at him.

He uncoiled, stepping into the tub before she knew he intended to. Catching her beneath the arms, he hauled her up and set her ass atop her neck pillow on the wide ceramic edge.

"I wanted to wait," he muttered, kneeling in the water and spreading her legs. "At least until after dinner."

He dove for her pussy, his mouth latching on to her tender core and tonguing her cleft. He pushed inside her and she gasped, her hips arching. His tongue slid in and out, licking quick and shallow, luring her slickness until she heard how wet she was. He groaned and tilted his head, thrusting deeper into her, drinking her in as if he couldn't get enough.

When she started to tremble, hovering on the edge of orgasm, he wiped his mouth on her inner thigh and stood. Darcy shivered at the look he shot her, the edgy hunger that seemed little appeased by their animal screwing on the couch.

He caught himself in hand and gently nudged her. A rough sound escaped him. "Fuck, I wanted to wait," he said again, with more vehemence. "You're swollen."

"I can't help it if you hit all my hot buttons." She gripped his hips to stabilize her perch. "You looked so damn hot in the shower. Turned me on watching you stroke yourself."

"You were looking at my dick like you'd die if I didn't give it to you. I almost blew my load in the shower." He began a slow slide into her, exerting minimal pressure to ease past tender tissues. "After what you did to me on the couch, I shouldn't have anything left to blow."

"I would have loved to watch," she said, breathless with lust. Every inch he pushed into her stole another piece of her sanity; every coarse word he spoke ratcheted up her need.

Cupping her cheek in one hand and her hip in the other, he shook his head, nudging deeper. His thumb pushed into her mouth. "I want this mouth first."

She drew on the callused pad, rubbing her tongue over it, watching his eyes darken.

"You'll suck my dick just like that," he said hoarsely. "I'll have you on your knees, deep-throating my cock. After this, it'll take me longer to come. I'll be fucking your mouth for a good, long while. I'll make it last because it's going to feel so damn good. Everything about you makes me feel good."

He pulled his thumb free and lowered his head to kiss her, his tongue thrusting into the warm recess in imitation of the act he spoke of. With his lips whispering over hers and his hand at her throat, he said, "You'll swallow every drop of my cum, sucking it from the tip of my dick until I've got nothing left to give you."

"Yes . . ." she breathed, wanting him in her mouth now. Wanting to see the pleasure sweep across his face as she took him to orgasm.

With a roll of his hips, he sank into her to the root. His groan hardened her nipples. "You're even tighter than before and your cunt was perfect then."

Tilting her head back, Darcy's lips and teeth followed the sharp line of his jaw. "You're thicker than before and your cock was big then."

"Because now I know how good it's going to feel when I go off." He leaned his head back to invite her attention to his throat. "How good it feels when you lose it and squeeze me like a fist."

"You make me come so hard," she whispered by his ear, licking delicately into it and smiling when he shuddered. She deliberately tightened her pussy around him.

Jared cursed and withdrew, then slid balls deep in a measured glide. "Play all you want, sweetheart, but you're not rushing me."

Gripping his taut ass in her hands, she squeezed and held him close so she could grind into him. She nearly came from the fleeting pressure of his pelvis against her clitoris, her sex spasming greedily around his erection.

"Shit." He groaned, reaching behind him to grab her hands and pull them away. He crowded her, forcing her to lean back. Then he pinned her hands to the tile with his own and gave her a breathlessly perfect stroke with a practiced swing of his hips. "You're not going to quit until I'm an idiot over you. A pussy-whipped, salivating piece of shit who can't think about anything but nailing you everywhere and every way he can, no matter how often he has you."

Darcy's head fell back with a mewl as he began to shaft her aching pussy with smooth measured thrusts. She couldn't speak for the pleasure, the fit of his thick, long cock so perfect it filled every centimeter of her. Eyes closed, she absorbed the rhythmic impact of his hips into hers and the arousing smack of his heavy balls against the wet curve of her buttocks. The push and pull of his erection was an erotic massage over her hypersensitive flesh, the wide crest rubbing over a spot that made her shake uncontrollably.

"I could do this all day," he growled. "All night."

"Don't stop, Jared. Don't. Stop."

His tongue flickered over her nipple and she nearly climaxed.

"Oh, yeah." His breath blew hot over her damp skin. "We're doing that later. I'm going to slide my dick into you, then suck on your nipples until your hungry little cunt milks me dry."

His lips surrounded the tip of her breast. He suckled her with drawing pulls that were perfectly timed with his plunges between her legs. His tongue lashed at the hardened nipple, flickering over it in a way that sent pulses of heated delight racing across her nerve endings. She heard herself whimpering, her body moving separately from her mind, her hips rocking to meet his and hold the incredible fullness of him deep inside her.

Jared released her wrists, his hands moving to cradle her spine and mold her body to his. It was the singularly most carnal experience of her life. And the most intimate.

"Yes," she breathed, suspended in his arms. "I'm coming . . ."

The orgasm swept through her like a gentle wave, lapping at her senses, gaining strength until she quivered uncontrollably. All the while he continued the leisurely thrusting of his rigid penis, swelling with his own imminent release, spurring her to climax again.

Wrung out and on an emotional precipice she hadn't expected, Darcy gave herself over to him. Let him pleasure her until she was certain she couldn't take any more, until her legs hung limply in the cold water and her nipples throbbed.

Only then did he let go, holding her torso against his scorching-hot skin, his chest heaving as he jerked violently and came endlessly.

chapter five

"They've actually made some good headway with the student list from the dance studio." Trish's voice came clearly through Jared's cell phone speaker, accompanied by the rustle of papers in the background. "They've already confirmed alibis for most of the repeat students going back one year. Miller is territorial, but he's got good instincts."

Jared slid the phone aside to make room for a cutting board on the kitchen counter. "My concern is whether or not the town's residents are a blind spot in his investigation."

"I'm working him around to thinking more along those lines. At least considering them."

"He lets you get a word in edgewise? You're a miracle worker." He deseeded a bell pepper, then chopped it quickly into small squares.

"He's not that bad," Trish said. "His only experience with federal law enforcement wasn't a good one."

"About that." He worked on an onion next. "I'd like the name and contact information of whoever was the primary on that case."

"You going to thank him or her for making our job so much easier?"

"Don't give me ideas." Using the knife, he scraped half the vegetables into a heated skillet. "It might be worth it to see if anyone in Lion's Bay rubbed the Feds the wrong way. Aside from Sheriff Congeniality."

"What time are you coming into the station tomorrow?"

"Not sure. I want to check out the other two locations in the morning. Why?"

"Wouldn't want Miller to be out and miss you."

Gripping the handle of the skillet, he jerked the pan to flip the sizzling vegetables. "I've requested courier manifests going back six months. While it'd be stupidly obvious to ship hazardous materials in and leave that trail—"

"We don't want to be the ones who overlook the obvious."

"Right. I'm hanging up now. Call if you need me."

"What is that noise?"

"Dinner. I'm hungry. Good night." Jared tapped the disconnect button on his phone and turned his attention to cracking eggs to finish up the omelets.

As he moved, he mentally cataloged the state of his body. His damned legs were jellied and there was an odd knotting in his gut that he told himself was hunger. He was having trouble staying focused, his thoughts drifting to the woman presently soaking in a fresh Epsom bath.

The sexpot fire inspector had fried his brain. A wild lay was not supposed to make a man feel strange. It was supposed to relieve stress, provide a workout, and clear a man's head. Instead, he didn't even hear Darcy enter the room until she spoke.

"Whatever you're cooking," she said, "smells delicious."

He glanced at her, cursing inwardly for being caught unawares. "Omelets."

"Awesome." She maneuvered around him and opened a cupboard to pull out plates. Dressed in jeans and a T-shirt, her composure irritated him. He'd tugged his pants back on because they were about to eat, but he'd left the fly partially open, exposing the waistband of his boxer briefs. He was shirtless and barefoot, comfortable and relaxed, while she looked like she was ready to leave the house.

"Where are you going?" he asked, scrambling the yolk with enough vehemence to make it frothy.

"Excuse me?"

"You got dressed." And her hair was damp and slicked back into a ponytail.

"I didn't know I was supposed to eat naked. You're not."

He unclenched his jaw. "You could have put on a robe."

Setting the plates on the dining table, Darcy returned to the kitchen. "I didn't want—" She exhaled harshly. "I don't want you to feel like I'm assuming anything or taking anything for granted. You made it very clear that things need to be simple."

"No assumptions, but you assume I'll get antsy if you follow the evidence that says I prepared to spend the night." He poured the eggs into the pan with the veggies, then added the ham he'd chopped before he called Trish. "Unless what you're not saying is that you're ready for me to go."

She straightened and approached him. "Sex doesn't improve your humor, I see."

"Maybe because I'm not done."

"Okay, then." She pulled silverware out of a drawer. "That's settled."

A moment later, Jared heard her moving the plastic shopping bag off the table. From the sounds of it, she was looking inside, perhaps noticing the toothbrush, antiperspirant, and razor sitting next to the two boxes of condoms. As far as he was concerned that wasn't optimistic, that was practical. He flipped the omelet with a deft flick of his wrist.

"I wish I had a camera," she said. "You look sexy as hell doing that."

She looked sexy as hell when he was doing her, all soft and warm and flushed. The memory of her in the bathtub was going to haunt him for a while.

He jerked his chin toward the table. "Sit down."

Darcy exhaled in a rush. "I wanted to put a robe on. Just so you know, I originally thought about ordering something in, answering any questions you might have about the case, and maybe watching TV if it wasn't too late."

"You should've gone with your instincts." He tossed some shredded cheese into the omelet, then slid it onto her plate in a practiced fold. "Dig in. Don't wait for me."

"This looks as awesome as it smells. Thank you."

Returning to the stove, he started cooking for himself.

She moaned, making his dick twitch with interest. "Jared. Wow. This is phenomenal. You're as good in the kitchen as you are in bed."

He watched her lift a second bite to her mouth, her eyes closing as she chewed and hummed her pleasure.

Swallowing, she went on. "Not that we've made it to the bed."

"Yet."

"Yet," she agreed. "You know, I should get some credit for being concerned about scaring you off. I'm giving you credit for being offended at the possibility of a brush-off."

Jared stared into the skillet. Simple would be taking the out she'd offered him and heading back to the motel to sleep in a solitary bed. Simple would be keeping his eye on the job he was here to do and his hands off the smoking-hot inspector who flooded his system with so much testosterone he couldn't think straight.

Rubbing the back of his neck, he said gruffly, "Keeping things simple means not making things complicated. You're overthinking."

Of course, *he* was hardly thinking at all. He was running on pure animal instinct when it came to her.

Darcy laughed softly. "You can't put this on me. I know how men work when they start off with the warning to keep it simple. That means don't get clingy. Don't expect me to be there for you when we're not fucking. I get that, and it works for me. That said, I know all men have hot buttons, but I don't know what yours are."

He grunted. As far as he was concerned, everything about her was a hot button. And this conversation had veered into a direction certain to drive him crazier than she did.

"You know what I'm talking about." She set her fork down. "Things that freak you into thinking the situation is becoming more involved than you want it to be."

He slid his own omelet onto his plate, returned the pan to the stove, and joined her at the table. Too late for the freak-out warning. It had been going off since he'd drilled her into the sofa. He had no control with her. No cutoff switch or throttle.

Darcy leaned forward. "You can't tell me that a woman assuming a sleepover when you're in a wham-bam frame of mind doesn't make things dicey."

Shoving a bite of his food into his mouth, he chewed through his frustration. He didn't want to analyze this . . . *them.* He'd rather stick with orgasmic ignorance. "I can tell you that as long as we're both in the same place at the same time wanting the same thing, I really don't give a shit."

Darcy pushed back from the table. "All right. Excuse me a moment."

He scowled at the sight of her half-eaten omelet, then glared at her retreating back. He'd give her five minutes to get her tight little ass back in her chair or he was going to drag her back in to finish eating . . .

She returned in a short white satin robe that revealed her bare legs and the lack of a bra. Jared forgot his aggravation.

As Darcy resumed eating with obvious relish, he leaned back in his chair, watching her.

"In a town of this size, with only one fire station, how does the city council justify paying for two fire inspectors?"

When she looked up at him, her eyes were lit with amusement. "A combination of nepotism, being willing to work part time, and a good word from Jim."

Jim. He reined in his irritation with a long, slow exhale. "Who's the family member?"

"My uncle. He moved several years ago, but memories are ageless in Lion's Bay."

"And the rest of your family is gone, too?"

"Yep. Although my parents didn't go far. They bought a place on Lake Horton."

Which wasn't all that far from his place in Seattle. "Why do you stay? What's here for you?"

Darcy pushed back from the table and picked up her plate. "Why not?"

He studied her as she came toward him to collect his plate, too. "It doesn't suit you," he said. "The town. This house."

"You don't know that."

Standing, he followed her to the sink. "I do."

"Maybe I'm not as easy to read as you think."

Jared backed off, noting the tension in her shoulders and the way she avoided his gaze. Coming up behind her, he pushed her ponytail aside and brushed his lips over her nape. He'd get the story out of her eventually. In the meantime, he wanted her soft and warm. He wanted to explore what it was about her that made him want to kiss her all over.

She turned to face him. "Why did you join the Marshals Service?"

He gripped the counter on either side of her, trapping her in the cage of his arms. She smelled sweet and clean, and he was hyperaware of the fact that she was mostly naked beneath the thin wrap of white satin. “Because the military and I were done with each other and there’s nothing else I’m good at.”

“You’re a good cook.”

“Thanks.”

Her hands went to his hips, her fingers twining in his belt loops. “You’re seriously hot. You could be a calendar model. Or a Chippendales dancer.”

“That’s not flattering.”

“You’re outrageously good in bed. Although monetizing that is illegal.”

“I like it on this side of the law,” he murmured, bending his head over her. “And I’m picky about who I go to bed with. I’d starve to death.”

“Well, that’s flattering.”

Darcy was a confident woman; she knew the force of her sex appeal. Since it was highly doubtful she would’ve picked up that level of sensual sophistication around a town of this size, where the dating pool had to be painfully small, he was even more curious about the time she’d spent away from this place. And what had brought her back. Maybe she was licking her wounds after a bad breakup, swearing off men for a while and retreating to a place where she’d be left alone.

He stepped back. “Wanna watch TV?”

Her eyes sparkled with silent laughter. She knew damn well he wanted another go at her, but he was going to hold off. He needed to be more careful or risk her burning out on him. He also needed to get a grip on himself.

“Find something you like,” she urged. “I’ll join you after I load up the dishwasher.”

He went along with the suggestion only because he wanted to get a closer look at her place without making her nervous about it. Moving into the living room, Jared took notice of all the details he'd been too lust addled to appreciate earlier. His gaze went to the now infamous couch first. Its modern lines and extra deep cushions were very much in keeping with how he saw Darcy, as was the sixty-two-inch flat-screen TV hung over the fireplace. Both were out of place against dated wallpapered walls. The coffee and end tables were sturdy wood pieces as retro in style as the dining table, while the knickknacks around the room were contemporary pieces.

Pausing by the fireplace, he looked at the framed photos on the mantel. Some were of Darcy with her parents, some were of her sister. He could tell the two apart easily, a difference confirmed by pictures of the two sisters together. The set of Darcy's shoulders and the cant of her chin were unique to her, displaying a self-possession and boldness that wasn't as evident in her sister's shy smile.

He turned away from the fireplace as she entered the room, his gaze hungry as it swept over her slender frame. He should be wrung out by the two explosive orgasms she'd already given him, and there was no denying she was sore. But that didn't stop her from looking at him like she wanted to ride him 'til morning or him from seriously weighing the pros and cons of letting her. He'd experienced potent sexual attraction before, but this was inexorable. Feeling his cock stir, he shucked his jeans but left his boxer briefs on.

"Don't get excited," he warned, when she caught her breath, "I'm just getting comfortable."

Catching her lower lip between her teeth, she gave him a deliberately provocative look. She ran a finger down her throat to her cleavage.

"Keep it up," he drawled, grabbing the remote before dropping into the corner of the couch where he'd had her pinned just hours before. He spread his legs and patted the spot between them. "Now be a good girl and lay here against me."

She came to him with a wry smile. "You don't strike me as the type of man who likes good girls."

"I like you." He wrapped an arm around her as she settled her back against his chest. "And I don't expect you to behave."

"You know me so well," she teased, raking her short nails across his thighs.

Not yet, but he would.

chapter six

The sun had barely risen when Jared finished poring over Darcy's files. Finding his cell phone a poor substitute for the big screen of his laptop, he availed himself of Darcy's office. He powered on her desktop, praying she didn't have it password protected. Whether she always slept like the dead or he'd just worn her out, he figured she needed the sleep, considering the demands he'd be making of her over the length of his stay.

When the computer screen flickered to life, he found himself looking at an image of Darcy and her sister, which served as the desktop wallpaper. They were children in the photo, not quite teenagers. Their hair was arranged in matching pigtails and they wore identical pale pink leotards. A reflection of their backs in a wall of mirrors was behind them, with a ballet bar that traversed the full width.

He tucked the image away along with the other bits and pieces he was collecting in his mental file for her, then he got to work. He accessed the Merkerson case files, comparing the information with what he'd just acquired from Darcy's. The similarities were irrefutable. In fact, they were nearly perfect.

The only anomaly he could pinpoint was the incendiary devices in relation to the rapidity of the timeline. Merkerson had started out with smaller devices, such as soda cans, but he'd been more intermittent. Months passed between arsons, until later in his rampage, when he advanced to using paint can–sized devices and striking every seven days. His illness had progressed to where he wanted the entire world to burn. Fire was his obsession and his mistress. This new combination of smaller devices and frequency melded his earlier work with his later freneticism, but whether that was evolution, devolution, or simply a poor fit to the pattern was debatable. And any of those options left the field wide open.

Jared drafted a quick report to his superior, giving a rundown of his thoughts and impressions. She'd lived the case the first time around, which gave her insight worth tapping into. He also asked for an update on the anonymous 911 call that alerted the authorities to the second fire. Miller had ascertained that the call originated in Seattle and was placed via a burner phone. But the sheriff had stopped investigating at that point, leaving the thread dangling. Why?

With that question in mind, he powered down Darcy's computer and checked the time. Seven thirty.

Heading back into the bedroom, he stopped by the nightstand and checked her alarm. It was set for eight, which gave him just about enough time. He looked down at her, finding her just as luscious while resting as he did when hit with the seething sensuality of the way she moved. She lay on her back with one arm bent around the top of her head and the other at her side. The sheet was loosely draped over her, exposing the upper swell of her tits and the bent knee of one leg.

He pinched the sheet between his fingers and tugged it down, exposing her body in delicious increments. She slept on, innocently luring him to start the day with a bang . . .

DARCY AWOKE WITH a gasp, heat flaring across her skin in a molten wave. As her brain lurched into awareness, another heated lash across her clit had her moaning and instinctively closing her legs.

But they wouldn't close. Strong hands held them down and spread for the next leisurely lick. Her heart raced with surprise and fear. Her eyes wrenched open, her hand thrusting downward to protect her intimate flesh. Her fingers sank into luxurious strands of thick hair, sliding through the mass to stroke over the scalp beneath.

A low masculine sound of approval slid across her skin like a caress.

The spearing of a tongue into her pussy woke her fully, arching her back and ripping a cry from her throat. Her mind was just catching on, but her body was already there, her nipples beaded hard and tight, and her sex clenching with demand for more attention.

"Morning, sunshine," Jared rumbled, his breath gusting warmly over her damp skin.

"Jared . . . ?"

"Who else?" He lifted one of her boneless legs over a thick shoulder and pushed the other up and to the side, opening her completely. "Now just lie there and come for me."

She opened her mouth to reply, but a slow, deliberate swipe over her clitoris stole her breath. Whimpering, she lifted her hips to him, seeking more.

"Umm . . ." he purred, nuzzling against her with his lips. "You have the softest, most succulent cunt."

Her head pressed hard into the pillow as he traced her folds with the stiffened tip of his tongue. Her pussy was creaming for him, her desire seeping from her body in silky skeins of moisture. He lapped at her, teasing the clenching opening of her sex with taunting flutters. Her womb tightened to the point of pain.

"Please." Her hips churned. "Fuck me with your tongue."

"Oh, yeah." He gave a shallow thrust, then circled her clit. "I'm going to do everything to you. Fuck you everywhere, in every way."

He moved sinuously, shrugging out from under her and gaining his knees. Pushing her legs up and back, he exposed her even more fully. Her hips were lifted from the bed, her shoulders supporting her weight as he bent his head and licked the length of her upraised slit. The vulnerability of her position only heightened the fever raging through her. His hands cupped the backs of her thighs, his thumbs holding her open for the tantalizing forays of his devious tongue. The scrape of his morning whiskers was an added stimulation, the slight discomfort soothed by the soft brush of his hair against her sensitive inner thighs.

And she could watch it all—the way his mouth sealed over her pussy as he pushed his tongue into her in a raw, erotic French kiss; the way his eyes darkened as she panted and fisted the bottom sheet; the way his lids lowered on a groan as she grew hotter and wetter.

His thumb slid through the building slickness, coaxing it lower, using it to massage the tender pucker of her ass. Lust shot through her like a strike of lightning while sweat bloomed over her skin in a mist of heat.

Jared's head lifted. "You want me here."

"I want you everywhere." She felt as if she no longer fit in her skin, as if she were trying to crawl out of it. Her hunger for him was raging through her, boiling through her veins and stealing every remaining shred of her sanity.

His thumb exerted the tiniest bit of pressure and she pushed out for him, flowering open and accepting his touch inside her. A violent tremor shook her, pushing her to the edge of climax. It had been a long time since she'd trusted a man to take her there. Too long. And even then, the relationship hadn't been so raw and sexual. Jared's unabashed carnality stripped her of her normal boundaries, violated her sensibilities, opened her to torment both physical and . . . otherwise.

Every time he touched her, she wanted more. More of him. More of who she was with him.

Squeezing her aching breasts, she tightened around his thumb. "Eat me 'til I come. Then fuck my ass until you come."

"Jesus." His skin stretched tight over his cheekbones. "You don't know what you do to me. How crazed you make me. I want to defile your body. Own it. Possess it . . ."

"*Yes.*"

"Beg me, Darcy. Beg me to do it all to you. Everything I want."

"Now. All of it."

He dove for the saturated flesh between her thighs, latching on with a greed that tore through her. His tongue fucked her spasming pussy hard and fast, his head angling to get deeper. His thumb thrust in and out of her rear, the dual shallow penetration making her mindless.

She begged as he'd demanded her to, pleaded with him to finish her, to make her come before she broke from the strain . . .

The moment his lips surrounded her clit, the climax hit her hard, bowing her back and blackening her vision. She cried out as he sucked her, drawing on her with rapid measured pulls. The orgasm barreled through her senses, building and building until she thought she might lose consciousness. Then it ebbed, taking her breath and energy with it. She melted into the bed, barely aware of the gentleness with which he lowered her.

"Darcy."

Her breathing rasped in the semidarkness of the bedroom. She struggled to open her eyes, finding Jared kneeling between them, pushing his boxer briefs down to free his raging cock. His balls were hard and full, drawn up close to the base of his heavily veined shaft. The wide crest was purpled by the need to expend the semen dribbling from the tip and he fisted it with a harsh curse.

As he had in the shower, he rolled his scrotum in one hand and jacked himself off with the other.

She watched with a dry mouth as he stroked his cock with a

brutality that pounded through her blood. It was a primitive demonstration of how wild she made him, soothing her with the proof that he was as lust crazed as she was.

Pinching and tugging on her nipples, she urged him on. "I'm imagining you in me—how deep you get, how thick you are just before you come. You fill me so full the pleasure is almost pain. I don't know how I'll bear it when you take my ass, but I know I'll love it. I'll—"

"Fuck." Semen exploded from him in a scorching stream across her torso. His fist flew, pumping the creamy fluid up the shaft to spurt over her nipples, coating her skin with the evidence of his virility. He came long and hard, cursing as his powerful body was wracked by wrenching shudders.

But when he finished, he was still hard, and the gleam in his eye was as rapacious as she'd come to expect.

The blaring of her alarm was jolting, kicking her racing heartbeat into overdrive. Reaching down, Jared caught her by the nape of her neck and lifted her to his mouth. He kissed her hard and swift, his free hand kneading his cum into her breasts.

"Saved by the bell," he said roughly.

Darcy spoke with her lips against his. "Later. We'll finish this later."

"I'm counting the seconds."

DARCY SET COFFEE to brewing while Jared showered, then turned her attention to the files on the arsons that lay on the dining room table. At some point during the night, he must have gone out to her car to retrieve them. She wondered what conclusions he'd drawn, if any, and if he had any theories or questions she might help him with.

The shower turned off, leaving a sudden void as the noisy pipes quieted. In the ensuing silence, she could almost hear her body humming. She felt strangely energized and exhausted, content and apprehensive. In less than a day, Jared had found a loose thread in her life and he was slowly pulling it, unraveling her at the seams. She didn't see how she would be able to continue the searingly intimate sexual exploration they were engaging in without becoming attached to it.

Already she craved him. Picturing an addiction to him wasn't that big of a leap.

"I'd kill to have some of that coffee I smell," he said, entering the kitchen with damp hair and nothing but his jeans on.

She drank him in, resisting the urge to run her fingers through the light dusting of hair on his chest. Truth be told, she couldn't stop her mind from imagining her tongue tracing the line of his happy trail from his navel to his cock below. Her mouth watered with the desire to lick and suck him to orgasm, to fully own his pleasure when he came. And her proprietary feelings extended beyond that to encompass the whole of him.

"Stop looking at me like that," he said sharply. "You're making my dick hard."

"Stop teasing me with your rockin' body," she shot back, stung and frightened by the sting, which hinted that she might be in too deep with him already. "How would you like it if I walked around topless all the time?"

He scowled. "I'd love it and you know it, but we have shit to do besides fuck each other's brains out. I need you to give me a break."

"You're one to talk," she muttered under her breath, turning toward the coffeemaker. He was irascible, grumpy, and rude as a rule. But that was part of his charm. Even if his gruffness did rub her raw at times. "How do you take your coffee?"

"Black."

Darcy pulled a mug out of the cupboard. She felt him come up behind her, then closed her eyes as he nuzzled his way past her ponytail to her nape. His arms came around her and she tensed, fighting to keep the tremors she felt on the inside from being discernible on the outside.

His embrace tightened and he spoke roughly. "I'm sorry."

Reaching for the carafe, she took a deep slow breath. "Nothing to be sorry about."

"Bullshit. I can't take it out on you when it's my own damn self I can't seem to control. We're on fire for each other. Keeping that in check is going to take work and some concessions. I hate putting clothes on when my skin's damp, but I'll get over it."

"Okay."

His teeth bit lightly into the muscle between her shoulder and neck, a primal possessive gesture that sent an unwanted thrill of awareness through her. "I love the way you look at me, Darcy. Like you want to eat me alive. It's not a bad thing, it's just inconvenient."

She slid the full mug to the side. "I'll work on looking elsewhere. Here you go."

Jared didn't move for a minute, then he released her with a muttered curse. He left the kitchen, and she took the breather to give herself a mental kick in the ass. She straightened when he returned, moving away and toward the living room as he passed her on his way toward the coffee she'd poured him.

They needed some distance from each other. They hadn't had any since they'd met and that was a mistake.

"Don't you dare walk out of this room," he said in a voice too even to be anything but dangerous.

"It's my house."

"And if I've worn out my welcome, you'll look me in the eye and say so."

Pausing by the dining table, Darcy faced him, feeling grateful that she wore her uniform, which gave her the look of having her shit together even if she didn't. Jared had put his shirt on. He was now leaning with his hip against the counter and his legs crossed at the ankle. The leisurely pose didn't fool her for a minute. He was coiled tight. Watchful. Ready.

She hit him with something certain to give him pause. "I'm feeling fragile this morning."

One arm crossed his chest; the other lifted his mug to his lips. He swallowed and nodded. "I'm a bit raw myself."

His confession made her feel better and she managed a smile. "I was thinking maybe it would be a good idea for you to work with Jim today. I'll see what I can do to help your partner and Miller. We can sleep off some of the hormones . . . pheromones . . . whatever, separately, and see how things look tomorrow."

There was a long stretch of silence, then, "I'll agree to the break, but it would be best for everyone if I didn't see Ralston again."

"He's damn good at his job. He trained me."

"He could be the best damn fire inspector in the country; that won't stop me from laying him out cold if he tries that territorial bullshit again."

"He had no way of knowing we'd made arrangements to hook up," she argued. "He was just trying to be a good friend, which is all he's been for the last couple of years."

Jared took another sip, his gaze locked with hers over the lip of the mug. "I'm a trained observer, Darcy. So is he. We both got the measure of each other from the first. He knew I was stepping in, and he pushed a little to try and put me in my place. He pushes again and I'm pounding him back."

Her anger spiked. "I don't need this right now. I don't have anything to give you. I'm all tapped out. You were just supposed to be a vibrator that didn't need batteries."

His eyes were as hard and beautiful as sapphires. "And you were just supposed to be a hot piece of ass. Instead, this is getting messy. Deal with it. I want you and I can't turn it off. And when I'm touching you, I don't want to turn it off, and you don't want me to, either. If you're hoping to shut us down with some distance, I'll roll with it just to prove you wrong, but we'll be back at each other in no time."

"It won't work out."

"I'm not taking your word for it. I'll see for myself." He finished his coffee and refilled his mug. "I need to change into fresh clothes and grab some things from the motel. Then I want to head out to the other two scenes. I'd prefer it if you'd take me, but if you're opposed to that, I'll work something else out."

"Opposed," she repeated, laughing without humor. "If only."

"We're in the same boat. If it sinks, we go together."

She stood and mentally dusted herself off. "Do you need to eat?"

"Not yet."

"Okay, then. I'm ready to go when you are."

chapter seven

Trish was just leaving the motel when Darcy pulled her BMW into a spot in front of Jared's ground-floor room. He climbed out and met his partner at the curb.

"Hey," he greeted her, frowning at her obvious agitation. "What's up?"

"Miller is champing at the bit to hold a press conference. He thinks if we put the heat on the arsonist, he'll move on."

"Genius," Jared muttered. "Make our torch someone else's problem."

"I reminded him—firmly—that this is our case and we'll decide how to proceed." Her pretty face was hard and her choice of attire betrayed her determination to establish her control of the situation. Usually a jeans and blouse sort of gal, she was wearing slacks and a blazer today.

"How well does he listen?"

She shrugged with a wry smile. "Well, he called me to give me a heads-up. That's something, at least. I'm going to head into the station and keep an eye on him. You heading out to the other two sites?"

"Yes. I've got the inspector's files for you to run through while I'm out. You'll find she's very thorough." He glanced at Darcy and gestured for her to join them. "We also need to follow up on the vacation homes. There's a steady stream of seasonal residents and rental transients running through the town. The full-time residents aren't the only ones who know the ins and outs of the area."

"I like your jeans, by the way," Trish said, as Darcy unfolded from behind the wheel. "They looked good on you yesterday, too."

He shot her a withering glance, to which she laughed. When Darcy came up beside him, he introduced the two.

"Can you pass the files on to Morales while I get what I need?" He moved on without waiting for an answer.

Entering his room, Jared unzipped his as-yet unpacked suitcase and pulled out a change of clothes. When he was done, he grabbed his laptop case and the sunglasses he'd left on the dresser the day before, then headed back out to the parking lot. He found Darcy and Trish standing with their heads bent over the front end of the Marshals Service's SUV he'd driven to Lion's Bay, discussing a file they had spread open on the hood.

Darcy glanced up when his room door shut. The way she looked at him was like a physical caress, and his heartbeat quickened. Her feminine hunger was a drug he couldn't quit. Even knowing it was fucking him up, he couldn't stay away.

Trish straightened, frowning at him. "I'll be interested in hearing your thoughts when you get through surveying all three scenes. On paper, I'm missing the connection. I find it odd that the subject would be so meticulous in his timing and the creation of the incendiary devices, and yet so random in his location choices."

"Join the club." Jared pushed his shades onto his face. "Once we find the connection, we'll crack this case wide open."

Darcy said good-bye and moved back to her car. He was right behind her. They headed to the fire station to change vehicles. It was just Jared's luck that the guy he least wanted to see approached Darcy the moment they entered the building.

"You didn't have to come in on your day off," Ralston said as she searched the rack on the wall for the keys to the department's truck. "I can help Deputy Cameron with whatever he needs."

Jared smiled grimly. The easiest card Darcy could have played to gain some distance was one she hadn't used—she wasn't working today. He took it as a good sign, as far as signs went.

"Actually, Inspector," Jared replied, "we could use your help reining Sheriff Miller in. He's pushing for a press conference, which will either feed the ego of our subject, run him off, or both."

Ralston sighed. "The last thing we need is media scrutiny. We'd never get anything done. We know that all too well. Don't we, Darcy?"

"He'll listen to you, Jim. You have a way with people."

"Chris will listen to you, too. He's still got a soft spot for you. Don't suppose you noticed that he keeps a picture from prom in his office."

"Oh, God. I didn't want to know that. I'm going to take Deputy Cameron up to the Animal Friends site, then back around to the Sweet Spot."

Stepping closer, Ralston lowered his voice and said, "Let me take care of the one for you. You shouldn't have to go up there again."

She exhaled harshly. "It's okay. You've got to deal with Miller, and Deputies Cameron and Morales need to make as much progress as possible before we have another blaze. The sooner we get through the sites, the better. I'll be all right."

"You keep saying that, darlin', but sayin' it doesn't make it so."

Jared took a step forward, reminding the other man that he was there. He did nothing overt, didn't reach out to Darcy or make any proprietary moves. He didn't have to. The look he shot the inspector said it all and more—evolution hadn't altered the silent communication between males.

Ralston sized him up again. There was no challenge in the once-over he gave Jared. Just quiet, calm curiosity.

"I can do this," Darcy said, oblivious to the exchange taking place over her head. "I probably need to."

Ralston glanced at her again. "Okay. I just don't want you pushing yourself into something you might not be ready for."

She responded with more assurances, then asked, "Do you know where the truck keys are?"

"Mitch had it around back, giving it a wash."

They went to collect the truck, with Darcy explaining that aside from two trained EMTs on payroll, the other firemen were local volunteers. "Mitch Quinn is one of the most active," she said as they rounded the corner and found a trim blond man in dark blue uniform drying off the pickup. "I'm hoping he'll get a permanent position if the city ever approves a budget increase. He deserves it."

She made quick introductions, then hopped in the cab, raring to go. They cleared the town quickly, then turned off the coastal highway and began climbing into the wooded area that scaled one end of the U-shaped ridge of hills that hugged Lion's Bay to the ocean. Darcy's knuckles turned white on the steering wheel and her lips thinned. Mentally, she drifted away from him, became lost in some thought or memory that absorbed all of her vitality.

"Tell me about this place we're going to," he said, engaging her because he wanted her with him. Wanted to be there for her, with her, while she dealt with whatever she was struggling with.

She jolted as if the sound of his voice had startled her. Looking at him, she revealed green eyes that were stark and lost. "What?"

"Your impressions of the animal shelter. Any thoughts you might have about its selection. What you know of its history."

"Oh. Right." She slowly came back to him, exhaling her tension in a rush. "The shelter was built with funds provided by the Darmody family, who've owned the land up here for three generations. Lucy Darmody spearheaded the project in response to teasing from her family that she was turning her house into a zoo, due to her tendency to pick up stray, wounded, and unwanted animals. When she passed away, her children didn't want the hassle of it, so they donated the equipment and planned on razing the building and kennels. Since then, it's been tied up in litigation. They can't agree on the best way to monetize the land."

"How often do you come up here?"

"Not a lot."

He studied her covertly from behind his shades. "But you used to."

"Years ago. My dad is a vet and he used to donate one weekend a month to coming up here to spay and neuter. He conscripted me and Dani—my sister—into odd jobs whenever he could. That's how Dani found out she loved the practice of veterinary medicine."

"Too tame for you."

She glanced at him. "Yes. I love animals, but it just wasn't a vocation for me."

"Where is she now?" Jared wanted to meet Danielle. He wanted to see Darcy with her sister, see the emotions and reactions she had to someone she loved and trusted.

"Near my parents."

Why was Darcy still here? he wondered again. Without family ties, what was rooting her?

They pulled into a gravel parking lot riddled with weeds. At the end of the lot, charred cement block walls outlined the building that had once stood there. The kennels were obvious, the chain link and cement having weathered the fire well.

Darcy entered the building, her shoulders high and tight, the beam of illumination from a Maglite leading the way. "This was the main office. There wasn't a whole lot left in here. Some built-in bookshelves and boxes of records for deceased pets. The boxes were moved into that corner there, with the incendiary device placed in the middle. We estimate the fire began sometime around ten in the evening."

"And the unidentified witness called at quarter after. From Seattle."

"With the timed delay, he could have set the stage and made the drive with time to spare."

He glanced at her. "Where's the fun in that?"

She stepped into a slender ray of light entering from a hole in the ceiling and gave an approving nod. "Exactly. What pyromaniac doesn't stick around to watch the show?"

"One who isn't obsessed with fire," Jared answered, which he knew was impossible.

"Then he's not a pyro, is he?"

"I'm following. We've already noted that the materials used to build the structures our subject selected were not the most flammable choices." Jared rested a hand on the butt of his gun. "What are some of the other reasons to start a fire? We talked about insurance payouts. Maybe revenge? Damn it, the incendiary devices are tripping us up. Like you said, they're too sophisticated, too meticulously built."

"Right. Someone loves them, loves working on them, loves imagining the destruction they're going to cause."

"So we're back to a pyro who doesn't get off on his own fires." He stared at her. "What are you thinking?"

"That maybe what you said about Merkerson passing the baton to a protégé is spot-on. What if they're working together, with Merkerson teaching the ropes, deliberately starting off with a small town and structures that are manageable?"

"A training ground."

"Yeah."

Jared's mouth curved grimly. "I'm liking this."

"It pulls more of the threads together."

Impressed, he asked, "How long have you been thinking along these lines?"

She stepped deeper into the building. "Since the tip came in.

How do you have a torch igniting a fire in one town and a tipster in another? Two people. Occam's razor."

"But you waited until the third fire to shout out for help?"

"It wasn't my call." Darcy opened a door that led outside, flooding the interior with dappled sunlight. "Then I made it my call."

He followed. "I'm hung up on something."

"You, too?"

"Those sophisticated time bombs you talked about—they're better than they were back in the day. If it is Merkerson, he's upped his game over the years. He's been honing his weapons of destruction, modernizing them, which means he's been somewhere he could acquire the tools and substances he needed."

"Not jail, then." She paused at the end of a walkway that emptied into a small patio surrounded by the kennels. Her eyes took on that faraway look again.

Drawing to a halt beside her, he asked quietly, "What are you seeing?"

"Memories." She pointed to a kennel and her breath left her in a rush. "Dani locked me in there once—for an hour—because I ripped the knee on her favorite pair of jeans when I borrowed them . . . without her permission."

He set his hand at the small of her back, offering what support he could. "I knew you were a troublemaker."

Darcy leaned into his touch. "I always thought it was stupid that so many fugitives stick around familiar locations. If they value their freedom, I'd think they'd want to get out of the country. Maybe that's what Merkerson did. Canada, maybe? Or Mexico?"

"We can share his photo and see if anything shakes loose." Jared took another look around. "But this location is remote. He would've had to hear about it from someone familiar with it, or he would've had to come here himself and find it on his own. Wouldn't be something he'd accomplish in a day."

"He might've stayed here awhile? Is that what you're thinking?" She turned toward him. "A snake in the grass, how creepy."

Cupping her face, he took her mouth. The kiss was slow and simmering, a gentle stroking of tongues and brushing of lips. He continued until his breathing was fast and she was pressed against him. Pulling back, he studied her eyes and found them dazed and hot with desire, which was a damn sight better than seeing them filled with shadows. "That's better. Now we can go."

DARCY'S LIPS WERE still tingling when they pulled up to the curb in front of the Sweet Spot. More profound—and infinitely scarier—was the warmth he'd pushed through her with his kiss, thawing the knot of ice that had settled in her stomach.

Jared got to her. Far too deeply and easily, and she didn't know how to deal with it. It was outside the scope of her experience.

She loved men. She was fascinated by them and enjoyed the hell out of them, but they were accessories. There was too much going on in her life, too many things that took up her time. Dani called her a heartbreaker. Darcy hadn't ever set out to hurt anyone, but it had been known to happen.

Looking at Jared over the hood of her work truck, Darcy wondered why *he* had to be the one to get under her skin. What was it about him? He was testy and brusque when he was in a good mood, and an ass when he was in a bad one.

One of his brows arched over the top of his sunglasses, a gesture that said, *What are you staring at?*

You. You're affecting me. Stop it. Instead she said, "You can't blame me for ogling. You're the hottest man I've ever seen."

"Keep thinking that way. Are you coming?"

"Not unless you need me. I don't have anything to add to my report." She couldn't face the ruins of another place she loved. The shelter had been bad enough. Visiting the site again had hit her harder than she would have expected. Because of Jared. He'd opened her up, found a way inside her through the hairline fractures he had created, and left her vulnerable to the reality of her losses in a way she hadn't been before.

With a curt nod, he ducked under the crime scene tape and stepped through the frame of what used to be a large front display window. It had exploded outward during the fire, showering the sidewalk with glass.

The proprietress of the adjacent jewelry store waved at Darcy through her matching window, then stepped outside. She was a statuesque brunette with cornflower blue eyes and bone structure to make a plastic surgeon weep in awe. With her waist-length black hair swaying around her shoulders, Nadine Bender glided over and joined Darcy in leaning into the truck. "Is that the Fed?"

"Deputy U.S. Marshal," Darcy qualified, her eyes riveted to Jared as he examined what was left of the shop. He got a particular look on his face when he was focused on work. It was laser bright, sharp as a blade, and sexy as hell.

Nadine whistled. "He's a looker."

"Absolutely."

"You sure can pick 'em. You've got a thing for men in uniform. Chris, Jim, and now this guy."

"Deputy Cameron," Darcy supplied as Nadine bumped shoulders with her.

They'd gone to school together, from kindergarten through high school. Like Darcy, Nadine had fled Lion's Bay as soon as she graduated, then came back. They joked that the town was like a vortex, inexorably sucking natives back into it.

"All I did was call in the cavalry." Darcy shrugged. "I can't take any credit for his hotness."

"And you snagged him straightaway. I can see it in the way he looks at you. If I thought you were purposely grabbing all the sexy men, I'd hate you. You've always been the biggest guy magnet. Makes me pea green."

"You're way prettier than I am, Nadine. Always have been."

"Doesn't matter. You have this vibe that drives men wild."

"That's not always a good thing," she muttered as a patrol car parked behind her truck.

Miller grabbed his hat off the passenger seat and unfolded from behind the wheel. His gaze was on Darcy as he set the hat on his head and shut the door.

"Hey, Chris," Nadine greeted with a wave. "How are you this fine early afternoon?"

"I've been better." He glanced at Nadine long enough to manage a smile. "How's the store?"

"A little worse for wear, but open for business. The insurance adjuster will be out later to take a look."

"Good." He nodded and came to a stop before Darcy, his warm brown eyes shaded by the brim of his hat. "Everything all right with you?"

"Yes, sir, Sheriff. Deputy Cameron is just checking out the scene."

Nadine backed away. "I'm going to head back to work."

Darcy shot her a look that said, *Don't you dare*, but the other woman just grinned mischievously and backed away.

Chris leaned back against the truck next to her. Too close. When he crossed his arms, his biceps brushed hers.

"Where's Deputy Morales?" Darcy asked.

"She was making some phone calls and Jim was helping her out with some things. So I thought I'd find you and see if you needed anything."

She exhaled softly, feeling that tiny twinge of discomfort that came with knowing someone's interest was deeper than could be reciprocated. She and Chris had dated in high school. He'd been prom king to her prom queen. They'd had fun together, been wild and reckless as kids usually were, and she'd enjoyed being with him, but it had never been serious for her. He was a good guy in a lot of ways. Plus, he kept himself in prime shape and was great looking. But he didn't get to her, not the way she needed.

"I'm set," she answered. "I've turned everything I have over to Deputy Cameron."

"I'd heard that." The intimation in his tone put her back up.

Darcy straightened away from the truck and faced him from the sidewalk. "Watch it, Chris."

"I think we need to talk about this. Why are you always going for a dead end? First Jim, then this guy—" He gestured toward Jared with a flick of his wrist. "I'm right here, Darcy. We're good together. You know that."

"Seriously? We dated when we were kids for chrissakes."

"We have history," he argued. "Who knows you better?"

"Honestly, Chris, you don't know me at all." She thought back to when she'd woken up to Jared in her bed. The things she'd said to him . . . the raw sexual things she'd demanded of him . . . She could never say such things to Chris. It didn't matter how long she'd known him. The connection she needed to be so open wasn't there. "Where is this coming from anyway?"

"I've been patient, Darcy." Pushing off his hat, he ran a hand through his thick mahogany hair. His eyes were hot with frustration. "I mean, you're back in Lion's Bay. I figured that was the big step. I knew you had some adjusting to do so I've kind of hovered on the side."

"Come on, Chris. Are we going to have this conversation now? Here? Really?"

"I know you're going through a rough time. You need someone solid, Darcy. Someone who can anchor you. Not Jim and not some fly-by-night outsider."

"We're not talking about this," she said, low and quiet. "You're under a lot of pressure at the moment. We all are. So I'm going to give you a pass today and forget you brought this up."

"I should've asked you out before now. Is that what you're saying? I tried to do the right thing by giving you some space, but I gave you too much space."

She sighed. "Who knows? Maybe if you'd asked me out when I first got back, I might have said yes. Maybe I wouldn't have. We'll never know. It's a moot point right now. I'm working. So are you. And I'm presently involved with someone."

"Involved?" he snorted. "He's passing through, Darcy. Don't forget that."

"I haven't, but *you* seem to have or your boxers wouldn't be in a twist and we wouldn't be having this conversation. We're going to collar our torch, Chris, and everything is going to go back to the way it was, then you'll be embarrassed over this conversation. Let's put it behind us."

Jared walked out of the building. "Everything all right?"

"Everything's fine," Darcy said. "Sheriff Miller just wanted to offer his assistance."

"You get Deputy Morales the list of part-time residents, Sheriff?"

Chris straightened and shoved his hat back on his head. "Your partner's got everything she asked for."

"Good." Jared bared his teeth in a semblance of a smile. "Morales will let you know if we need anything further."

She waited until Chris had driven away to say, "See? You underestimated yourself. You worked with him just fine . . . without your fists."

"He managed not to talk too much." He looked at her. "But he was laying it on thick for you. You handled that well."

Shrugging, she moved to the truck. "That wasn't his style. This case is really getting to him, I guess."

"Or the thought of you with another man is." He opened the passenger door and paused, looking at her. With one arm draped on the roof of the cab and the other resting on the window frame, he looked casual, relaxed, and extremely delicious. "You know, being so easygoing with your brush-offs make them harder to accept."

"Why?"

"Because women are supposed to be emotional. Pissed off, vengeful, sad . . . whatever. Something. Brushing a man off like a gnat makes us realize we never got to you at all. Or that we were much too easy to get over."

"That's sexist."

"Maybe. No one's ever accused me of being PC." He pushed his sunglasses up, revealing cool blue eyes that scorched her. "I want to go to Seattle, take a look around the area where the tipster placed his phone call. And I want to take you to lunch. Since it's your day off, it's not a problem for you to get away, is it?"

"No." And she wouldn't have to wear her uniform. She was looking forward to hitting him with something flirty. "I just need to change my clothes and my ride."

His slow, sexy smile did a number on her. She stood there a moment, absorbing the sensation of being so highly attracted to a man. Not just physically, but in every way. He'd called her easygoing and she thought that was true. She'd long avoided drama with men and anyone who was high maintenance. But her irritable lover wasn't scaring her away. She wanted more of him, the good and the bad, the rough and the smooth.

"Ready?" he asked.

"No," she said honestly, "but that's not stopping me."

chapter eight

Jared wondered what the hell he'd gotten himself into when Darcy came out of the house. She'd changed into a strappy, fitted red dress that bared toned arms and lithe legs that ended in heeled sandals. Her dark hair drifted around her shoulders, and she'd touched up her eyes and lips with a light application of cosmetics.

His breath caught. More than her physical attractiveness, it was her sultry confidence that riveted him, the indefinable essence of her that so perfectly aligned with something deep inside him.

"Are you still there, Cameron?" Supervisory Deputy Holt asked through his cell phone's speaker.

"Yes, ma'am. Sorry."

"We've pulled the photos and video from the surveillance cameras around the payphone. They're not very helpful. The subject wore a hooded sweatshirt and kept his head down, but they're being e-mailed to you. Maybe one of the locals will see something familiar in the body language."

"We'll run it through. Thanks." He straightened as Darcy reached him. "I'm going to visit the location myself. I want to time the trip and see if something in the vicinity jumps out at me. It's possible he picked the payphone at random, but just in case, I'll check it out."

"Send me an updated report by morning."

"Yes, ma'am." He killed the call, shoved the phone in his pocket, and caught Darcy by the hips to pull her close. "You look amazing."

"Thank you, Deputy." She accepted the compliment with an easy self-assurance.

A heartbreaker, he thought grimly. The kind of woman a man was never sure he possessed completely. That aloofness stirred his most primal proprietary instincts, and he was slightly irritated that he was no more immune to her allure than any other member of the male species.

But then she'd confessed today that they were "involved," and she wasn't the type of woman to use one man as an excuse to extricate herself from another. For now, she was his. It was up to him to decide if he wanted to keep her, and if he did, take the steps necessary to make that happen.

"You're scowling at me," she pointed out wryly, her cool fingertips smoothing the line between his brows.

"Sorry."

"What's wrong?"

Jared shook his head. "You're perfect, Darcy. Just the sort of uncomplicated and undemanding female a guy like me hopes to pass some time with. It's driving me fuckin' crazy."

"That makes absolutely no sense," she said wryly.

"Tell me about it. Kiss me."

"All right. Don't move."

He forced himself to relax. "Go for it."

Stepping closer, she brushed her mouth across his. The kiss was soft as a butterfly's wings, barely there. Her tongue darted out, licking the seam of his lips, dipping just a tiny bit inside. He groaned, fighting the urge to drag her close and take over. He wanted her to give to him whatever she chose, however much she chose.

Her hands went to his shoulders, then the one not holding her little clutch purse cupped his nape. Her head tilted and she sealed her mouth over his. She deepened the kiss, unraveling him stitch by stitch. He couldn't say why, couldn't figure it out. She was a pretty woman he'd met twenty-four hours before. They'd fucked like feral rabbits, which should've worked her right out of his system. Physically, he'd been thoroughly satisfied. Yet he couldn't catch his breath because of a chaste kiss. His lungs heaved and burned, his heart pounded violently.

Pressing her forehead to his, Darcy exchanged gasping breaths with him. "I need you to touch me."

He heard the tremulous note in her voice and caught her close, banding one arm around her hips and rubbing his hand up and down her back. He wondered if she'd ever really *needed* anything from any man. What twist of fate had aligned his ferocious need to take her with her unrealized need to be taken?

"Are we a pair or what?" he murmured with his lips to her crown.

"We're something."

"Yeah." Jared rubbed his cheek against the top of her head. "We're something."

THROUGH THE LENS of his camera, Jared stood on the street corner and photographed every possible angle from the phone booth.

"Seems so wide open," Darcy said. "Where do you take an investigation from here?"

He lowered the camera. "Cross-check local businesses with Lion's Bay residents. Check cab fares from that day and time and this general vicinity. He probably drove, but maybe he was cautious enough to take a cab from a parking garage to somewhere nearby. Of course, if he's that careful, he probably paid cash, but we'll tie off that thread to be sure."

She looked at him grimly. "You're keeping yourself busy while we wait for him to strike again."

"Building a case." He put the cap back on the lens and put the camera back in its bag. "I'm done. Hungry?"

"There's a great little café around the corner, although we might have to wait a bit for a seat."

"Let's go." He caught her hand and led her straight to the restaurant. It was crowded, with a line out front and a harried-looking hostess who instantly brightened when she saw him.

"Jared." Tiffany smiled and grabbed a menu. "Just in time for your reservation."

He felt Darcy's grip tighten on his and knew she caught the undercurrent of familiarity. He didn't have a reservation, but Tiffany always found a spot at the counter for him . . . and time after work when he was in the mood for more than food.

"For two," he pointed out gently, pulling Darcy up to his side.

Tiffany's brows rose and her smile widened. "Absolutely."

"Uncomplicated and undemanding?" Darcy asked softly, following his urging to precede him to their table.

"Yes." And suddenly far less appealing. Not that he didn't note and appreciate Tiffany's beauty. It just didn't hold his attention. Instead, he found himself focused on the number of stares directed at Darcy. She looked like a million dollars and carried herself as if she was worth ten times that.

God, she was fucking hot as hell.

And he had it bad for her.

Jared pulled out her chair and took the one next to her rather than across the table. The smile she gave him was warm and it stayed warm as she accepted the menu from Tiffany.

"I know exactly what I'm getting," she announced when they were alone.

"Do you come here often?"

"Only a couple times, but Jim ordered this phenomenal pasta once. I've been dying to get a plate of my own ever since."

Jared set his camera on the table and made sure that when he spoke his voice was smooth and unchallenging. "I'm still not getting the Jim thing."

She set her menu aside. "Back in high school, Jim was the hot older guy all the girls crushed on, and he was a fireman, which made him even sexier. When I moved back to Lion's Bay, some of that adolescent infatuation was still there. Turned out he'd thought I was pretty hot, too, but I'd been jail bait before. We had unfinished business, so we wrapped it up. Like I said, it was never serious."

"Have you had any serious relationships?" He knew something had to be the catalyst that drew her back to Lion's Bay.

Her lips pursed as she considered the question. "I've had long-term boyfriends, but I've never been engaged. Have you?"

Leaning back in his seat, he shook his head. "I'm a busy guy, Darcy. I mostly work this region, but I'm also a SOG deputy—the Marshals Service's Special Operations Group—which means I'm on call to go anywhere at any time. I haven't had any serious relationships. My last long-term girlfriend was back in high school and that lasted less than a year. I don't have commitment issues, but I haven't met anyone who was worth the inconvenience of trying to get a relationship off the ground." He took a slow, deep breath. "Until now."

She stared at him, her gaze darting over his face. Their waiter approached and Darcy ordered, then turned her attention to laying her napkin across her lap as he did the same.

He didn't say anything when they were alone again, thinking he'd lobbed the ball into her court and she could either keep it in play or drop it. Maybe the duration of the case was all he'd get from her. He wondered if staying out of her bed would make it easier to walk away at the end or harder. It wasn't a situation he'd faced before. So he asked her, because he suspected she knew. Not from her point of view, but from the perspective of the other guys in her life who'd wanted the piece of her she kept to herself.

"If I stop fucking you," he asked in a low, even tone, "will it be easier to stop wanting you?"

Twisting in her seat, she faced him. "I'm not sure what you're proposing, Jared. More of this?" She gestured at the interior of the restaurant with a sweep of her hand. "More dates? Or just an understanding that we'll have sex occasionally when the mood strikes and we're in the vicinity of each other? Actually, aren't they both the same thing when a relationship is too erratic to be steady? One just comes with food and/or entertainment, while the other allots that bonus time to fucking instead."

"How the hell am I supposed to know what to ask for? I've never done this before." He drummed his fingertips into the tablecloth and tried to figure it out.

"Jared." Her voice had the slow, conciliatory note of someone about to impart bad news. "I don't think we can have a casual relationship. The attraction between us . . . it's too intense."

"I figured that out when the first sight of you hit me like a two-by-four between the eyes. Listen . . . I'm not talking about fitting you into my life as it is. I'm talking about changing things to fit around you."

"Making me a priority?"

"Yes." He held her gaze. "With the expectation that you'll make the same effort for me."

"Maybe you should wait a few more days before you decide I'm not going to lose my appeal."

"Don't start playing games. It insults both of us."

She exhaled in a rush. "Sorry. You freak me out. And the really scary part is I don't care. As freaked out as I am, it's not enough to get me to blow you off."

"Good." The rush of relief he felt almost made him dizzy. "So we make it work."

"It's going to be work. A lot of it. We're too volatile. Too . . . greedy."

"Like a thirst you can't quite quench," he agreed softly. "The flip side being that every time you take a drink, it's the best fucking thing you've ever tasted. If that's not worth working for, what is?"

Darcy set a hand over her tummy and offered a tremulous smile. "Yes. I suppose you're right."

The rest of lunch became a slow exploration of the basics of who they both were. Jared talked about SOG—the Shadow Stalkers, as they were called—and some of the experiences he'd had that he could share. He told her about his sister, Casey, who fell in love every other day and was unable to keep a secret to save her life.

For his efforts, Darcy talked about growing up in Lion's Bay, with most of her anecdotes featuring her sister, Danielle. He learned quickly that he'd pegged the sisters right. Darcy was the trouble-maker; Danielle was the good girl.

Jared was sorry when the meal ended, wishing the day was already over so he could take her home to bed. The sharp bite of lust for her was always with him, but it was the sense that he was really *inside* her when they made love that he craved. She was cool and collected everywhere . . . except in bed with him. When he was inside her, he knew he had all of her. Every fascinating centimeter of her.

"I'm going to freshen up before we go," she said when the check came.

"Meet you outside?"

"Sure."

He'd just shouldered his way past the dwindling line at the front when his cell phone rang. Pulling it out, he didn't recognize the number. "Cameron."

"Deputy Cameron, Special Agent Michelle Kelley here. Your partner left a message that you had some questions for me."

"Agent Kelley, yes. Thanks for getting back to me so quickly. I wanted to ask you about your impressions of Lion's Bay and its residents, particularly anyone who struck you oddly."

She snorted. "It's a small town, Deputy. Everyone there is a bit odd in one way or another."

"Right. Small town. What are the odds that two sets of Feds would end up there, investigating crimes with known MOs?"

"Zilch," Kelley said bluntly. "But the MO of our Unsub was off. The basics were textbook perfect. It was the details that deviated to an unacceptable degree. I liked the mystery boyfriend, but we never got close to him. Never even dug up a name. In a town that small, where everyone knows everything, no one knew the victim had a man in her life. Not even the sister, who was—by all accounts—very close to her. But then, she hadn't known the victim was six weeks pregnant, either."

"Jesus."

"Yeah, got to me, too. I don't see how this is helpful to you, though."

"Maybe it isn't." He adjusted his grip on his camera. "The arsonist is familiar with the area. He's got a local's knowledge, but no one is pointing any fingers. I thought maybe someone might've rubbed you the wrong way, give me someone to look at."

"I'm sorry, Deputy. I wish I had something for you, but the residents of that town gave up nothing. That case still haunts me. What was done to the victim . . . She was so young and pretty. A vet, for God's sake. Lived in Lion's Bay her whole—"

"A veterinarian?" The sounds of the traffic and conversations faded from Jared's perception, leaving a stunned silence. "Michaels?"

"Yes. Dr. Danielle Michaels."

chapter nine

Darcy slid behind the wheel of her car and tucked her legs in as Jared closed the door behind her. He rounded the trunk and reached through the open top to set his camera on the backseat, then climbed in beside her.

"Wanna stop by your sister's place?" he asked, looking out the windshield. "She's in Seattle, right?"

She took a deep breath, then let it out. "Okay."

Backing out of the parking garage spot, she hit the road. Her grip was too tight on the steering wheel, but she couldn't ease up. There was a block of ice in her gut and her throat was tight. It didn't matter how many times she saw Dani's headstone, it still had the power to break something inside her.

When they drove through the open wrought iron gates of the cemetery, Jared reached over and set his hand on her thigh. The knot inside her loosened. She set her hand over his and squeezed. "You're not surprised."

"I was when I found out." He glanced at her, pushing up his shades so she could see his eyes. "Now I'm just glad you're letting me in."

"That's why we're here."

His fingers linked with hers. "Is it so bad? Letting someone in?"

"No. I'm . . . grateful. It's just . . . I can't come here with my parents. They need me to be okay. And I try to be. For them."

"But you're not."

"Dani was half of me."

She followed the road for a couple miles, then pulled over to the side and parked. They got out and she led him across the lawn to the Michaels family plot. Jared didn't say anything as she stood over Dani's grave and felt her eyes burn. He just came up behind her and wrapped his arms around her waist, setting his chin on her shoulder. They were there a long time, long enough for her to find her voice and tell him about the early-morning call that had irrevocably changed her life.

"There was talk of a boyfriend," he said softly. "You didn't know who he was?"

"Oh, I know him," she said grimly. "I just don't know his name. When Dani made it clear his identity was a secret, I knew he was someone familiar to me and she didn't want me razzing her about him. That's a big reason why I moved back to Lion's Bay after she died. I wanted to figure out who he was and what he might know. I thought he'd come forward by now . . . that just looking at me every day would shake him up."

"Do you know how fucking dangerous that is?" His voice was rough with fury. He turned her around to face his glare. "After what was done to her?"

She'd identified her sister's body, although everyone in town had known who Dani was and one look at Darcy's identical face proved it. The coroner had draped Dani's body in a sheet from the neck down, but Darcy was aware of what the Prophet was known for . . . the sick mutilations he did to his victims' bodies. "I can't let Dani go while her killer's still out there, Jared. And honestly, with her gone, I'm half dead anyway."

"Bullshit. I've been inside you. When I'm touching you . . . fucking you . . . you're so alive you burn me up with it. I see you trying to get out of this shell you're just surviving in, living a life that doesn't suit you one damn bit." He cupped her face in his hands. "I'm going to get him, Darcy. He's going to pay for putting that look in your eyes. I promise you that. Let me do my job. Let me keep you safe."

Her breathing picked up. "You think he's in Lion's Bay, too?"

"I think it's likely, yes. The candy shop—your sister have any connection with that?"

Darcy frowned. "She was a customer. Dani had a sweet tooth. She stopped by there almost every day to buy a dollar or two of candy to carry around in her lab coat. And we celebrated our twelfth birthdays there. Why?"

"Every place our torch has hit has been tied to your sister in some way. You being in Lion's Bay *is* shaking this guy up, sweetheart. He's systematically wiping your sister off the map. First by taking her out, then by taking out places associated with her."

She caught him by the wrists. "If he wants Dani gone, why not take out the woman who looks like her?"

Jared's gaze darkened. "If I'm right, he's saving that pleasure for last."

"I KNOW HOW it sounds," Jared muttered into his cell phone as they entered Darcy's house.

She watched him cross through her kitchen into her living room, then begin to pace. Something inside her shifted as she watched him move, his stride powerful and predatory yet utterly silent. Armed and dangerous. A trained hunter. And he was now on the hunt for the man who'd killed Dani. The morass of emotions churning in her tummy had no outlet and she had no way of dealing with them. She'd never felt like this before.

Because he was also hunting *her.* Deliberately. Systematically. And he wasn't going to stop until he'd captured her. She wasn't going to let him stop.

Whatever it was she felt for him, it was important. With a little time, a little compromise, and with no effort at all, she could fall in love with him. And part of her really, really wanted to. Wanted to experience the magic she'd only ever felt faint echoes of. She could have it with him. He wanted it, too.

"What have you got on your plate now?" he asked his partner, running a hand through his hair. "Okay. Good. When you head back to the hotel, give me a buzz and I'll meet you there. We'll order pizza and tear into this."

He was hanging up when she walked past him toward the bedroom, their eyes meeting in a long meaningful glance. She gave him a cheery smile because she didn't want him to worry any more than he already was. He'd been even edgier than usual since they'd left the cemetery; he didn't need any more on his plate.

She was crying silently before she reached the bedroom. She closed the door far enough that there was no gap, but didn't push it all the way—she didn't want him to mistake her desire for privacy as a desire to shut him out. Then she undressed and entered the bathroom through the door in the master bedroom. Forgoing the bath, despite how tempting it looked, she got in the shower and welcomed the brief shock of cold before the heat kicked in with a vengeance.

The tears flowed freely, mingling with the water. Darcy stood directly beneath the spray, letting it course down her face like a veil, hoping to prevent puffy eyes that would give her away. She hadn't cried since the flight that brought her home to Dani's dead body lying in the morgue. She knew she was due, but that didn't make the dam burst any easier to bear.

She felt him come in behind her and was grateful he couldn't know that she was falling apart. Setting her hands on the tile in front of her, she bent her head as if she was directing the strength of the spray on her neck.

Jared's arms embraced her and he curled around her curved back. He didn't say anything when an unexpected sob shuddered through her.

She tried to shake him off, feeling stupid. "I need a minute."

"Take all the time you need."

When he didn't let go, she found her mouth curving ruefully. She turned in his arms. "You're a menace."

He shrugged. "I was trained to press every advantage."

Her mouth quirked, her grief lifting at the gleam in his eyes. His beautiful face was stern and his sinner's mouth unyielding. Such a hard man in so many ways, yet he could be tender. She'd like to see him with the sister he spoke of with gruff fondness and the parents he clearly admired and loved deeply.

His hands cupped her face, his thumbs brushing at her cheeks. "I can't imagine your pain."

"Good. I wouldn't wish it on anyone."

I'm still crying, she realized when the rough pads of his fingers stroked over her face again. "You know," she said hoarsely, "I was trying to spare you a weepy woman."

"Don't. My job's going to put enough between us as it is. We need to be brutal with the rest in order to make it."

"For a guy who doesn't do relationships, you seem to have a good handle on how they work."

"I have a good handle on what I need." His fierce blue gaze riveted her. "I expect that you'll tell me what you need."

Her hands slid down his damp back, caressing the hard slabs of muscle bracketing his spine. Steam billowed around them, but the warmth she felt came from inside her. "I don't know what I need. It's been a long time since I've thought about it."

"So while I'm out tonight, think about it. Just make sure I'm in there somewhere."

"I'll be wishing you were in *me*." She reached between them and fisted his erection. "You're a deadly weapon all by yourself. Did you know that, Deputy?"

He snorted, his grip tightening on her hips.

"I bet there isn't a woman alive who's said no to you in your life. I'm just one of the many to fall under your irascible charm."

"Look who's talking. You're a man-eater."

With a two-handed grip, Darcy stroked him from root to tip. Her gaze lowered to the thick column of flesh in her hands, her heartbeat quickening at the impressive length and thick network of veins that coursed along it. It was a brutal-looking instrument of pleasure, as primal as Jared's sexuality. That dichotomy—his powerfully elegant build and fallen-angel face paired with a curt temperament and raunchy sensuality—fascinated her.

"What a lovely idea," she murmured.

Backing up a step, she sat on the tiled bench seat. It put her eye level with the object of her desire, which caused a hot flutter in her belly. She licked her lips, surprised at how turned on she was.

"What are you doing?" he asked gruffly. "You're not sucking my dick."

Her brows rose. "The hell I'm not."

He slapped her hands away when she tried to tug him closer. "Christ, Darcy. You were just bawling your eyes out. The only reason I'm naked is because I haven't got a change of clothes and the only way to get to you was to get wet."

Her mouth twitched with the urge to grin. He looked so affronted. As sexual as their relationship was, it wasn't all he wanted from her. That was good to know. Wonderful actually. Because as much as she wanted his body, she wanted more from him, too.

She pointed at his cock. "He's ready to play."

"What's new? I've had a perpetual hard-on since I met you. Since I first laid eyes on you."

"I cause the problem; let me take care of it."

"It's not a problem and I don't want you to take care of it," he snapped. "I want to take care of you."

"I'm okay." Darcy held his gaze, let him see the clarity of her eyes. The ache in her chest would never totally go away, she knew, but it was easier to bear than it had been just that morning. That she could feel differently was a miracle to her after living with it unchanged for so long, that her chronic pain could be alleviated at all. God . . . it had been so nice to lean on someone in the cemetery and have her grief accepted without reservation. "You wanted to make me feel better and I do."

"Fuck that." He scowled. "I'm a selfish bastard. I wanted to make myself feel better. Seeing you hurting was killing me. Watching you suck me off would make me feel worse. Hell . . . I'm not a douche."

"When did I give you the impression that I was the type who went down on a guy without really wanting to?"

His scowl grew fiercer.

"Right." Her gaze lowered. Her mouth watered. "You have the most perfect cock, Jared. Did you know that? It's a thing of beauty."

"You're scrambled."

"Actually, I'm ridiculously pleased with myself. I managed to snag exclusive access rights to your delicious body, which I'd like to exert now."

His hand moved to grip the object of her desire. His fingers curled around it and stroked from root to tip. "I have work to do."

"So stop lagging and let me have it."

Releasing himself, he stepped forward and cupped her face in his hands. He searched her features, his gaze softening. "Are you okay, Darcy? *Really* okay? Or are you feeling shaky?"

She caught him by the wrists. "I think you're feeling shakier than I am. I've had three years to deal with this. You're the one who's been blindsided by a cold case."

"And a hot woman." His thumbs slid gently over her cheekbones. "You're an occupational hazard."

"Step a little closer and I'll make it worth your while."

One of his hands slid down, the pad of his thumb gliding across her parted lips. "You already have."

He didn't stop her when she reached for him again. He set one hand on the tile above her head and turned down the temperature of the water with the other. The spray beat down on his right side, running in rivulets down his muscular torso and washboard abs. She started there first, tracing the ridges with her tongue, her hands caressing his cock with soft, gentle pulls.

Jared's palms pressed flat to the wall, his head hanging over her, his breath quickening. As his skin heated beneath her hands, his raw sexuality slipped its chain. She could almost see its smoky tendrils curl around her, intoxicating her. Primitive need burned in her blood, melting what few inhibitions she had. She was like a bitch in heat with him and she liked it, liked the wanton freedom his acceptance gave her.

Fisting him, she made him harder, made him shudder. She nuzzled his cock with one cheek and then the other, before moving lower to fondle his balls with her lips.

"Fuck," he gasped, his cock jerking her grip.

Darcy took one full, heavy testicle into her mouth, sucking gently, rolling it around with her tongue. He was such a primal male. Big and hard and virile everywhere. There was a part of her that reveled in that, celebrating her claim on such a potently desirable masculine creature.

His thighs began to shake, his lungs heaving. "Payback's a bitch,

Darcy. Stop torturing me and suck it, sweetheart. Suck my cock in that hot little mouth."

She purred and pumped him with a two-fisted grip. She wanted to eat him up, every mouthwatering inch of him.

One of his hands cupped the back of her head, his fingers flexing spastically in the soaked strands of her hair. "Wrap your lips around me, Darcy baby. *Yes* . . . just like that."

Her mouth flowed over the thick crest, her eyes closing at the feel and taste of him. Warm satin over stone. Her tongue rubbed the sensitive underside of his cock head, every sense focused on his responses. His low groans. The tension gripping him. The sound of his teeth grinding.

"So good," he bit out. "Your mouth is so damn good . . . hot . . . fucking perfect. You're perfect."

She sucked hard on the wide, sensitive crown, moaning as a hot wash of pre-cum spilled over her tongue and made her ravenous for more. She stroked him with her hands, milking him, as his other hand tangled in her hair. His hips began to move, his grip holding her still. He fucked her mouth at the depth and pace he needed, his hips lunging in a steady unfaltering tempo, his stomach clenching and releasing as his cock slid in and out.

Darcy looked up at him, their eyes meeting. Holding. As raw as the encounter was—her mouth filled with his thrusting cock, his abdomen sheened with water and sweat, the muscles flexing powerfully—it was intimate in deeper ways. His pleasure was hers, hot and sweet. Fierce.

He hissed when her cheeks hollowed. He swelled further, making her pussy ache to feel him tunneling deep into her. "Shit. Just like that, sweetheart. Suck it just like that . . . I'm gonna come so hard for you."

Her pussy spasmed as his flavor sharpened. She moaned and

squirmed, so turned on by an act that had never gotten her hot and bothered before. She liked it well enough, but it'd never aroused her to a fever pitch, never burned her with the stark eroticism of the act.

His fingers tightened in her hair. His face twisted in a grimace of agonized pleasure. "Fuck yeah . . . you're making me come."

Greedy, she sucked him like a woman possessed. Her head bobbing. Working the pulsing length with both lips and hands. Urging the furious spurts of semen to flood her mouth. Jared shouted a curse, his entire body wracked with violent spasms as he released stream after stream of hot, thick cum over her stroking tongue, his hips pumping his spending cock to the back of her throat.

His hands were shaking when he finished, when he tried to pull her off. She continued gently sucking, wanting everything he had. Every drop of his pleasure. Moaning in triumph when she pulled one last pulse of semen from his still-rigid flesh.

She was startled when he hauled her up and pushed her against the chilly tile, his hand dipping between her legs to thrust two long fingers into her. He took her mouth, his tongue delving into the depths that tasted of him, his moan of pleasure vibrating against her lips.

Hooking her leg over his, he set his foot on the bench, stealing her balance and opening her completely. His fingers began to rub inside her, sliding through the silky skeins of her desire, expertly finding all the tender spots and capturing her gasps of pleasure in his mouth.

Darcy clung to his shoulders, her nails digging in as he pressed his taut frame against her and pushed every thought from her head but him. "Jared—"

"You're so fucking sexy," he growled, his fingers sliding free of her pussy to rub the pucker of her ass. "You make me so hard. I've never been this hot for a woman, never felt like I'd die if I didn't touch her. Taste her. Make her come screaming my name."

She cried out as one finger slid into her rear, only to retreat and come back with two fingers. Ferocious pleasure pumped through her with the maddened beat of her heart.

Watching her with that fierce blue gaze, he pushed deep, then withdrew. "Only you, Darcy. You're the only one to make me want to crawl out of my skin and into yours."

"Yes," she gasped. "In me."

His fingers were driving her mad, fucking her anally with a steady, wickedly knowledgeable tempo. Her hips circled without her volition, trying to get him deeper. Harder. As close as they were, it wasn't close enough.

"Oh, I'll be in you, sweetheart," he promised darkly, his breath gusting fast and hard over her ear. "Bare and deep. I'm gonna pump you full of hot, thick cum while I'm riding your ass as hard as you can take it. Pounding into you until I can't tell where I end and you begin. You turn me into an animal, Darcy. You make me want to invent new ways to fuck just so I can own every inch of you."

Jared's thumb slid into her pussy and she cried out, so close to orgasm it was painful. Even the cool water couldn't cool the fever for him in her blood, a need that grew with every hour she knew him.

He caught her breast in his free hand, squeezing with a tenderness so at odds with the ferocity of his passion. She gripped the back of his head with both hands and ate at his mouth, sucking his tongue and moaning as the orgasm hit her with the force of a hurricane. He choked out her name as she tightened around his thrusting fingers, her body trembling so violently she thought she might break apart into thousands of tiny pieces.

It was Jared who held her together as the pleasure raced across her nerve endings like an electrical charge. He sank onto the bench and pulled her into his lap, his arms banding around her as she shivered with sweet, fiery aftershocks.

chapter ten

Jared finished his list of unusual package deliveries to investigate and began gathering up the items he needed to take with him to the motel. When Darcy's doorbell rang, he straightened and moved toward it, waving her back when she headed for it, too.

"I've been perfectly safe for three years now," she reminded dryly, but she backed off and let him get it.

Finding Jim Ralston on her doorstep with a six-pack of beer in his hands made Jared immediately irritable. He'd never been the possessive type, certainly had never cared who his lovers had fucked before he'd come along. But the animalistic drive to claim Darcy as exclusively and irrevocably his extended beyond the bedroom. He fought it back with effort.

"Inspector," he greeted the man.

"Deputy," Ralston returned, his eyes lit with amusement. He was dressed casually in black jeans and a button-up shirt that was rolled up at the sleeves and open at the throat. His civilian clothes made him look younger and gave Jared his first inkling of what might've prompted Darcy to have a friends-with-benefits relationship with the man.

Darcy rounded Jared with a welcoming smile. "Come in, Jim. Ah, and you come bearing gifts. Deputy Cameron's heading out for pizza with his partner, which has got me craving some. You up for that?"

Ralston stepped into the house, the storm door gliding closed behind him. "I'll have to take a rain check. I've got a date with the insurance adjustor who's looking over Nadine's shop. She called after I'd already left the house to say she was running late, so instead of driving all the way back and waiting around, I figured I'd make a pit stop here until she calls again."

Her eyes brightened. "Yeah, a hot date trumps pizza. Good for you."

Returning to the coffee table, Jared grabbed what he needed along with the keys to the BMW. "I'll be no more than a few hours. I'll call if I'll be back later than that."

Darcy came to him, looking just as hot in stretchy pants and a V-neck T-shirt as she had in the red dress she'd worn to lunch. "You know where to find me."

"Walk me out." He glanced at Ralston, feeling marginally better knowing the man was going out to get laid tonight. "I'd like to see you tomorrow, Inspector. Go over a few things with you."

"Absolutely." Ralston gave a curt nod. "Buzz me and we'll work out a time."

When they reached Darcy's car, Jared dropped his stuff in the back through the open roof, then turned toward her to catch her close. He brushed his lips across hers and murmured, "When Ralston leaves, lock up the house."

She looked prepared to argue, then seemed to think better of it. "Okay."

"Thank you." He kissed the tip of her nose. "For everything."

"It's been my pleasure, Deputy."

"I'll be back quick as I can." He smacked her ass cheeks with both hands and squeezed playfully, lifting her to her toes against him. "Set out some lube on the bedside table. Bottled water, too."

"You're a machine."

Flushed and sporting kiss-swollen lips, she looked like a woman who'd been fucked long and well. It suited her. If he had his way, she'd be looking just like that every day from here on out.

She grinned as if she knew his thoughts. "Lucky for you, I can take it."

He pressed his temple to hers, needing her safe and happy and close. He needed the time and space to explore the connection between them, both physical and emotional.

Backing away, Jared admitted that his emotions were still raw from their interlude in the shower. She was deep under his skin already. "Yeah, lucky me."

WAVING, DARCY WATCHED Jared drive away in the car that was her last real piece of her former life. She clung to it for that reason and because she loved it. Thankfully, her parents owned the house outright and she didn't have to pay rent. Otherwise, she wouldn't have been able to afford to keep the car with what the town paid her.

"Things are moving pretty fast with you two," Jim said, coming out of the front door with an open beer in each hand.

She accepted the one he handed her and smiled. "That's an understatement."

Together they walked back up to her porch and sat on the swinging bench. With one leg tucked beneath her and the other on the ground, she rocked them gently.

"He likens it to being smacked upside the head," she said. "I have to say, I did feel like I'd been sucker-punched when I first saw him."

"I've been hearing the women around town talking about him. I gathered he's considered very attractive."

"That helps. But it's not everything."

"That's true." He tipped his bottle back and took a long drink, the muscles of his tanned throat working with each swallow.

She looked away. The sky was deepening into shades of pink, purple, and navy blue. The breeze grew in strength, cooling slightly and carrying a tinge of salt from the nearby ocean. "We're due for another fire, aren't we?"

"Yeah," he said. "And we're just sitting here. Makes me so goddamn mad that we know he's out there and there's nothing we can do about it."

"Deputy Cameron thinks Dani's murder and the fires are connected."

Jim froze, his green eyes going wide. "What? Why?"

"He can explain it better than I can, which is why he wants to hook up with you tomorrow, I'm sure."

"Wow." He shook his head. "I'm speechless. Not a conclusion I would've jumped to."

"I know, right?" Darcy took a pull on her beer. "Fucking insane. All of it."

Reaching over, he set his hand on her bent knee. "I'm sorry. This has got to be really tough for you."

She looked at the spot where her car had been and thought about Jared. Knowing he was working on Dani's case was keeping her grounded and, for the first time in a long time, optimistic. Placing her hand over his, she squeezed. "I'm okay. Been a long time since I was able to say that and mean it."

Her smile faded as the sheriff's vehicle pulled up in front of her house. She watched as Chris got out and put his hat on his head, his gaze holding hers as he shut the door of his cruiser and rounded the front end. "Hey, Darcy. Jim."

Jim returned the greeting, but she waited until Chris joined them on the porch, his boot-clad feet thudding heavily over the wooden planks and his leather holster creaking.

"What brings you out this way?" she asked.

"I need to speak to Cameron."

"He's not here."

Chris cursed under his breath. "Where is he?"

"With his partner. Working the case."

"Fuck. Did you know he thinks Dani's murder is related to your arsonist?"

"Yes."

"He's in town two damn days and he's going to wrap up a cold case along with the arsons? That's bullshit."

Her brows rose at his vehemence, but she wasn't overly surprised. Chris didn't like others digging into his cases and she couldn't blame him. She knew how she'd feel in his shoes. "It's an angle, but it's not his only angle. I watched him compiling information—he's covering a lot of bases."

Leaning forward, Jim set his elbows on his knees, holding his beer in both hands. "Chris."

Something about the way Jim said his name had Chris stiffening. Darcy frowned.

"What?" Chris snapped.

Jim stared at him.

"Don't look at me like that, Ralston. You don't know shit."

Darcy's gaze shot back and forth between the two men. "What doesn't he know, Chris?"

Chris glared at Jim. "Nothing. Absolutely nothing."

Putting both feet on the deck, she stood. "That's crap. Don't lie to me. Not about this."

Jim pushed off the swing, too. "Dani told me."

"Bullshit." Chris ripped the hat off his head. "That's fucking bullshit."

"Dani told you what?" she demanded, her temper flaring.

Jim kept looking at Chris. "It's going to circle back around to person of interest."

"Fuck you, Ralston," Chris shot back, turning to leave.

Darcy focused on Jim. "Jim?"

As his mouth opened to reply, his cell phone rang. "Damn it. Hang on, Darcy." He stepped to the other side of the porch to take the call.

She set her beer on the little glass table by the swing and watched as Chris stalked back to his cruiser. She followed. "What the hell is going on?"

Then it hit her. *Person of interest*. There had been only one person of interest in Dani's case . . .

"It was you, wasn't it, Chris? You were the one seeing Dani."

"No. Damn it." He spun around halfway down her front walkway, his face red and eyes fierce. "It wasn't like that."

Darcy's heart raced. "What was it like, then, Chris?"

He stared down at her when she came to a stop in front of him, his handsome face taut with strain. "She changed after you left, Darcy. A lot. She started dressing different, acting different, styled her hair and makeup different."

"You were attracted to her."

"No, I wasn't." He crossed his arms, looking ornery and defensive. "You're the one I want. No one's like you, Darcy. What we had . . . You can't tell me you don't think about it. We couldn't get enough of each other."

"Jesus, Chris." She exhaled harshly. "We were kids. Teenagers for god's sake. We were hormonal, and frankly, there wasn't much else to do around this town."

"I still get hard thinking about the things we did. Your mouth and hands on me . . . the noises you make—"

"What the fuck does that have to do with Dani?" Her sister wasn't like her. She had been softer, sweeter. Sex had been highly personal for her. Darcy enjoyed sex for sex; Dani had equated sex with emotional commitment.

"She stopped by my house one night. Dressed like you, smelling like you. She came on to me like a freight train. I couldn't help but think of you."

"Oh my God . . ." Darcy turned away, feeling sick.

"I know you don't believe me. You're thinking Dani wasn't like that. She was the quiet one, the good girl. But she wasn't that way after you left. It was as if she wanted to be you."

She barked out a humorless laugh. "Please. Dani was perfectly happy being Dani."

He grabbed her by the arm, squeezing hard enough to bruise her, yanking her back around. His face was so hard and furious she recoiled from it.

"Hey," Jim yelled from the porch. "Watch it, Miller."

"I wasn't the only one banging her," Chris bit out, releasing her. "Because I'm not the one who knocked her up."

She slapped him before she knew she was going to.

"You won't want to do that again." His voice was low and deep, his gaze dark and hot. The imprint of her hand glowed red on his cheek, intensifying the look of fury on his face.

Her tummy quivered with fear.

"There was someone else," he insisted. "I gave her what she wanted that night and once more afterward. That was enough for me. She wasn't you, couldn't even come close. It was done and over long before six weeks prior to her death."

"You're an asshole. A Grade A prick."

"For taking what was thrown in my face? Repeatedly? Does it make you feel better to lie to yourself?"

"Nothing can make this better." She backed away.

"Don't fucking look at me like that." He stepped closer. "You know me. You know I couldn't do what was done to her."

The awful thing was, she couldn't imagine anyone she knew hurting Darcy the way she'd been hurt. But what did she really know about anyone, if Chris could've hidden this from her?

Jim came up beside her, his hand gently gripping her elbow. "You should go now, Sheriff," he said grimly. "Go find Deputy Cameron and tell him what he needs to know."

"Darcy . . ." Chris stared at her for a long minute, then cursed under his breath. "We're going to talk about this. We need to talk about this."

She turned her back on him and walked to the house.

"THAT'S THE WACKIEST theory I've heard in a long time," Trish said bluntly. "Maybe ever. You're trying to pin first-degree murder and arson on the same subject, with years in between crimes. It's highly unlikely."

Jared met her gaze and nodded grimly. "I know. But there are connections. After looking over Kelley's notes, I found out Danielle's obstetrician's office is catty-corner to the phone booth where the tip came in for the shelter fire."

"Could be coincidence." She sat back in her chair at the small table in her motel room and rubbed the back of her neck, her dark eyes capped with a frown. "Think of the premeditation required to copy both the Prophet's and Merkerson's MOs."

"I've requested a cross-check of library lendings of true crime stories on both. It's a long shot, but at least we'll tie off that thread." He looked at his laptop screen and the case files Kelley had sent his way. "There was DNA from the fetus, but not one man in this town—regardless of age—volunteered a sample to rule himself out. Not one? And no probable cause on anyone to justify a warrant, because no one pointed a finger anywhere. Everyone knows everyone's business in this town, but not who's intimate with the vet, a woman who's lived here her whole life?"

"They don't believe he's one of them. Everyone's innocent, so there's no one to be guilty." She sighed and grabbed another slice of pizza out of the box they'd tossed on the bed. "Small towns. When everyone knows everyone else's business, they can't believe there's something they *don't* know."

"You sound like you speak from experience."

"I grew up in a small town. Some things are universal."

He filed that information away for further pondering. "Our subject has no imagination. He hasn't been thinking about killing and burning for years, as we'd expect, or he'd have his own pattern, his own style. Instead he has to borrow someone else's, right down to the tiniest details. And when he's done what he set out to do, he puts the urge away. Goes back to being himself. Forgets about it. Because he's crazy as a loon, but his crazy doesn't eat at him every day. Something has to set it off."

"So we need to figure out what set him off. Maybe it was the baby the first time around. Maybe the guy's married. That's why they kept the relationship under wraps. I'll look up the men in this town who were married at the time and see what shakes loose."

He looked up at her. "We also need to find out what happened in the last year or so that set off the fires, with a cushion for the learning curve required to build those incendiary devices. Then we can try and tie that back to the murder. I've already started searching through the local paper's archived articles on the web, but they didn't have a website three years ago, so I'll have to hit the microfiche at the library if we need to go back further."

"It's a wide net we're casting." Trish wiped her mouth with a napkin.

"Inspector Michaels is working on drafting a list of locales in town that had some special tie or significance to her sister. All three locations so far met that criterion." He closed his laptop. "We'll need Miller to cover surveillance on the best options."

She snorted. "That may be asking a little too much from our friendly sheriff. He didn't take it well when I mentioned your theory."

"He'll get over it." Jared pushed back from the table and stood. "I'll meet up with him tomorrow and get him on board."

"You going back to the inspector's place?"

He shot her a look.

"Hey." Grinning, she held up her hands. "Just surprised is all. You're different with her, in a good way. I hope it works out."

He'd do whatever was necessary to make sure it worked out.

He was shoving his laptop into the padded sleeve in his workbag when a faint hiss caught his awareness. He stiffened as the hairs on his nape prickled with warning. His nose twitched; his gaze darted to the door, then to the vent in the wall near the ceiling. Sleek tendrils of smoke reached into the room like skeletal fingers, curling sinuously. He yanked the bedspread off the mattress, sending what was left of the pizza flying, and tossed the floral material over Trish's head.

"What the hell, Cameron?" she gasped as the fire sprinklers in the ceiling sputtered to life. She lifted the comforter over both their heads, shielding the table as he swept everything into his open bag.

He'd barely yanked the door open when the room exploded.

chapter eleven

Darcy forced herself to loosen her white-knuckled grip on her phone. "How could no one know about Chris and Dani, Nadine?"

"Hell if I know. I can't believe it. How could I not know? I didn't even suspect."

"God."

"But Chris is the sheriff. If anyone would know how to cover their ass, I guess it'd be him. Not because he killed her. I could never believe that. If anything, he hid it because he knew he'd blow any shot at getting back together with you if you found out he'd tagged Dani."

Inhaling a deep shaky breath, Darcy swiped at the tears coursing down her cheeks. It was impossibly painful hearing that Dani had changed so much. She still couldn't quite believe it, couldn't in any way picture it. "What the hell was she thinking? Did she love him? She had to have . . . How long had she loved him? And if he's telling the truth about ending it long before she got pregnant, who else was in her life?"

Nadine sighed. "I don't know. Maybe she missed you. Or maybe she'd been jealous of you for a while. Jealousy can make a woman lose her mind. Or maybe she was just stretching her wings and she took your example to the extreme. I'm not a shrink, doll. Or a psychic. I don't have the answers for you. I'm sorry."

"I have to go."

"Want me to come over? Or is your hunky deputy with you?"

"I'm fine. Thank you, Nadine. I'll talk to you later." She hung up, gasping for air and drowning in grief as if she'd lost Dani all over again. She'd sent Jim off on his date, then she'd locked herself in the house, feeling too exposed to associate with anyone but Jared, who'd already seen her bared to the soul.

Clinging to the receiver, she paced, fighting the urge to call him. He had more important things to do than listen to her breakdown. Besides, their relationship was so new and had already been weighted by heavy issues. The least she could do was give him a little time to get away from her and do his job in peace.

She jumped when the phone rang in her hand. Glancing at the caller ID, she saw it was dispatch and her stomach clenched.

Another fire goddamnit.

"Michaels," she answered. "Where is it?"

Her heart missed one beat, then stuttered back into a panicked rhythm. "*My God . . .*"

DARCY SAW THE smoke and flashing emergency lights long before she reached the scene. She parked her work truck on the street and hopped out, her heart racing as it had been since she'd received the call from dispatch twenty minutes prior. Not having a car had held her back, forcing her to beg the use of one from a neighbor to get to the fire station.

Jared.

She climbed out of the department's truck and grabbed her field kit, forcing herself not to run or appear as panicked as she felt. It wouldn't be fair to lose him now. It was too soon. She'd had only a taste of what he could bring to her life. Not nearly enough . . .

Her attempt at decorum was forgotten the moment she saw him

sitting on the back of an ambulance with an EMT examining him. Her pace picked up.

Although he couldn't possibly have heard her coming with all the chaos around them, his head lifted and his gaze met hers. He pushed to his feet, saying something to the female paramedic without taking his bloodshot eyes off Darcy. He was soot-stained but alive, making him the most beautiful thing she'd ever seen.

Shoving her kit at a passing firefighter with a hasty thanks, she broke into a run. Jared met her halfway, catching her up and squeezing the air out of her.

"I'm okay," he said hoarsely. "It's all right."

"You scared me half to death." She held on to him with every bit of her strength. "I c-can't let you out of my sight for a minute."

He cupped the back of her head and pressed her close. They clung that way for a long moment, their hearts pounding in a synchronized beat. The cold knot in her stomach eased at the feel of him against her, warm and strong.

She pulled back to examine him. "How's your partner?"

"Well enough to be in the front office typing up a prelim report. This riled her up." He brushed his fingertips over her brows. "Walk me through the scene with you. The sooner we get through it, the sooner we can get out of here."

Darcy drew herself together with a deep breath, then stepped back and went in search of her kit. Her hands were shaking as she reached for the box.

Chris intercepted her. "Where's Jim?"

"On his date. He knows what's going on. I told him I'd handle it, and if I had any trouble, I'd give him a call."

He nodded, then yanked off his hat to shove a hand through his hair. "Hell, Darcy. Five of the rooms were occupied. A half dozen people could've been killed."

"Was anyone seriously injured?"

"Tear gas in the air duct system pushed everyone out before the fire started."

Jared stepped into Chris's line of sight. "You keep tear gas in inventory, Sheriff?"

"Already looking into it, Cameron."

She looked at the two-story building, noting the area with the most damage. "The fire started in Morales's room?"

Jared set a grimy hand on her shoulder and squeezed. "Yeah."

"Shit." She reached up and set her hand over his, needing to deepen the connection.

Chris's gaze narrowed. "Someone wants you dead, Deputy."

"Wouldn't be the first somebody." The raspiness of Jared's voice made her wince in sympathy.

"Let me do my job," she said. "And we'll see if we can find something that gets us closer to figuring out who our torch is."

She moved toward the obvious point of origin with a brisk stride.

Jared drew abreast of her. "You're aggravated with him."

"Some things have come up since I saw you last."

"Oh?"

"Ask me about it when we get home."

IT WAS JUST after midnight when they got back to Darcy's house. Jared could see how exhausted she was but knew more than the length of the day was weighting her slender shoulders. He decided not to press her to talk, to let her decide when she was ready to share. She was a solitary woman in many ways. Joining her inner circle was going to take time and patience. The latter wasn't one of his strong suits, but he'd make the effort for her. Not that he had a choice; he wanted her too much.

In the meantime, he showered, then made them both some cold sandwiches while she typed her preliminary report for Ralston.

When they crawled into bed just after two in the morning, she turned into him, wrapping herself around him. With her legs tangled with his, her palms pressed to his back, and her face in his neck, he dropped into a deep sleep.

He woke up alone. Glancing at the clock, he noted it was barely six. He left the bed, then the bedroom, looking for Darcy. He found her in the living room, curled up on the couch beneath a chenille throw. She was watching a muted television, her eyes marred by dark circles. An open box sat on the floor by the coffee table, holding a variety of loose items, including framed photos of Darcy and Danielle.

"Hey," he said softly. "Let me join you."

She sat up at his urging and he settled behind her, taking her weight against his chest. He ran his fingers through her hair, brushing it back from her forehead. The feel of her bare skin against his soothed him. As the explosion had thrown him out into the parking lot, his thoughts had been with Darcy and how he'd be damned if some sick asshole blew him to hell before he figured out what he had with her.

"You wanna talk?" he asked softly.

Turning her head, she pressed her cheek to his chest. "I don't even know where to begin."

"Wherever you want." He kissed the crown of her head, hating the misery that radiated from her and his helplessness to alleviate it. "I can pull it all together later."

"How much crap can I dump on you, Jared, before you run screaming?"

"I never scream and I damn sure never run away." He gripped her shoulders, resisting the urge to give her a little shake. "Spit it out."

In a low halting voice, she told him about Miller's visit and her subsequent talk with Nadine. "I knew she had to be with someone familiar to me, but Chris . . . ? I can't believe she didn't say anything. I wouldn't have been upset."

"A lot of people have secret lives. Their loved ones are shocked when they come to light. It's no reflection on you."

"I can't help thinking that I fucked up somewhere and that's why she couldn't trust me with this."

"It sounds like it was a couple random encounters. Maybe she was embarrassed. Heat-of-the-moment type thing that she regretted."

"Even more reason to tell me, so we could've laughed it off and put it away." She exhaled harshly. "And Chris . . . Wow. He had a responsibility to disclose his affair with her to the Feds. Why didn't he, if he had nothing to hide?"

"It's definitely a problem. But at least we've got enough to get a DNA sample from him now."

"I've known him forever. He was my high school sweetheart. I thought I *knew* him." Her exhale shuddered out of her. "I wanted to vomit when he said he slept with Darcy as a substitute for me. It's so sick."

"How far would he go to keep you from finding out about it? Especially if he's the one who got her pregnant?"

She twisted to look into his eyes. Her gaze was so haunted it gored him like a dull knife.

"I hate that I was thinking the same thing," she whispered. "He was important to me at one time. How could I be so wrong about two people I thought I was close to? The Dani I know couldn't stomach casual sex. She always became emotionally attached when things got physical. And Chris . . . he's a sheriff, for chrissakes."

Jared brushed his fingertips over her cheek. "It's killing me that you're hurting and I can't do a damn thing about it."

"You're here. That's what I need more than anything." Leaning into his palm, she sighed. "The answers will come later. We'll find them."

"Did she have a bad breakup shortly before her involvement with Miller?"

Her gaze softened. "You really do pay attention when your sister talks, don't you? Yes, she met a fellow vet at a conference, and it was hot and heavy for a while. Then she found out he was married and that she was just a piece of ass on the side. She took it hard. I thought she'd sworn off men."

"Or became determined to prove she didn't give a shit about them."

Darcy sat up, the throw falling to pool in her lap. "And I'm her example for that? What the fuck does that mean?"

"That she had issues," he said calmly, "and she didn't know you all that well. You like men just fine. You just hadn't met one you liked enough to get serious about."

"Until you."

He inhaled deeply at the admission, knowing how important it was to her. And to him.

She stood, gloriously naked, agitation pouring off her in waves.

Straightening, he tossed the throw aside and held her gaze. "None of this is your fault, Darcy."

"Right." She paced, her lithe muscles flexing through her thighs and buttocks. "You know, you say 'commitment' and I get butterflies."

"You've had commitments before. This one scares you because it's the last one you'll have." He set his elbows on his knees and linked his fingers together. Between his spread legs, his cock was hard and thick, thrusting upward hungrily in appreciation of the sight of his woman. "Even I find that scary."

She paused midstride, staring at him. He saw her chest expand on a slow breath and her eyes darken with both grief and longing. Her turmoil was tangible, and unable to bear it, he pushed to his feet. She plowed into him, nearly knocking him back into the couch.

Catching him by the nape, she yanked his mouth down to hers. His teeth cut his inner lip and the sharp metallic flavor of blood stirred him violently.

Lightning in a bottle. It had struck the moment they'd laid eyes on each other. Sexual creatures that they were, they'd both mistaken it as lust at first, and certainly that was a major part of what they knew about each other so far. But lust could be appeased. Sated. What they had ran much deeper, was more voracious than mere desire.

Gripping her by the elbows, Jared lifted her to her tiptoes and took over the kiss. His lips sealed over hers, his head tilting to find the perfect fit. The stroking of her tongue along his was as arousing as if she'd licked his cock.

She reached down and grabbed his ass, grinding against him, massaging his dick with the soft firmness of her lower belly. "Fuck me."

"Darcy." There's nothing he wanted to do more, but the rapid-fire switch in her mood gave him pause. He couldn't afford to screw things up with her. As fragile as she was at the moment, the intensity of their lovemaking could be too much. "Easy, sweetheart. I'll take care of you."

"I need you inside me, Jared."

He caught her face in his hands. "Let me set the pace. I know how to give you what you need, when you need it."

Her nails dug into his flesh. "I need it now."

She dropped to her knees and took him in her mouth. The drenching heat, followed by powerful sucking, nearly sucked the cum right out of him. Her tongue fluttered. Her cheeks hollowed with deep, drawing pulls. Maddened by her greed for his body, his balls drew up tight, the urge to blow his load almost too great to resist.

Catching her beneath the arms, Jared yanked her up. If he didn't get a handle on her, she'd have him so spiked he'd bang her on the couch again, rutting on the woman he was falling in love with like an animal in heat. On any other day there'd be no problem with that, but not today. Today they both needed more than a quick, furious orgasm.

"We're doing this in a bed this go-round," he muttered, lifting her feet from the floor and carrying her to the bedroom. She wrapped her legs around his hips, wiggling, trying to align their bodies. When the satiny soft lips of her cunt slid across the crown of his dick, his step faltered, his chest vibrating with a groan.

Darcy caught his mouth, latching on to his tongue and sucking. His knees buckled and he cursed, leaning heavily into the wall to keep them both upright. "Behave, damn it. Before I nail you on the floor."

"Yes . . . Do it."

Cursing, he stumbled into the bedroom and dropped her on the bed. As she dove for his cock again, he snatched his handcuffs from the nightstand and intercepted her. He had her hands restrained at the small of her back before she knew what hit her.

She froze prone on the bed, her breathing quick and shallow. "What are you doing, Deputy?"

"Pacing us, Inspector." He was going to give her the love and tenderness she needed, by any means necessary.

"No."

"No?" He ran the pad of his index finger down the length of her spine, finding the sight of handcuffs against her bare back the most erotic view of his life.

"I want you *now*." Her voice was even breathier than usual and it did crazy things to him, taking him to the very edge of his control.

"You're going to get me now, sweetheart. All you can take and more."

chapter twelve

Darcy absorbed the feeling of heavy metal around her wrists, then she processed how she felt about it.

Jared arranged her carefully with effortless strength, until she found her feet on the floor and her torso draped across the mattress. With her hands bound, it was a vulnerable pose. A shiver of anticipation coursed across her skin in a wave of goose bumps.

His lips whispered along her arm from shoulder to fingertip. "You're so fucking hot in handcuffs."

Hearing the lust in his voice spurred her into a feverish desire. Her breasts were tender, the nipples furled tightly against her rumpled sheets. Her pussy was damp and swollen, aching for the feel of his big cock pounding into her.

"Jared . . . I need you." She felt cold inside. Distant. As if a part of her had shied away and retreated, like it had when Dani died. Jared had lured her out when he'd entered her life, made her start thinking beyond the moment, enabling her to envision a day when she might be able to put Dani's death behind her and get her life back. She needed him to do it again, make her *feel* again.

"I know." His hands slid under her and cupped her breasts. He nuzzled his lips just below her ear. "I need you, too."

He caught her nipples between thumb and forefinger, tugging

gently. His cock brushed against her hands and she clasped him, her eyes closing when he groaned and thrust into her touch.

He was hard as a rock and hot. She squeezed her thighs together, fighting off the building throb. She'd wanted to make him come in her mouth, wanted to hear his pleasure. Taste it. Drink it down.

"Let me suck you off," she said in what might have passed for a plea.

"Later."

Darcy heard him move behind her, felt his hands cupping the backs of her thighs in the crease just below the curves of her buttocks. His breath gusted gently over the slick lips of her sex. She tensed in expectation.

"Such a pretty pussy," he murmured. "I'm going to eat this cunt every chance I get for the rest of your life, Darcy. I'm going to shove my tongue in your hot little hole and tongue-fuck you so often you'll feel strange when my mouth's not buried between your legs."

The rawness of his passion for her continued to astonish her. It mirrored her own in a way that felt like . . . kismet, a concept her rational mind scoffed at. But there was no denying that being with Jared felt like being half of a whole, two individuals drawn to one another by a fiery magnetic pull that was irresistible.

She bit her lip and quivered violently as he licked leisurely through her cleft, tracing her folds slowly and so gently that the touch of his tongue was like the kiss of a butterfly's wings. Her hips circled into the teasing strokes, but he wouldn't be rushed. When he finally pushed into her as he'd promised, she moaned into the bedding, so close to coming she could taste it.

Pushing her legs apart, Jared opened her farther, thrust his tongue faster, showing her with his greedy voracity how much he loved going down on her, how much pleasure he took in the carnal intimacy. His groans made her hotter. Wild and desperate. His morning stubble scraped along her tender skin; the rough silk of his hair brushed over her in a whisper of a caress. She gasped and writhed, her skin misting with sweat as his tongue fucked relentlessly into her, making her cream for him until her inner thighs were wet with it.

"My clit," she begged, her muscles trembling with the strain. "Lick my clit."

Instead, he moved in the opposite direction, rimming the pucker of her ass with the pointed tip of his tongue. Darcy cried out, the tight ring of muscle flexing in delight. With a groan, he took her there with a lush dark kiss, pushing into her and thrusting shallowly.

Aroused beyond bearing, her body shook so hard the mattress vibrated with her, her hands fisting and releasing in mindless spasms. Pushing to her tiptoes on the floor, she lifted into his mouth, urging him on. Her entire body was a live wire, arcing with crackling sensual electricity.

"Yes," she gasped. "Oh . . . it's so good. I'm going to come . . ."

Spreading her cheeks with his thumbs, he held her open and pushed her into climax with rapid-fire licks. She ground her sweat-slick face into the sheets, muffling her scream as the release tore through her with brutal power, singeing her nerve endings and flushing her skin like a fever.

Then his fingers were there, slick with lube, expertly preparing her with deep leisurely thrusts into her rear. She pushed back into his hand, riding those two wicked digits with a barely tempered hunger. They stroked along her smooth inner walls, twisting and pumping until she thought she might go mad with the need to feel him filling her with his big, beautiful cock.

He stood. His lips touched her shoulder as his fingers left her. "How are you doing? Your arms okay?"

"Don't stop," she said hoarsely.

"I won't. Not until you beg me to."

There was the sound of foil crinkling, then the soft snap of latex. When he pushed into her pussy, Darcy jolted in surprise.

"Easy," he murmured, steadying her with a hand on her hip. He paused a moment at the midway point, his breathing deep and even. Then he drove into her with one smooth, forceful thrust.

She came in a startled rush, crying out his name as the sensitive tissues rippled greedily along his thick length. He felt like heated stone inside her, stretching her to her limits and yet so—

"Perfect," she breathed, closing her eyes, feeling his warmth spreading through her. Soothing her, just as she'd needed.

The terrible anxiety that had been ripping her apart since Chris's visit the day before eased, dissipated by her bone-deep surety that she'd found the one man she could share herself with absolutely. Jared had come upon her during a terrible time and accepted it, accepted *her* as she struggled through it. Offering support and comfort in just the way she needed it. His quiet strength and determination gave her hope that Dani would have justice after all and that she might have a life without Dani in it, one that would fulfill her and give her a reason to strive forward every day.

But most importantly, Jared was the man she wanted to offer all those things to in return, with everything she had to give and more. She'd learn to be more for him. She wanted to be everything to him, everything he needed and wanted.

"Perfect," he agreed, nuzzling against her temple. "It's so good, Darcy. Do you feel it?"

"I feel it. Feel you . . ."

"Yes," Jared groaned, his grip tightening on her hips. "Feel me."

He began to fuck her with slow, deep thrusts, his rhythm perfectly controlled and fluid. He wielded his long, wide shaft with breathtaking expertise. Knowing just how to please a woman with it, but more, knowing just how to please *her.* Noting the nuances of her helpless response and focusing on what drove her to the edge. Stroking the thick crest over and over the sensitive spot inside her that made her insensate with pleasure.

"Feels so good . . ." she slurred, floating into a melting simmering orgasm with a breathless cry. He ground his hips against her, rubbing the deepest point of her, prolonging her pleasure.

"I'll never get enough of you coming around my cock." Flexing his fingers on her hips, he began shafting her pussy again. "Once more, sweetheart. Let me feel you."

But once more wasn't enough for him. He drove her to orgasm twice before pulling free and unshackling her wrists. He rolled her gently to her back, his mouth surrounding an aching nipple and sucking softly, his tongue flickering over the hardened point.

Darcy whimpered, so boneless she scarcely had the strength to run her fingers through his sweat-soaked hair. He was drenched all over, betraying the effort he'd exerted to make love to her with such selfless tenderness. He hadn't come, forfeiting his own needs to give his attention to hers.

"Take what you need," she urged. "Take it how you need it."

Rubbing her bent knee against his flank, she urged him on. With his gaze on hers, he rolled the condom off and wrapped it in a tissue from the bedside table, tossing it in the trash can beside it. Moving quicker now, he caught her leg and lifted it into the air to prop against his shoulder, then he did the same with the other.

He stared down at her, his features harsh with lust, his blue eyes dark and soft with emotion. "I'm crazy about you, Inspector."

He positioned his cock's head against the lubricated pucker of her ass, groaning as the eager orifice flexed in invitation. She flowered open for him, catching her breath as the thick crown pushed past the tight ring.

With her heels in the air and her ass cupped in his hands, he pushed into the slick passage, his gorgeous face twisting in a grimace of tortured ecstasy as she clenched around him like a fist.

"Darcy, sweetheart, you're so tight." Sweat coursed down his temple and glistened on his flexing abdomen. "So damn hot. You're scorching my dick."

Her neck arched, her head pressing into the pillow as surrender radiated outward from the place where he pressed inexorably into her.

"Jared." She moaned as pain mingled with her pleasure. The surfeit of sensation pulsed through her, tightening her chest and quickening her breathing.

"I'm right here with you," he said hoarsely. "Ah, God, I'm gonna come before I get all the way inside you."

"Please . . ." She wanted that. Wanted to feel it. Wanted to know that there were no barriers between them physically, just as there were none between them emotionally.

Adjusting his grip on her hips, he pumped deeper, sliding over highly sensitive nerve endings. Her hands fisted in the disheveled sheets; her head tossed from side to side. It felt as if something feral were trying to claw its way out of her skin. She surrendered to it, surrendered to him, the uninhibited lover who took the sexuality she'd always embraced and enhanced in a way that made it new. Made it his.

Pushing onto her elbows, Darcy looked at where he entered her, her mouth drying at the sight of the thick veins pulsing along his rigid erection. He was at the limits of his control, yet still he held back for her. "Jared."

His gaze was hot as it met hers. She tightened down on him and he jerked violently, sliding deeper. With a growl, he thrust in to the root and started coming, spurting hot and thick in the depths of her rear.

She writhed as her pussy clenched on the verge of climax, then screamed as he placed the pad of his thumb over her clit and rubbed, hurtling her into orgasm with him. They arched together, straining against the vicious ecstasy, Jared thrusting mindlessly as he pumped his semen into her willing body.

As the tension eased and her body sank limply into the mattress, Darcy came to the awareness of the unabated erection sliding in and out of her ass. Blinking heavy-lidded eyes up at Jared, she moaned as his gentle fucking stimulated overworked and hypersensitive nerves.

"You just . . ."

"I did." His voice was gravel-rough and sexy as hell. "And I have more to give you. Everything I am, Darcy. Everything I have. It's yours."

She set her hands over his where they gripped her hips. "Give it to me. All of you."

chapter thirteen

Jared ran his fingertips up and down the arm Darcy had draped over his abdomen and ran the gathered data through his mind for the hundredth time, searching for what he might've missed.

When Darcy bolted upright without warning, his arm shot out, his hand grasping for his weapon.

Breathing heavily, she stared at the gun he had aimed at the door, then met his gaze. "Dani never said a word to me about Chris, but she told Jim. I didn't know they were close, her and Jim. Close enough that she'd share a secret lover with him."

"Okay," he said carefully, returning his gun to its holster. "You're following the same train of thought I had. I e-mailed Ralston's name to Agent Kelley. She might have some questions for him."

She pushed her hair back from her face. "I don't want to make trouble for him. He doesn't deserve it."

He propped some pillows behind his back. "You deserve answers and I'm gonna see that you get them."

"You don't think he has anything to do with this, do you?"

"He wasn't one of the subjects the Feds interviewed, so technically he didn't lie to them, but it's never a good thing to withhold information. It smacks of having something to hide."

"Or someone to protect."

Reaching for her hand, he linked fingers with hers. "How close is he to Miller?"

"Not very. But I do think he said what he did yesterday to protect Chris. If you tie the arsons and the murder together—which is what Chris came looking for you to talk about—outing Chris's relationship with Dani absolves him of both. He has an airtight alibi for the first arson, he was out of town for three days prior to it—his sister just had a baby. And the night of the shelter fire he was in the station when the call came in, working on evaluations. Unless you find out differently, that makes it impossible for him to have been the one to set the fire or make the call from Seattle."

He tugged her close, urging her to snuggle up with him again. "Can you get Ralston to talk to you?"

"Yes." She laid her cheek against his chest. "When I talked to Nadine yesterday, she said jealousy can make a person crazy. If Chris isn't the father of Darcy's baby, there was someone else in her life. Maybe he found out about Chris and lost it."

"We'll figure out the why when we figure out the who. We'll get there, sweetheart."

She looked up at him. "I'm ready to put this behind me."

"Where was home for you before you came back here?"

"Albuquerque. I wanted something arid after growing up with so much rain."

"I can do arid."

Her gaze softened. "Would you?"

"Sure, I can transfer."

"When I left New Mexico, I thought it might be a while before I figured out what was next. I quit my job, sold my condo . . ." She ran her hand over the light dusting of hair on his chest. "I can start over anywhere."

"I don't care what the plan is, as long as it includes you."

"After losing Dani and then last night . . . I could've lost you, too. A few minutes here or there and you wouldn't be here now. I don't want to waste any chances, Jared."

He hugged her tightly. "We won't. We won't waste a thing."

DARCY PULLED INTO the parking lot of the fire station and waved at Trish, who waited for them with Ralston by the open apparatus bay doors.

Jared stopped her from exiting with a hand on her arm. "I don't want you leaving town. Even the animal shelter is too far. And I don't want you in the car with someone else if you're not behind the wheel. Don't go anywhere private with anyone. And text me as you move around so I know where you are."

"All right. I'm just going to pick over the motel scene with Jim, then come back here to the station to expand on my prelim report. If that changes, I'll let you know."

Dressed in her uniform, with her lush hair restrained in a ponytail, there was little evidence of the insatiable wanton who'd shredded him just hours before. Except in her eyes. The way she looked at him made his chest ache.

"You be careful, too," she said quietly.

"Always."

They split up and he watched her pull out of the lot a few minutes later, driving the pickup with Ralston in the passenger seat.

"You okay?" Trish asked.

"I've been better." He faced her. "You?"

"Fired up. I want this shithead's ass in a sling."

His mouth twitched. "We're starting here because of a volunteer named Mitch Quinn. There have been a few suspect shipments to the station, all under Quinn's name. Inspector Michaels says he should be here today."

"All right. Let's talk to him."

They found Quinn in the kitchen, putting away groceries. He looked up as they came in, his frown melting into a wide smile. With his shaggy blond hair and pale blue eyes, he had the look of a surfer about him, an impression strengthened by the seashell and hemp necklace visible through the opening in his uniform collar.

"Hi," he greeted them. "Are you looking for Inspector Michaels?"

Trish returned his smile, but her game face was on, her eyes flat and watchful. "We're looking for you, Mitch."

He paused, then shut the refrigerator door. "What can I help you with?"

Jared stepped up to the island. "We need to talk about some of the deliveries coming through this station—"

Quinn shoved the groceries across the tile at Jared and fled.

"Well, shit," Trish muttered.

Jared leaped over the oranges and apples spilling off the island onto the floor, and gave chase.

DARCY PICKED THROUGH the charred remains of the motel while Jim jotted notes in his folder.

"Your prelim was well done, Darcy."

"Thank you."

He closed the folder with a decisive snap. "When are you going to ask me why I didn't say anything about Miller and your sister earlier?"

She faced him. "I was waiting until we got through the scene first."

"All right. We're finished for now. Since I was out all night, Columbo missed his morning walk. How about we pick him up and we'll talk about it away from here?"

"Sounds good." They headed back to the truck. She closed up

the evidence collection boxes in the bed of the pickup and said, "I take it from your overnighter that the date went well?"

"Yeah . . . not bad. I appreciate you handling things last night."

"You needed the break and I knew we'd need daylight to get the full scope." She slid behind the wheel and headed to his house.

"You know Chris isn't responsible for what happened to Danielle, don't you?"

Darcy glanced at him. "I can't believe he'd do it. I can't believe anyone I know could do that to another human being."

Setting his elbow on the window ledge, Jim rested his head in his hand and sighed. "He wasn't wrong when he said she'd changed. There's no easy way to say this . . ."

"So just say it."

"She was . . . seeing a few men at the same time."

Darcy's grip tightened on the wheel. It was painful realizing there'd been a widening gap between her and Dani, and she hadn't realized it. "Go on."

"One of the guys was Mitch."

"What?" But the moment she asked the question, she knew it wasn't so surprising after all. Mitch was the sort of hardworking, good-humored type Dani had been drawn to. "Okay."

"When he caught on to her having other interests . . . it hit him hard. She was special to him and he hadn't realized that feeling wasn't mutual. So I went to see her, talk to her, try to get her to let him off the hook easy. Turned out she was upset because he'd been following her. Angling to catch her in the act, I suppose. She told me she'd been trying to cut him off for weeks and if I was really worried about him, I'd tell him to knock it off or she'd have Miller arrest him."

She felt him look at her, his gaze heavy on the side of her face. "Darcy . . . I bluffed when I said she told me about her and Miller. There was just something in her voice. I wondered. When he showed up at your place so upset about tying the arsons in with the murder—I took a shot in the dark."

Pulling up in front of his house, she parked and twisted to face him. She thought of Jared asking her about Mitch that morning and wondered what had drawn his attention in that direction. "Do you think Mitch killed my sister?"

"No! Hell, no." He shook his head violently. "If I even suspected that, I would've driven him to the sheriff's office myself. Danielle was driving into Seattle a lot. I figure that's where she met the guy, whoever he is."

She shoved the door open and got out, needing to stand and suck in air to get past her sudden nausea. "I really need that walk."

"THAT WAS A real dumb move, Mitch." Trish circled his seat at a metal interrogation table in the sheriff's department. "Running from a marathon man like Deputy Cameron."

Through the two-way mirror, Jared watched Mitch Quinn sprawl insolently in his chair and shake his head. "I wasn't running from the deputy. I left some ice cream in the truck."

"Um, ice cream. What flavor?"

"Vanilla."

"Ah, too bad. I like chocolate myself." She settled in the seat across from him. "So, let's talk about some of the packages that have been shipped to the station to your attention."

Quinn met her gaze directly. "All packages coming into the station are addressed to me. Stuff was getting lost before. I keep things organized."

"You're meticulous, aren't you, Mitch?"

"I am, yes."

Trish nodded. "I bet building a precision incendiary device

would be child's play for a dedicated, meticulous, organized fireman such as yourself."

He bolted upright. "Now, wait a minute! You're not pinning the arsons on me. I fight fires, I don't start them."

"But in a town of this size, there's no budget to take on more permanent firefighters, is there? Unless there was suddenly a rash of fires in the area. An arsonist setting up shop here would be almost a blessing for a long-suffering volunteer."

"That's sick."

"I agree. The supply room here in the sheriff's office is missing a can of tear gas. Did you know tear gas was used in the motel fire last night? Our arsonist didn't mind charbroiling me and Deputy Cameron, but he wanted to get the other guests out. You were in the supply room yesterday, Mitch. What for?"

"Because there was a note on the dry erase board in the station telling me to grab a box labeled LBFD—Lion's Bay Fire Department, if you couldn't figure it out."

"Who left the note?"

"I don't know."

"You didn't recognize the handwriting? A meticulous guy like you?"

Quinn's gaze was icy. "I didn't look at it that closely."

"All right." She pulled out her cell phone. "I'll text Deputy Cameron to snap a picture of it and bring it over."

"I erased it after I finished the job," he bit out. "That's what we're supposed to do, so we don't have guys trying to do jobs that have already been done."

"That's a shame. Or maybe I should call it convenient?"

"This is a witch hunt. You're looking for a scapegoat to keep your record looking good and I'm the lucky guy. No way. I'm done talking. I want a lawyer."

"Fuck," Miller muttered from his place beside Jared in the observation room. "This is why I should've interviewed him. He'd trust me enough to hold off on lawyering up."

"Too risky," Jared said, although he'd already said it before. More than once. "If the arsons in any way tie back to Danielle Michaels's murder, you and I both have a conflict of interest. This way we're keeping it semi-clean."

His cell vibrated and he pulled it out of his pocket, reading the text from Darcy that said she'd gone to Ralston's house and that he'd pegged Mitch Quinn as one of Danielle's lovers.

Trish pushed back from the table. She'd gone casual today with jeans and blouse paired with a Marshals Service Windbreaker, but there was nothing soft about her approach to the job. "Maybe your lawyer can explain why you checked out three different books on Reginald Merkerson from the Seattle public library."

"That's a goddamned lie!" Quinn lunged to his feet, knocking over his chair and putting Jared on alert for his partner's safety. Quinn's eyes were wild and hot, his face pale. "I've never been to the Seattle library in my life."

She pulled a copy of the library check-out list from the folder in her hand and set it on the table. "This says different."

"I'm being set up!"

"Tell it to your lawyer." She reached for the doorknob.

"Why the fuck would I drive to Seattle for books on Merkerson when Jim Ralston has copies of the actual case files in his office?"

"Check the dates on the paper there, Mitch. Those books were checked out before the fires started. Months before. Plenty of time to figure out how to make nasty little toys like Merkerson was known for."

His jaw tightened. "Someone's setting me up."

"Who would do that to a nice guy like you?"

"I don't know. What I do know is that I didn't start those fires. A dedicated, meticulous, organized guy like me wouldn't leave such an obvious trail."

"Ever date Dr. Danielle Michaels?"

Mitch was clearly knocked back by the unexpected change in topic. "We hooked up a time or two. Why?"

"You wanna talk?"

He sat back down and crossed his arms. "I want a lawyer."

chapter fourteen

"Hey, boy." Darcy dropped to her haunches and wrapped Columbo in a big hug. "You're looking handsome. Miss me?"

The energetic German shepherd greeted her with a bark and a tongue swipe across her cheek. She rubbed him down with both hands.

Jim set his notepad down on the dining table and pulled the leash off the rack by the door. "He does, of course. I told him after things settle down around here, he'll see you more often."

She stood. "I need to talk to you about the settling down part."

"Oh?" He hooked the leash onto Columbo's collar. "Shoot."

"I know I'm pretty superfluous around the station . . ."

He arched a chastising brow at her. "That's not true."

"Okay, I'm copping out," she admitted, shoving her hands in her pockets and rocking back on her heels. "It wouldn't matter if I was indispensible. The thing is, if you really need someone to do what I've been doing, you should start putting out feelers."

"Why?"

"Because." She took a deep breath. "It's time for me to pick up the life I left behind."

Holding the leash loosely in one hand, he leaned casually into the wall and crossed his legs at the ankles. "Is this because of Deputy Cameron?"

"He was the spark, maybe, but the fire is my own." She pulled out one of the dining table chairs and sank into it. "Time has been flying by and I didn't realize it. I've been in a daze, I think, since Dani's death."

"And a couple nights of hot sex snapped you out of it?"

She shrugged, then smiled sheepishly. "It is really hot, but I've had great sex before. There's something there, you know? Something more."

"Yes, I know." He pulled the chair out beside her. "So what are you thinking? You're just going to drop everything and run off with a guy you've known a few days?"

"I dropped everything to come back here. Getting on with my life eventually had always been my plan, although I lost track of that for a while—"

"I think you're losing track of what you've got here."

"I've never been really happy here in Lion's Bay, Jim," she reminded softly. "It's why I left in the first place."

"And Deputy Cameron doesn't have anything to do with your decision?"

"I already answered that question."

He rubbed the back of Columbo's ears. "When are you going to grow up, stop being flighty, and commit to something?"

"Excuse me?"

"One guy to the next, one town to the next. Without any concern for the people who care about you and went out of their way for you?"

"You sound like Chris." Darcy slid her chair back and pushed to her feet, unnerved by his unexpected and provoking remarks. "We'll talk later, once we're both thinking straight."

"Sit down."

"I don't think so."

"Sit the fuck down."

She stared at him, finding the harshness of his words very much at odds with his calm voice and demeanor. A chill ran down her spine. "What the hell is the matter with you?"

"I've done a lot for you." He gave her a mocking smile. "Don't you think I have the right to get pissed when you throw me over for a gung-ho deputy who'll be in and out of your cunt as fast as he's in and out of this town?"

Darcy turned away, heading around the opposite side of the dining table to get to the front door.

Columbo started barking violently. She'd scarcely registered the addition of a third voice in the conversation when the leash whipped around her neck and yanked her back.

Her head slammed into the edge of the table and her vision blackened . . .

JARED WAS SEALING up the contents of Mitch Quinn's locker at the fire station when the hairs on his nape prickled with warning. He paused, knowing he was wasting time closing off an avenue that was a dead end to begin with. In the meantime, something was wrong. It hit him in the gut, and he knew better than to ignore it.

He pulled out his phone and called Darcy. When he reached her voice mail twice in a row, he went to the contact list hung on the station's wall and called Ralston. When he got no answer there, either, he returned to the sheriff's department and entered the interview room to confront Quinn.

Setting his palms on the table, he asked, "Why did you run?"

"I didn't run, I—"

"Listen, I don't give a shit, Quinn. The recorder isn't on. It's just you and me."

Mitch shot him a look. "Do I look like a moron?"

"You look like a guy who's being set up. You have no one to corroborate your alibis for the nights of the fires, you have electrical wiring in your locker similar to the type Merkerson was known to use . . . With everything else we've got, it's not looking good." Jared saw cold defiance shift across Quinn's face and changed tactics. "You consider Darcy Michaels a friend, don't you? I know she's real hopeful that you'll be promoted to full-time soon. I bet she puts in a good word for you every chance she gets. Does that mean anything to you? Or do you just care about yourself?"

Jaw ticcing, Mitch said, "I like Darcy."

"I think it's possible the person responsible for the fires is responsible for Dr. Danielle Michaels's death, too. I think it's possible they're going to go after Darcy Michaels at some point. And I think it's really fucking unlikely that you had anything to do with any of it, but someone wants to deflect attention from himself by drawing it to you. Someone who knows something about you that would make you antsy, make you run, make you lawyer up right off the bat so you look guilty and waste my time. Who would know you're into something shady, Mitch? Who would know your schedule? Gimme a name. Help Darcy after all she's done to help you."

Mitch scrubbed a hand over his face. "I don't trust you."

"You don't have to." He bent closer and lowered his voice. "Miller? Ralston?"

"No way. Both of them are gonzo over her." He gripped his head in his hands. "The chief makes the schedule. He knows my hours and days."

Jared straightened, remembering his brief introduction to the Lion's Bay fire chief. "Chief Sendak?"

"He's gay, dude. He wouldn't have been messing around with Dr. Michaels."

"But he has access to your locker, your schedule, and the mailing room?"

"Listen." Mitch leaned closer and lowered his voice. "Occasionally—*rarely*—some of the guys have things shipped to them at the station that they don't want their wives finding out about. You know? Aside from that, there's nothing hinky going on. The guys are all straight up."

"Fuck." Leaving the room, Jared pulled out his phone and called Darcy again. As it rang, he went by Miller's office and found it empty, then crossed through the bull pen to the desk and the blond deputy who manned it. He hung up when he got Darcy's voice mail.

"Hi, Deputy," the blonde greeted him.

He managed a brief, distracted smile. "Where's Miller?"

"He left while you were at the fire station."

"Where did he go?"

She shrugged and smiled prettily. "I don't know. He took personal time."

"Get him on the radio. Please." He watched her make the attempt a few times with no answer before he turned around and looked for Trish. She was pouring a cup of coffee but sensed his gaze. She looked at him with a frown, then set the carafe down. She was walking toward him before he gestured to her.

"What's wrong?" she asked.

"I don't know. Something's bugging me. I need to find Darcy."

"I'm coming with you."

He didn't question her assertion, knowing her instincts were as keen as his own. He looked at the deputy at the desk. "I need Chief Inspector Ralston's home address. And Sheriff Miller's, too."

TRISH DROVE WHILE Jared continued to try to reach Darcy. When his other line beeped, he looked at the screen and saw Kelley's name.

"Cameron," he answered.

"Cameron, it's Kelley. I got your e-mail about Sheriff Miller. Thanks for keeping me in the loop."

"It's your case, Kelley. I hope you can close it."

"I'm on my way to the airport now. I'll be back there to talk with Miller myself tonight, but in the meantime, in the spirit of sharing, I thought you'd be interested to know that I poked around his background a little this morning and discovered his second cousin was aide to the lead detective on the Prophet case in Memphis."

"Well, shit." He glanced at Trish and mouthed, "Miller."

Trish adjusted the GPS and changed direction.

"Thank you," he said to Kelley. "Have a safe flight."

"Try not to get blown up before I get there. It'd be nice to meet you in one piece."

DARCY WOKE WITH a groan, her head throbbing. Blinking, she tried to move and found her wrists bound. Awareness shot through her like a bullet, setting her heart racing. Her jaw ached from the ball gag that stuffed her mouth. She turned her head from side to side, trying to figure out where she was. Something wet touched her cheek, followed by the soft stroke of a tongue.

Columbo. The German shepherd lay beside her on the floor in an unknown bedroom. The room was shrouded by drawn curtains and cloaked in eerie quiet.

She rolled to the side and managed to prop herself up with an elbow. The room spun and her stomach roiled. She fought off a wave of nausea, knowing she'd choke with the gag in her mouth. Leaning against the side of the bed, she sucked in air through her nose like a swimmer too long underwater. Her gaze fell on a badge lying on the floor near an antique dresser.

Chris's sheriff badge.

A chill moved through her as she remembered his angry voice intruding on her conversation with Jim just before she'd lost consciousness.

Darcy managed to sit up, her gaze falling to the standard-issue handcuffs on her wrists. Chris's cuffs. Fear settled like a rock in her gut.

She jerked as she heard a door open somewhere in the house, then close, followed by heavy boot steps crossing hardwood floors, increasing in volume as they drew closer. The doorbell rang and they paused.

Struggling to her knees and then her feet, she was frantic to get to the door and get help.

The bell rang again and the screen door creaked open. Knocking ensued.

"Miller? It's Deputy Cameron."

The sound of Jared's voice brought tears to her eyes. She was fumbling with the knob to the door when it opened. Stumbling backward, she fell onto the bed. Relief poured through her when Jim stepped into the room.

Then she saw the gun in his hand.

"Make a sound," he said softly, "and I'll shoot Cameron as he comes in. Understand?"

Outside, Jared knocked and called out again. Tears coursed down her face, her brain trying to process the feverish brightness of Jim's eyes. She'd never seen him look that way, never had him eye her coldly as he was doing now . . .

"He can't come in here without a warrant," Jim said calmly, as if he weren't brandishing a deadly weapon. "If you're quiet, he'll leave and live another day."

It seemed like an eternity before Jared gave up.

Darcy's lungs heaved for breath, spots swimming before her eyes.

Jim raised the gun to point at her chest. "After everything I've done for you . . . Damn it. It breaks my heart to have to kill you again."

* * *

JARED STARED AT the police cruiser parked at the curb in front of Miller's house and shoved a hand through his hair. He called the station and asked what kind of personal vehicle the sheriff drove.

Trish stood on the sidewalk with her hands on her hips. "Miller is hugely territorial, but we get a suspect in custody and he bails?"

"He knows something we don't."

"You like him for this? The fires or the vet? Or both?"

He went to the cruiser and set his hand on the hood, feeling the heat that told him the car had very recently been driven. "Do you?"

"No." She looked at the house. "I'm not keen on Quinn, either."

"Let's run by Ralston's."

As they pulled away from the curb, the unsettled feeling in his gut grew. He dialed Darcy's phone again.

DARCY LIFTED HER gaze from the barrel of the gun and looked into Jim's eyes. Fear slithered through her veins like ice water, chilling her to the bone. She flinched when he stepped closer.

"Scream and I'll shoot you." He released the ball gag with one hand.

Flexing her aching jaw, she asked, "What are you doing, Jim? Where's Chris?"

"Thinking about taking up with him again? After he blew you off like a whore?"

She frowned. Chris hadn't broken it off with her; she'd ended their relationship, as gently as possible. That was common knowledge. "We're in his house, right? I figured he'd be around."

"He's around."

Her chest expanded on a sharp inhalation. "Can you take the handcuffs off, too? Please."

"Don't be sweet now. You fucked everything up by sending for the Marshals Service. If you'd left things alone, none of this would have happened."

"None of what? The fires?" Her lower lip quivered violently. "Dani?"

"The fires were bringing us closer together again. You were staying the night at my place . . . We were working the case during the day . . ."

A choked noise escaped her as her chest tightened painfully. "You targeted places that meant something to me. You wanted me vulnerable, so I'd turn to you."

"Cameron had no right to come in and push me out of the picture." Jim leaned into the dresser, looking totally relaxed. His easy demeanor was scarier than if he'd been a raving lunatic.

"The people who owned those businesses you torched are our friends. They trusted you to keep them safe. You've ruined their lives, stolen their livelihoods—"

"No, I didn't. I know exactly what kind of hazard insurance covered each of those properties. They can rebuild better than before."

She gaped at the man with whom she'd shared her body but didn't know at all. "You're insane."

His jaw hardened. "If I am, you've made me that way. I gave you everything, I was committed to you, and you got pregnant with someone else's baby. Who the fuck do you think you are, playing with people like that? After the way Miller treated you, you of all people should know how it feels."

"I've never been pregnant in my life," she shot back, anger slowly chasing away the terror. "I'm not Danielle. Did you kill my sister, Jim? Did you cut her up and do those horrible things to her?"

"I know who you are," he snapped, his free hand waving with agitation. "And Dani killed herself. She was screwing everyone, most especially anyone who had a tie of some kind to you. When I found out she was banging Mitch, I confronted her. We had a relationship. I expected you to be faithful, damn you. I was."

Darcy pushed slowly to her feet, alarmed by his shifting perceptions of who she was.

He straightened, tension stiffening his frame. "If you hadn't tried to leave, I wouldn't have reached for you. You shouldn't have pulled away. If you'd stayed where you were, you'd never have fallen. You'd never have hit your head."

Unsure of what to do, whether it would be wiser to play into his delusions or keep reminding him of reality, she asked, "So what now?"

He exhaled harshly. "I hate that you're making me do this. We were happy together. I don't understand why that couldn't be enough for you."

"It's this place." She tried to swallow, but her mouth was too dry. "It's Lion's Bay. I can't take it here, Jim. That's the reason I spent time with Deputy Cameron—he's going to leave and take me with him. But maybe you'd take me instead? We can be happy anywhere, and with the fires . . . it's better if we leave."

"I'm not stupid. Don't try to play me."

"I'm being practical, for once. I know you can make me happy. I don't know Cameron at all."

Jim's mouth thinned grimly. "It's too late for that. I don't trust you anymore. You've whored around one too many times."

"You're digging yourself a hole you won't be able to crawl out of," she warned, hoping he had some sense of self-preservation left.

"No one's looking at me, Dani." His finger twitched on the trigger. "And when they find your body with Miller's and pin the fires on Quinn, this will all go away and I can get on with my life."

Thinking her time was just about up, Darcy took a risk and launched herself into him.

* * *

"STOP THE CAR," Jared said.

Trish braked to a halt. "What?"

He hopped out. "We don't both need to check out Ralston's. I'm heading back to Miller's. If you catch Darcy, tell her to fucking call me. Now."

"Be careful," she called out, then she drove off.

Jared headed the two miles back at a brisk pace, spurred by a sense of urgency he couldn't qualify. He was still two blocks away when he heard a gunshot. He broke into a run. The house came into sight and he drew his weapon, racing past curious neighbors who straggled onto the sidewalk.

"Get back in your homes," he shouted. "Call nine-one-one."

He'd just reached the lawn when the door to Miller's house burst open and Darcy stumbled out, her wrists handcuffed in front of her. Relief burst through him, followed immediately by blood-chilling fear.

He darted forward, catching her and pulling her to the side of the house, out of the line of fire. "Are you hurt?"

"N-No . . . no, I'm okay."

"Where's Miller?"

"I don't know." Her lower lip quivered. "It's Jim. He did it all. Everything."

Peering around the corner, he eyed the porch. "Where is he?"

"I tackled him into the closet in a bedroom on the right side of the hallway."

He glanced at her, his heart finally slowing from its frantic pounding. "A fucking crazy thing to do."

She sucked in a rasping, shaky breath. "God, I'm glad to see you."

Another shot rent the quiet.

"Oh, no . . ." she breathed. "Columbo."

He stood in a rush. "Someone else is in there?"

"Yes. No. It's Jim's dog. I tripped on a runner in the hall and Jim was behind me with the gun . . . Columbo took him down. The gun went off and shot into the wall, but Columbo had his arm and he was snarling—"

Cupping her nape, he gave her a quick hard kiss. "Stay down."

Jared moved quickly and silently down the side of the house, looking in each window. The silence was brutal. When he saw blood and gray matter spattered on a paned window, he knew what the crime scene unit would find inside.

The dog was fine. It was his owner they'd have to scrape off the walls.

DARCY WATCHED THE frenzy in the police station with an odd detachment. Jared was bent over a desk, talking with the federal agents who'd arrived just a few minutes before. Outside, night had fallen and she was cold, but she suspected that came more from the inside than out.

"Coffee?" Deputy Morales sank into the seat beside her and held out a paper cup filled halfway with steaming java.

"Thank you."

"I checked with the hospital. Sheriff Miller's fine. He has a nasty concussion, so they're going to keep him overnight, but he'll be good as new after a little time off."

Exhaling in a rush, Darcy's eyes stung with grateful tears. "I'm glad."

"Cameron's going to drive you home in a bit." Morales studied her. "Are you all right? I mean, as much as you can be under the circumstances?"

It took Darcy a moment to gather her thoughts into something coherent. "I don't know how I feel about what Jim did . . . today."

"It was pretty much inevitable that he'd self-destruct. I don't know if that's any comfort or not. There's nothing you could have done differently. You're alive, that's what matters."

Darcy rolled the warm cup between her bloodless hands. "I expected to feel a sense of justice when I found Dani's killer. Instead I still can't believe it was Jim. I don't know if I'll ever understand it. And Columbo . . . That dog loved Jim, but he turned on him like he was a stranger."

"Dogs are smarter than we are. They sense things we can't."

"Dani used to say that she couldn't trust people who didn't like animals, but more than that, she couldn't trust people that animals didn't like."

Morales patted her knee, then excused herself, getting back to work.

A few minutes later, Jared walked over. He crouched beside her chair and caught her free hand, his thumb stroking over the minor cuts and bruising left by Chris's handcuffs. "Let me take you home."

Her gaze met his and her heart warmed. "Are you done?"

"I'll have to come back, but you need a hot bath and your bed. I'll hurry and get back to you as quick as I can."

Her mouth curved. "Don't rush for me. I understand the job."

"I know you do, just like I'll understand yours when it takes you away from me. It's one of the reasons why we fit so well."

"Is that what it is?" Her widening smile betrayed the sexual undercurrent of her thoughts.

He blew out his breath, looking relieved. "You're going to be all right."

She realized then how worried he'd been that she wouldn't be. "Yes. I'll be fine." Standing, she said, "Take me home so I can get out of your hair."

Jared linked his fingers with hers and started toward the door. "Won't matter. You'll still be under my skin."

"Good. That's right where I want to be."

epilogue

The closing of the rolling metal door on the back of the moving truck was loud in the otherwise quiet afternoon. Darcy leaned into Jared as he draped his arm around her shoulders and they watched the truck drive away.

He nuzzled his lips against her temple. “Anything left inside?”

“A couple boxes.” She glanced at her childhood home, now sporting a Realtor’s sign in the lawn. “I’m glad to be going, but I have fond memories of this house.”

“So do I,” he murmured, his mouth curving against her cheek.

She laughed softly, then jumped a little when he gathered her close and squeezed her tight.

“It’s good to hear you laugh, sweetheart.”

“I’m getting there.”

“*We’re* getting there.” He pushed his fingers into her hair and cupped her scalp. His blue eyes were clear and warm, filled with a tender heat that never failed to touch her deeply. “And we better get moving. We’re supposed to be at your parents’ house in a few hours.”

Placing her hand in his, Darcy whistled for Columbo. Together, they went into the house to gather the last of her things.

ABOUT THE AUTHOR

Sylvia Day is the national bestselling author of more than a dozen novels. A wife and mother of two, she is a former Russian linguist for the U.S. Army Military Intelligence. Sylvia's work has been called an "exhilarating adventure" by *Publishers Weekly* and "wickedly entertaining" by *Booklist*. Her stories have been translated into Russian, Japanese, Portuguese, German, Czech, Italian, and Thai. She's been honored with the *Romantic Times* Reviewers' Choice Award, the EPPIE Award, the National Readers' Choice Award, the Readers' Crown, and multiple finalist nominations for Romance Writers of America's prestigious RITA Award of Excellence. She's now hard at work on her next book, but would love for readers to visit her at www.SylviaDay.com.

The Unwilling

shiloh walker

chapter one

Slumped in a beach chair, a bottle of beer in his hand, Colby Mathis was on his fifth mantra of, *This is the life.*

Early retirement from a government job. He had very few responsibilities and most of those were centered around running an already thriving bookstore. That was a walk in the park compared to his old life.

Nobody's life depended on him.

He didn't have to worry about somebody dying if he fucked up.

He got to spend his days on a sunny beach.

He got to stare at pretty ladies in small bikinis.

A far cry from working on some task force in the FBI where most of the agents were as fucked up in the head as he was—even if the rest of them hadn't screwed up the way he had.

Dez . . .

Brooding, he tipped the bottle of beer back and let it run down his throat. Twenty-three months earlier, he'd made a judgment call that had nearly ended with one of his fellow agent's death . . . and the death of a child. Dez—Desiree Lincoln had survived. The child had survived. No thanks to Colby. He'd quit the FBI, and no force on earth, including his former boss, could make him go back.

No, he had a good thing going here. The beach. Girls in bikinis. Beer.

He didn't quite believe it. But he had another two hours to convince himself of just how good his life was before he had to head in for his afternoon shift at his dad's bookstore. The store that would be his in a few years—well, technically, a third of it was his now. He'd ring up books. He'd point tourists to good spots to eat, drink, fish. Whatever they wanted. It was Wednesday, it was June, and it was gorgeous out. They'd be busy until around nine thirty that night and then it would slow down.

After work, he'd head home, have a quiet night. Actually, he planned on having a quiet night, accompanied by copious amounts of Jack Daniel's. He was brooding too much and that meant he was about to start with the nightmares again. He'd rather drown them out with alcohol.

If he didn't wake up with a hangover, then tomorrow, he'd get up and go fishing again.

Thursday was his day off. He could take the boat out.

He could relax. Forget all about his failures. About the job, the people he'd failed. Forget about all of it . . .

He needed to do just that. He'd left that life behind. It didn't involve him anymore—

Abruptly, his heart started to race. A weight landed on his chest, all but crushing him. Blood roared in his ears. The bottle in his hand started to feel awful damn heavy. Black dots swarmed in front of him for a minute and then they faded out, his vision taking on a startling, surreal clarity. The weight in his chest grew heavier and he could feel every brutal, pulsing thud of his heart—it felt like that thing was trying to come out of his chest. It didn't exactly hurt, but it wasn't pleasant, either.

Anybody else might have thought they were having a panic attack, maybe even a heart attack.

Colby knew better. It wasn't a heart attack. He almost wished it was, though.

Because *this* was the last thing on earth he wanted. He couldn't do this, couldn't do this anymore. *Fuck* no—

Colby had been a teenager when the psychic gift came on him, and it had come on him strong. Sometimes, the visions were intense. Others, not so much.

This one was almost enough to suck all the air right out of his lungs.

Slamming up the shields in his mind, he shook his head. "No." He reinforced the shields, drew a deep, steady breath. "No."

That wasn't for him—it couldn't be.

NOT FOR ME—

It took most of the next two hours to throw off the heaviness of the attack. He could have gone home, fallen into bed, and slept for ten hours. It often hit him like that, the first initial waves of warning. Hell, sometimes it hit him like that when he was working, unless he had his anchor—another psychic to keep him grounded. It flat-out left him exhausted and sleep was the best thing for him.

His dad would have understood.

But that would have been admitting something had really happened. And Colby was damn determined to not do that. So he finished his not-so-relaxing morning at the beach and walked the mile to the store.

By the time he got there, his legs felt like jelly, but that was good—very good, because it gave him something to focus on besides that sense of impending doom. He was good with having something else to focus on.

Although maybe what he should have focused on was finding a way to keep his dad from really looking at him. One glance was all it took for the older man to realize there was a problem.

"You okay, Son?"

"Yeah." He forced himself to smile. "I'm fine."

He lied. His dad probably knew. But he'd fake it until he was fine. "Fake it until you make it," that was the saying, right? Whatever it was, it would fade, and it would fade without him doing a damn thing.

"You sure you're okay?"

Shoving it aside, Colby looked at his father, held his gaze. "Yeah. Just didn't sleep very well."

The look in his dad's eyes was measuring. "It's starting again, isn't it?"

"No." Colby cleared his throat and wished to hell he could have sounded more convincing. Not that it mattered. It wasn't starting again, because he was done. He was *done*. "No, it's not."

chapter two

She screamed as he came closer. Begged. Pleaded. "Please . . . can't you just stop?"

"Stop?" He smiled, amused. "No. I can't stop until I'm done. And I'm not done." He wouldn't ever stop.

Her broken sobs were like music in his ears as he got to work, singing under his breath as he laid out his tools. He already knew what he was going to do to her. It was going to be . . . unique.

Would this be the one to break her?

As he made the first slice, he sang softly, "Would you dance . . ."

Her body jerked as she screamed.

". . . if I asked you to dance . . ."

Carefully, he wiped away the blood, waited for her screams to fade. He wanted her to appreciate his song, after all.

"Would you run and never look back?"

He made another slice, listened as she screamed again. And he smiled.

By the time he got to the chorus of the song for the first time, she was all but mad with fear, and screaming so steadily he couldn't hear himself sing.

It didn't matter . . . He knew the lyrics. He knew them by heart. And as he continued his work, he sang.

* * *

"WHAT IN THE hell did he do to her?"

Lieutenant Mica Greer stood over the body, vaguely aware of the fact that two of the officers—younger guys, she thought—were fighting the urge to puke. It was hot out, too. Heat and death were a bad, bad mix.

Although she'd slept only a few hours, she was clear-eyed, focused on the ruin of the body in front of her.

Focused on the fact that there was now a third victim.

There will be another one, a slippery little voice murmured in the back of her mind. An echo from her dreams. Dreams that had been interrupted that night by a call—*this* call. She left dreams of death to come and face it.

Her belly was steady, but her heart ached as she stared at what had been done to the woman.

She'd been pretty once.

Not that one could tell by looking at her. But he always picked the pretty ones. Sick fuck. The media was calling him the Surgeon, although they would change their supposedly clever nickname if they got any idea what he'd done this time.

The surgical precision might be there, but the rest . . . ? This didn't even resemble any sort of surgery, macabre or otherwise.

Her gut knotted.

"We sure it's the same guy?"

She didn't look away from the victim. Every second was focused on memorizing the details. Although, seriously, how could she forget this?

"Greer?"

"It's the same guy," she said quietly. They hadn't found the calling card yet, but they would. She didn't need to see it to know it was the same guy.

She just knew.

She'd been trapped in dreams she couldn't understand. Visions of white. Dark blooms of flowers. A wash of crimson blood. And the hideous music of screams. And everything tried to fade the minute the telephone jerked her into wakefulness. But she'd known. Even as the sleep had struggled to clear from her mind, she'd known.

You knew sooner.

She shut off the quiet, sly little whisper in the back of her mind. It had no bearing on the case. Dreams, an incomprehensible knowledge, none of it had any bearing. The only thing that mattered was finding this fucker. Nailing this fucker.

"Well, if it's him, we'll find whatever shit he left for us. Where do you think he left it?"

"I don't know." She angled her head and crouched down to study the woman's dead, sightless stare. "We'll find it."

Her partner, Barry Phillips, echoed her, kneeling down. He had an unlit cigarette dangling between his lips. He hadn't smoked in three months. But sometimes he still had one on him—claimed it helped him to think.

"You mean *you* will find it," Barry said, keeping his voice low.

She wished she could pretend she hadn't heard him. Wished she didn't know what he was talking about. Bile churned in her throat. The endless lines carved into the woman's body hadn't made her ill, but thinking about that . . .

So I won't think about it. She resolutely pushed it aside. "I wonder if she was a dancer or something. Our first vic, she used her mouth. Phone sex operator." She'd had her tongue cut out. "The second one, she did massages." Her hands had been cut off.

"And other stuff," Barry interjected.

Mica slanted him a narrow look. "Possibly other stuff. But her clients found her through the massage place—he took her hands."

"Did a nice, neat job, too. There's nothing nice or neat about this."

"Yeah, there is." She studied how the victim had been carved up. There was blood, but not much. Most of it came from where she'd struggled against the ropes. She'd been killed here, and although she had to have bled, a lot, there wasn't much other than where she'd struggled against her restraints.

Carefully, Mica eased the body up, noticing the dark, mottled flesh where the fluids had pooled after death. She hadn't bled out. Although her throat wasn't bruised, Mica suspected the woman had asphyxiated somehow, smothered perhaps. "She should have bled from this. A lot. But there's not much blood here. He took his time to clean her up as he went."

Phillips grimaced. "That's . . . fucked up."

"Yeah." She blew out a breath, aware of the stink of decay and death. It hung in the air, a cloying stench that seemed to line the inside of her nose, the back of her throat. "But what did you expect? Decency?"

Phillips just grunted under his breath and continued to study the body. After a minute, he said, "A dancer. So why not a prostitute?"

"Because a prostitute gets her money by selling something other than her body, but he tore her body up to hell and back," Mica replied. She didn't want to think about what the killer would cut up then.

"Huh?"

"Sex," she said. "A hooker sells sex."

Mica didn't bother to wait for the picture to connect. Instead, she started to roam around the deserted warehouse. It was a busy enough part of town during the day. But come nightfall, not too many people hung around these parts. Had the killer known that?

She tried to ignore the voice as it whispered, *Yes . . .*

Hard, though, because she wasn't able to completely shut the voice out right now. She needed to find it—that calling card. It was here. She knew it. And that voice . . .

Closer.

Closer.

She was almost to the window now. A smudged, dirty gray window. It had an arrow on it. Frowning, she followed the direction the arrow pointed—east. It pointed east. "What are you trying to tell me, you son of a bitch?"

She didn't know.

And that was a puzzle she'd have to figure out later.

A few levels down, she found what she was looking for.

His calling card. It was his victim's clothes. Neatly folded. On top of them was a flower. People into gardening would probably know that it was called a Queen of the Night. It looked like a tulip to Mica. She knew the name of it only thanks to the reports from the previous victims. When she was able to examine it closely, she'd see that it was a dark, dark purple, almost black. Almost but not quite. Their expert would tell her the same thing she'd heard before—it was a fine specimen. But nothing exotic. Nothing that a hundred, a thousand, a million people couldn't grow in their backyards.

She would also find the victim's ID, more than likely, her purse, whatever she'd had with her. The guy wasn't much into keeping trophies.

He doesn't want trophies. He wants their fear—he wants to hurt them.

"Shut up," she muttered.

"Greer? You okay?"

She glanced up, biting back a curse as she realized that Phillips had come up behind her and she hadn't heard him. Damn it. Way to look like a basket case. "I'm fine. I think we found his calling card." She pointed out the window. "There's an arrow, too. Points off to the east. Wonder if it's from him?"

It is. He's showing you something.

Mica steadfastly refused to acknowledge that quiet whisper, just as she refused to acknowledge her dreams. She'd figure it out on her own. She was a damn good cop—she didn't need help.

"WE NEED HELP, Greer."

"Captain, if we go to the media, it's going to be a disaster—"

Captain Alice D. Kellogg held up a hand. The captain had played basketball in high school, all throughout college, and she ran four miles a day, rain or shine. She stood six foot one in her bare feet, and she had a fondness for high heels and sleek suits. Mica wasn't short, but when she stood next to the captain, she felt like a small, grubby child.

"We're not going to the media. I want you to make a call."

Mica's gut went tight. She knew exactly what the captain was going to say. Exactly.

No. Oh, *hell* no.

As Kellogg reached into her desk, Mica stared at a point on the wall past the other woman's shoulder, working on focusing her breathing, her vision, her temper. *I'm not doing this. I'm not doing this. I'm not—*

The captain held out a card. Mica accepted, staring at the card. Oh, hell.

"I realize you may be resistant to the idea."

Resistant. She shifted her gaze to the captain. "Why would you think that?"

"The fact that I can see a vein throbbing in your forehead is one reason. The other reason? You are standing there looking like you want to kick my ass."

"Captain, I don't want to . . ." She scowled and turned away. "I have no desire to kick your ass." Even if she had the desire, she doubted she could. Mica was used to being able to win the fights she got into—she fought mean, she fought dirty, and she fought hard. Somehow, she suspected the captain would trump her on all levels.

"You have connections that might prove useful." Kellogg stared at her, her hazel eyes penetrating, deep. "You and I both know that."

"I disagree. I don't know that."

"Then that's because you're being obtuse." She continued to study Mica with knowing eyes. "You have connections. You can cut through red tape."

"If we call the FBI, they'll just string us along. There's no reason for them to help us."

"Officially?" Kellogg nodded. "You're right."

"They have no reason to talk to me."

Nobody owed her any favors. She didn't even know if anybody who knew her still worked in the unit. Except the head guy, of course. Taylor Jones would be the last one standing. But the others . . . She'd heard Taige Branch was gone. The others she'd trained with . . . and the one man she tried not to think about. Ever.

Colby.

Colby Mathis.

A shiver raced down her spine as his face flashed through her mind. Blue eyes . . . eyes that saw straight through her. They'd always haunted her.

"Give them a reason." Kellogg's voice, hard and flat, cut through the fog of memories, jerking Mica back to the present. "We have three women dead in three weeks, and you know as well as I do, if we don't find him, we'll be looking at another dead body in a week."

If only Mica could pretend the captain wasn't right . . .

"I DON'T HAVE a team I can spare to send down there."

Mica, torn between relief and frustration, listened as Taylor Jones, the special agent in charge of a task force that technically didn't exist, told her all she needed to hear to report back to her captain. They couldn't send anybody.

That meant they had to rely on good old-fashioned police work. And that meant Mica didn't have to relive the freakiest time of her life . . . right? The hardest. The happiest. The most heartbreaking.

"I've only got three teams, and all of them are out right now. But . . ."

As she heard paper shuffling, the bottom of Mica's stomach dropped out. "But, Jones?"

"Impatient, as ever, aren't you, Ms. Greer? Actually, it's Detective Greer, isn't it?"

"Lieutenant," she corrected. "I'm afraid I've got three murders to solve and one to prevent, Jones. I don't have *time* to be patient. Since you can't help me—"

"I can't send a team. I didn't say I couldn't help." On the other end of the line, Taylor Jones studied a picture. The file had been sitting on his desk for the past week, although he didn't know why he'd had Gina pull it for him. It wasn't as though Colby Mathis was likely to come back to the unit. The man didn't trust himself anymore. Still, Taylor had known he needed to pull that file. That was the extent of any gift he might have, he knew. Just that minor glimmer of knowing.

It wasn't much. But he used what he had.

Absently, he wondered if Mathis had any clue that his former lady had moved to Texas all those years ago. She was only an hour away from him.

An hour. Not much time at all.

Had he been having dreams?

If he had . . .

"A former agent of mine is living not too far from you, Lieutenant. One of my bloodhounds. He may not be able to help you keep the woman from being grabbed, but if he's brought in, you may be able to stop the killer from completing his mission."

"One of your bloodhounds." *Shit.* Mica knew. She just knew.

Her gut twisted, but she couldn't say it was dread that filled her. Her pulse started to race, but she couldn't say it was fear.

"Who is this bloodhound?"

"Just head to the beach in Galveston. You'll find him. Or he'll find you."

Then, before she could try to demand any more information, Taylor Jones hung up on her.

Swearing, she lowered the phone and glared at it. "This isn't happening."

But even as she tried to convince herself otherwise, she knew better. And her heart continued to race . . . with anticipation.

IT HAD BEEN one bad, seriously bad week.

Three days has passed since that first episode, and each day, Colby had been hit with another one.

Yeah. A bad week. Screwed up six different ways to Sunday, and Colby knew it wasn't going to get any better. Then the dreams started. Nothing psychic—just shit where he screwed up. Again. And again. And again. But they weren't going away. He could have dealt with that. Either dealt with it or drowned the damn dreams out with alcohol; he was fine either way.

Those heavy, pressing attacks were another story. Sneaking in to wrap greedy fingers around his heart and soul, sucking the life out of him, whispering to him of death and pain.

You're not done, his conscience tried to tell him as he pushed through the door of the bookstore. *You're not finished and you know it.*

The hell I'm not. He wasn't risking it again—wasn't risking that he'd cost somebody their life. He was done, very, very much done. All he had to do was wait until the dreams went away, and they would.

Somebody else could answer this call. The only damn calls he took anymore were the ones in the store. He'd be taking plenty of *those* today, but that was it. He had to work, and he needed to think about that, about the store and all the shit he still needed to learn there. Not about vague dreams and anxiety attacks—

"Colby."

He met his dad's gaze. Those blue eyes, so like his own, held a look that made the bottom of Colby's stomach fall out. "Yeah?"

"You had a call."

"Did I?"

In response, his dad nodded to a slip of paper lying on the counter. There was a sand dollar on it, acting as a paperweight. Blood roared in Colby's ears as he read the message. *You'll be getting a visitor today, I think. Sorry, Mathis. She needs help. Instinct says it's you that can help her.*

There was no name, but it wasn't necessary. He already knew who it was from, and the longer he stared at it, the louder the roaring in his ears became. Finally, he slanted a look at his father. "Jones."

"Yes." His father lowered his gaze to the glasses he held, polishing them absently on his shirt. "I suppose you wish I hadn't taken the message."

"Nah. You're too polite for that." He made himself smile.

"This visitor, I suppose she's going to come here."

Now Colby looked at his dad. "I guess she will. But I'm not going to be here. I can't help anybody, Dad. It's no good."

He turned around and left.

THE BEACH.

Mica would find him at the beach.

Even though she wanted to pretend it was *anybody* else, Colby Mathis was the one she'd find at the beach. She knew it in her gut.

In her bones. In her heart. As she climbed out of her car, she wished she'd remembered to get that haircut she'd been putting off. Wished she'd thought to put on makeup. Wished she'd put on something other than the serviceable jacket and trousers she wore. Wished she'd look halfway . . . well, *nice* when she saw him again.

And even as she wished all of those things, she wanted to kick herself. She was here about murder. How she looked shouldn't matter at all.

"Okay," she muttered to herself as she studied the beach. "Where to now?"

The beach was a pretty damn vague destination. He could be anywhere. Yet she found herself heading up the coast—not aimlessly, either. Almost like she was being pulled that way. The longer she walked, the more excited she got, too. The faster her heart raced, the hotter she felt. And it had nothing to do with the June sunshine beating down overhead.

Her breath hitched in her throat as she neared a bend and she knew.

He was there.

And then she rounded it and she saw a figure standing on the edge of the beach.

"Oh, hell."

chapter three

The dread he'd been feeling all day had finally eased up a little.

Colby wanted to think he'd managed to avoid whatever in the hell was out there trying to call him. But while the dread was gone . . . other things weren't. His heart continued to race like he was out running in a fucking marathon. His mind was crowded with whispers. *You can't outrun it, you can't outrun it, you can't, you can't, you can't—*

He would have done damn near anything to stifle those damned voices. *Anything.*

And then, abruptly, everything went silent.

Like the calm before the storm.

Even before he turned his head and saw her, he knew. Some part of him did, at least. He didn't even know if he could claim it was any sort of psychic knowledge. Certain things, people didn't *need* true psychic skill to know—just instinct—and this was probably every bit as much instinct as anything else. The instinct that trouble was coming his way.

Trouble . . . five feet nine inches of trouble and most of it was leg. Black hair was pulled back in a braid so tight he wouldn't have known it was curly. Except he had spent many, many hours with his hands fisted in those curls. She hated them . . . He'd always loved them. Her eyes, a deep, strange shade of blue violet, so much darker than his own, were hidden by sunglasses, and he could only imagine the derision he'd see there. And it would be there. He knew it just by the sight of the slight sneer on her pretty face.

Mica Greer had never much cared for psychics. Strange, considering she *was* one. Or maybe not so strange, he supposed. Denial wasn't just a river in Egypt and all that.

Mica's gift, like his own, had been unstable. Unlike him, she hadn't learned to stabilize it through practice alone. She'd needed a partner, and she'd turned out to make a damn good anchor. For a while, the two of them had worked together in training. Her gift had grown, bloomed . . . as had some crazy thing between them.

Then she'd decided she didn't want all the "crazy shit" in her life.

She pulled out. Not just out of the unit, but out of the FBI altogether.

And from him—

Don't go there, he thought. Blowing out a breath, he shifted his attention back to the ocean, trying to reach for some inner peace. It wasn't going to come, though, and he knew it. If she was here, on top of the insane coming at him, then it was for a reason.

I can always pretend she's here because, after all this time, she realizes she's still in love with me. He laughed deprecatingly. Yeah, like that was going to happen. Fifteen years . . . fifteen fucking years. How had those years slipped away from him like that?

She came to a stop next to him, standing almost shoulder to shoulder with him. He waited for her to say something, but it didn't happen. Of course, he'd also waited for her to come back to him . . . that hadn't happened, either. After a while, he'd stopped waiting. But he'd never stopped wishing. Never stopping wanting, either.

The waves crashed against the sand just a few inches from his feet, and he stooped down, raked his fingers through the wet, watched as it filled back up in eddies and swirls before another wave came. Mica remained silent at his back.

He could feel her turmoil, if he let himself. Even without lowering his shields. All he had to do was concentrate . . . and there.

There it was. She didn't want to be here, she worried about whether or not his gift had gotten stronger, whether or not he could pick anything up from her and damn it—why did he . . . ?

He smiled a little as her thoughts tumbled to a stop, almost like she'd sensed him. "You never did learn to stop projecting so loudly," he said softly.

"You never did learn to mind your own business," she snapped.

He shrugged. "I can't help that I hear people shouting at me from the next room. You don't like it . . ." He slanted a look at her through his lashes. "Don't shout. You can tone your thoughts down. You learned how."

Yeah, she'd learned how. But back then, he hadn't been quite as good at picking up random thoughts, or even direct thoughts. Not that Colby was going to point that out to her.

Mica curled her lip at him. He hated that he still found that so fucking appealing, hated that he wanted to reach up and tumble her down into the sand next to him and strip her naked. So what if doing the dirty in the sand got grit in sensitive places? The ocean was right there if they wanted to clean up after. And his house wasn't too far away.

It was a strong enough impulse that he could even see himself doing just that, and somehow, he doubted she'd resist him if he gave it a try. Her breathing kicked up as she stared at him. No. She wouldn't resist. Not at all.

With a heated curse, he tore his eyes away.

"Whatever you want, Mica, I can't help you. Go away."

"You don't know what I want."

He thought of the blood-splattered images, of terror and death. The fear, the darkness that hung over him like a cloud. "I know enough," he said softly.

A shadow fell across him and he braced himself as she crouched down beside him. She was still a few inches away, but closer . . . damn it, too close.

"You're not with the unit anymore."

"No." He continued to play with the sand. Better to do that than reach for her, he decided. And he was so damn tempted to reach.

"Since when?"

"Almost two years ago." Okay, playing with the sand wasn't going to cut it if she was going to sit there and chitchat. He swished his hand through the next wave to get the grit off and rose.

"You aren't here to chat about old times, what I've been up to in the past fifteen years." *Ever since you walked out on us.* He kept that last bit trapped behind his teeth. It didn't matter anymore—*they* didn't matter because *they* didn't exist. "I've already told you that I can't help you with whatever the trouble is."

"You don't know that," she bit off.

"Yeah. I do. Because I *won't.*" He went to push past her—he had to get away from her. Had to get away from here.

But Mica wasn't going to let it go that easily. She caught his arm and that touch almost froze him. Her bare hand on his arm—the shock rippled through him. Memories raged. *Their* memories. Not just his. Blood roared in his ears and a fog of need and want, and a love she'd walked away from, rose inside him . . . For the briefest moment, it drowned out everything.

It faded too soon, and now, it wasn't memories that blinded him.

It was a bloodless massacre.

She'd lowered her shields and now she wasn't making *any* attempt to silence her thoughts or memories.

These were recent memories.

Staring through her eyes, he could see it all in vivid Technicolor—everything, from the toes of her boots to the way her bangs kept falling in her eyes . . . and the way her eyes tracked over the still body lying tied on the ground.

There was very little blood—disturbing, because the victim was covered head to toe in cuts.

Cleaned her up as he went—

This isn't done—

I need to find it. No, *not find, I know where it is—just like I knew this would happen . . .* fuck!

As her thoughts became louder and louder, Colby pulled back, breaking the physical connection and putting distance between them. It cut the line between them, but he couldn't do a damn thing about what he'd seen.

He'd seen worse deaths. There were always worse. But just because he'd seen worse didn't make it any easier to view that through Mica's memory. Hissing out a breath, he spun away. "What in the hell do you want?"

"I need your help."

"You're picking up on something—figure it out on your own."

He heard the soft, broken sound of her sigh—the utter defeat in it. It wasn't what he'd expected. He expected her to deny it. To fight it. Something. "I can't. I'm . . . I'm not good enough, Colby. I left before I could let myself get good enough. I can't control it and it's easier to just . . ."

"Hide?"

She stared back at him levelly. "Yes."

"And that's my problem . . . how?" He slanted a narrow look at her.

"It's not *your* problem. I wasn't equipped to deal with what was happening to me, especially once they paired me with you."

He curled his lip. Better to let her see his anger than to show the pain. "So it's all my fault."

"No." She took a step toward him. "It's mine. But our problems aside . . ." She looked at the file she held. He hadn't noticed it before then, so fixated on her, so fixated on everything raging inside him. But now it was like a lure, a bespelled one. He couldn't take his eyes away from it.

Shit. Shit. Shit—*I can't do this . . .*

She opened the file and handed him a picture. The moment he touched it, he was assaulted with images of bright flashes of illuminating the darkness, the low, sensual throb of music—eyes gliding all over the woman as she danced.

"She was a dancer," he said gruffly. "She stripped."

He didn't notice the way Mica's lashes flickered, the tightening around her eyes. The scene deepened for him. Excitement—she felt excitement. It was a lot of money, an easy hour. She could pay off some bills and go shopping . . .

Just barely, he resisted the urge to crumple the picture in his fist. Through his lashes, he stared at Mica.

She stared back, her gaze level. "I walked out on you. Screw walking away from the agency. If I didn't want to work with Jones, then I didn't have to, that was my call. But I walked away from you because I couldn't handle how much things changed when we used our gifts together. I just wasn't strong enough. I felt like a coward because of it, and I couldn't be around you and not feel weak, stupid. So I left." Now she lowered her gaze down to the picture he still held. "You want to hate me for that? Go ahead. Be angry? Feel free. You don't owe *me* anything. But there's at least one more woman who'll die. I know it. I *feel* it, and I don't know if that's because of my . . . ability, or if it's just instinct. But I'm right. As far as the investigation is going? We're drawing blanks. Another woman will die without help—and she hasn't done a damn thing wrong."

Colby took the file from her hand and tucked the picture back inside. He couldn't hold it another second. Not right now. Then, with his gaze out on the water, he held the file back, waited for her to take it.

It took her a few seconds, and from the corner of his eye, he saw the slight tremble in her hands. "Damn it, Colby . . ."

He said softly, "I'll help."

He didn't have much choice now.

He'd seen the dead woman's face—not through Mica's memories, either. That, maybe, he could have walked away from.

But the woman had been happy . . . had been excited about a job, excited about going shopping. About life. She'd been happy and somebody had stolen that from her.

She was his now. He couldn't walk away without at least trying to stop the monster responsible for turning that happiness into horror.

chapter four

How had this happened?

Colby Mathis stood inside a hotel room, the cool air blowing over his skin, his eyes adjusting to the bright lights and his head still spinning.

He was in fucking Pasadena with Mica Greer.

Mica—a lieutenant in the police department. Working a nasty couple of homicides and she wanted his help.

His help.

After all this time . . .

"Shit."

"Everything okay, Mathis?"

Mathis. Apparently sometime in the last fifteen years, she'd forgotten that he had a given name. He shot her a narrow look over his shoulder and stormed into the hotel room. "Everything is just roses, Lieutenant Greer," he said, not bothering to keep the edge out of his voice.

He had to do this again. Damn it. It filled him with terror. What if he fucked it up? What if he was wrong again? What if somebody—

A hand touched his shoulder. "What's wrong, Colby?"

"Nothing." Carefully, he moved away. That light touch, even though it wasn't her bare skin on his, was way too much. She couldn't touch him right now. He needed to get focused first. Get focused, get grounded . . . make sure he wasn't going to have a mental breakdown—

It would help if you'd stop being such a damned coward. That voice, cool and deprecating, managed to cut through the fog that tried to overwhelm him. *You've done this work before and you didn't fall apart. You've done it solo and you've been fine. You can do this again.*

He closed his eyes as a mental battle started to rage inside him. *And if I fuck it up, then what?*

Then somebody dies. But if you go by what Mica is picking up, then somebody is going to die anyway. At least if you try, there is a chance to stop it. Are you going to be a coward, or what?

Blowing out a breath, he opened his eyes and realized he was standing on the balcony. He barely remembered entering the hotel room, much less coming out here. Sucking in a deep draught of hot summer air, he shoved aside the doubts and worries and fears. They'd eat him alive if he wasn't careful. Hell, they were already trying to do that. Inner demons were a bitch to deal with.

Turning, he saw that Mica was standing just a few feet away, eying him warily. Her lovely, midnight eyes were unreadable, but he still had a good idea what she was thinking. Just then, it had something to do with his sanity and whether or not he could handle this case. He had a feeling she was also considering a call to Taylor Jones.

You and me both, sugar.

"I need to see where they were found," he said, forcing the words out through a throat gone tight with nerves, need, and fear. *Focus on the job—do that, and don't think about anything else.* "Also, I need to see the reports, evidence, everything you can give me."

Mica cocked a brow. "I'll see what I can do on evidence. I can probably get some—"

"All." He strode to the bed and dumped the duffel bag he had yet to set down. "I can't help if I'm working totally blind."

She blew out a slow breath. "Look, Mathis, I'll do what I can, but these guys aren't used to working with . . . your type."

My type? For some reason, that made him smile and managed to ease some of the tension inside him. *My type—just what is my type? Psychic? Psychotic? Or maybe just neurotic.* All three probably applied just fine, really.

Still smiling, he slanted a look at Mica. "They work with you."

Her mouth tightened.

"Now isn't that a surprise." With a wry grin, he shifted his attention back to unpacking. Not that it took a lot of attention, but it was easier to look at his clothes than it was to look at her. "They don't know, do they?"

"There's nothing for them to *know*."

"Uh-huh. And how do you explain it when you manage to figure things out ten steps before the rest of them? Good instincts? You're just smarter than the rest of them?" He pulled out jeans, socks, underwear, and T-shirts, dumping them in a haphazard pile on the bed. "Bet that wins you a lot of friends."

When she didn't answer, he glanced back over at her. "You can't hide what you are. What you do."

"There isn't anything to hide," she snapped, and her eyes flashed blue fire.

"You don't believe that."

Not entirely. He could feel that much. It was complicated—very complicated. Narrowing his eyes, he studied her and waited.

She opened her mouth, then snapped it closed, shaking her head. "I'm not *like* the rest of you, Colby. I wasn't as strong after I left. And I never could make it work the way you all could. I had to have a partner, had to have help. Shit, even *you* managed to make it work without a partner. I never could. After I left, things just . . . fell apart."

With a sigh, she tucked a stray lock of hair behind her ear, moving to stand near the window, staring out over the paved expanse of parking lot. "There's nothing to explain to anybody."

"So you don't have an unusual knack for solving things? Making weird calls that the others can't quite understand?"

Under the light jacket she wore, he could see the way her shoulders tensed, the way her spine went rigid.

"So you're still hiding," he said softly. Gathering up his clothes, he moved to the dresser and dumped them in there. He slid it closed, but instead of turning around, he rested his hands on the dresser. A mirror hung over it and he could see Mica's profile, averted as she stared out the glass. "Fifteen years of hiding what you are, Mica. Doesn't that get old?"

She cut him a dark glare. "I'm not *hiding*. I just can't use what I have the way you all did. And I can't *cope*. I'm not made the way you all are, Colby. I'm not good enough—not strong enough for it, I guess. This way, I can still help, but I won't lose my mind. I'm sorry if that's not what you wanted to hear. But it's the best I got."

"The best you got." He sighed. Shoving away from the dresser, he cut a wide berth around her—as wide as the small hotel room would allow, at least. "At least you can admit it. More than I can do."

"Colby?"

He ignored her. He needed air. He needed to walk. Clear his head. "Get me those records, Lieutenant."

"Damn it—"

He shut the door. The rest of her voice was muffled, and the farther he got from the hotel room, the fainter her voice. He ducked into the stairwell just as he heard the door to his room open.

TWO HOURS LATER, Mica was still brewing over the fact that he'd walked out on her. *Walked out*. In the middle of a fucking conversation. And just demanded she show him whatever, like it was that easy—

"Make sure he gets whatever he needs to help."

Mica slanted a look at her boss over her desk. "I'm sorry, Captain. I was . . ."

The captain waved a hand. "You've been pulling crazy hours. The agent—I was asking about him. I just want you to make sure he has everything he needs to do . . ." She grimaced and wiggled her fingers. "His thing."

"His thing?" Mica echoed. Then she wondered why she was surprised. Of course the captain was going to want Colby to have what he needed—if for no other reason than because fate would demand she look silly for arguing with him earlier. *Now you're being paranoid,* she told herself as she signed the paperwork needed to make his consultation on the case official. Handing it over to the captain, she said, "He hasn't signed this yet, but I'll take it to him later."

"Hmm." Kellogg looked it over. "Just ask him to keep things quiet. I'd rather people not know I asked a psychic to consult on this."

Mica resisted the urge to fidget. *Don't want people knowing, do you?* Not that it was a surprise. There were certain people in the world who didn't blink at the idea of psychic ability. Certain professions where it wouldn't necessarily incite laughter and sneers. Being a cop wasn't one of those.

And wasn't it just sheer irony and utter hypocrisy that Mica felt pissed over the fact that the captain wanted to hide Colby's presence? Feeling the weight of an intense gaze, she looked up.

The captain was watching her. "That piss you off?"

"No reason why it should," she said. A nonanswer was the best. If she didn't say anything, she wouldn't give herself away.

Kellogg smirked. Propping an elbow on the arm of the chair,

she said, "No reason it should piss you off, hmmm? You do realize that I'm aware of the connection you have with the FBI, right?"

The knowledge glinting in the captain's gaze didn't do much to ease the tension ratcheting inside Mica. She rested a hand on the desk, just barely managed to keep from curling it into a fist. "There's not much of a connection there, Captain. I briefly entertained the idea of joining the FBI."

"Yes . . . started the training and everything." Kellogg straightened in her chair and leaned forward, her dark eyes unreadable. "I know about SAC Jones. I have . . . contacts, you could say."

"Contacts."

"Yes." She shifted in the chair, crossing her legs and smoothing a hand down a skirt that cost more than Mica made in a month. "And I won't deny the fact that I wasn't at all bothered by the connection you have to his unit."

"I don't *have* a connection to him, to his unit, and barely the sketchiest connection to the FBI," Mica snapped. She didn't like the direction this conversation was headed. Not at all. As a matter of fact, it was well past the point where she was pissed off and veering into *explosive* territory.

"Sure you do. Just like you have a connection to me."

"I *work* for you. I don't work for him, and I never did. I *would* have, if I'd stayed."

"Still a connection," Kellogg said. "And while I can understand your displeasure, you can simmer down—you're here because you're a damn good cop. You stay because you're a damn good cop. The fact that I'm not opposed to using any weapons at my disposal bothers you, and I understand that. But I'm pretty damn bothered by murder and I know you are, too. We all suspect he's not done." Her eyes narrowed on Mica's, and for a moment, neither of them spoke. Then, finally, the captain said, "But you don't suspect, do you?"

In the moment, Mica felt stripped bare. She knew. Damn it, the captain knew.

Kellogg cocked a brow. "I know my cops, Greer. I know their strengths, their weaknesses."

My weaknesses? She fought the urge to laugh hysterically. What Kellogg probably thought was a *strength* was actually Mica's biggest weakness. She was a failure, a fraud. Swallowing the bubble that likely blocked that hysterical giggle, she asked quietly, "Is there a point to this?"

Her hands were sweating. She did her damnedest to keep it nonchalant as she pulled them off the desk and swiped them across her trousers.

"I just want you aware of that. I know my cops. And I also want you aware of the fact that you have my okay to show the agent whatever he needs to see." Kellogg stood up.

Her okay. As she stood there, Mica thought about how helpless she felt, how useless . . . and then she thought of how calmly Colby had told her to get that information, how easily Kellogg was about turning it over.

Maybe it was petty of her. Mica didn't care. As Kellogg strode toward the door, she called out, "He's not an agent."

Kellogg paused, looking back at Mica with narrowed eyes. "Excuse me?"

Mica jerked a shoulder shrug. "You kept assuming. I called Jones and he said he couldn't spare anybody to send, but he did know of a former agent in the area." She gave the captain a what-can-you-do look and shrugged. "It was the best he could offer."

"So we have a psychic. A former agent." Kellogg rolled that around, obviously not pleased with the information.

Mica supposed she could have mentioned it earlier, or found a more diplomatic way to deliver it. This worked for her, though.

"Why is he a former agent?"

Now Mica had wondered that more than once herself. But all she did was shrug. She couldn't answer that question because she hadn't asked—getting personal with Colby Mathis wasn't what she needed to do. *Ever.* "That's kind of his business, I figure. But Jones wouldn't have pointed me in his direction if he couldn't do the job."

That elicited a grunt. Then, without saying another word, Kellogg was gone.

THIS WASN'T WHERE she had died.

This was where she had danced.

Danced under hot, bright lights for too little money, and sometimes, the men had gotten a little grabby. But she'd had dreams of something bigger. Something better. She hadn't been angry about her life . . . she'd been excited.

In front of the squat, simple building, Colby waited. Patiently, he untangled all the lines tugging on him and focused on the one he needed. It took longer than he'd like. He was out of practice, he didn't have a decent anchor, but in the end, he let the woman be the anchor. He let *her* pull him in and steady him, this woman who had died too soon.

Head bent, eyes closed, hands jammed into his pockets, he stood there and worked a puzzle he could see only in his mind. A hundred, a thousand writhing lines, all pointing toward him and ending in a snarled mass.

But *her* line flared hotter, brighter. Her soul. Her life . . . and her death.

Finally, he had a good enough grasp on it to separate himself and open his eyes. Although there wasn't much to look at. Shades shielded his eyes from the white-hot brilliance of the sun as he studied the strip joint.

The bright sunlight didn't do a damn thing for the place. Except to highlight how tawdry it looked, maybe.

It was made of cinder block and painted white. Not exactly a dive. A few steps up. The woman hadn't been totally down about working here, but she'd had dreams of dancing someplace better. She'd been happy when she left here.

Alive.

Yeah, Colby could already feel that much. She'd been alive when she left here.

But for how long?

Had her killer found her through here or had he already known her?

Once more, Colby closed his eyes and let those emotions wrap tighter and tighter around him, pulling him deeper and deeper. He heard the echo of the music she'd danced to, the whisper of her voice, a young, girlishly high voice as she told her boss she couldn't work late. He felt her excitement, heard her wondering if she should have gotten her hair done, a fresh manicure.

There was a vague sense of disquiet as she started to walk—her legs were tired and the heels were killing her feet, but she ignored it. Part of the job, part of what she did. If she got this job, she could get better shoes and her feet wouldn't hurt so much—

His heartbeat kicked as he sensed the exact moment her excitement started to change. When happiness trembled and then stopped. When the fear bloomed.

And as much as he hated it, that was what he needed. Her excitement and her nerves might tug at him, but her fear, it would guide him and suck him straight in—it was the strongest anchor he could hope for.

Without hesitation, Colby grabbed it, pulled it closer.

He heard a low voice—it reeked with evil, but Colby couldn't describe anything beyond that. Young, old, male, female, who knew.

Instinctively, as it always did, his mind tried to jerk away from the fear, but he refused to let it.

He didn't know how long he stood there, but it had probably been a while. When he opened his eyes, he had an idea which way he needed to go, which way he needed to walk. Sweat was trickling down his spine and running into his eyes, but he didn't pay it any attention. He'd dealt with worse than the Texas sun before. As he started to walk, he slid the backpack off his shoulder and pulled a bottle of water out of it.

Colby didn't know how long this would take.

It could take five minutes. Or five hours.

Experience told him it would probably be somewhere in between.

The line in his gut pulled him in a slow, drawn-out ramble from the strip joint, heading west. The route meandered, up and down streets, through alleys, back and forth. What could have taken a few minutes to drive took him hours as he followed that slowly unfurling line.

And every step made the hum in his head grow louder.

By the time he stopped, that hum was a scream.

He found himself standing in front of a towering crumble of a warehouse. It took up most of a city block and half the windows were busted. Graffiti appeared here and there in random spots. It didn't look like anything had been done to clean it up, although considering the area, that wasn't a big surprise. This wasn't exactly prime real estate. Some of the gaping squares were boarded over. Others weren't and those empty holes seemed like eyes, staring at him.

The entire place felt of death.

Here.

She had died here.

She had died with her screams trapped in her mind, because she hadn't had the breath to voice them. She'd died in pain and terror, choking on it.

Closing his eyes, he fought his way past those screams to find *something*—something that would help. Something that could end this. He stood there, lost in the moments of her death, his lungs aching, his throat burning.

There was an echo of pain that danced all along his body, and if he'd been able to think it through just then, he would have realized it was probably related to the dozens and dozens of shallow cuts all over her body.

There had been the rasp of a rough towel as her killer had soaked up the blood, the glint of madness in his eyes as he crouched over her.

Look at him closer, sweetheart, Colby thought. He needed to see better. Needed to see the man's face.

But all he could clearly make out were the eyes. The eyes of a man who knew he was insane . . . and didn't care.

In the back of his mind, Colby could hear a voice. A man.

He was singing.

Singing.

"*Would you dance . . . if I asked you to dance . . .*"

"THERE'S SOMEBODY STANDING outside the warehouse."

Mica looked up at her partner as she stuffed the files into her workbag. "Huh?"

"Where the latest victim was found. A couple of uniforms were doing a drive-by and they saw him. He's just standing there." Phillips flipped his phone around and showed it to her.

But even before she saw the lousy image, she knew. Mentally, she swore. *Okay, Captain, and how do we keep it quiet* now*?*

She kept her face blank as she peered at the image. "Don't worry about it. He's a friend of mine—I've asked him to consult on the case with me."

"The captain know about that?" Phillips studied her with a narrow look.

"I told her I'd be exploring a couple of avenues."

"And you didn't bother to fill me in?" He took a step closer to her, lowering his voice. Disgust and irritation darkened his eyes.

Of course, that wasn't all that different from any other day, she knew. Phillips lived to be pissed off at the world in general. And he reserved a special level of *pissy* for her. Refusing to let him get to her, she calmly said, "Right now, there's nothing to fill in but a big blank. This could be a dead end. He hasn't given me anything and I don't know if he will." *Liar.*

He crowded into her space. "That isn't how this works, damn it. What you know, I know, got it?"

"You want to take a step back there, Phillips?" she suggested, her voice mild.

He didn't. He loomed closer, his eyes level with hers as he demanded, "What's going on, Greer? You're keeping me in the dark more and more, and it's pissing me off."

With a vague smile, she eased away, forcing some distance between them. She could finish the damn case with him, damn it. Finish it, and then talk to the captain. If that didn't do it, she'd put in for a transfer. She hadn't been overly thrilled when the department stuck her with Phillips. He'd been bounced from just about every other member of the squad, and if he didn't stick with her, the captain would have more problems on her hands as she figured out what to do with him.

That wasn't Mica's problem, either. She didn't care. She just plain didn't care.

"You going to answer me?" he demanded. "What in the hell is going on?"

"Right now, nothing. This probably isn't going to add up to much," she lied baldly. "If it does, I'll bring you in. But for now, no reason for both of us waste to our time."

He wasn't buying it. She could see it in his eyes.

Yet one more thing she didn't care about. Riffling through the files, she pulled out the one that had been their priority for tomorrow. "Why don't you head back to her work, see if you can't find anybody she talked to that last day? Somebody had to know *something.*"

He took the file but lingered there a moment, tapping it against his leg as he studied her. "We're supposed to be a team, right? We work it together. Not I take off this way, you take off that way."

"Except when that's the best way to do it," she said easily. Then she pushed around him, hefting the strap of her bag over her shoulder. She didn't have time for this. Besides, she wasn't quite ready to share Colby's abilities with the biggest asshole in the squad—talk about potentially compromising the case.

She could just see it now—"Supposed Psychic Hired to Help Find the Surgeon."

If that happened, the shit would hit the fan, and no telling how their killer would react.

chapter five

Would you dance . . . if I asked you to dance . . .

If I asked you to dance . . .

Dance . . .

Dance . . .

The vision of bright lights, the flash of the woman as she strutted across the stage whirled through his mind, over and over.

Would you dance . . .

Colby couldn't find any respite from it, no matter what he did.

Would you cry . . .

He saw the first victim. Bound, bloodied, brutalized, her mouth open in a silent, traumatized scream, revealing the bloody stump of her tongue.

She wouldn't have been able to cry anymore, Colby knew.

The second victim had fought, and she would have screamed long and loud. The broken, discordant tunes of the song bumped around in his head without truly connecting.

The first victim—he'd cut out her tongue.

The second—he'd taken her hands.

Which had killed them, he wondered? The shock, the blood loss? They'd been alive when he mutilated them.

Would you dance . . .

"Colby."

He managed, just barely, to keep from flinching. The sound of Mica's voice was an interruption but a welcome one—it pulled him from the blood and despair. Slowly, he turned and watched as she came striding across the busted-up pavement of the parking lot, the worn heels of the boots she wore crunching over the gravel, busted glass, and cigarette butts.

Without saying anything, he turned his attention back to the warehouse.

The broken chords of music still sounded in his mind, but they were faint now.

She came to a stop next to him, standing almost shoulder to shoulder. Although the summer sun was still burning white-hot, she wore a light jacket to cover the weapon at her side. The wind teased the ends of her ebony hair, and he found himself thinking of a time when he'd had the liberty to do the same thing, toy with her hair, maybe curl his hand around her neck and pull her close.

Not anymore.

It had been a long, long time since he'd had the freedom to touch her as he wanted.

That really sucked.

If he had that freedom, he'd . . .

"What are you doing here?" Mica asked.

The fantasy shattered before it barely had time to form. *Figures,* he thought sourly. He could have used a few seconds lost in a hot daydream after spending an eternity trapped in a nightmare of death.

"This is where she died." He shrugged, letting it go at that. There wasn't much of anything else to say beyond that as far as he was concerned. The victim had died here—was it really any surprise to Mica that she'd found him here? He doubted it.

The victim's soul, her spirit might cling to this spot the longest. And it was possible that she'd already moved on. But her emotions would linger, and that was what he needed.

Those emotions, and the ability to tap deeper into them.

"Guess I should have figured you'd find it," Mica said softly.

"Yeah. Probably." From the corner of his eye, he could see her measuring stare.

He knew what she'd ask before she even asked it. "Have you found anything?"

He closed his eyes, once more letting his mind drift to the sound of that hypnotic voice, the discordant little tune. "He sings to them."

Mica stiffened.

Slanting a look at him, she asked levelly, "What do you mean, he *sings* to them?"

"Just that. I don't have all of it yet, don't know if it's anything other than toying with them."

He slid her a look and watched as she grimaced, saw it when the wheels began to spin inside her head. "What song?" she demanded.

Colby lifted a brow. "I just said, I don't have it all yet. Just a line here or there, and frankly, pop music isn't my thing. I'll figure it out."

"Sing it to me."

Colby just stared at her.

She glared at him and then turned away, started to pace. "So is he, like, trying to serenade them or what?"

He watched her, vaguely aware of the soft mutter of her thoughts pressing against his shields. After a moment, Mica shook her head. "No. That doesn't feel right."

"He's not serenading them. Not exactly," he said quietly, shifting his gaze back to the building, the pull of death tugging at him once more. *Would you dance . . .* He jerked himself away, forced his mind to focus on the moment, on Mica. It wasn't as easy to separate himself as it had once been. Wasn't as easy to do this shit solo, without any anchor at all—the darkness wanted to suck him under. "It's not a serenade and this isn't a seduction thing for him.

He doesn't *want* these women. He wants something, but it's not them."

Colby closed his eyes again, tried to tune in more on that song without letting it pull him completely in. It danced in his mind, moving further and further out of reach now. Unless he went deeper . . . Sighing, he turned away and met Mica's eyes full-on. He saw the intense focus there, the determination.

He saw the frustration as he said, "That's it. I'm done for now."

"Done?" She shot a look between the warehouse and him. "What do you mean, you're done? I need to know more about the singing. What are the words? Do you know the tune?"

"Just a line or two. I'll figure it out after I have a minute at my laptop." Colby shrugged and started to walk. He had to pause a minute and think—which direction had he come from? Instinct had led him here, but it wasn't going to do a damn thing to get him back to the hotel. And he needed to get back. Soon. Now that he'd cut the tether between him and the mess that had pulled him here, he was teetering close to a mental crash.

"Damn it, Colby."

He looked back, lifting a brow as Mica came storming toward him. "Yeah?"

"Are you listening to me?"

He rubbed the back of his hand over his mouth as his head started to roar. "Ahhh. No. I guess I wasn't. Not intentional."

Hotel. Food. Bed. He placed one foot in front of the other. Five steps. Ten steps. The roaring in his head got louder, his vision spun until it felt like *he* was spinning. Okay. Maybe reevaluate. Food. Then cab. Then hotel. Then bed. As the roaring turned into a deafening cacophony, the summer sun beat down on him with brutal intensity, and he swallowed, feeling his stomach churn. There was nothing in it but water.

Still, he felt like he was going to puke—

Mica's hand gripped his arm. "Shit, it still hits you this hard?"

"Don't worry about it," he said brusquely, pulling back. No. It didn't *still* hit him this hard. When he wasn't following the trail of something, he was just fine. When he had a partner to anchor him, he was fine. But on his own, it was still tricky. And he was out of practice. Psychic skill wasn't any different than any other gift—if you didn't train it, it got harder to control, harder to manage.

He shrugged her hand off and got back to walking, digging the phone out of his pocket. Up ahead, he could barely make out the familiar yellow arches of a McDonald's. The cab could pick him up there—where was *there*, though?

"Colby, if you walk away from me one more time, I swear, I'm decking you."

He sighed as Mica planted herself, all five feet nine inches, in front of him, a hot light glinting in her eyes. Shoving his hand back through his hair, he looked away. "Damn it, what do you *want*, Mica?"

"You're not walking," she said quietly. "And you're not going back to the hotel where you'll just drop, either." She held out a hand.

Eying her palm with distrusting eyes, he flicked her a quick look. "What—you going to smack my hand, now?"

"No. I'm getting you food. And then I'm getting you to bed."

Even the thought of that made her belly ache, Mica realized. Getting him to bed. *Alone!* she insisted. *Alone.* Not exactly how she wanted things and it didn't help the way he was watching her. It was a sleepy, lambent look from under his lashes, and she couldn't help but think of the times when he'd looked at her in just that way after they'd spent some time tearing up the sheets.

Although the memories really shouldn't be clear, so vivid in her mind. Not after all this time.

Hell, she shouldn't be thinking sex at all when she looked at him. Not now. *Stupid, stupid, stupid*—

Until he'd swayed on his feet, she hadn't realized he'd been caught under the crashing weight as the vision ended. It had hit him like that before—before they'd started working together, and when they'd first started trying to figure out how to mesh their abilities. But she'd expected . . . hell.

She guessed she'd expected him to get better about it, because if he was still prone to going through this hell, yet he still kept at it, how much more of a coward did that make her?

Not right now, she told herself, staring at him, at the endless blue of his eyes, at the tumbled, gold-streaked brown hair as it fell into his face, and at the mouth she so desperately wanted to feel against hers. Again. Not just one time, not just for one more night, but . . .

A car drove by, the engine rattling, the music booming from shitty speakers, shattering the moment. Mica dragged her gaze from his and swallowed. "Come on. You need to eat—we both know it. The last thing you need is a two-mile walk back to the hotel."

chapter six

If she'd thought a meal might do a damn thing to break the tension between them, she would have been wrong. But she hadn't been banking on that. There was too much still left between them, things unsaid. Things that should probably *remain* that way.

If she was wise. Because if she started saying all the things that were still unsaid, she'd probably start wishing she could do the things that were still undone—and maybe even the things that *had* been done. Just not recently. Making love with him. Lying in the bed next to him and listening to him breathe as he played with her hair. Laughing with him, talking with him . . . and before it had gotten to be too much, even working with him. Just *being* with him.

Yeah, she didn't need to start thinking about all of that, and if she spent too much time with him, she would. She needed to be smart. Except she knew she couldn't be. She'd thought she'd been smart all those years ago when she ran from something that overwhelmed her.

Since then, she'd spent years regretting it.

Years . . . years regretting the one decision she'd thought she *had* to make, listened to what she'd thought was the voice of reason. Since then, she'd asked herself more times than she could recall if she hadn't made a mistake. And now . . . she just didn't know. The only thing she did know was that she couldn't leave him yet. Not yet.

She was certain she'd start to question herself any second now. Yet again that voice of reason would rear its ugly head and she'd start to think . . .

But it was strangely silent.

There was no reason for her to go with him, really. Unless she counted the information she had in her workbag. She could have given that to him outside. For that matter, she could give it to him here.

She didn't want to do that, though. He'd look through it. And he needed to rest before he did any more. She could see the dragging exhaustion in his eyes.

If somebody wasn't there to make him put the work aside, he wouldn't do it.

So I could have waited until tomorrow . . .

They didn't have time, though.

No time. They just didn't have time for him to spend the next twelve hours in bed.

You don't want to walk away, you don't want him walking away, and you can't wait until he's gotten the sleep he needs. But with anybody else, you could let them sleep a few hours and then *call. So either admit what you want . . . or just go home and call in six hours.* So now the voice of reason had become the voice of insanity, temptation, and sluthood. The voice was sly, almost gleeful as it added, *Just admit you can't leave yet. You* can't *walk away yet. You need him too much—just do it already.*

Just do it?

Just do what . . . *him*?

Admit what she wanted? Like there had ever been any question of that.

Abruptly, she crashed into Colby's back and realized he'd stopped in front of the door. She mumbled an apology under her breath, looking everywhere but at him. He was looking nowhere *but* her.

She could feel it, that intense, focused stare, all but searing her flesh. Her breath hitched in her lungs and her bones threatened to melt, to turn to water.

"Okay, Mom. You made sure I got home at a decent hour," he drawled. "You can stop worrying now."

Jerking her gaze to his, she made a face at him. Golden brown hair tumbled into his eyes as he stared at her, a sardonic smile on his mouth and that attitude of his should have shattered the moment, should have ruined everything for her.

It didn't.

"Oh, shut up," she muttered, hating how breathless her voice sounded. She sounded like a damn hussy. *He* sounded and looked completely unaffected. Just how fair was that? Shit, what if he *wasn't* affected? What if he . . . *Stop it. You can't do this. Just stop,* she told herself. Hiking her bag up on her shoulder, she stared at him. "Are you going to open the door and let me in?"

"Why?"

I don't know—okay, she couldn't say that. So she fell back on that handy little excuse tucked into her bag. It was also another good excuse to look away from that compelling blue gaze. Damn him. Why did he still have to get to her like this, after all this? And if he did have to get to her like this, then why didn't *she* get to him? Or had he just gotten over her?

Hell, it's been fifteen years . . . Swallowing the knot that formed in her throat, she forced herself to clear her throat, to focus. She had a job to do, right? Except she had one more thing that loomed large in her mind. One crucial thing—*has he gotten over me?*

Riffling through her workbag, she pulled out the file and held it up. "You asked for information. I've got it."

"Then let me have it," he replied, lifting a hand.

"Sure. When you let me come in. There are things about the case you won't find in the reports."

Things I don't need to know yet, Colby thought. He could have mentioned that to her. But he didn't. If there was a day when he was strong enough to walk away from the chance of being alone with Mica Greer, he'd be damned surprised.

He wasn't here just because of a damned job—it was entirely possible he could have worked this case without stepping foot out of his home. It wasn't an option that had occurred to him until he had been driving to Pasadena with Mica, but it *had* been an option. All he'd needed was evidence. Before he'd quit, he'd worked a few cases while being on the other side of the country. No reason he couldn't do this one from an hour away.

If he hadn't cared about being around her, it would have occurred to him sooner.

But he'd needed to be around her again. Needed it like he needed to breathe.

He was here because he hadn't been able to turn her away.

He was here because, in the end, he still loved her.

Wasn't that a damned joke? Damn her anyway. She stood there staring at him, her cheeks pink, her dark, blue violet eyes unreadable, and he could all but feel the need emanating from her. But she'd leave again.

She'd leave because they couldn't be what she wanted. Not together. Damn her. And damn himself, too. Swearing under his breath, he turned to the door. He jerked the keycard from his pocket and swiped it, using a lot more force than the task needed—the same went for the door. He shoved it open, but stupid hotel doors, they were so heavy, it didn't even give him a good smack.

He didn't need this.

He didn't need to look at those reports, not until he'd rested.

He didn't need to be alone in a room with Mica, not after all these years, and not when he still wanted her. Not when he still loved her.

He didn't need her . . . Oh, shit. That was the problem. He *did* need her, but if he was smart, he'd steer clear, stay away from the heartbreak and the pain she'd bring back to his life. It would happen. She couldn't be who she was, not if she was still hiding from it, and even though he wouldn't let himself use his gift anymore, he wouldn't deny what he was. He couldn't live the way she did. He didn't believe in living lies.

But the knowledge didn't keep him from stepping aside and letting her enter. It didn't keep him from taking a deep breath and flooding his head with the scent of her. It didn't keep his body from going on red alert, like somebody had just flipped a switch.

As he watched her saunter into the dim, cool hotel room, he admitted silently that somebody had flipped his switch, all right. The same person who'd flipped it all those years ago.

Jamming his hands into his front pockets, he stared at her. "Okay. Spill."

"Spill?" She turned to look at him, her head cocked. "Just like that?"

"Yes." *Before I lose my damn mind and grab you.*

Mica wasn't in the mood to help him out, though. She bypassed the bed, thank God, and settled herself on the couch, the bag at her side. Her eyes met his and he saw the heat flickering there before she lowered her lashes, shielding it. When she looked back at him, her gaze was once more unreadable. But that one glimpse had been enough to drive him insane.

Or more insane than he already was.

Clearing his throat, he made his way over to the bottled water left on the desk by hotel staff. It would cost him a few bucks—or rather, it would cost the local police, since they would be picking up his tab, but he needed a drink and he needed it now. "Exactly what do you need to tell me, Mica?"

"You need to rest."

"You bully your way in here to tell me that?" He slanted a look at her over his shoulder. "Not exactly groundbreaking news."

She sighed and rubbed her hands over her face. "You can't give me your best if you're dragging. And I need your best."

"You'll get it." Granted, his best pretty much sucked, but he'd give it to her. Twisting the bottle open, he took a deep, long drink and then lowered it, watching her with a lifted brow. "Now that you've assured yourself of that, why don't you give me whatever information you have and then head on out?"

Her brows dropped low over her eyes. "What bug crawled up your ass?"

"Well, you already pointed out that I need to rest. I'm *tired*, Mica," he drawled. *Tired. Horny. Going out of my mind, and just looking at you makes it worse . . .* How had fifteen years passed without this changing? It was like it had been all those years ago—like the time between them hadn't changed at all.

But he couldn't let her know. So he gave her a cool smile as he continued, "I'm dog tired and it's not going to get any easier until we put this thing to bed, so I want to sleep before I totally immerse myself in it."

He did look tired. It was there in the slump of his shoulders, in the strain in his voice.

Mica really should just leave.

Instead, she found herself curling her lip at him in a sneer. "You know, I haven't had more than a handful of hours to sleep each night since this started, and I've been working it, on top of my other cases, for weeks. They make it so fucking easy in the FBI that you can cut out whenever you want for nap time?"

"Oh, yeah. It's all fun and roses. Maybe that's why you left." He glared at her.

"I left because I didn't *belong* there," she snapped.

"You left because you didn't *want* to belong," he corrected. "And you know what? That's fine. I'm not there anymore because I don't belong. Now what in the hell do you *want*?" Fury glinted hot in his eyes as he advanced on the couch.

Refusing to let him loom over her, she stood up, glaring right back at him. "We have a case to solve—three murders, and probably one more. And you're whining because you're tired?" *Damn it,* shut *up*! she thought. Whining? He wasn't whining—he just wanted some rest . . . and he wanted her gone.

That was the problem, she realized. It wasn't that he wasn't able to help her as much as she needed just yet. It was because he didn't want her there. He didn't want her there and it hurt. Damn, it hurt. He may still *want* her, although she couldn't be entirely sure of that. But if he did want her, he didn't want her enough.

Sucking a breath, she stared past his shoulder. "Okay, time-out. I . . ." Blood crept up her neck—she could feel the heated crawl of it spreading higher and higher, and she knew she'd be blushing hard in a matter of seconds. Edging around him, she grabbed her bag.

"I don't know where that came from," she lied, hoping her walls were still holding steady. The last thing she wanted was for him to get a glimpse inside her.

"You're right. Once you get us on the right trail, we'll probably be running night and day to get this thing wrapped up, and until that happens, you're going to be pushed. Hard." She pushed a shaking hand through her hair and then hefted her bag higher, rooting through it. Pulling out the file, she left it lying on the narrow work desk. "So you should rest. You can go through this whenever. I'll . . . um, I guess I'll call in a few hours. You can rest and then go through it and . . ."

She let her words trail off as she headed for the door. Get out. That was what she needed to do. Get out of here.

She almost made it to the door.

But Mica made the bad mistake of looking backward.

Looking . . . and falling into Colby's gaze. He'd followed her and he stood only a wish away. Blue eyes, darkened by so many shadows, held hers. A hand came up, touching her cheek lightly. She felt that touch tremble through her entire body—it was like a shock wave. He went to pull away and she caught his wrist.

This is a bad, bad idea, she thought.

Very bad. And still, she found herself reaching for him with her other hand. When he just stood there, she went to him.

Lashes lowered over his eyes, shielding them.

"Mica."

She pressed her lips to his chin, then brushed them along the line of his jaw. "Yeah?"

"This isn't smart."

"No. You're right." She pushed her hand into his hair, memory flooding her as it twined around her fingers. "I don't much care."

Tipping her head back, she stared into his eyes. "Do you?"

"I should." He closed his eyes. "I probably will . . . later."

As his mouth came crushing down on hers, she thought, *Let's hear it for later* . . . That was her last sane thought for quite some time.

As his hands came around her waist, everything became a rush of heat, and touch, and need. She felt the wall against her back and him at her front, leaning into her, letting her feel every hard, muscled line of his body. Lean, too lean, but she didn't care. Letting her hands roam over his shoulders and arms, she memorized those lean, lean lines, letting her fingers learn the feel of his skin all over again.

Between her thighs, she felt the heated length of his cock, throbbing, pulsating. She whimpered and rocked against him. That was something else she wanted to relearn, she knew. Desperately. *Now.* When his hands skimmed up her sides to push her jacket backward off her shoulders, she shuddered from just that light touch. Against her side, she felt the solid weight of her gun and she groaned, letting go of him with one hand. She fought with the side holster and managed to get it halfway off.

Then he pressed his mouth to her neck.

The heated press of his mouth against her skin had lights exploding behind her eyes, and the neurons in her brain started to sizzle, then pop, one by one.

Hissing out a breath, she let her head fall back against the wall. She gave up fighting with the side holster and reached up, curling her hand into his hair and pressing him close.

Colby wasn't as big on the idea, though. He toyed with the leather of the harness and muttered, "You really do need to lose this thing."

Just the feel of his lips moving against her flesh was enough to drive her insane. He skimmed them up to nip on her earlobe, still toying with one of the straps of her holster. Mica groaned and pressed closer, hating everything that separated them . . . The clothing. The years. The distance . . .

A distance you caused, a sly little voice whispered in her mind.

Determined not to think about that, about anything but this, she leaned back and stared at him through her lashes. "If you want me to lose anything, other than my mind, you need to quit touching me for a minute."

"I don't like that idea." One hand slipped under the hem of her shirt, and the feel of his touch, his calloused hands on her naked flesh, had the bones in her legs dissolving. "I think I went long enough without touching you as it is. *Too* long. Now you want me to let go?"

"I don't much like the idea of you letting go, either, but if you don't, I can't think." She turned her face into his neck, breathing in the scent of his skin. "If I can't think, I can't make myself get rid of the holster or anything else."

"Hmmm. Maybe I'll do it." Then he did just that, stripping the holster away with quick, efficient hands. Her own hands were shaking. *She* was shaking. And then she was reeling, struggling to catch her balance as he straightened up and pulled away.

"Hey," she protested, reaching for him.

"Shhhh." He pressed a quick kiss to her neck and moved away, setting her weapon down on the table just a few feet inside the room. "Can't exactly go and drop that, can we?"

Hell, right then, she didn't *care*. The safety was on. That's what the safety was for, right? "Just get back over here."

"Yes, ma'am." Colby's grin, wicked and hot, flashed across his face as he returned to her, his hands going to her waist and pushing up. As the fabric of her shirt rode up under the press of his hands, he dipped his head once more to her neck. "Don't you think we should move to the bed, though?"

"I don't care. I just want you touching me." *Too long?* He'd said it had been too long and he'd been right. Desperation, burning and bright, settled in her belly, tugging on her. With every breath she took, with the beat of her heart, the need just got worse. Wrapping her arms around his neck, she sought his mouth with her own. "Just touch me, Colby."

JUST TOUCH ME, *Colby . . .*

The soft, husky timbre of her voice went straight to his head. If he hadn't already been mindless for her, the sight of her, the sound of her, that's all it would have taken. The faint flush creeping over her skin, the hungry glint in her eyes . . . and the way her hands trembled as she stroked them over his shoulders. The tremble in her voice, the way her breath caught in her lungs. "I've missed you," he rasped just before slanting his mouth over hers. Damn it, he'd missed her.

Over the years, it had gotten easier, at times, to not dwell on the might-have-beens, but then there were times when memories of her would creep up out of his subconscious and sucker-punch him, turning him into tangles and making his heart ache as he thought back to the one time in his life when he'd felt whole. Complete. The one time . . . and he'd lost it. Lost her.

And now she was here again, her long, sexy body pressed against his, her skin hot, her mouth wicked and soft. Skimming his hand down, he pushed his fingers inside her trousers, past the barrier of her panties, dipping them inside her slick, wet channel. Hot. Wet. Tight. She closed around his fingers even as her mouth opened under his. He caught her lower lip between his teeth, tugging gently.

Mindless for more, he used his free hand to fight with the buttons of her simple white blouse, stripping it away. It wasn't so easy to do her bra one-handed, though, and he wasn't about to stop touching her, especially not once she started riding his hand.

"Take it off," he muttered, lifted his mouth just long enough to pluck at the silk and lace. She smiled against his lips, stripped out of her bra, then reached for his shirt, all but tore it away. Even the act of leaning away to pull the material off was too much distance in that moment. "Still wearing too many clothes, damn it," he said against her mouth.

"You, too."

He'd have to stop touching her . . . for a few seconds. Just a few seconds.

Those few seconds took too long, passing in a hot, hazed blur as they fought free from the clothing and then, *finally*, he could touch her, all of her. He could feel her, all of her. And taste . . . skimming his lips over her shoulder, then lower, lower, he sank to his knees in front of her, pressing his mouth to the V between her thighs. Mica whimpered and fisted one hand in his hair, the other clutching at his shoulder.

As he caught one thigh and lifted it, she gasped out, "Colby . . ."

And then, when he opened his mouth and licked the tender flesh, a strangled scream escaped her. She groaned, pressing closer.

"Fuck." Closer . . . but still not close enough. Too damn long. With the taste of her hot in his mouth, he surged to his feet and leaned against her, his cock cuddling against her middle. "Please tell me you've got some condoms or something with you."

She stared at him, blinking sleepily. "Now what kind of woman would that make me, Colby?"

His brain struggled to process that. She . . . fuck. She didn't have anything?

Then she was pressed against his chest. Dazed, he eased away, collapsing against the wall, struggling to breathe. Damn it. He knew he couldn't die of terminal lust, but he sure as hell felt like he might.

Watching Mica, he frowned as she bent over and snagged her bag. He heard the rasp of the zipper. Then she turned back to him, a smile on her lips and a box in her hand. "I guess it would make me a prepared woman." Still smiling at him, she tore into the box.

"Let's hear it for preparation," he muttered, refusing to think about the fact that Mica was ever practical. Maybe she frequently carried around protection. And maybe . . .

She returned to him, one foil packet in hand. "I bought these earlier. I can't look at you without wanting you, and I can't breathe without needing you. There's no way I thought we could work together and this not happen."

Her words hit him straight in the heart. And somehow, it managed to make his stomach go tight and icy, too.

There's no way we could work together and this not happen . . .

This—sex? Something more? But he didn't want to think about that right now—didn't want to think about anything but her. Having her. Finally. After too many years. Taking the rubber from her, he tore it open. Now it was his turn for his hands to shake. As he rolled the latex down over his aching cock, his fingers trembled. It seemed everything inside him trembled as well, and that sensation only strengthened as he reached for her.

"Come here," he muttered, catching her hand and drawing her close.

Her body, long and sleek with those subtle, sweet curves, pressed against his. Her eyes, dark and warm, rested on his as he turned, positioning her back against the wall. "Want to move to the bed?" He nipped her lower lip as he nudged her thighs apart.

"No . . . I want to stay here. Right here." Mica wrapped her arms around his neck, lifting one knee and rubbing it against his thigh. She tugged him near, stroking one hand down his chest to close around his cock. "Right here . . . although I do need you a little closer to me now."

Colby stroked his hands down her back and gripped her hips. "Hold on to me, Mica."

Hold on to me . . .

The words echoed deep, deep inside her as she wrapped her legs around his waist. *Hold on* . . . That was all she wanted to do. What she wished she would have done years ago. Regret tried to claw its way inside her, but she shoved it down. It had no place here. Not now. And as he pressed the thick, blunt head of his cock against her, it was easier to forget. So much easier, for now, to think about the hot, sleek length of him as he butted against her entrance, as she yielded and opened for him. So much easier to think about nothing except how good it felt as he slowly sank inside her, feeling the stretch of her muscles around him.

Her breath caught, and despite herself, despite the need to stare at him, to watch him, her lashes drifted down.

"No." Colby tangled a hand in her hair and tugged. "Watch me. Let me watch you."

Forcing her eyes open, she stared into his dark, turbulent blue gaze. Against her shields, she could feel the heat of his presence in a deeper way, and although she knew it wouldn't be wise, she wished she could let those shields down, too. So that nothing separated them.

But she wasn't about to strip herself so bare.

Yet as his mouth came down to brush against hers, Mica's determination to keep some piece of herself apart from him trembled. How was she to keep herself apart from him when all she'd wanted was to be back *with* him?

He sank deeper inside, so deep that nothing save herself separated them.

Flesh slicked against flesh. Hunger bloomed, raw and endless. Yet as desperate for him as she was, as desperate as he seemed to be, there was a gentleness to it. His mouth took hers, a deep, drugging kiss, and all the while, he watched her. Like he couldn't stop. She understood the feeling, because she really didn't want to stop watching him.

The world spun around her—no. It was them, Colby pushing away from the wall and moving deeper into the room, still gripping Mica close, his hands on her hips, her legs twined around his waist. Then they were on the bed and she shifted, moving her legs until she sat astride him, her hands braced on his chest.

Their gazes locked as she began to move. A whimper escaped her as the throbbing ridge of his cock rubbed against her in just the right way. The need, the hunger . . . all of it, swirled tighter, faster inside as she rode him. When his thumb brushed against her clit, she moaned, her head falling back. Back and forth, back and forth, he stroked her and then she shattered, unable to hold back any longer.

With a cry, she climaxed, and as she sagged down, collapsing on his chest, she felt him stiffen and swell inside her. The hands on her hips tightened and he started to move faster, angling her hips until the head of his cock butted up against that same, sensitive little spot with each stroke. She hissed out a breath as it triggered another mini-explosion, her muscles gripping his length, her nails biting in his skin.

"Colby." His name was a broken, shaken sound on her lips and then his mouth caught hers, one hand streaking up her back to tangle in her hair.

Here, once more, was that raw, desperate need, the tenderness lost, replaced by hunger . . . deep, endless hunger.

chapter seven

She fell asleep in his arms.

Colby knew the best thing for him to do was to close his eyes and try to get some rest of his own. But he couldn't. Not yet. And oddly, he felt more rested than he had in days. Rested . . . at peace, almost. Just because of Mica. She was once more in his arms and it didn't matter, at the moment, that he knew this wouldn't last. The job would end, he would leave, and Mica would go back to pretending she belonged in a world she didn't. A world where the people were normal and they didn't hear whispers in their mind, or see ghosts, or hear a killer as he sang a death song to his victims.

It would happen, he knew.

If Mica wanted to accept who she was, she would have done it before now, he suspected. His sudden reappearance in her life wasn't going to change things. Especially as he suspected she hadn't particularly *wanted* his reappearance.

But for now, it didn't matter. He'd think about the heartbreak that awaited him when he had to. For now, all he was going to think about was Mica.

Reality was going to press in soon enough.

He could already feel it—a heavy weight pressing ever close, like a thunderstorm.

Brushing his lips over her shoulder, he settled more comfortably on the bed. She still felt so right in his arms. She'd always felt so right. He'd sensed her before he'd seen her, and when he had seen her that first time, it had all but made his heart stop. *She's the one . . .* He'd known it just by looking at her. The only one. And they'd clicked—damn, had they clicked. Not just physically. Not just emotionally. Even their gifts had meshed in a unique way—they'd made each other stronger.

Then Mica decided she couldn't belong to that world. Their combined gifts had been too much, and instead of waiting to see if they could work through things, she'd walked away. Because he hadn't been able to keep enough of his *gift* inside him. Because he'd spilled too much of it into her.

He might not hang around monsters anymore, but he couldn't stop himself from being who he was, either. He couldn't pretend to be normal. Mica wanted to—he couldn't. No, this wouldn't last, but he'd enjoy it while he could.

With that thought in mind, he pressed a kiss to the nape of her neck and closed his eyes.

She was too restless to sleep for long. He suspected she sensed some of the same shit he did, even if it wasn't as clear for her. She felt something and it had her in knots. Even through her shields, he felt that turmoil. So if he wanted to make it through the next few days without being a total zombie, he needed to sleep.

HE'D EXPECTED SOME nightmares. Rarely a night passed for Colby without at least one. And sure enough, the nightmares found him the minute he slid deep enough into sleep.

But they weren't *his* nightmares . . .

Not his nightmares, not his dreams. Not his visions.

It was Mica . . . her memories. Through her eyes, he could see the victim. Mutilated, pale, and pitiful, she lay on the floor. Her legs were marred by scar after endless scar, forming a macabre sort of map all over her flesh. There was so very little blood around her. If he hadn't known better, he would have thought perhaps she'd died elsewhere—those injuries, there would have been blood.

But he knew she'd died here. He could even hear the faint, ghostly echoes of her screams . . . through Mica's ears.

Just as through her ears, through her eyes, he watched, waited, listened while she spoke with the other cops. Watched and waited as she rose and dusted her gloved hands off. Watched as she walked across the dull gray floor to a window. She knew it was there. Waiting for her. All but calling out her name. When she peered through a window, there it was . . . a grim, nasty little gift left by a killer.

A flower.

A lovely, dark flower.

The dream shifted, narrowed down to tunnel vision, and all he could see was that flower. The air seemed to burn in his lungs and he needed to breathe, needed to move, but he couldn't.

In the dream, something shattered. Shifted. And when it reformed, he saw what looked like an endless wave of those dark, lovely blooms, drifting gently on a breeze. He heard the low sound of a man singing. And the awful music of a dying woman's screams.

The sounds mingled and ran together, spinning through his mind in endless, dizzying circles, pulling him under, pulling him in. Darkness danced ever closer, and with a rush of adrenaline, he snapped free of the dream, snapped free of the vision.

Lying in bed, breathing raggedly, Colby closed his eyes.

Those screams. He could still hear those screams echoing in his mind.

The screams of the woman who had just died?

But in his gut, he knew the answer.

No. This was the next one.

The killer had already selected his next victim.

The dream tried to fade—vision or not, it was a dream and they always tried to fade. He clutched the remnants tight, forcing the imprint on his mind. A dream, yes, but so much more, and he had to remember.

Next to him, Mica stirred, a soft, tortured sound escaping her.

Rising up on his elbow, he stared at her, watched as she slid a hand down low, protectively cradling her lower abdomen. A harsh groan, a gasp, then a strangled scream. He wasn't the only one plagued by nightmares tonight, it seemed.

Whatever haunted her, it was dark, tortured. Terrible. He felt the weight of it pummeling against his shields, threatening to shatter them through sheer force. He wasn't about to have that happen—nothing good would come of that. Easing his shields down he focused his mind until it was receiving only what he wanted.

Not that he really wanted to take in those dreams, but . . .

Instinct drove him.

That dark, awful weight had become a dark, awful whisper. There was something important. Something he needed to know . . . *Sorry, Mica,* he thought as he rested a hand on her arm. And stiffened as the images flooding her mind reached out to him as well.

The first, clear vivid thought was that of the pain. Horrid and bright as it tore low through his belly.

THE MINUTE SHE woke, Mica knew something was wrong.

The tension in the air was thick enough to choke her.

Swallowing, she sat up, clutching the blanket to her chest as she sought Colby out in the dim room. The shadowy form by the covered windows might have made her heart bump if she hadn't already known who it was. But she'd know him anywhere. Day or night. Whether she saw him or simply sensed him.

She'd know him anywhere . . . and she'd also know when things weren't exactly right.

Things were so far from *right* at the moment she could feel her hands start to sweat.

The harsh, heavy burn of anger was a slap against her senses, and she winced under the weight. Even as the echo of the emotional blow started to fade, she realized something . . . she shouldn't have been able to feel it that heavily. Not unless . . .

Oh, hell.

Immediately, she slammed her admittedly shoddy shields into place as she clambered out of the bed. Oh, shit. Oh, *shit.* The strange, jumbled dreams that had plagued her through the night leapt to the forefront of her mind and panic rose in her throat. She hadn't fully been able to make sense of them. Instinct had been guiding her on these murders, and the dreams were tied to it, she knew, but there was a lot about the dreams she didn't fully understand.

Somehow, she knew Colby did.

Damn it.

"He wants you dead."

He wants you dead—

Closing her eyes, she let those words echo through her mind. This wasn't a shock. She'd suspected it. Felt the malice in those dreams, a malice that wasn't *just* directed at his victims. It had felt like . . . *more.* She'd been right.

Her hands trembled minutely as she fought to secure the sheet. She couldn't do this naked. She would have a hard enough time getting through this without breaking.

Oddly enough, she was more scared about the fact that she had to face what was happening within her than the fact that some psychotic might want her dead. She had faced that before. Facing herself was another issue, but somehow, she didn't think Colby was going to let her hide anymore.

"Maybe he doesn't want me dead." Swallowing, she made herself look up, meet his eyes in the dim room. "Maybe I just get in the way." She shrugged and even managed to give him a fake smile. One he wouldn't believe, she knew. She didn't even believe it. *Way to face yourself, Mica.*

"Get in the way," Colby said, his voice dry and mocking. "That's why he decides he's going to cut out your eyes, cut off your hands?"

The image from that dream, so faint and insubstantial, suddenly solidified in her mind. It was one thing to think about your death—another thing to actually see how it would play out. Closing her eyes, she shook her head.

"It's not going to happen," she said quietly, with a lot more calm than she felt. Colby wouldn't let it. Mica didn't plan on letting it happen, either.

"Glad we're clear on that." He folded his arms across his chest. "Interesting pal you picked up there—wants your eyes and your hands?"

"Well, it's easier for him than the brain." She gave him a faint smile. "That's the top tool of my trade, but maybe he's too squeamish to cut that out."

"You're smiling about this." He shoved off the wall and stalked closer, his blue eyes glittering with fury. "I just watched him kill you and you're treating it like a joke."

"He didn't *kill* me. I'm right here. And as long as I'm right here, and I'm careful, I can avoid whatever he plans." She didn't shrink away, despite the weight of his anger as he came closer. Colby was the only one who'd ever connected with her on this level—she saw bits and pieces of the future, and with an anchor, somebody who worked with her, those visions were stronger. But with Colby, her gift became a different beast entirely. It had terrified her once.

Now . . . now she just didn't know. No, she did know—she was still terrified, but through their connection, those hazed memories from her dreams were becoming more real.

Giving her something to focus on. Something to hunt.

Yes. She was scared. But she was also determined—she wouldn't let this stop her, and she knew Colby wouldn't stop, either. That meant they could stop *him*.

"You knew this." His voice shook. "Damn it, you knew this going in and you let me find out like that?"

"No. I—no, Colby." Staring at his face, seeing the horror in his eyes, she started to feel sick. Shit. What had she done? Sinking down on the edge of the bed, she buried her face in her hands. She took a deep breath and willed the fear in her mind, the adrenaline, everything else to fade as she focused on Colby. Quietly, she said, "I didn't know."

"Don't give me that—" he bit off.

Surging off the bed, she said louder, "I didn't know!" With a soft curse, she turned away and stared at the bland, impersonal painting that hung over the bed. It was a mess of geometric shapes, gold streaks of color—the sort of painting one would see in a thousand other hotels. Focusing on one of those gold streaks, she said again, "I didn't know. None of the dreams are ever clear and I barely have even the memory of the dead woman when I wake. That doesn't even happen until after it's too late to save her. It's like I'm seeing a movie I'd forgotten I'd seen or something. Bits and pieces are there but that's it."

Behind her, Colby was silent. The heavy weight of his rage finally lessened after several moments, and she listened as he dragged in a deep breath.

"You had no idea he'd focused on you like that?"

Mica shrugged restlessly. "Not exactly. There was a weird sense of malice that would linger even after I woke, and things have felt off ever since this started. But damn it, three women have been murdered. Why *shouldn't* something feel off?" She rubbed her temple, but it didn't do much for her headache. *If it was me in his shoes, I'd be pissed, too,* she thought. Slowly, she turned. "I'm sorry. I'm sorry you saw that—it shouldn't have happened."

"You're damn right it shouldn't have," he growled, stalking closer. Heat, fear flashed through his eyes, but there was also something else . . . something she couldn't quite name.

But as he lifted a hand to cup her cheek, Mica felt her heart stutter, then sigh. "You should have warned me, Mica. You know that."

"Yeah." She swallowed and nodded. "I know. I just . . . I swear, Colby. I didn't know. I couldn't know. I'm still . . ."

"You're just still hiding."

"Yes," she agreed with a twist of her lips. "I'm still hiding."

His hands closed around her arms and he jerked her close. "No more hiding, Mica. *None.*"

Startled, she slapped her hands against his chest and the sheet fell to the floor. Damn it. Maybe she was going to have to do this naked. Nose to nose, she stared at him. His eyes all but glowed. "Tell me you'll stop hiding," he whispered, leaning in until his mouth brushed against hers as he spoke.

The naked need in his voice, in his eyes, called out to her. She could feel it, too, wrapping around her and pulling her in. *Damn it, I can't do this—*

Except she already was. And she knew it. Haltingly, she nodded. "I'll stop hiding."

"And you're going to have to stop fighting what your gift is trying to tell you, damn it. Starting now."

The command in his voice had her stiffening. "I don't much care for being bullied into things, Mathis. And you know it. I'm not . . ."

His hands came up, cupping her face. "Just how much have you seen of those dreams, baby?"

"I . . ." She shook her head, unsure how to answer that.

Colby knew, though. He knew and she saw the blue of his eyes darken just as he lowered his shields. She had no defense. Through the connection that had tied them together from the very first, Mica finally saw what her shadowy, incomplete dreams had been trying to tell her.

chapter eight

She was still pale.

Hours later, they bent over the files, rarely talking. Colby watched her when he could, and her pallor left him feeling sick. Maybe he'd been too abrupt and maybe he should have warned her somehow.

But she had to see.

Colby knew how her mind worked, knew how she'd insist on hiding, right up until she had no other choice. And this time, it might be too late. It had been a risk, letting her see everything he'd seen—there had been a possibility she'd push him away for daring to breach the cold, steel walls she'd built around herself.

He hadn't given a damn. If it kept her alive, that was all he cared about. As long as she didn't end up—

No. He shoved that thought aside, forcing himself to think about other things. Like the fact that he was here now. Having him in the game changed things. Having her aware of what could happen, that changed things, too.

Together, they'd figure this out before the next victim was grabbed.

At least he hoped they could prevent that.

Shifting his eyes away from Mica and back to the file, he flipped through it. Nasty, dark little fingers tugged at him, but he kept his shields up tight and thick. He couldn't do jack for her if he kept getting pulled back into the same visions over and over.

What he really needed was to go *deeper* into one of those visions. See something more. Something different. Preferably the killer. Although he couldn't make it work on quite that level. *If only it was that easy* . . . Heaving out a sigh, he stroked his thumb down the edge of the picture—it was one of the pictures from the autopsy. In death, she was pale, the bruises on her flesh standing out in stark relief against her pallid skin. Her hair was dark, short, skimmed back from her face so that nothing detracted the eye. All one could see when staring at that picture was death.

Dimly, Colby heard that deep, melodic voice.

Would you dance . . . if I asked you to dance . . .

Closing his eyes, he muttered the words.

Next to him, Mica stilled. "Colby?"

"The song." He glanced at her. "That's what he sang to them." Scowling, he flipped through the file, saw another picture, another, another . . . but there was another.

"Colby." A hand touched his.

Bare skin on bare skin.

For a moment, heat sparked and then he slammed a hand against the table, swearing in a low, raw voice as the darkness swarmed up and sucked him under. If he hadn't been reaching for this very thing on his own, it never would have gotten its hooks in him so deeply. But for a moment, he'd reached.

And now it had him. It dragged at him . . . voices sounding in his mind. Screaming at him. Brutal splashes of color—bloodred on white. Bloodred on gray. Bloodred on everything . . .

Blood splashed across a face, highlighting a dark, dark pair of eyes, so cold and so clinical. So fucking crazy.

A voice rang in his mind, soft, deep . . . melodic. Yet still a monster's voice.

Would you run . . .

And Colby watched as the landscape sped by in a rush—through a woman's eyes. As she started to run, terror a vivid, ugly smear inside her mind. He was lost in her memories, seeing through her eyes, hearing through her ears. Everything was distorted, and he had to pull back a little, had to look. Not real, not real, not real—he shoved past the terror, struggled to see things on his own, even from within the mind of another.

The image snapped, and for a moment he couldn't breathe as he was flung from the mind of one person to another. And now, all he saw was flowers. Just flowers. What was with the damn flowers?

They flooded his vision for long, endless moments and then finally faded, revealing something else. No—some*one* else. Or at least his hand—a man's hand. White male. A smattering of dark hair on the back, nails neatly clipped. Bared wrist, a forearm. Strong but not bulky. Long fingers toyed with one of the blooms and then the man selected one perfect flower. Colby saw what looked like glass—

Look up, you bastard, look up—

The image faded. Flickered. Fell apart.

A harsh voice, loud and demanding, sounded in his ear.

Gritting his teeth, he let the connection fade and looked up, found Mica glaring at him. Her eyes snapped in the dim light of the room, and she had one hand lifted, gripping the front of his shirt like she wanted to shake him. He was sitting flat on his ass in the middle of the room. He could hardly breathe. His cheek stung—he had some dim recollection of her shouting his name. Slapping him. And when he hadn't answered—

"Damn it, Colby, what's wrong with you?"

Blinking, he forced his eyes wide open, made himself swallow although most of the spit had dried in his mouth. When he stared at her, it was like he saw through a fog. And energy spiked off her.

Her energy. As he stared into her gaze, he saw an eerie overlay of the girl he'd seen.

Mica.

Damn it, it was Mica—that was the connection he needed. Why hadn't he seen that already?

His voice raw, he said grimly, "Give me your hand."

HE'D SCARED HER.

For a moment there, he had really and truly scared her. There were a few times when he'd all but stopped breathing.

She'd touched him and then he'd . . . Shit, she couldn't explain it. His eyes had taken on a locked, almost dead stare. His skin had paled. And the air around him had been so charged, she half expected one or both of them to self-combust, and not in that fun, sexy-tension sort of way.

All because she'd touched him. Now he wanted her to do it again.

Scrambling backward, she said, "Are you insane?"

He reached out and caught her ankle, the cloth of her trousers a faint barrier. She could feel the heat of his hand, but it wouldn't happen until they touched bare skin to bare skin. "I saw something," he replied, his voice gruff. "It went deeper this time. I . . . I wasn't expecting it, but if I know it's coming, I can control it. I need to go back there. Look again."

"And if you can't control it?"

"I always did before," he said simply. "Even after you walked away and I had to rely on somebody else to anchor me."

"You almost stopped breathing a couple of times," she whispered, shaking, staring at his extended hand.

"Then I pass out. That's happened. It's a built-in off switch. If I stop breathing in a vision, all I'll do is pass out. Then the connection is cut and it's done." He waited, hand still held out.

Gently, he reminded her, "You said you wouldn't keep running."

He was still half sick inside. She could feel it. There was terror and adrenaline and nerves sparking all around him—she could all but *see* that. And it didn't matter to him. It didn't matter what the gift cost him.

She'd always hated her own abilities, but Colby had accepted them, let them tear him apart inside. But he never let it stop him.

"No more running," she whispered. Throat tight, she lifted her hand. As she reached for him, she slammed her own shields down tight. When their fingers touched, she grounded herself, just as she'd been taught all those years ago—it took a few precious, shaking seconds, but she stabilized, steadied. Some lessons, it seemed, were never forgotten.

As their fingers twined until they touched palm to palm, she lifted her gaze to his. "Don't make me regret this," she whispered quietly. "This shit is no good for me."

"It's no good for me, either. But all we can do is just deal with it . . . or let somebody die."

Stark, simple words. In that moment, she all but hated him for being stronger than her. Better. But she pushed it all away. Had to, otherwise, she'd fail him. She'd done that once, when she walked away.

She wasn't doing it again. "I'm ready," she told him.

WOULD YOU DANCE . . . *If I asked you to dance . . .*

Would you run . . . and never look back?

The voice echoed in Colby's mind, stronger now. It echoed with malice, and need, and an insatiable desire to hurt.

Time blurred together and lost all meaning.

The woman was there, once more. Completely unaware she was being followed. Walking to the bland, borderline seedy little strip joint, a bag bouncing against her hip. Her head shifted to the left, the right, and it would have seemed she knew what was going on around her.

But she didn't. The threat was behind her. Far, far behind her and nobody ever looked at him twice.

That *amused* him. That *pleased* him. And *that* gave Colby a line—an anchor. Drawing on it, Colby let the bastard suck him in. Through that connection, and his connection to Mica—the one that grounded him, everything became clearer.

All at once, death unfolded. It was everywhere.

Women, already dead and gone. Some left alone in alleyways. Some buried. And then there were the latest three. Their faces flashed before him, one right after the other—the petals of a flower stroked down their cheek, the mocking sound of laughter.

Would you dance . . .

The voices of three women rose in Colby's mind, echoing along with that mocking laughter. And there were other voices.

Lost in the cacophony, Colby couldn't make sense of them even as he reached out and tried to focus. As he tried to grab on to one voice and separate it from the rest. It wasn't happening, though. The voices became a blur, background noises as the faces spun in dizzying circles and then stopped.

Now there was just one woman.

A fourth victim . . . a hooker, Colby suspected. Chosen for just that. The man didn't want her, didn't want anything from her. Beyond her pain. Beyond her screams . . . beyond her torment.

That was what he wanted, and that was what he took.

There was a fifth woman, too. Her image spliced itself over everything else. Colby saw her walking through a building—cop shop.

Now *this* woman, the man wanted. Colby felt the burn of that anger, even as he felt the burn of lust for the woman as he stared at her, watching her as she huddled over her desk, her black hair pulled away from her face, her eyes narrowed in concentration.

Need sparked. Yearning wrenched through him. He wanted her. She wasn't like the others—she wouldn't be so easy to catch, so easy to break . . . and he wanted that.

The vision shifted, swirled. The killer was alone. Walking through a darkened house, into an equally dark bedroom. Change jangled in a pocket, clothing whispered. Colby, still wrapped in the vision, watched as the killer dumped loose coins on his dresser.

Followed by a gun.

Colby tensed, startled. The vision shifted and swayed, thrown by his brief break in concentration. He struggled to steady it, still staring at the gun, sheathed in simple, utilitarian holster, the kind somebody would wear to keep the weapon tucked against the ribs. The kind a cop might wear.

A cop . . .

Even as Colby thought that, something was placed on the dresser by the gun.

He saw a glint of gold, still tucked in the leather wallet.

A fucking cop.

"YOU'RE WRONG, DAMN it."

Nearly an hour later, Mica glared at Colby from across the hotel room. It was nearly dawn. Neither of them had gotten more than a few hours of sleep the night before, and she knew he'd gotten even less than she. But damn him, he looked fresh-eyed and focused.

She felt like death warmed over, still wearing her clothes from yesterday, her hair a tangled mess, and despite her attempts to ignore it, she knew she still smelled of him. It made it that much harder to concentrate on what he was saying—and figure out how to prove him wrong.

"It's not a cop. I'm not buying it."

"Why?" he asked easily. He'd thrown off the lingering sluggishness that had hit him after the vision and now he looked ready to go again, to plunge himself into the death, the darkness, the despair.

So he could look for more clues that made him think their killer was a fucking cop.

No evidence. He's never seen by anybody, leaves no sign. Plus, these killings are too perfect—he's killed before, but we can't connect him to anything . . .

Swearing, she turned away from him and started to pace. *Anybody* could figure their way around leaving evidence, it seemed. Thanks to crime shows, the Internet, and all that shit, there was a ton of information found with a simple Google search.

They still fuck up. They forget things. But this guy's kills were all as clean as it could be.

She didn't want to think it was a fucking *cop*. But if she didn't . . .

Mica groaned. She stopped by the window and thunked her head against the glass. Other possibilities. If she refused to look at them, then she ran the risk that a killer would go free.

Even if those options were as unpleasant as a fellow cop being the killer.

"All you saw was a gun," she said quietly. "Plenty of people have guns."

"You're right."

"You didn't even see his shield, not for certain. You didn't see his face, nothing. Just his damn weapon. It doesn't have to mean jack shit."

She turned, slumping against the window, exhaustion dragging her down.

Colby's blue eyes met hers. There was no condemnation in his gaze, no disgust, no anger. Just patience. Ever the patient one. Like he would wait forever for her to accept this.

But they didn't have forever.

"Where did you see the fourth victim?" she asked, pushing away from the window. First things first. Focus on what she *knew* for now.

But the bad thing was . . . thanks to Colby's vision, she had new knowledge she didn't want to accept.

In her gut, she knew the killer very likely *was* a cop.

She was hunting one of her own.

chapter nine

"Has he learned anything?"

Kellogg's low, quiet voice drew Mica's attention away from the selection of coffee offered by the vending machines. She had a choice of bad and even worse. Or she could save her stomach lining by getting a Coke. She needed the caffeine punch, though. Desperately. The coffee was akin to sewage here, but it would wake her up better than a Coke would . . . except she valued her stomach lining.

Under the pretense of fishing change from her pocket, she didn't meet her commander's eyes as she replied, "He's picking up on a few things. Nothing solid."

Not a complete lie. They didn't have what they needed for Mica to find him, after all. And if she laid it out before the commander without having proof, she'd have her ass handed to her. Before she told the woman in charge about Colby's suspicions, she wanted proof. Something tangible, and then she'd tell the commander.

And how are you going to get that? He hasn't left anything so far . . .

"He doesn't have anything useful?"

Mica shrugged. "This isn't like a book or something—you can't just open his brain and find the answers."

"Maybe he *needs* to open his brain and find the answers," Kellogg said, her voice edgy and harsh. "We only have a few days at most—I don't want another dead woman on my hands, Lieutenant."

Mica didn't particularly want that, either.

"Neither do I," she said quietly. Slanting a look at the captain, she added, "He's doing the best he can. Sometimes this is like shooting in the dark. You've got to let him work."

Kellogg sighed as Mica shifted away from the vending machine, an icy-cold can in her hand. The captain stood in front of the machine now, eying it with a look of acute dislike. "This stuff is going to eat my stomach alive," she mused as she fed a few quarters into it.

"That's why I went with the Coke."

"I need more caffeine than that," Kellogg murmured. "Has your partner figured out what's up with the . . . consultant?"

Mica jerked a shoulder. "He was asking about him, but I've managed to dance around answering. Telling Phillips what Colby is doing will not help anything."

"Colby?" Kellogg cocked a brow as she took her coffee.

A dull flush threatened to spread across Mica's face, but she shoved it down. "The psychic," she said smoothly. "But I'm not going to be able to avoid giving Phillips an answer forever. We're heading to the latest victim's place of employment again today, and I imagine he's going to keep on pushing."

"He's not an easy partner to work with, is he?"

The woman already knew the answer—Mica could see it in her eyes. "I don't need easy. I just need him to do his job."

Kellogg sipped the coffee, a grimace twisting her mouth. "Do you want to go ahead and tell him?"

No—

Before the response could show on her face or in her eyes, Mica pushed it down. *Careful . . . be careful here,* she warned herself.

"At this time, until we have something more concrete, I think it's best we keep his involvement down to an absolute minimum. Only those who absolutely need to know."

Kellogg studied Mica appraisingly, one brow lifted in speculation. "And I take it your partner isn't one you'd consider an absolute."

"Right now, I only consider those who already know the circumstances an absolute," Mica replied honestly. It was nothing less than truth, after all. Mica already knew about Colby, and Kellogg was the one who'd wanted him in the first place. No reason anybody else needed to know anything.

"You're holding back on me," Kellogg murmured.

"Not entirely. I'm still just putting things together." She gave the commander a game smile and said, "The pieces aren't all fitting together yet. Once I have a clear picture, I can say more."

"SO YOU GOING to tell me what's up with this friend of yours that's consulting?"

As they crossed the busted, broken pavement of the strip joint where their last victim had worked, Mica replied, "At this point, nothing is up, Phillips."

He snorted cynically and reached into his pocket, pulling out a battered cigarette.

She wished he'd either smoke the damn thing or just throw it away.

With it hanging from his lips, Phillips said, "He's been in town for two days, and I bet you're spending the evenings with him on the case. But you still don't want to bring me in."

"There's nothing to bring you in on," Mica replied. Sweat trickled down her back. They'd left the cool comfort of her air-conditioned car for the sweltering ninety-degree temps. It wasn't even eleven and it was already this hot out. It was going to be a miserable summer, she imagined. "Right now, he's just going over the evidence we've got. If he has some earth-shattering revelation, I'll let you know."

"Generous of you, giving me the information I need to do my job. Shit, you won't even tell me what kind of consultant he is. But you'll let me know if he has an earth-shattering revelation."

Logically, she had every reason to bring him in. But her gut warned against it. Not until they knew something. Not until they had something solid. She didn't want to tell her commander, her partner, nobody.

"Our job," she reminded him. "And hell, it's not like you don't have sources of your own. You don't exactly share those with me. Besides, once I *have* something, I'll let you in. Right now, there's just nothing to share." They came to a halt in front of the tinted glass of the front door. She couldn't make out a thing behind the painted glass. "You ready to turn on the charm in here?"

She didn't wait for an answer as she reached up and hit the doorbell.

This was the first of several stops today, and the last thing she wanted was to get into another argument with her so-called partner. Granted, this time he actually had a reason to be pissed off. That didn't make it any easier to deal with him, though.

"THIS IS A fucking waste of time," Phillips snarled three hours later. They were talking to the victim's friends, people who lived in her neighborhood.

Mica agreed. Sighing, she shoved a hand through her damp hair. "Waste of time or not, it's necessary." Necessary, because it was part of the job. And she also never knew what was going to call to her. If something called to her, then it would likely call to Colby.

Still, she suspected she wouldn't find anything hitting the

streets. Her best bet at finding anything was when she talked to Colby . . . and let him get his fingers, psychic and otherwise, over the evidence she'd slipped into her bag.

He needed another connection—and she had an idea that something personal would have a stronger kick than autopsy photos. She was going to give him just that.

All she had to do was finish up what was turning out to be one very endless day.

chapter ten

"Any luck today?"

"Depends on what kind of luck you're hoping for," Mica said as Colby adjusted the seat to fit his longer frame. "I got to listen to my partner bitch, had to dance around questions from my commander about you, and ran into one dead end after another in the investigation. So all kinds of *bad* luck."

"Why are you dancing around questions with your commander?" Colby shot her a frown. "She knows what I do."

"Yeah." Mica huffed out a breath as she put the car into reverse. "She just wasn't expecting you to come out with this idea that it's a cop. I'm not ready to break that to her without proof."

"So you're basically working this solo."

"No," she said softly. "I'm not solo. I've got you." She slid him a look and a faint smile. "I'd trust you over just about everybody in my department anyway."

Reaching into her bag, she pulled out the evidence bag. "And the luck wasn't all bad. I brought you something." The earrings in the bag had belonged to the third victim—a pair of silly, dangly little hearts, and when Mica had touched the bag, her fingers had buzzed.

She hoped that was because this was the right thing to do.

But she wasn't going to know until she turned it over.

Taking a deep breath, she held it up, letting it hang between two fingers. She'd tried to keep from handling it any more than necessary, even though she doubted it would matter much. Colby was too good at what he did to let some minor interference get in the way.

His eyes lingered on the bag, a humorless smile on his lips. "Thanks, but they aren't exactly my style."

Watching the skin tighten around his eyes, she waited.

He didn't make her wait long. After taking a slow, deep breath, he held out a hand. "Just the earrings. Hold on to the bag."

She nodded and pulled it open. She didn't let herself think about the procedures she was breaking here. If the captain hadn't wanted her doing this sort of thing, she wouldn't have given her carte blanche. As it was now, it would be a lot like closing the barn door after the horse had gotten away.

Colby cupped the small pieces of jewelry loosely in his palm, keeping his fingertips away from the metal.

She swallowed and held out a hand. "Do you need . . ."

"No." His lids drooped. "I've got it already . . ."

Then he went silent.

And something started to happen.

The air in the small car sparked, snapped. It seemed to wrap around her and dance along her skin, a light, electric touch.

Seconds ticked away, turned into minutes. She suspected nearly twenty minutes passed before he opened his eyes and stared at her. In a low, raspy voice, he murmured, "Drive."

The intensity of his voice sent a shiver down her spine, but she ignored it. This was what she'd been hoping for. Swallowing, she said softly, "What direction?"

He slanted a look out the front window. "East. It's somewhere east."

* * *

THE PLACE WASN'T in town this time.

Outside of the city limits, a good forty-five minutes away. The traffic on the highway was scarce and the silence in the car was almost oppressive, heavy and tight as Mica drew it in. She could smell Colby and the sun-scorched earth.

It didn't seem like there was anything else around for miles, but that was deceptive. It was easy to feel lost out there, under the big, blue bowl of the sky, with nothing around by the wide-open land and the road.

And Colby.

The intensity emanating from him was still enough to leave her skin buzzing. She probably would have felt it even without any psychic ability, but as it was, it was almost too much. "We're getting close," he murmured.

Scowling, Mica cast another look around. *Close to what*? she wondered. But as they veered around a bend in the road and up a slight incline, she saw the wire fence and, in the distance, an old, abandoned ranch.

Because of the bends in the road, the house kept disappearing from sight. It was the outer buildings she was able to make out the easiest—especially the dilapidated barn that had fallen into disrepair.

And she knew it, even before he said it. She didn't bother waiting for him to speak before she eased up on the gas.

"It's here," he said softly.

"Somehow I knew you were going to say that." Sighing, Mica hit her blinker and shot another look at the spread of land.

What was here, though? And just *where* was it?

chapter eleven

They didn't stop at the broken, busted-up barn.

She waited for some sign from him that he knew what he was looking for, but he remained silent. Once she reached the house, she pulled the car to a stop and shut it off. "Is whatever we're looking for here?"

"We'll see." A faint, humorless smile curled his lips.

"Any idea what we're looking for?"

Without answering, he climbed out of the car. She did the same, grimacing as the heat hit her square in the chest. She stared at him through the lenses of her sunglasses, watched as he just stood there, staring at the house.

"Colby?"

He glanced at her finally, one shoulder rising in a restless shrug. "I don't know what I'm looking for. I'll know it when I see it."

THE SIGHT OF the greenhouse in the back of the house shouldn't have looked so ominous, Colby knew. It was just a building, constructed of glass and metal, the windows reflecting the light all around.

Unlike the rest of the house, it looked like somebody had been taking care of it. There weren't any busted windows and he was pretty sure he saw plants and shit inside. Somehow he doubted there would be that much green in there if this place was completely abandoned.

"The greenhouse," Mica murmured, echoing his thoughts. She swiped the back of her hand across her forehead and slid him a look. "Why do I get the feeling we have to go into the greenhouse?"

"I don't know." Colby smirked. "Maybe you're psychic."

She scowled at him as she started forward, muttering under her breath.

It was an improvement, he thought. She wasn't swearing at him.

A few minutes later, they were surrounded by the moist heat of the greenhouse and he couldn't breathe without smelling wet earth and growing things.

It didn't seem right that he also felt death.

But he did. Moving to the center of one narrow aisle, he closed his eyes. As he did, the vision came over him—he saw hands. A man's hands. Doing whatever in the hell one did with flowers—pruning, snipping, clipping. Fading blooms fell around those hands like rain, the petals falling to the ground around a pair of beat-up work boots.

And some of those petals were almost midnight black.

The flowers . . . over and over again, he saw those flowers.

Dozens of them, and then just one. Being meticulously chosen from the growing blooms, cut from its stem, wrapped carefully. In the background, the entire time, he heard singing. Loud, getting louder. And he saw a woman . . . swaying to the music.

Endless moments passed. It could have been minutes. It could have been hours. The vision shifted, shuddered, and fell apart and Colby opened his eyes.

Turning his head, he found himself staring at a neat little patch of flowers.

Tulips, he thought.

They were tulips. With blooms the color of midnight.

* * *

COLBY'S DAMN SPELLS hadn't gotten any less creepy over the years, Mica thought. He'd been out of it, his eyes closed, breathing almost nonexistent, for a good twenty minutes.

When she heard the car engine, she swore, easing away from him with as much silence as possible. Not that it would matter how much noise she made just then—the world could end, with earthquakes rumbling and volcanoes erupting, and Colby Mathis could be completely unaware if one of his visions came on him. Slapping him might jerk him out of it. Rocks hitting him in that hard head of his. But noise wasn't going to do it.

Moving to the doorway, she peered outside. Damn it, don't let it be an owner, don't let it be an owner . . .

The sight of her partner's car pulling around the corner of the house almost had her gnashing her teeth together. If that bastard was following her, she was going to beat him bloody.

A shiver danced along her spine and she shot a quick look over her shoulder, saw that Colby had finally opened his eyes.

And he was staring at something.

The sound of a car door slamming had her swinging her attention back to her partner, though. *Ex-partner,* she told herself. She was having it out with the captain very shortly. She was off the clock, on personal time . . .

Working the case with somebody not *your partner,* a dry, cynical voice pointed out mentally.

Shit.

"We have company," she said in a flat voice as Colby glanced in her direction. Those blue eyes were all but glowing. What had he seen?

But it would have to wait. He wouldn't discuss it in front of somebody else, and somehow, she didn't think she could get Phillips to go merrily on his way.

She slipped outside just as Colby opened his mouth to say her name. Her mind was spinning as she tried to come up with a plausible scenario.

Phillips stood by her car, staring at it with disgust all over his lean face. It was a damn shame the guy was such a jerk, she thought absently. Then his dark, liquid eyes cut in her direction and she saw the typical aggression reflected there. Planting her feet, she cocked her head and studied him.

"I'd ask what you're doing here, but I bet I already know," Phillips said.

"Oh?"

He sneered at her. "Don't try and act like you didn't get the same anonymous tip I did." With his lip curled and animosity flashing in those dark eyes, he continued, "When in the hell did you get it? How long have you known about this place?"

Anonymous tip?

"I just found out about this place."

"Just found out—as in earlier today? Before or after we called it quits? Before or after we spent a wasted afternoon doing interviews?" He started toward her, shaking his head. "The message on my voice mail came earlier this afternoon. I answered after we finished our shift, because you were so fucking set on doing those interviews."

She opened her mouth to tell him she hadn't gotten any fucking anonymous tip, but what was she supposed to do? Tell him her psychic pal had led her out here?

Dancing around the subject, she said, "I didn't find out about it until after we'd finished up for the day, Phillips. You need to throttle back."

As the door behind her squeaked open, she saw Phillips's gaze shoot to the man at her back. Colby rested a hand on her shoulder. She gave him a tight smile. "Colby, this is my partner, Barry Phillips."

* * *

COLBY'S BRAIN WAS a rush of blood and pain. Screams all but sounded in his ears, and as he stared at the man approaching them, he had a hard time separating himself from the visions in his head. Blood-splattered flowers. Lifeless women. And that single woman . . . who danced to the music.

Shifting his gaze toward the house, he stared at it, searching for answers. But they weren't there.

Or maybe they were—he just couldn't hear the whispers over the roars.

Resting a hand on Mica's shoulder, he reached for that steady peace—it was insane how they fit. Without each other, they were both chaos. But when they linked . . . harmony. When she let it happen.

And this time, she let it. As the voices in his head faded to a dull rush, he opened his mouth to tell Mica he needed to talk to her. But the asshat masquerading as her partner turned on his heel, heading toward the house. "I'll fucking find out what's here myself," the man snapped over his shoulder. "You two keep on playing whatever game you're playing."

Under Colby's hand, Mica tensed. He felt her anger whisper along that connection. Then she pulled away, stalking after her partner. Phillips. The guy's name was Phillips—Barry Phillips. Colby lingered a moment, watching as they mounted the steps.

Phillips banged on the back door. Walked around, peering inside windows, with Mica trailing after him.

Uneasy, Colby let his shields lower.

Death. Death. Death.

It was all around him. But it was so fucking heavy, and *everywhere*. He couldn't focus on any one line just yet. Especially without Mica standing there. She'd cut herself off when she stepped away, and although he could reach out to her, reestablish that connection, he didn't want to do it. Not yet. He needed her focused on what she was doing. Not on him.

As the two of them disappeared around the corner of the building, Colby slipped a hand into his pocket and pulled out his iPhone.

The wonders of technology, he mused as he pulled up the map.

MICA SWORE WHEN Phillips paused by the doors of the storm cellar. She knew that look. Damn it, she knew that look. He crouched down, peering at the lock and then looking at her.

"Somebody busted inside here."

Lifting a brow, she said, "Could easily be the owner." Yeah, she could see the signs that somebody had broken inside. Saw the shiny new lock. She wasn't blind. "We have no reason to enter a private residence."

"Oh, yeah. I know that. I just . . ." He cocked his head. Frowned. "Did you hear that?"

"Hear what?"

She glared at him. She hadn't heard anything.

"It sounded like a voice—muffled." His eyes narrowed and he stood up, swearing. He started to kick around in the grass.

"Damn it, Phillips, I didn't hear—" Mica stiffened as something drifted across her shields. Incomplete. Fragmented. A plea . . .

But she didn't know if it was real. Shifting her gaze from Phillips to the cellar doors, she swallowed as her heart started to race away. She couldn't focus it, couldn't make it connect. But what if Phillips was right?

The killer is a cop, Mica. Colby had told her that. In the dead of night, only hours earlier as they sat side by side in the hotel room.

A cop.

She wanted to scream. Wanted to reach out to Colby.

She couldn't *not* go in there. But she couldn't walk in blind, either.

He wants you dead—

Was it Phillips?

THE PHONE BUZZED in his hand and Colby read the text from Jones. *Too long for text—sending e-mail.*

Swearing, he hit the icon for e-mail.

The e-mail was still loading when he glanced up.

It was too quiet.

His gut in a tangle, he started toward the house.

The e-mail finally loaded and all he needed to see was the first few lines.

By then, he'd heard the heavy clang of metal on metal.

And he felt the whisper of Mica, her mind reaching out to his, unsteady and erratic, but determined.

SHE'D ALREADY DESCENDED into the darkness, but her gut was screaming it was a mistake.

There was the smell of death in the air. Fresh death. Old death.

Phillips's voice came back to her, soft, quiet. "Smell that?"

"Yeah." How could she *not* smell it? "We need to call this in."

"And what if it's just a dead animal?"

As her eyes adjusted to the darkness, she watched as he came to the bottom of the steps, fiddling with the door there. It was too fucking dark and his body blocked the door. The skin along the nape of her neck started to crawl and she swallowed the spit pooling in her mouth.

Mistake—*fucking mistake—*

He kept his back pressed to the wall as he eased the door open.

There was no screech of rusty metal, no squeak of untended wood. It glided open smooth and easy—too easy. "I'll go high," he murmured, sotto voce.

"We need to pull back," Mica replied. He wouldn't, though.

So did she?

Indecision screamed in her mind. Going in that house alone . . .

There was a brush against her mind. It was a wordless reassurance and an insistent demand, all at once. Colby. He was coming and he wanted her *out*.

Out . . .

Her skin continued to crawl. Yeah. If she backed away now, that would be a big, fricking red alert, letting Phillips know she'd figured out something was wrong. If she was lucky—*assuming* she was reading her instincts right—he'd just follow them out of here and then slip back, ditch whatever evidence was here. If she wasn't, she'd be facing her partner's gun the second she inched backward.

There wasn't much question.

She had to go forward. And she went forward with her weapon ready, knowing Colby was coming along quietly at her back.

The best she could hope for was that Phillips didn't know much of anything about Colby.

Well, that . . . or that she was just plain wrong.

THE SMELL GOT stronger with each step into the darkness. Unable to take standing in that dark hole, not knowing what was around her, she pulled her flashlight out. "I'm turning on my light," she warned, keeping her voice casual.

There was a faint light from behind them, where the door lay, and she wanted to be away from it so Colby's shadow wouldn't give him away any second.

Phillips just grunted. "There's a door here. It's jammed . . . there. Got it."

In some part of her mind, Mica kept thinking, *What the hell are we doing? How do we explain—*

The other part of her was too focused on Phillips to worry about explaining anything. He was no longer moving through the place like a cop. In the bright, vivid beam of the small light she'd pulled from her pocket, he strode around with way too much confidence, absolutely no caution. Straight down the middle of the floor.

Mica had her back pressed against the cool concrete behind her and she checked the ground carefully with her toes before setting her foot down.

He wasn't acting right—

"The smell is coming from here," he said. But he wasn't bothering to whisper now. And there was something in his voice . . . a sly, almost smug laugh dancing under the words.

Mica stiffened. *Watch out*—the voice in her mind warned.

And then he hit the lights.

Mica jerked her weapon up even as she saw he had his pointed square at her.

INSTINCT GUIDED EVERY step.

Colby didn't dare go the same way they'd gone. He didn't question how he knew better than to do that, and he didn't hesitate, either.

He just moved. He had his lock picks, and the door opened under his hand with ease. Through a kitchen that looked unused, down a dark and dim hall—the doorway at the end. It all but pulsed. Red and evil and angry—

He went to put his left foot down and stilled, shifted it to the left a few more inches. The board would squeak. He could hear it in the mind of the killer—the cop who was downstairs alone with Mica. Alone with *his* cop. He continued down the hall, placing each foot carefully, taking too much time but managing to avoid any noises that would have given him away.

There were stairs—he could see them in his mind. The first, third, seventh, and eighth steps squeaked. Somebody, a woman—Colby could hear her voice—had wanted to repair them, but there hadn't been money. And then there hadn't been her.

He eased the door open, one bare inch at a time, staring down. There was light, very faint. At the bottom of the steps, he should find the washer and the dryer, except it had been taken out. There was just a bare space now . . .

Focus, he told himself, viciously jerking his mind under control.

Down the steps, bypassing each one that made noise, his attention spread out, locked on any small sound.

He heard voices now . . .

THERE WERE DEAD flowers.

Everywhere.

And lying on a bed, tucked against a wall, there were the skeletal remains of a woman. Dark hair. An ivory dress . . . a wedding dress. And in her hands there were the crumpled, dried stalks of flowers.

There was a table by the bed. Mica saw that, saw the glint of light on crystal. She took it all in through her peripheral vision, keeping her gaze focused on Phillips.

"If you're going to shoot me, you better do it fast," she advised, going against everything she knew she *should* say. She'd already screwed this up enough, no reason to start playing it by the book now, she figured. Besides, the *one* thing she knew about Phillips . . .

he was about as likely to do what she *told* him to do as he was to sprout wings and fly.

Maybe he'd even avoid shooting her for just long enough.

"Why?" He smiled at her. "You want me to think you have people coming? Other than that pretty-boy consultant?"

"That pretty-boy consultant is a problem. You can't convince him that I shot myself." If it had been anybody but Colby, she wouldn't have dared risk them. But this was Colby . . . and it wasn't a risk for him. If he couldn't handle this . . . she didn't know a soul who could.

Phillips just smiled. In his eyes, she saw the light of madness. Not just a sick bastard, but a crazy one. They weren't one and the same, she knew. *Okay, this is bad* . . . If he was convinced it didn't matter if he killed her, well, she'd end up *dead*.

Something stroked across the edge of her mind. A calm, cool presence. Although there were no clear words, she felt Colby's response clear as day. *Stop*. He wanted her to stop. No thinking about dying.

Stall.

She needed to stall.

Colby was coming. They were deep enough in the other room that Phillips couldn't see the door now.

Colby would come. He would . . . but if he didn't, and she saw Phillips's finger so much as twitch on that fucking gun, she was going to blow his damn head off.

She felt another brush from Colby. A stronger, almost clear thought this time . . . *Don't die, Mica* . . .

She had no plans on dying anytime soon—she had too many reasons to live.

ONCE HE HAD the hard, solid concrete under his feet, Colby felt better. It wouldn't squeak, creak, or make any other fucking sound. Keeping his back pressed to the wall, he held the weapon he hadn't touched in months—it was a Glock 26, light and small, easily concealed . . . deadly as hell.

It was also a reminder of the life he'd left behind, whether it was his personal weapon or not, and he hadn't wanted any reminders.

Now he just hoped he hadn't gotten too fucking rusty, because when Colby saw that bastard, he was going to put a bullet between his eyes.

Calm—be calm—

He eyed the distance between him and the end of the wall. Eighteen inches. He could see shadows. Hear voices—and that fucking song. Damn it. The air was the heavy, cloying stink of rotting flesh. He could feel Mica's horror and rage battering at him—and her determination.

Fifteen inches. She had a gun on her—the man had pulled a gun. It was another instinct, nothing Colby saw clearly, but that was because he wouldn't let that connection click.

Couldn't, not if he wanted to get her through this—

Twelve inches.

He was sweating. Hotter than hell under the layers he wore. That putrid stench made him want to gag, but he shoved it all aside. *Focus . . . focus . . .*

Harder, though, to shove aside everything he felt coming from Mica. Especially when it solidified into one bright, vivid spike—

INSTINCT.

It can save a life—Mica knew that. It could also cost lives—and it just might cost *her* life, she realized, as something flashed through Phillips's eyes.

Knowledge.

Some sort of knowledge. He knew—

She dropped her shields, a desperate measure that just might be the end of her, she knew. But she had to—

He was full of hatred, rage, and need. It was a twisted need, though. One she couldn't fully understand. She also felt the one thing *she* needed—the warning just before he could squeeze the trigger.

"You shoot, I shoot," she cautioned softly. "You know that."

"You shoot, I shoot . . ." he echoed. Then he smiled. "But I think I want to go first."

COLBY CAME UP behind him. "I think *I* want to go first," he said, pressing the muzzle of his gun to the base of Phillips's head.

But if he'd hoped that would throw Phillips off, he'd been dead wrong. Phillips swung around, already dropping.

Colby compensated, pulling the trigger. He saw the neat little hole appear in the man's forehead—then an explosion of red as the bullet tore through the other man's brain and ripped out the back of his skull.

At the same time, he felt the massive pain rip through him. It spun him around and the world went dark.

MICA SCREAMED.

She didn't notice. She ran to Colby, not even pausing by Phillips's side. He was dead—beyond dead, his brain and blood leaking out on the floor.

Colby . . . he was all that mattered, lying facedown on the floor.

Breathing—

Thank God.

He was breathing. Touching a hand to his neck, she checked his pulse. A little fast.

"Okay . . ." she whispered to herself. "He'll be okay."

Gently, she eased him up by the shoulder. Had to get a look . . . She frowned, feeling the odd, bulky thickness under her fingers. No blood. Nothing—

As she got him onto his back, the relief crashed through her, and if she'd been standing, she would have collapsed. Her world had been going black, the air disappearing. But now, bit by bit, the light returned and she could breathe.

He'd be okay. He would live.

He would *hurt* for a while. But he would live.

The fucking man had been wearing a vest.

"Colby . . ." She laid a hand on his cheek, but he didn't stir.

Closing her eyes, she bent over him, rested her brow to his. Just a minute, she told herself. She needed just a minute. God. Thank God. He was alive.

And before she realized what she was going to do, she pressed her lips to his. "I love you . . ."

chapter twelve

"Fractured ribs."

Mica leaned against the wall as Colby eased himself up in the bed.

It was dark. Hours later. She'd just managed to get away from the scene, and the entire time, her mind had been here. Here, with him, nearly an hour away while he was getting worked over, poked and prodded by paramedics.

She wasn't done, and she knew this wasn't where she should be.

It was simply where she had to be. For a few minutes, at least. Even though he'd been awake well before the paramedics arrived, she'd had to come see him.

As his blue eyes cut to hers, she moved deeper into the narrow little cubicle, her hands inside her pockets. He was pale, fine lines fanning out from his eyes, bracketing his mouth. But when he saw her, a faint smile curled his lips.

She resisted the urge to smile back. "Fractured ribs. Bruised insides. Shot at point-blank range. That how they teach you to do things at the FBI, Mathis?"

"Only when you have to go backing up hotheaded cops who do things they know they shouldn't," he responded easily. He went to stand up but stopped when she came to stand in front of him.

"You really need to be moving around?" She barred his way, figuring he'd hurt too much to go around her or try moving her.

"Yes. Because I really need to get out of this hospital." A grimace twisted his mouth. "I hate hospitals. I can't get out of here until I move off the bed."

She rested a hand on his shoulder. "You just got shot."

"Yeah, well, the vest took most of the damage."

Catching her lip between her teeth, she reached out and caught the V opening of the button-up shirt he'd scrounged up from somewhere. Probably bullied it out of a doctor or charmed it out of a nurse, she figured. The mottled bruising was spreading all over the upper part of his chest, and she couldn't even see the worst of it that well, she suspected. "It looks like you took enough damage. You should be still . . . rest."

"I will. When I'm someplace other than here." He closed his fingers around hers and pressed a kiss to the back of her wrist.

"Colby . . ."

"Mica . . ." Sliding her a look from under his lashes, he said, "You've got a case to wrap up, don't you?"

She froze. Something warm and hopeful had been working inside her heart for . . . hell. Almost from the moment she saw him on the beach. It had damn near died when she saw him go down, only to flare back to vibrant life, and now, he was shooing her off?

Swallowing, she pulled back. "Yeah. Yes, there's a case to wrap up." Carefully sidestepping all the various crap medical types managed to cram into an ER room, she made her way back to the curtained door. "Should I have the captain contact you, fill you in once it's wrapped up?" she asked coolly.

"Nah. It's not necessary."

"Okay, then. Have a nice life, Colby."

HE WATCHED AS she disappeared, just barely resisting the urge to go after her.

The problem was, right now, he'd almost have to crawl.

And that wasn't happening.

She didn't realize he'd heard her.

That whisper through the darkness had guided him, made it easier to get past the pain.

I love you . . .

Yeah. He was holding on to that. And the two of them were going to have to face each other, figure out how to live with each other.

Because he loved her, too, and he wasn't letting her go again.

Part of that, though, included figuring how to live with *himself* again.

"GOOD WORK." CAPTAIN Alice Kellogg finished the report and then settled back in her chair, studying the woman before her.

Mica stood with her hands linked behind her back, her face blank. There were signs of sleepless nights visible in the shadows under her eyes, but she didn't care. She looked like shit. Big deal. Who was there around that would even care anymore?

The captain studied a photo wrapped in an evidence bag.

"You look like her."

Mica glanced down and then away. Phillips's wife. Her name had been Christine. She'd divorced him eight years ago, and according to what Mica had unearthed, Christine Phillips had left the country with her lover shortly after the divorce. There was even a marriage license for them filed in Jamaica . . . and a house. One that had been abandoned. There had been no sign of her or her new husband in nearly five years.

She didn't need the captain pointing out the similarity—she'd seen it. The same dark, curly hair, the same tall, lean frame, even their eyes had looked similar from what Mica could tell. Mica had been eerily disturbed when she'd watched Phillips's wedding video—their wedding song had been "Hero" by Enrique Iglesias—the song Colby had heard the bastard singing over and over to the women he'd killed.

It had been damn freaky seeing that man dance with a woman who had looked so much like herself. Damn freaky. Christine, though, had a softness to her that Mica didn't. A gentleness, perhaps.

Abruptly, Mica figured something out. And even as that mystery revealed itself, she wanted to kick herself. Mica looked in the mirror every day and saw strength—she just hadn't ever really realized it before. *Strength*—she had strength inside her. She wasn't the coward she'd once been . . .

Aware of the captain's gaze, Mica forced her thoughts back to the case. Away from her self-realizations. She could deal with those later. Clearing her throat, she nodded to the wedding photo the captain still held. "Did you notice the flowers she's holding?"

"Yes. The Queen of the Night, right?"

"Yes. She was a horticulturist—she doesn't have any family living, but I was able to track down some friends. She was very fond of that breed of tulip." Shifting her gaze away, she stared out the window into the burning-bright light of the afternoon.

"I heard from a friend of yours a short while ago."

Mica cut her eyes back to the captain as her heart stuttered in her chest.

Colby—

"Jones called. Apparently, he got a text from his former agent while you all were out there. He didn't go into much detail, but he did want to make sure I had the relevant information about the house's owner . . . It had belonged to the wife's father. Phillips has been quietly caring for it all this time, which you already know." Kellogg tapped the report with a pen. "I'd say once Mathis made the connection, that's what pushed him into the house. I have to guess at that . . . seeing as how your report was sketchy on those details."

Mica tensed.

"Any reason you didn't get me those details?"

"He left the hospital," she said stiffly. "Left town. Seeing as how you wanted his involvement kept to a minimum during the case, I didn't see why you'd want to change that now."

"Hmmm. Good cover-up." Kellogg continued to stare at her. "I almost believe that."

Then she bent back over her desk. "You need a few hours off. Take the afternoon."

"Captain, I—"

"Take the afternoon," Kellogg repeated, looking up with a steely glint in her eyes.

AS MICA DISAPPEARED through the doors, Kellogg rose from the chair and moved to the window.

Considering her angle, she doubted Mica had been able to see him.

But he'd been out there for the past hour, leaning against Mica's car. Unmoving. Patient as the sea.

Considering he'd just taken a bullet to the chest not that long ago, Kellogg hadn't been able to make him wait any longer.

THE HEAT WAS a bitch.

Colby took another drink from his water bottle and shifted on the car.

His chest was aching like hell, and if she didn't come outside soon . . .

It was past lunchtime.

He'd spent those hours loitering around the front steps, certain she'd head out to grab a bite from the deli across the street, but she didn't.

So now he was just waiting for her shift to end.

He figured he could have gone to her house.

He knew where she lived, although she hadn't ever given him that information and it wasn't exactly public knowledge. And he *would* go there, if he had to. Just . . . not yet. Not until he actually had to pull that desperate, I-can't-live-without-you stalker routine.

Something warm and sweet bloomed inside his mind.

The heart inside his bruised and battered chest started to race.

Lifting his head, he saw her.

Striding out the door, shoulders set, a look on her face that said, loud and clear, *I'm pissed . . . lemme alone.*

"Sorry, baby."

She stilled. Almost like she heard him.

But he imagined she only sensed him. The way he sensed her. The way he'd sensed her all those years ago. Need, a heavy ache, throbbed inside his veins. Desire pulsed hot and bright. And love, so pure it hurt, beat inside his heart. He didn't want to be without her. He'd done it before and it had made him miserable. He could be whatever, do whatever he had to . . . as long as she was with him.

Her head lifted, and across the hot, shimmering heat of the parking lot, their gazes locked.

Knowing he'd pissed her off, and good, he figured he might as well make it a challenge for her. After all, if he pissed her off, she was much less likely to storm back inside, at least not until she'd torn a strip from his hide. Right?

It took everything he had to paste a smug, smirking smile on his face, to tip his water bottle in her direction in a cocky salute.

But it worked.

She came storming in his direction, the light of battle in her eye.

* * *

HE WAS HERE—

Mica's heart started to race.

He was *here—*

"It doesn't mean anything," she muttered, squaring her shoulders as she continued on her way toward him. She resisted the urge to fiddle with her hair. Resisted the urge to tug at her shirt. It clung to her skin already, but hell, it was summer in Texas. What did she expect?

She stopped barely two feet away, hands hanging at her sides.

"Yeah?"

A spark glinted in those endless blue eyes. A smile tugged at his lips. He looked tired, though. She couldn't help but notice it. Was he still hurting? Shit, why wouldn't he be? It had been only four days.

He opened his mouth and her gaze dropped to said mouth as her heart started to race. *Stop it, Mica. He booted you out, remember?*

"So did you wrap up the case?"

She lifted a brow at him. "You came down to ask that? You could have called."

"I could have." Then he reached out, quick as a wish, and hauled her against him. It was so sudden she barely had time to blink. As she crashed against his chest, he muttered, "Oomph." Then he covered her mouth with his. "But then I couldn't do this."

Couldn't do—

That was about as far as she got before her brain shut down and her body turned on, taking control from her. As his tongue slid along the crease of her lips, she opened for him. Five seconds passed—ten, twenty—

And then she shoved off his chest, stumbling away, panting.

"Ouch," he muttered, wincing and pressing a hand to his chest.

She almost apologized, but then she bit it back. "What in the hell are you doing?"

"Was I doing it wrong?" he asked, lifting his brows.

Mica gaped at him. Doing it . . . What . . . Shaking her head, she skimmed her hands along her hair, straightening the disheveled ponytail. "What do you want, Colby?" she asked, turning away, staring out in the distance. Buildings, large and small, filled her vision, kept her gaze focused on something other than him.

"This." He didn't move. He spoke quietly, but with such intensity the word reverberated through her. "I want this."

She glanced at him, the question forming despite her best intentions otherwise. But then it lodged in her throat as her gaze locked on what he held in his hand. It was a small, blue, velvet box. An open one, one that displayed a ring that reflected the rays of the sun in a dazzling rainbow.

"This was my grandmother's," he said quietly. "My dad's mother. I was going to give it to you fifteen years ago . . . I even had it planned out. But you left."

Shaken, Mica jerked her gaze to his. "Colby . . ."

He moved then, finally, shoving off the car and closing the scant distance between them. He snapped the box closed and lowered it as he used the other hand to press against her mouth. "I loved you then. I love you now. I loved you every fucking day in between . . . and I'll love you until I breathe my last. I can live without you in my life, Mica. But I sure as hell don't want to."

Tears clogged her throat. "This . . ." She cleared her throat and shook her head. "But you pushed me away. It's only been four fucking days and you pushed me *away*."

"I was flat on my back in a hospital bed," he said, quirking a smile at her. "And I didn't want to say this when you had to be rushing off to finish up a case, when I was still floundering around trying to figure out what I needed to do with my life. I took a few days to make sure I knew the answer to that . . . and to make sure you didn't have those loose ends."

"You planned on coming back." She stared at him. Desperate to believe that. He planned on coming back. "You planned on coming back for me."

He cupped her chin in his hand and lowered his head. As he brushed his lips against hers, he whispered, "Pretty much from the second I saw you on the beach, I think some part of me was planning to come after you, Mica."

Shaken, she slid her arms around his waist. "And everything else? You . . . I mean, you said you had to figure things out?"

"I'm going to freelance and shit. I've got a contact in Georgia who can probably point me in the right direction, and I doubt Jones would mind tossing some stuff my way if he had a use for me. I . . ." He sighed and shifted his gaze past her shoulder to stare off into nothingness. "I've been hiding from myself for too long and I can't keep it up. I won't try to . . ."

He trailed off and she reached up, touched his mouth. "I can't keep hiding, either. I figured something out earlier—I'm not as weak as I always thought I was. Or maybe I'm just tired of being that way. But I'm done hiding."

"Mica." He threaded his fingers through her hair, tugging out the band that held it confined. "You were never weak. We all just adjust at our pace, that's all." He nuzzled her mouth again and then whispered, "What do you say . . . you think the two of us can do the rest of the adjusting . . . together? Will you marry me, Mica?"

Easing back, she stared into those endless blue eyes—those eyes, his face, *he* had haunted her. From the time she'd walked away. No more, she told herself. "Colby," she whispered, leaning forward and pressing her mouth to his. "You bet your ass I'll marry you."